FROZEN GRAVE

Lee Weeks was born in Devon. She left school at seventeen and, armed with a notebook and very little cash, spent seven years working her way around Europe and South East Asia. She returned to settle in London, marry and raise two children. She has worked as an English teacher and personal fitness trainer. Her books have been *Sunday Times* bestsellers. She now lives in Devon.

ALSO BY LEE WEEKS

Dead of Winter
Cold as Ice

FROZEN GRAVE

LEE WEEKS

SIMON &
SCHUSTER

London · New York · Sydney · Toronto · New Delhi

A CBS COMPANY

First published in Great Britain by Simon & Schuster UK Ltd, 2014
A CBS COMPANY

Copyright © Lee Weeks 2014

1 3 5 7 9 10 8 6 4 2

Simon & Schuster UK Ltd
1st Floor
222 Gray's Inn Road
London WC1X 8HB

www.simonandschuster.co.uk

Simon & Schuster Australia, Sydney
Simon & Schuster India, New Delhi

A CIP catalogue record for this book
is available from the British Library

PB ISBN: 978-1-47113-360-2
EBOOK ISBN: 978-1-47113-361-9

Typeset by M Rules
Printed and bound by CPI Group (UK) Ltd, Croydon, CR0 4YY

For Ginny and Robert, with love and thanks

Prologue

The January gloom that made everything grey also made Olivia's white Fiat shine luminescent on the deserted street in Woolwich. Her bright red lipstick was vivid in the gloom. She reread the message on her phone:

I'll be waiting for you.

Her mouth was so dry that she found it hard to swallow; the ends of her fingers tingled as she slipped her hand beneath her coat and felt her warm bare skin between the lace and silk; she shivered.

She got out of her car and pulled her coat tightly around her. Her heels echoed on the cobbles as she crossed the road. Stopping outside number 22, Olivia placed her bright red nails on the peeling paintwork and pushed the door open just a little. She looked back at her car. She had only to run across the road and jump in and she would be safe. She turned back to number 22 and loosened her coat; her flesh glowed in the darkness as she stepped inside.

Chapter 1

DC Willis got out of the passenger side of the black BMW and looked down the street past the SOCO van.

'Who found her?' DI Carter asked her whilst putting on his coat. He pulled up his collar as the cold hit him.

'Anonymous caller, guv,' Willis answered, studying the row of derelict buildings that had once been large commercial properties, some still with a shop face, but now boarded up and covered in graffiti. Across the street from them a 1990s tower block marked the start of the sprawling Hannover council estate. On the other side of Parade Street was a smart new row of red-brick terraces in a Victorian style.

'Accent?' Carter tied his Armani scarf loosely around his neck.

'English. Male. Well-spoken.'

Parade Street was cordoned off at both ends, with police officers stopping anyone entering. No one had tried while they'd been standing there the last three hours because no one lived on the condemned street except rough sleepers.

As Carter swivelled round to get his bearings, the pathologist's car drew up and parked up behind them. Dr Jo Harding switched off the engine but stayed where she was, talking on her phone.

'Were there any cars on this street when you arrived, Officer Gardner?' Carter asked the officer standing outside number 22 with the crime-scene logbook in her hand.

'Three, sir, and they have been traced to their owners. One was abandoned, one belonged to a couple on a night out who left it and got a cab home and the other is owned by a woman who lives on the next street.'

'She *chooses* to park it here overnight?'

'She's new to the area. She's waiting for a resident's permit, sir.'

Carter looked up and down the street. He was searching his memory banks. He turned to Willis.

'Do you recognize this place?' Willis shook her head. 'Must be before your time then. I reckon it was five years ago when these buildings first started being pulled down and we had a murder here. Polish immigrants, one was kicked to death over a row about drink. You'd think they would have done something with these buildings by now.' Willis zipped up her jacket. Carter was still surveying the outside of the building. He looked up and his eyes filled with the deep blue of the cold winter sky. 'Council ran out of money maybe.' He turned back to PC Gardner. 'Have all the buildings on the street been searched?'

'Not yet, sir.'

A tall, white-suited figure emerged from number 22,

taking the mask from his face as he did so. He came round to the back of the SOCO van and opened the doors.

'Sandford?' Carter said by way of greeting to the crime-scene manager. Sandford looked at him but didn't answer; he nodded at Willis. He liked her. He wasn't so keen on Carter. Carter had a laddish brashness, a chunky bit of gold around his wrist and wax products in his black hair. That, so far as Sandford was concerned, constituted what people termed 'chavvy'.

'Are you getting déjà vu here?' Carter asked. 'Must have been five years ago at least.' Luckily, Carter never minded or noticed Sandford's low opinion of him.

'Yes.'

'Is it the same sort of thing this time?'

Sandford looked down at his forensic suit and his soiled knees. 'Same filth, it's come right through the suit, difference is – it's a woman this time.'

Dr Harding got out of her car, took out her bag from the boot and joined them.

Sandford began pulling out packets of forensic suits from the back of the van and handing them out.

'Carter – extra-small?'

'Yeah, funny.' He passed the suit on to Dr Harding. Willis was an inch taller than him at five ten. 'What about the rest of this street?'

'I want my team to go through this one first. This whole street is used by rough sleepers – we need to start where we have a chance of finding something.'

'Is it okay for us to go in?' asked Carter.

'Only as far as the inner entrance and be careful what you step on and what you step in.'

Harding took the overshoes from Sandford and sighed impatiently.

'Sooner we get in, sooner we get her out,' she said, zipping up her suit.

Willis took off her black quilted jacket and put it in the back of Carter's car.

Carter waited until she'd thrown hers down then he folded his overcoat and put it neatly on the top along with his scarf. He eased the elastic hood of the forensic suit over his hair and straightened out the suit so that it fitted better. Sandford looked down at Carter's expensive shiny shoes and then reached in and pulled out two more pairs of overshoes.

'You'll thank me for these.'

He shut the doors on the back of the van and picked up his Croc box containing an assortment of variously sized evidence bags. 'Follow me.'

Dermot, the scenes of crime officer, stood to greet them as they stepped inside.

'That's far enough,' Sandford said, leaving the detectives at the entrance as he crossed carefully on stepping plates to the far side of the room. There were battery-powered LED lights in the corners. The only other light was filtering in past boarded-up windows and through the open entrance.

Carter switched on his head lamp and pulled up his mask against the smell of human waste mixed with cigarettes, alcohol and dog shit.

'Christ – what a place to end up. You wouldn't want an animal to die in this, let alone live,' he said, looking around.

'I reckon this is home to about twenty people,'

Dermot said, shining his torch into the far left-hand corner of the room. 'And it looks like they left here in a rush,' he said as his torch beam lit a mound of broken glass. 'Besides all the empties, I found half a bottle of Smirnoff over there and three of these – used recently.' Dermot held up a crack pipe in his hand.

'Party time,' said Carter.

Willis stepped round to stand beside him and get a better view as she shone her torch into the room. The woman's body was lying on the far side near the back wall; the pale skin of her flank glowed in the dim light. Above everything else, all the obvious smells of dirt and defecation, Willis could smell the unmistakable sweet overtones of clotting blood.

'I need more light on her,' Harding said as she stepped across on the plates and squatted down beside the body.

Sandford picked up one of the LED lights and brought it nearer.

'Rigor mortis is fully established,' said Harding. Sandford knelt beside her, to help roll and hold the body on its side.

The corpse sighed.

'Lividity is established too. She died here.' Sandford rolled the body back. 'Extensive bruising around the pelvic area and the hips, top of the thighs. Evidence of sexual assault, rape. Lacerations,' said Harding. 'There are also large areas of bruising around the shoulders, ribs and collarbone. Consistent with pressure being applied,' she continued.

'So she was held down and raped,' said Carter.

'There are multiple footwear marks around the

body,' Sandford said as he angled the light for Harding.

'Which would explain the hasty exit,' said Carter. 'Everyone in here was involved in this in some way.' He looked around. 'Maybe she came in here with someone. Maybe this wasn't her usual place to sleep and she drifted onto someone else's turf. She pissed someone off.'

Carter was watching Dermot as he moved a mattress and propped it up against the wall then knelt to examine it.

'Someone's been bottled by the look of it. There is fresh blood on the mattress – still wet.'

'No evidence of wounds consistent with being bottled,' said Harding. 'It looks like someone tried to strangle her though.' She moved to one side so that the detectives could see the ligature around the woman's neck.

Dermot stood and held something in the air for them to see.

'Expensive knickers.'

He walked across and passed them to Carter.

Carter looked at the label. 'La Perla. Very posh.'

'There's also one half of a pair of stockings attached to a suspender belt,' Dermot said, taking the knickers back from Carter and putting them into a crime-scene bag. He handed the stocking across. 'Just one so far.'

'The other one is round her neck,' said Willis, who was squatting level with the body and leaning into the room to get a better look.

'This is expensive lingerie,' Carter said, holding the

stocking. 'This outfit must have cost a hundred quid – probably two. La Perla is expensive, isn't it, Doctor?'

'Yes.'

Carter knew there was no point in him asking Willis. Dermot walked back across the plates and resumed his examination of the mattress.

'Do we know the cause of death, Doctor?' asked Willis.

Harding turned the woman's head away from her.

'There is a crush wound to the skull, a lot of blood lost here, and possible brain injury.' She shone the light onto the woman's face. 'But there are so many other poss—' She paused mid-sentence. She moved the light closer. Her voice quietened: 'We'll have to get someone else to perform the post-mortem.'

'What's the problem, Doc?' Carter moved towards the body, stepping on the first plate.

Dermot stopped working and stood upright.

'I know her.'

'You sure?' asked Carter.

'Yes . . . of course I'm sure – I wouldn't say it otherwise. I don't know her well but I've met her a few times. Her name is Olivia Grantham. Early forties. She lives in Brockley, south-east London. She works for a solicitors' firm in London Bridge, near the Shard.'

'Any idea what it's called, the place she works at?'

'Spencer and Something. As far as I remember, she's a junior partner.' Harding started to pack away her kit.

Sandford and Dermot were poised, listening to the outcome of the conversation.

'When was the last time you saw her, Doctor?' Carter asked.

'Not sure, about six months ago, probably.'

'Could she be sleeping rough here, Doctor?' asked Willis.

'Don't be ridiculous!' snapped Harding. 'You don't go downhill that fast. The last time I saw her, she was drinking cocktails and hoovering a line of coke.'

'How exactly did you know her?' Carter asked, interested now that Harding had painted a scene and accidentally painted herself into it.

'Through friends. Social events. That kind of thing.' Harding stood, ready to leave. 'I'll organize for some- one to do the post-mortem for me and I'll let you know what time it's happening.' She turned to Sandford. 'When you're ready for her to be moved, phone me and I'll send someone down to collect her.'

As Harding passed him, Carter turned and fol- lowed. By the time he got outside, she was already half out of her forensic suit.

'You all right, Doc? It's not easy when it's someone you know.'

Harding didn't look at him. She opened the boot of her car and deposited her bag inside.

'I told you, I didn't know her well. Merely a social acquaintance.' She glanced his way as she got into her car.

'But still ...'

She held his gaze. 'But still, nothing, Inspector. Don't read into it.'

Carter hovered by the door. 'Do you know what street she lived in?'

'No.'

She slammed the door.

Carter was watching her drive away as Willis came out of the building and joined him.

'What was that all about?' he said, peeling off his suit. 'She was even more abrupt than usual. She couldn't wait to get away, could she?'

'She had to, guv – difficult position to be in. I guess she must have felt really bad seeing her friend like that.'

'Yeah, right . . . she doesn't have any friends.' Carter looked around as he made a mental map of the area. 'The nearest station is Woolwich Arsenal,' he said. 'And that's a good eight, ten minutes' walk, especially in heels. She'd got to have been wearing heels with that outfit. I think she would have got here by car – she drove or took a taxi. We need to find out all the local taxi firms; see if there's any CCTV as well.'

'Yes, guv.'

He took out his phone to make a call to the crime analyst back at the office.

'Robbo? We have a possible name for the victim: it's Olivia Grantham, early forties. Dr Harding recognized her. She thinks she works in a solicitors' office at London Bridge – Spencer and Something. See if you can find it and an address in Brockley for her. There was a fight here; someone got bottled; check the A&E departments as well. Do you know what, Robbo? This place is the same derelict buildings where we had that Polish man kicked to death a few years ago. That's progress for you.'

He ended the call and looked back towards the entrance of number 22. 'What a place to end up in: "Shit Central",' he said as he discarded his suit and handed Willis a bag for hers. 'Got to hand it to Sandford and that lot in there – it's a shit job but someone's got to do it.' He smiled a little at his quip. Willis didn't react but took the bag from him as she stared down the street.

'Don't get it, guv. Who comes to a place like this on a Sunday evening dressed in expensive lingerie?'

'I agree – I don't know many women who wear stockings unless it's to add spice to the bedroom. This is certainly *not* a romantic setting to slip into your La Perla. If Harding is right about her, then Olivia Grantham didn't need to slum it.'

'I've seen some women in the changing room at the gym wearing them,' Willis said. 'Coming straight from work, I suppose.'

'Really?' His eyes glazed over for a few seconds. 'Okay, well maybe some women wear them for work as well, but I think the majority of women put them on especially. But *not* especially to come into a shit-hole like this. Plus, it was sleeting last night. Not the kind of night to walk around in your underwear.'

Willis bagged up her suit and signed it off in the logbook as she thanked PC Gardner.

Carter took out his coat and handed Willis hers. Willis was studying a street map of the area on her phone.

'See if Robbo has that address for Olivia Grantham's place and we'll go there now,' said Carter.

'He's already sent it – 103 Station Road, guv.' Willis began reading it from her phone. 'Runs from the High Street to …' She stopped talking and began running towards shouts coming from the end of the street.

Carter shouted across to Gardner.

'Call for back-up but stay here, tell Sandford what's going on.'

Willis reached the officer and helped him up from the ground.

'You okay?'

'Yes. I'm okay. I couldn't stop him, I'm sorry. He came out of nowhere and the dog charged me.'

'What did he look like?' asked Carter as he got to them.

'In his late twenties, scruffy, blood on his face, hands … he had on a grey woolly hat pulled down over his ears. His dog looked like it had been in a fight too. It's light-coloured – one of those big ugly ones. He came out of the space behind the bins over there on the second to last property.'

'Did you see where he went?'

'He ran off into Hannover Estate.'

'Okay. Help is on its way. Be ready. There could be more people hiding.'

They started towards the estate. Carter reached inside his jacket for his phone, dialling as he ran.

'We're going after a suspect in Hannover Estate – entrance opposite Parade Street … I need a car around the back of it. Looking for a white male with dog. He's injured. Be careful – the dog will attack.'

They ran past the row of scruffy garages and lock-ups in the parking area. Carter signalled to Willis that he had seen something and was headed towards the gap between the tower block and the four-storey building that flanked it. She began to follow but then slowed as she heard a sound coming from the garages.

She went to call to Carter but he was already twenty
metres away.

Willis walked towards the last of the garages, plastered in graffiti, spray-painted in blocks of colour and
covered with the name 'Hannover Boys'.

'Police.' She waited for a reply. 'Come out and
show yourself. Come out now.'

Carter was out of sight by this time. She stepped
towards the door and pulled it open.

'Police – come out. I need to see you.' She took a
step inside the garage and shone her torch around. The
walls were covered in graffiti. There was silence. She
heard a shout go up from Carter and a dog bark. From
somewhere outside she heard running. She turned to
leave but stopped – in front of her was a man wearing
a woolly hat, his face slashed by a gaping wound that
ran over the top of his nose and split his eyebrow
before it pierced his cheek in a semi-circle. He was
holding the dog by its collar as they blocked her way.

The dog reared and snarled as it bared its teeth.

'It's okay. Keep calm. Make sure the dog stays
under control. Are you all right?' The man didn't
answer. He was breathing hard. The front of his
T-shirt was soaked in blood. 'Look, you need help –
your face needs seeing to. Let me help you.'

He held the dog's collar in a stronger grip with one
hand as he touched his face, then looked at the wet
sticky blood on his fingertips.

'Something happened on Parade Street last night.
Did you see it?'

He didn't answer. He looked nervously towards the
sound of someone approaching outside.

'You need to come with me.' Willis took a step closer and the dog lunged forwards at her. She held up her hands for calm. 'I can help you.'

He shook his head, released the dog, and ran.

Chapter 2

The dog lingered in the doorway, snarling before it turned and followed its master. Willis ran outside – both man and dog were gone. Carter was jogging towards her.

'I thought I saw him but it turned out it wasn't him. Where were you?' he said as he got within earshot and stopped to catch his breath. He looked at Willis's expression. 'Are you okay? What happened here?'

'The suspect was hiding in here with his dog,' answered Willis.

'What happened?'

'Nothing – he ran. He looks like he's been glassed or bottled.'

They heard a police siren, then four officers came running their way.

Carter met them.

'Two of you get back in the car and see if you can find a white male with a dog. Willis?' He turned to her to finish the description.

'Twenty-five to thirty-five. Grey woolly hat. Dark blue jacket, combat trousers. He is bleeding on his face. His dog is sandy-coloured – a cross-breed, bull mastiff, bulldog type. It will attack.'

'The other two of you get some crime-scene tape and cordon this area off. Get the keys from the council,' said Carter. 'I want all of these garages searched. I want SOCOs here. We're looking for a match with the scene at 22 Parade Street. That lad must have left his blood somewhere. Willis?'

'Guv?'

'We'll leave them to it and head over to Brockley.'

As they drove south of the River Thames, they were snagged in a morning queue of traffic. Carter tapped his thumbs on the leather steering wheel as he watched the traffic inch forward. He looked across at Willis.

'Oy!'

He shifted in his seat so he could turn more towards her as the traffic was stationary.

'I wish you'd shut up – you're driving me mad with your constant chatter.'

She shook her head apologetically. 'Just thinking it through.'

'Think and talk. Tell me what we've got here.'

Willis took out her notebook.

Carter put the car into first gear, eased a few feet further into the traffic jam, then started the conversation:

'The woman … Olivia Grantham … goes in there, dressed for sex. She goes in there and she can't get out.'

'Yeah – the men get carried away; fights break out

and she gets killed; then they get scared and do a runner,' said Willis.

'Where did they go then?' asked Carter, not waiting for an answer as he continued: 'We need to get officers going into every hostel, every empty building where they sleep; we'll start with those within a mile radius and then we'll widen the net if we have to. I need all the off-licences in the area contacted, to go through their tills and see who paid for that brand of half-bottles of vodka we found in there. Who are the heroin and crack dealers in the area? Also, I want officers all over that estate. Someone must have seen something.'

'I think we should post extra officers on the surrounding streets too, guv,' said Willis as she made notes. 'The people who sleep there are bound to try and come back.'

'Exactly. We will. We'll round them up. Bring them in, fingerprints, DNA samples.'

'We might find some evidence in the lock-up, guv.'

'Ring Sandford now and tell him what we found.'

Willis got off the phone to Sandford.

'He'll get over there as soon as he is able. He says to wear suits when we go into Olivia Grantham's flat. He's going to want to go in there next.'

Carter laughed. 'Tell him to get his head out of his arse and do his job – we'll do ours – pompous git.' Carter went back to drumming his thumb on the wheel.

The caretaker answered his buzzer at the entrance to the mock-Georgian block of smart flats where Olivia

Grantham lived. He was expecting them and handed them the keys to her apartment.

'Do you know if Miss Grantham had a car, sir?' Carter asked. The caretaker was a retired Met officer now living rent-free in exchange for handyman duties.

'Yes. She had a white Fiat 500.'

'Where is it parked?'

'She had a car-parking space around the back of the building – but the car's not there now. She left in it yesterday evening and didn't return.'

'Did you see her leave?'

'Yes. I talked to her.'

'What time was that?' Willis wrote in her notebook as Carter asked the questions.

'About six. I was saying goodbye to my friend here at the door when she came by us.'

'What did she say to you?'

'She complained about her tap dripping in her kitchen. She asked me to fix it.'

'Did she say she would be gone long?'

'She said she was going out for at least an hour. I said I would mend it for her while she was out.'

'Was she a friendly sort of person? You didn't mind helping her on a Sunday evening?'

He shrugged. 'I didn't mind. She didn't ask for much. She was quiet. She worked hard.'

'Any boyfriend on the scene?'

'I don't think so.'

'And can you tell me what she was wearing when you saw her last?'

'She was wearing a blue coat.'

'How did she look to you?'

'She looked like she was going on a date. She had perfume on. Make-up: red lipstick, nails. She'd made a big effort for someone.'

They took the stairs up to the second floor and changed into forensic suits before going in. As they opened the door they heard the sound of a radio playing.

Carter walked on into the lounge straight in front of them. The curtains were closed; he switched on the light. Everywhere had magnolia walls, cream carpet. There were insipid abstract paintings of orange and purple swirls on the walls. He turned off the radio.

'Can't see any couples photos,' Carter said as he walked around. 'It looks like a rented apartment – no clutter, no mess.' Willis lingered in the hallway, writing up what she saw and drawing a diagram of the flat. 'This place is corporate, chic,' continued Carter. 'It looks like the type of place anyone could move into tomorrow – especially me. Reminds me of my flat before Cabrina arrived and then finished off her offensive with a smelly baby.'

Willis glanced at him. 'Making of you, guv.'

'Ha!' He grinned. 'You could be right – jury's out on that one.' He walked through the lounge, looking at Olivia's choice of gadgets. 'Great Bose sound system. Blu-ray, 3D television. She definitely had money.'

The hallway carried round to the right and Carter opened the door to a neat and tidy kitchen with spotless surfaces and shiny taps that had the smell of having recently been cleaned.

Willis scanned the cupboards. 'Cereals in here mostly.'

He opened the fridge door. 'Looks like Olivia drank in but ate out a lot. There are several bottles of wine but little else.'

They moved back out into the wide hallway and into the first of the two rooms.

'It's like a hotel bedroom.'

Carter ran his hand across the silk bedspread as he walked round to the far side of the bed and opened the wardrobe; he pulled out an inner drawer.

'Impressive.' He stood back to show Willis the neat racks of hanging clothes and the lingerie in the drawer that went from dark to light, left to right. 'Colour-coded, even her underwear.' He looked back to the bed and closed the drawer. 'Which side do you think she sleeps?' he asked.

'Left side.'

'I see the way you're thinking but not everyone would want to attack an intruder. Most people would want to be furthest away from the threat and have more chance of running.' Willis didn't answer. 'But you're right – so would I. Anything on your side?' Carter asked as he pulled open a drawer beside the bed that had tea lights inside, a pink vibrator and a packet of variously sized condoms. 'She sleeps this side,' he said. 'She was a runner then, not a fighter.'

Willis ducked down and pulled out a small case from beneath the bed. She opened the lid and took out a hooded ball gag.

Carter came round and knelt down beside her.

'Welcome to Olivia's toy box,' he said. 'Welcome to her secret world.' He stood with a harness in his hands. 'Tell you one thing we need to know – we need to know how Dr Harding knew her. Because, like I said' – Carter was distracted reading instructions and turning the harness around to try to work out how it was fastened – 'Harding doesn't have female friends.' He gave up and put it back in the box. 'We'll leave these for Sandford. This will be right up his street. If Harding met her outside work then they had something in common. The only hobby I know that Harding has outside work is having sex with people she shouldn't. If this woman doesn't have a husband to interest Harding – she must have something else.'

After he left Hannover Estate, Mason's feet didn't stop running until he reached the arches beneath the railway bridge in Shadwell where he had made a home tucked in beside the road and the fencing that bordered the car park. In the day, cars parked there but from six it was empty. Mason crawled into his makeshift cardboard tent and pulled his sleeping bag up over his legs. His heart was pounding; his lungs burning.

Sandy stayed on sentry duty until she sensed that there was no more danger, then she looked around for water and found a puddle.

Mason's breathing slowed as Sandy came to lie beside him and the warmth from the dog soothed him, her heartbeat calmed him; the sound of her breathing made him feel safe. He closed his eyes and sank back onto the blue cashmere coat that still smelt of the woman.

Chapter 3

It was late morning when Carter and Willis arrived back at the office, both loaded down with boxes of Olivia Grantham's paperwork taken from her flat. They parked in the car park alongside SOCO vans and squad cars and took the lift up to the third floor. They were part of MIT 17 – the murder squad – which was one of three Major Investigation Teams in Fletcher House. Fletcher House was a concrete three-storey building adjoining Archway Police Station, separated by just a door on level one. All the officers serving in Archway Police Station referred to the MIT teams as 'the Dark Side'.

They carried the boxes down to the crime analyst Robbo's office. It was the crime analyst's job to work out the sequence of events, analyse statements, pull everything together and highlight any gaps in intelligence. It was his job to work out how it all fitted or didn't. He worked in there with Pam, his 'work wife', and there was usually at least one other researcher working alongside them – at the moment it was Hector, a young detective constable who was recovering from a knee operation and on desk duty.

Hector looked up as Carter and Willis entered the room. The door to Robbo's office was always propped open. Robbo had a desk from where he could look through the glass partition and right down the corridor but it was tucked back against the wall. Behind his chair was a large whiteboard, where he made notes on the case he was working on and pinned up photos and diagrams, location maps. Olivia Grantham's name was written at the top of the board with photos of Parade Street and stills from the crime scene.

Pam looked up and smiled at Carter.

Carter winked at her. 'All right, Pam? Have a nice holiday? Is that an all-over tan?'

Pam blushed. 'It was. It's fading already.'

'Has the family been notified?' Willis asked Robbo as she placed her boxes from Olivia Grantham's flat on Hector's desk.

'Yes, we found a relative,' he answered. 'She has family in Yorkshire. Her dad is coming down late tonight and he'll identify the body tomorrow morning.'

'We need to get the post-mortem done before then,' Carter said as he watched whilst Hector shifted the boxes on his desk. 'Is Dr Kahn doing it?'

'Yes,' replied Robbo. 'Dr Harding is handling the arrangements. She said it's scheduled for this afternoon at two. Do you want to attend?'

'Yeah, we have to; personally speaking, *want* has nothing to do with it. The top box is her bank statements,' added Carter, as he placed his boxes beside the others.

'She's not the paperless type then,' Hector said as he removed the top from the box and looked at the reams of statements.

Robbo came round to look at the boxes and their contents. 'Solicitor, remember. Make a spreadsheet of her spending in the last six months, work backwards, Hector,' said Robbo as he held out his hands for Hector to hand a box over to him. 'Give one to me – I'll make sure it's in order for you.'

'What have you found out about her, Pam?' asked Carter.

Pam changed her reading glasses and skimmed down the research she'd done as she read out the bullet points from the page in front of her:

'Age forty. Originally from Yorkshire. Only child. Solicitor in family law. Never married. I talked to work colleagues this morning. There doesn't seem to be much of a social scene at her workplace. They didn't know of any friends outside work. She was on Linkedin, so I'm tracing her contacts there. I'm still building up a picture of her but so far she seems a private person.'

'Any boyfriend on the scene?'

'Her work colleagues didn't think so. She never brought anyone along to any company events.'

'Okay, well, we need to keep digging.'

Robbo turned to Willis. 'What were your thoughts when you saw the body?'

Willis was standing in the centre of the room. She hadn't moved since she put the boxes down on Hector's desk. She looked as if she were in a world of her own.

'She was never meant to be in there,' she replied.

'What are we saying? Drugged, drunk, you think?' asked Robbo looking at Carter.

Carter shook his head. 'Our only suspects and witnesses are the people who sleep in there. They are not going to be the most reliable. We have to look to Olivia's lifestyle for answers.'

'I hear you had a run-in with one of the men?' Robbo said, looking at Carter.

'Willis did.'

'What did he look like?'

'He looked freaked out,' she answered. 'He was scared, hurt.'

'Did he look like he slept rough every day?'

'Yes.'

'Well he won't be able to get into most of the hostels with a dog so he'll be on the streets somewhere. The Dogs' Trust care for the dogs on the street. They might know this man,' Robbo said. 'Did he say anything?'

'Nothing. He ran for it when I tried to approach him to bring him in. I pushed too fast. I was trying to catch him off-guard. I messed up.'

'No, you misjudged – you didn't mess up,' corrected Carter.

Robbo was making notes as they talked.

'We don't know if he speaks English then. We need to find him and to know exactly who uses that building,' he said. 'There must be a mainstay of sleepers in there.'

'The foreigners tend to stick together. The drinkers do too,' said Hector.

Robbo made notes. 'Right. People stay in their social groups,' he said. 'I'll get hold of Social Services for the area and see if they have had any information about Parade Street.'

'Hannover Estate is a rough one,' said Carter. 'Looks like the gangs are rife in there. There was graffiti everywhere.'

'We know them,' Robbo agreed. 'The Hannover Boys are a well-established gang. There are sparodic outbursts of trouble in there. There has been a lot of activity there recently. Robbery around the neighbouring streets and the usual muggings, phone theft.'

'What about the serious stuff?' asked Carter.

'They are thought to be responsible for three murders in the last two years – gangland turf wars – a beef about territory. Twelve rape charges down to them but didn't make it to court. Gang rapes are their speciality. Five of them are in prison for the rape of two girls held hostage in a flat in the tower block. They were kept for thirty-six hours. Both families had to be given witness protection and moved out of the area. The girls were thirteen. Mahmet Balik is the man behind most of these attacks.'

'Jesus – well within their capabilities then: murder, rape. Balik seems to be unchecked,' said Carter.

'Mahmet Balik and his deputies,' said Hector. 'I was part of the Met's drive to sort out the gangs on that estate when the Trident Operation changed brief to include the gangs. I had to help a family there. The fourteen-year-old daughter had been caught carrying weapons for male gang members. She'd been passed around as a piece of meat within the gang, sexualized from the age of twelve. She was in a mess. Already on crack. We had to relocate the whole family because they lived in fear of reprisals. Mahmet Balik was the main one they were scared of. He's escaped a murder charge a few times now. There's been insufficient evidence to get him but he's getting cockier all the time.'

'Okay. We need house-to-house in there then. Let's see what people are saying on the estate,' said Carter. 'We also need to find Olivia on CCTV on her way there, if we can.'

'We have her car reg now,' Robbo said as he went across to pour coffee into five mugs. 'We have patrol cars looking out for it.' He handed the mugs out.

Carter took his coffee and sipped appreciatively. Robbo was a coffee connoisseur. He had been given a machine that made it from pods for Christmas but it was still unopened in its box. He preferred to grind his mix of coffee beans and brew it in a cafetière. That and Haribo gummy bears were his biggest weakness, and added to his thick waistline. It didn't help that he never wanted to move from his office. His agoraphobia was never completely under control. It took managing – it didn't like surprises.

'So ...' said Robbo. 'Not only did she come to a derelict building in a condemned street, she came in a suspender belt and stockings.' He turned to Willis. 'She went in there by mistake? Was she meeting someone? Did someone take her in there?'

'We looked in the drawers in her bedroom,' said Carter. 'Bondage gear and ball gags and some sort of complicated-looking harness.'

'That's why she went in there then, was it? The thrill of a lifetime?' asked Robbo.

'Maybe ...' said Carter. 'She wasn't careful what she wished for.'

'What about the body itself?' Robbo turned to ask Willis.

She walked across to the whiteboard and the crime-scene photos. A map of the area was pinned up and a close-up of Parade Street.

'The area around the body was heavily scuffed – marks associated with kneeling, stamping, bootmarks, palm-prints, belonging to several different people,' she said as she pointed to the diagram on the board. 'Her collarbone was broken. Her jaw too. She had genital lacerations, not sure how deep they went – probably caused by an instrument. The amount of blood at the scene indicates that she was alive, her heart was still pumping blood around, for the duration of the attack. Large deep head wound, fractured skull and possible brain damage. The ligature around her neck was probably not sufficient to kill; although it might have cut off the blood supply to her brain and caused her temporary unconsciousness.' The office went quiet.

Pam stopped typing. 'Let's hope so. Poor woman.'

'Poor woman with a lot of money to spend on getting laid.' Hector ruffled a sheet of paper in the air. 'Were talking over a hundred quid a month on sex sites.'

Robbo walked back round his desk to take a call. Carter waited expectantly.

'What's up?'

'They've found her car.'

Chapter 4

Carter parked the BMW behind Olivia Grantham's white Fiat 500. Her car was parked at an angle, one tyre forced against the pavement. It was under a tree and covered in pigeon excrement.

'Anyone see anything?' Carter asked as he showed his badge to the patrol officer.

'The owner of the grey Ford over there said he parked here at 8.10 last evening and he didn't see it then.'

Carter squatted down by the driver's side and felt beneath the wheel arch.

'I checked there, sir,' the patrol officer said. 'No keys.'

Carter stood and peered in through the windows.

'No sign of her shoes, coat. Nothing left on the seats. But, it looks messy and there is a definite print on the driver's door frame,' he said as he cupped his hands against the glass to keep out the glare. 'Some kind of substance on the back passenger's window; smears on the seat covers. Someone's been in here who shouldn't have. Plus ...' He stood and looked down the street. 'She wouldn't have walked from here – too far.' He looked back at the car and up at the tree above it. 'She didn't park it here either. Even if she only intended to park here for an hour, she wouldn't have left it *here* like this. Not at that time of night when the pigeons are roosting, and she'd have parked it straight.'

Carter moved round to the back of the car and looked through the rear window, before stopping to listen to the noise of people coming from further down the street.

'What's down there?' he asked.

'The Church of Light, sir. It's a multi-denominational church,' replied the officer.

Willis began looking it up on her phone. 'It's also a bad-weather shelter run by a religious charity called Faith and Light,' she said, reading off the information.

Carter turned to her. 'Did you remember seeing any religious stuff at Olivia's flat?'

Willis shook her head. 'No, no crucifixes, no Buddhas. Not sure what else to look for. What does multi-denominational look like?'

'Let's find out,' said Carter as he locked up the car.

They walked down the road and crossed a car park to a flat-roofed, two-storey block next to a small steepled church. Three people were sharing a cigarette in the church entrance.

Willis kept reading the information from her phone: 'It has accommodation for up to twenty people sharing rooms.'

'That must be in one of those buildings behind,' Carter said, glancing around the car park.

The smell of breakfast greeted them as they opened

the door into the hostel. It was coming from a small canteen, just a handful of tables, straight ahead. Immediately to the right was a busy area where there were three PCs and people sitting around waiting to use them. There was the noise of dishes and chatter. The place was busy.

'Hello, mate – sorry to interrupt. Who's in charge here?' Carter asked a young man waiting for the computer.

'Simon. Over there.' He nodded in the direction of the café counter and to a dark- haired man in a white overall disappearing through double doors behind.

'Appreciate it.'

They walked behind the counter and through to the kitchen beyond. There were two women inside, clearing up, loading a dishwasher. The man they'd followed in was about to start drying pots from the draining board.

Carter showed his warrant card. 'Simon – are you in charge? Can we have a word?'

'Yes, of course.' His voice was soft public school. He put down his tea towel, took off his overall and hung it on a row of pegs to the right of the door.'We can talk in my office.' He had curly dark hair, long on the top, almost shaved at the sides. He had a pensive look with a ready-made frown line across his forehead. His dark eyebrows and brown eyes gave him a Spanish look, although his skin was too pale to be Mediterranean. He was very young-looking, thought Carter.

He escorted them through to a room off the kitchen and closed the door after him.

'I'd ask you both to sit but there's only one chair, which you're welcome to. Please?' He smiled. His eyes flitted from one detective to the other.

'No need.' Carter smiled. The room was small enough to have been a storeroom at one time. It had no window. 'We won't keep you long.'

He sat with his back to his monitor, his hands in his lap, waiting.

'How can I help you?'

He pushed his hair away from his forehead. The floppy collar on his polo-shirt was half sticking up.

'I'm Detective Inspector Carter and this is Detective Constable Willis. You are Simon . . . ?'

'Smith. How can I help?'

'A woman died near here last night, Mr Smith – on Parade Street,' said Carter. 'Do you know it?'

'Yes, I do. What happened?'

'We don't know exactly. Her body was found this morning after a tip-off from an anonymous caller. We think she went into the building early yesterday evening. What do you know about the street?'

'There are problems there all the time, fights over drink. It's where the younger drug addicts congregate as well as the older drinkers. It's not somewhere you'd expect a woman to sleep. It's too dangerous.'

'We are pretty sure we know the identity of the victim,' began Carter. 'Her name was Olivia Grantham. She was a lawyer working in London Bridge. Does that name mean anything to you, Mr Smith?' Simon shook his head. 'We think several people would have seen what happened to her and might have been involved. Her car was parked just

down the road from here. As this is the nearest homeless centre to Parade Street, we were hoping that
someone here might know something. Did you notice
anything that made you think that something wasn't
right yesterday evening or this morning?'

'No, sorry. Last night there were the usual in. It's
always chaotic. And I've been rushed off my feet this
morning. The cold weather is bringing everyone in for
some hot food.' He paused, looked at Carter's face
and shrugged. 'Sorry. I tend to be so busy with the
hostel I don't have time to look a couple of streets
away. But a lawyer sleeping rough? It wouldn't be the
first time – it can happen to anyone, you know.'

'Yes. But she wasn't homeless.'

Willis could see the tension building in Carter's
shoulders. He had the same problem talking to
Sandford when they first started working together.
Carter had an issue with posh accents.

'We believe that there would have been a substantial amount of blood,' said Willis. 'Both from the
victim and from fighting that seems to have gone on
around the time she was killed.'

'They would have been high on drink and other
substances,' added Carter.

'It's not likely to be someone from here then.
Substance abuse is carefully monitored her. We don't
allow people in here who are high on anything.'

'What about any of your staff? Might one of them
be able to help us – they might have seen something?'
Carter's stocky presence filled the small office, his feet
planted wide in his expensive shiny shoes, his hands in
the pockets of his overcoat. He tipped his weight

slightly forward over the desk, where Simon was now sitting half-turned towards his PC monitor, his hands rested on a pile of papers on his desk.

He shrugged. 'Ask them, by all means.'

Willis said little. She was trying to guess Smith's background: expensive public school, family money. The kind of person you would expect to be in a job with a massive salary for doing very little. But this wasn't the set of *Made in Chelsea*. This wasn't the least bit glamorous.

'How does it work here?' she asked. 'How does someone find you?'

'People are referred to us, by their GP, by the local police, council homeless department, mental-health crisis management – several ways. There are forms to fill out and then they have to pay in advance for their next-day accommodation if they want to secure it. If we have room, we take them in.'

'So who are the ones that don't get a place in here?' asked Carter.

'They have to be sober and to be non-users. We can't cope with addicts in here or dogs.'

'Do you know of a man who has a light-coloured dog – one of those tough-looking breeds used for fighting?' Willis asked. 'We think he needs help – he got bottled.'

'I don't think I do – sorry.'

'And you are sure you didn't notice anyone behaving strangely last night?' she asked.

'Stranger than usual? No. It's a difficult time for so many people. Lots of people who come in here are damaged. So many rough sleepers have mental-health issues.' Simon shrugged again, his eyes went from Carter to Willis and he shook his head. 'Sorry I can't help. But – I'll do my best and look into it for you.'

Carter took out his wallet and gave Simon a card. 'Appreciate a call when you do.'

As they all walked back through the kitchen, Carter stopped to talk to the woman loading the dishwasher.

'Excuse me, miss. I'm Detective Inspector Carter and this is Detective Constable Willis.'

'Lyndsey,' she said, looking at Simon anxiously.

'Can we have a word, Lyndsey?'

She picked up a towel and dried her hands. She was a woman of mixed British and Asian descent. She had her long black hair tied back in a plait.

'I'll finish that', said the older, auburn-haired woman who'd walked in with a tray of dishes. 'Breakfast is over so you can sit in the canteen now.' She was speaking with a Glaswegian accent. 'I've just cleared the last of the tables. I'm Sheila, by the way.' She set the tray down.

'Thank you, Sheila. Could we have a chat with you too at the same time?'

'No problem. Shall I bring out a cup of tea?'

'Magic.' Carter turned to Simon, who was still with them in the kitchen. 'We won't bother you further. Once we've finished talking to Sheila and Lyndsey, we'll head off.'

'Of course.' Simon smiled, a little uneasy. 'Sorry I couldn't be more helpful.' He went back through the double doors, in the direction of his office.

They went into the canteen and found a table, Sheila following with a tray with four teas on it. The

PC corner was still busy with people waiting their turn.

'Sugar's on the table.'

'Thanks very much.' Carter took the teacups from the tray and waited for Sheila to sit down opposite Willis. Willis took out her notebook and pen.

'Have you two worked here long?' asked Carter.

'I have,' replied Sheila. 'Lyndsey's only been here a couple of weeks but she fits right in.'

'How did you come to work here, Lyndsey?' asked Carter.

'I saw their advertisement for "volunteers needed" when I walked by the church one day.'

'What about you, Sheila?'

'I used to be homeless. I lived in a hostel at King's Cross.'

'So you've been through the system – you can advise people?'

'Yes. I hope so. Everyone needs a helping hand in life, eh?'

'Yes. Absolutely.' Carter looked over at the people chatting by the PCs. Their voices were becoming raised.

'You get to know people well? See the same faces?'

Sheila looked at Lyndsey and they both nodded.

'This place has its characters,' said Lyndsey. 'You see the same people most days; you start to take an interest in what happens to them.'

'I'm sure. Were you both here yesterday evening?'

'Yes, we were,' said Lyndsey.

'We served Sunday lunch. We were out of here at six,' Sheila added.

'So you didn't see the people who stayed here overnight?'

'Not last night; Simon deals with things overnight on Sunday. We saw some of them at breakfast this morning.'

'Can I ask you if you felt there was a strange atmosphere then?'

They looked at one another and nodded. 'We kept asking, "What's going on?"' said Lyndsey.

'What was it that bothered you?' asked Carter.

'The whispering. The worried faces,' said Lyndsey.

'The cuts and brusies too,' Sheila added, shaking her head. 'But there was so much of that secret stuff going on. No one would talk to us.'

'What is it? What has happened?' asked Lyndsey.

'A woman was killed in the derelict buildings on Parade Street,' Carter answered.

'Dear God ... was it Martine?' Sheila gasped, looking at Lyndsey.

Willis shook her head. 'It was a woman named Olivia. She wasn't a rough sleeper. We think she was on her way to meet someone. Her car is parked just up the road. We are working on the theory that she was not meant to be in there – either she was forced or she was drugged – we're waiting for the post-mortem results.'

'Dear God – she shouldn't have gone in there. It's not safe.'

'Who is Martine?' asked Carter.

'She is one of the younger ones,' answered Sheila. 'She sleeps on Parade Street sometimes. She sleeps in lots of places.'

'Have you seen her this morning?' Both women shook their heads. 'Have you seen any of those who sleep on Parade Street?' Willis asked.

'I saw one of them – Toffee.' Sheila looked at Lyndsey, who nodded.

'Yes, I saw him too, as I was coming in this morning. I think he was waiting to speak to Simon.'

'Toffee?' Carter sipped his tea as he noticed Willis empty another packet of sugar into hers.

'He's like a father figure to Martine and the others,' Lyndsey answered. 'To the younger lot.'

'Is he around now?'

'No. I didn't see him after I passed him this morning.' Lyndsey turned to Sheila. 'Did he come in for breakfast?'

'I didn't see him there either,' Sheila answered. 'He was definitely upset about something if he didn't even stay for breakfast. He likes to line his stomach in the morning.'

Willis looked up from her note-taking.

'Toffee? Is that his surname?'

'It's his nickname because he talks posh,' said Sheila. 'I don't know what his real name is.' She looked at Lyndsey, who shook her head.

'So there is a group of people who come here to eat but who sleep on the streets?' Carter asked.

'Yes. They prefer it sometimes, or they just can't give up the substance addiction. Or they have a dog and the dog means too much to them to give up – sometimes it's the only thing that makes life worth living for them. But having a dog keeps them on the streets.'

'And Martine?' Willis looked at Sheila for a reply.

'Martine is anorexic – an abuse victim. She'll come here for tea in the morning, soup at lunchtime, but she won't stay long. She spends a lot of time on her own. The regulars know her at the train station. If the right person's on duty, they'll let her sleep in the toilets. When she does pair up, she stays with Mason; he's about the same age. It's then that she sleeps on Parade Street. Mason has a dog.'

'What's Mason like?'

'He's about thirty. He wears a grey hat pulled down over his ears. He's a quiet lad. His dog is called Sandy. She's ugly-looking but soft when you know her.'

Willis was still making notes.

Carter was watching a heated discussion that had broken out at the PCs.

'Is there anyone that comes here you think we should speak to about this incident?' he asked.

Sheila stood and glared at the group who were arguing over the PCs. She looked down at Carter.

'You should speak to the lads from the estate, that's who.' She leant forward, spoke now in a hissing whisper: 'They kill someone for nothing. They kill as part of some bloody initiation rite. They're always making trouble. They have attacked rough sleepers from this area before now.'

Willis was watching Lyndsey stare into her teacup.

'Is that your judgement too, Lyndsey – that it could be someone from the estate?'

She looked up and shrugged.

'I don't know the area like Sheila but I know the people who come here will lie about most things –

they'll tell you anything they think you want to hear but I would not expect any of them to commit murder.'

Simon Smith appeared then, to sort out the dispute at the PCs.

Carter stood. 'Thanks for your help, ladies, and for the tea,' he said as Willis closed her notebook.

Simon stopped them on their way out.

'Any good?'

'Sheila and Lyndsey have been a great help, thanks. I wanted to ask you about a man named Toffee. Did you speak to him this morning?'

'Toffee? Did I speak to him? Yes, briefly.'

'What about?'

'Just chit-chat, really.'

'Nothing to concern you?' Simon shook his head. 'If you see Toffee again, can you ask him to get in touch with us, please. You have our direct line.'

'Of course.'

Chapter 5

They got outside and walked to the car. Carter got in and slammed the door shut.

'Christ Almighty, you'd think he was doing us a favour. A woman died here, probably killed by some people that Smith was serving breakfast to. Stuck-up twat.' He looked across at Willis as she closed her door.

'Simon Smith was a strange mix,' she said as she did up her seat belt. 'He looked and talked like a confident public-school boy but then he's working in a homeless hostel. There must be more to him.'

'Doesn't need to work, probably,' answered Carter. 'Daddy's money. Maybe this was his do-gooder phase, a project. Maybe Mummy says he needs to find out about the real world.'

'But it's a strange choice of project. It's hard work. It must have something to do with the religious aspect. He didn't stop smiling.'

'Smug.'

'He looked like he was but I'm not sure.'

'We need to find out about him and the church,' said Carter.

'It's things like – I would have thought he'd know

his regulars; he'd make it his business to know them. He must get out and walk around the area,' Willis added. 'But he said he didn't know them.'

'Maybe he gets a taxi back to Knightsbridge every evening.'

Carter looked in his side mirror and saw Simon jogging across to them. 'Hello? Talk of the devil,' he said under his breath.

He wound down his window. 'What can we help you with, Mr Smith?'

'Sorry, I realized I must have come across as unhelpful. Look – I want to help. But it's difficult for me. I'm not only the warden here – I'm a minister.' He looked at each of them in turn, waiting for a reaction. He got a look of begrudging respect from Carter, who had had a broadly Catholic upbringing: dragged to church until he was too big to be cajoled or bribed or threatened. But his Catholicism affected him in many ways. It stopped him from getting married to Cabrina. He couldn't risk the marriage failing. Simon got a look of suspicion from Willis, who had little regard for religion of any kind.

'I have more than just an obligation to respect privacy. It is a matter of faith – them having faith in me and me sticking to mine. I don't want people to stop using this centre. People around here rely on coming here when the weather gets cold like this.'

'I understand.' Carter was about to try his charm, thought Willis. He usually managed to win people over – male or female. She was intrigued to see what angle he'd take with Simon. 'But, if the press get hold of the fact that a group of homeless people are involved in the murder of a hard-working family-law solicitor, well . . . after all . . . it's a tricky thing for the public to get their head round. Even if it turns out to be nothing – it might be too late to stop more prejudice from creeping in. I can see how hard you work here and what a good job you do. I know how much you rely on funding.'

'It has nothing to do with this hostel and we get funding by various commercial means. We are not reliant on government grants.' Simon looked exasperated. He took a deep breath. 'I was given something to look after this morning.' Simon took a phone out of his pocket. He handed it to Carter.

Carter switched it on. 'It's hers,' he said as he handed it to Willis. 'Phone Robbo.' Carter turned back to Simon. 'Who gave this to you?'

'Toffee. The man you mentioned.'

'What did he say when he gave it to you?'

'He asked me to look after it.'

'You didn't ask him where it came from? You didn't look at it?'

'No, I was busy this morning. I was still working when you came in, if you remember. I hadn't had time to look at it.'

'So Toffee gave it to you this morning; what time?'

'At eight. I found him outside when I opened up.'

'What did he look like?'

'He had a few cuts on his face. He looked agitated, upset. He looked a mess, but then he often does. I tried to make him come in but he wouldn't.'

'We asked you if anything strange had occurred and you didn't think to mention this?'

'Because it isn't strange for here. Fights are common. Injuries happen every day when people live in these circumstances.'

'Where do you think he will have gone?'

'I don't know exactly. He hangs about with another man, Spike. He's not here either. I think if you try the parks, bus stations – just about anywhere there's shelter and they can sit and drink. They never go far.'

'Do you have a photo of him?'

Simon shook his head. 'Sorry. He's about five nine, very thin. His hair is grey, curly. He wears a brown jacket with a lighter-coloured collar.'

'And Spike?'

'He's shorter, bald; with a spider's-web tattoo on his neck; he's an ex-con. He's more vocal. He gets drunk faster. We've had to throw him out of here for fighting.'

Sandy woke instantly from a deep sleep when she heard someone approach. She had learnt to stay absolutely still, next to her master, and to strike at the last minute if the threat came too near him. She would not step away too far from the man she had to protect.

As the man got within a few feet, she leapt out and wagged her tail and pushed her big head inside the man's hand to lick his palm.

'All right, girl. Stay quiet now.'

Mason groaned. 'Toffee?' He was having difficulty opening his eyes – they had swollen up as he dozed. Toffee sat down on the blue coat and he examined Mason's face. Mason brought up his hand to cover it.

'You're in a state, lad.'

'I'm okay.'

The pair sat for a few moments in silence as they listened to the train thunder past overhead. People were getting in their cars in the car park. Doors slammed, laughter hung shrill in the air.

Toffee turned to watch Sandy as she went across to the next archway, to look for food amongst the rubbish.

'Why did you go back?'

Mason shrugged and propped himself up. His head tilted back on the side of the stone. He squinted at Toffee, shook his head. Then he closed his eyes again.

'That face will get infected. You need to clean it, stitch it up. We can't take you to A&E – they'll be watching. I'll go and find you something to do it with and get you a drink too – help to ease the pain. I'll be back. Stay here. Here's some money, in case you need it.'

He rolled two twenty-pound notes tightly before pushing them into the lining of Mason's coat.

'I don't want it.' He shook his head.

'Take it. You earned it, lad.'

Chapter 6

After they watched Simon walk back into the hostel, Carter started the car. He called Robbo again.

'We're bringing in Olivia Grantham's phone but I need a team of officers to go in to Hannover Estate within the next hour. I want to hit it quickly and a message sent out to signal we mean business. If we leave it too long, gang members will have had time to intimidate any possible witnesses and time to cement stories. Make sure the gangs know we're not going anywhere. I need a team of ten officers, in pairs. Have armed police on standby. We need to find Mahmet Balik—'

'Guv?' Willis interrupted. 'I want to go in as part of the team.'

Carter nodded. 'Robbo – correction, we'll give this phone to a patrol car to bring in to you and we'll coordinate the search of Hannover Estate ourselves. Pick officers who know this area where you can; we'll wait at the entrance to Parade Street.'

Hannover Estate was an amalgamation of post-war red-brick council housing and newer high-rise concrete towers. The two had been botched together with social housing based on small streets and balconies, gardens and civic pride. The reality had been the opposite. Families who didn't care for the community had been dumped there and the place became a breeding ground for gangs. There had been no more building since the early 1990s. The estate was slowly being left to decay from the inside out, as the council stopped maintaining it in the hope that it would slowly empty of residents when their lives became intolerable.

They waited in the car with a map of the estate up on Carter's iPad and worked out how they were going to cover the whole of it.

'It will take several days to make sure we catch the people at work,' said Carter as he moved the map on the screen. Willis jotted down the names of the various areas.

'We will split the estate into five sections and you and I will take the one here, nearest to the crime scene. This is also the roughest end, where the gangs are causing the most trouble. We'll try and catch them by surprise. Where is Balik supposed to be living?'

'In one of the four-storey blocks, Drydon House, apparently – that's the one beside the tower block.'

'Okay, we'll go straight there when the rest of the team arrive; we all start at exactly the same time, so that we have a chance of seeing who we flush out.'

As they sat waiting at the end of Parade Street, they saw Sandford coming out of 22. He was stretching out his long back as he went across to his van, then took something out from the rear.

'People never die where it's easy to get at them, do they, Eb?'

'No, they're never so obliging, are they? They must be getting ready to move her soon.'

They stared down the street in silence as they watched Sandford go back inside the building.

'This street reminds me of where I grew up,' said Carter. 'It was here in the East End in Shadwell before it was upmarket. None of your swanky restaurants and private clubs then. Good honest people that took care of one another. People lived alongside one another. My nan lived in a tower block – she and the other residents took it in turns to wash the stairs.'

Willis was watching the council estate – it seemed peaceful. It was school time. Monday midday. A few mums were chatting and pre-school kids were running around the green bits between the buildings. Dogs were coming out to defecate. She looked back at Parade Street and at Carter, who was still being nostalgic. A police van drew up behind them and uniformed officers got out.

'Okay – we'll brief the team and get on with it.' Twenty minutes later the five teams of two were ready to move into the estate. Two of the teams got back into the van and were taken to start at the other end of the large estate.

'Keep in constant touch with each other. Anything you think should be followed up then call Detective Willis or myself and we'll pursue it. We have armed officers ready to assist should we need them but I want to keep this friendly. This is an exercise to find out if anyone saw anything last evening and to locate Balik.'

Willis and Carter made their way past the garage block where Willis had encountered Mason and his dog, Sandy. They headed towards the flats to the right of the tower block, where Carter had thought he'd seen someone run. They walked past the flats at ground level, with their small back yards where kids were playing. The place had the feel of a ghost town. Litter blew past their feet. In the kiddies' park was one of the children on a squeaky sea-saw, whilst his mother leant on it with one hand and talked on her phone with the other. She watched the officers approaching and her eyes went up to the block of flats behind her. Willis looked up and heard a dog barking.

No one wanted to talk to them. They got a call from Team 3, the two officers who had taken the middle section of the estate.

'Sir? Found someone willing to say something about the gangs. Mahmet Balik stays with his grandfather on the sixteenth floor of the tower block at your end. They didn't know what number it was but they said his flat looks over the kiddies' playground.'

'Okay, thanks.'

The entrance door to the tower block was propped open. The entry phone had been dismantled.

'Don't touch the banisters,' said Willis. 'Sometimes they Sellotape used syringes underneath.' Carter retracted his hand quickly.

'I forgot you spent time with your mum in one of these estates.'

'Not such a bad place when you know the rules,' said Willis. 'Not a place I can get sentimental about though.'

Carter turned back, walked towards the lift and pressed the button.

'Miracle, it works,' he said and recoiled as the door opened and the smell of urine hit them. It had crystallized on the floor. He stepped inside, followed by Willis.

'Better than walking up to the sixteenth,' he added. 'But only just.'

They got out to the sound of a baby crying somewhere along the corridor. There was the smell of breakfast lingering in the hallway.

'Got to be this way if it overlooks the playground,' said Carter as he walked along the landing and took a right. They stood and listened. Only two of the five flats had any noise coming from them. The first one appeared unoccupied.

They knocked on the second and waited. A dog barked on the other side of the door.

'Hello, Mr Balik?'

There was the sound of a chain being latched across. An old man swore at the dog.

'Yes, what do you want?'

'Can we have a word?'

They stood back from the door as it opened and the dog forced its head through the gap to snarl at them. It had the body of a punchbag and the head of a gargoyle.

The old man poked his head round the door too.

'Mr Balik?' repeated Carter.

'Yes?'

'We are police officers.' He showed his warrant card. 'Is Mahmet around?'

'Who?' The old man tried to get around the dog as he held on to the collar.

'Your grandson.'

'No.' He started to close the door. Carter put a hand on it to keep it open. The dog went berserk.

'Is that your dog?' he asked.

'No; I'm just looking after it.'

'He's not very friendly, is he?' said Carter. 'Whose is it? Are you allowed to keep a dog here?'

'I'm only looking after it for someone – it will be gone soon.'

'Who are you looking after it for?'

'What?' He looked like he didn't want to say.

'Is it Mahmet?'

'He's coming to get it in a couple of days,' said the grandfather.

'If we need to come in, Mr Balik, we need that dog under control and I don't believe it is.'

'Yes. It's a good dog. It just doesn't like strangers.'

'Tell Mahmet we need to speak to him, Mr Balik. Tell him we will come back with a dog handler and we will have this dog destroyed if it's found to be a dangerous type, which I'm pretty sure is the case. Are you listening, Mr Balik?'

'Yes. Yes.' He was struggling to keep the dog back as he closed the door.

Carter talked through the closed door.

'You need to get help with that dog, Mr Balik.

'Poor old fella,' Carter said as they walked away

back down the corridor. 'We'll start knocking on doors at the other end of the corridor. Mahmet is obviously still around if he's left his monster of a dog here with his granddad. He can't have gone far.'

Chapter 7

Dr Kahn had finished cataloguing Olivia Grantham's external injuries on the body diagram by the time Carter and Willis got through the traffic and were suited up for the post-mortem.

Kahn greeted them, apologized for having to start without them, then nodded to his assistant, Mark, that he was ready for him to make the first incision. Kahn was a patient man and a lot slower than Dr Harding. He did not spend his time irritably tapping his pen or scalpel whilst waiting for Mark to get a move on. Willis and Carter hovered nearby. Willis was looking over Mark's shoulder, watching what he was doing, out of interest. Kahn had the kind of demeanour where nothing bothered him. He was semi-retired now and looked forward to being called in to help when needed; it got him out from under his wife's feet, so everyone was happy.

Mark picked up a scalpel from the tray and leant across the body as he started at the left-inside shoulder and guided the knife with just the right amount of pressure as he cut through the skin and fat. He made another incision from the right shoulder, down to

meet his first at the sternum, then he applied more
pressure to cut in a straight line down to the pubic
bone. He ran the knife over the cut again, in a couple
of places where the layer of fat was thicker, and then
opened the skin, cutting as he went, as if he were fil-
leting a fish, exposing her breastplate and a mass of
wobbly intestines. He stopped with the rib shears in
his hand and pulled out an implant from inside the
breast.

'A 34 Double D, I would say – silicone; bad choice.
Saline's so much more natural.' He turned it over in
his hands like a dead jellyfish.

Dr Kahn came forward to clamp off the lower
intestine and remove it in one block. He examined the
cavity as he cut out her spleen, removed the membrane and held it in his hand.

'Damaged beyong repair.' He passed judgement on
it before cutting out her liver and making cuts at one-
centimetre intervals along it. 'Bruising – otherwise a
healthy-looking liver. But there is bleeding in the peri-
toneal cavity. She has taken quite a beating.'

Mark snapped through each rib with the shears and
lifted out the breastplate whole.

'Any sign of clots?' asked Kahn as he came forward
to look at the heart and lungs. Mark shook his head.
'Mind if I take a look?'

Mark loved this side of working with Kahn. He was
treated with respect – his opinion mattered a lot more
than it did with Harding. But Harding was a genius
and if Mark died under suspicious curcumstances,
he'd want Harding to find out how and why.

Kahn waited until Mark had finished cutting open

Olivia Grantham's neck and then he watched him pick up the electric saw and carfully cut into the incision around her skull. Kahn opened it with a twist of a small chisel, used like a key to pop out the skull section, and then he cut through the thick white membrane and paused as he leant over to study the brain at eye level.

'We have already photographed the injury to her skull from the outside.' He handed the piece of skull to Mark, who began stripping out the membrane. 'But now we will get a better look at it.' He was still squatting in front of the exposed brain. He wiped it with his hand.

'I see damage here that corresponds with the position of the fracture-skull injury. This could have been enough to kill her – we will see when we get the brain out.'

Kahn took a pair of curved scissors from the tray and reached inside, to cut through the optic nerves and prise the brain out of its shell, cutting through the brain stem.

Willis was studying the skull portion with Mark.

'It's a crack of four centimetres straight and then a right-angled crush injury at the end of that,' she said as she took a photograph. Mark drew it on the diagram. Whilst he was doing that, Willis was sketching the dimensions of the wound.

'It looks like a square-shaped instrument. It's a tool, a hammer maybe.'

'Yeah – not sure . . .' She was looking at her drawing. 'It's left a rim shape, a space in the middle where there is no bruising.'

'Yes –' He beamed at Willis – 'you're right.'

Kahn coughed. They turned to see him holding the brain in both his hands. 'Mark ... please take this from me.'

As they cleaned up, Carter got a call from Robbo.

'A group of homeless men have been spotted by a patrol car; the officers haven't approached but they say a couple look about right for the two we're looking for. They want to know what you want them to do.'

'Where are they?'

'In the area in front of Shadwell Station. Another thing – they've spotted Mahmet Balik nearby. He was seen talking to the rough sleepers outside the chemist's shop earlier on.'

'Okay. We're on our way. Tell the patrol to make themselves scarce. I don't want them to run.'

They finished up fast at the mortuary and drove down to Shadwell. They parked nearby and continued on foot towards the entrance to the station.

'Guv?'

'Yeah – I've seen them.' A group of men were sitting against the station wall.

'Can we have a word?' Carter said as they approached, and were met with a volley of abuse from the bald man sitting at the end of the group. As he turned away from them, a blue web tattoo was visible on his neck.

'Oy – big mouth – watch your language,' Carter said as he got near and pointed to the carrier bag. 'What's in there?'

He already knew what was in it. White Ace cider, sold from under the counter of newsagents' and grocery stores. The group began making moves to leave.

A new man approached from an adjoining street. He had a light collar on his jacket and was carrying a chemist's carrier bag. Carter saw him at the same time as Willis did and she edged left of the group. The man dropped his bag and bolted through the station and then through the open ticket barrier. They chased after him. As Willis sprinted over the railway bridge, she lost eye contact with the platforms below until she looked down from the top of the stairs to see the man running along the tracks and Carter keeping pace on the platform above.

She flew back down the way she'd come and sprinted along the platform, shouting at people to get back. The oncoming train was so close that she could see the train driver's panic-stricken expression.

Carter had jumped onto the track and was trying to drag the man to the side, shouting at him to move. Willis was within a few metres of Carter when the man gave up any movement and sank to his knees. Her voice was drowned out by the noise of the train passing. She reached out ready to grab Carter as she turned her face from the whoosh of air, the squeal of metal on metal and the scream of pain.

Chapter 8

'Guv? You okay?'

Carter stood outside the station with his head bowed as the man was being loaded into the ambulance.

'Christ . . . I should have been able to lift him off the track,' he said – angry with himself.

'He was a dead weight, guv. You did your best. He's still breathing. He might live.'

'Yeah – hope so.' Willis looked at Carter's face. He was ghostly pale. 'Pretty sure that's Toffee. He matches the description and he definitely didn't want to talk to us.' Carter leant over, catching his breath.

'Think so, guv. Looks like his mates have gone. Shall we get back in the car and search for them or do you need a coffee first, guv?'

'No.' He looked up and smiled. 'I need a Scotch . . . and a bloody big one.' He straightened up. 'That's enough of an adrenalin rush for one day. Ring Robbo and make sure Toffee's kept under guard at the hospital. I want to talk to him as soon as he's able and if he makes it. The patrols will have more luck finding Toffee's mates than we will. You're right – I need a cup of coffee.' Carter took off his coat and began beating the dust out of it with the back of his hand. 'I don't reckon these men will have gone far.' Carter looked forlornly at the dirt on his sleeve. 'Christ Almighty – if there's one thing I hate!'

They stopped at a café Carter knew well – he ordered aubergine pasta bake whilst Willis had a burger and fries.

He stared at her eating. It was something that both repulsed and fascinated him. 'You eat like it's your last meal and you've only got seconds to eat it,' Carter said as he picked at his food.

Willis didn't answer; she opened the burger bun and squirted on more ketchup. Carter's phone rang whilst they were eating. He talked and ate one-handed.

'Robbo? How did they say he is? Both legs? Shit! Yes, I'm fine. Have the patrols located his mates yet? What about Balik? No, we'll keep looking when we finish here: we'll call in at a few more homeless hostels in the area, and then we'll head over to the hospital.'

He finished his call and continued to watch Willis eat.

'I thought you were going to take a holiday after Christmas, but you came straight back to work. What happened – you changed your mind?'

She shrugged as she licked ketchup from her fingers.

'I thought you and Tina had it all planned. You were off to Cancún or somewhere? To drink buckets of booze and party hard?'

'I decided to wait a while.'

'For what?'

She pushed a chip around the salt on her plate.

'Just wasn't the right time.'

'You okay?'

'Yes, guv.'

'Don't "yes, guv" me, Ebony Willis. I want to know what's up with my partner.'

She stopped eating and pushed her plate away.

'My mum tried to commit suicide.' She made fleeting eye contact with him and then she took a sip of her Coke.

'Shit. When?'

'Christmas Day.'

'Jesus ... I didn't know she wasn't coping. Sorry – I've been so preoccupied with my dad and his cancer, I had no idea, Eb.'

'She's been self-harming.'

'Shit, Eb. Any idea why?'

'I missed some appointments to go and see her. I've been busy and ... I found excuses, I guess.'

'Stop there, Eb... ' He leant in to emphasize. '*Do not* blame yourself for anything your mother does or doesn't do. She's a past master at manipulation.'

'Yeah. I know. But she is still my mum and I should have gone to see her.'

'Okay, go and see her then. Can I suggest you go soon and get it over with?'

'We're busy.'

'I can spare you for a couple of hours.'

Chapter 9

'Is he awake?' Carter asked the nurse escorting them through to Intensive Care later that day – she had a sweet fresh face that belied the fact she'd been out partying the night before and was chewing gum to hide the smell of alcohol. Her badge said *Ivy Miller*.

'Has he said what his name is, Nurse?'

'Yes. Michael Hitchens. He came round briefly before he went down to theatre – he's had both legs amputated from the knee but he has complications that we are keeping an eye on. He sustained a head injury. He asked me to ring the man who runs the hostel where he stays sometimes, to come and be with him.'

'Simon Smith?'

'Yes. That's right. I asked the front desk to phone him.'

Carter glanced at Willis. She knew what he was thinking.

'Can we see him straight away, please, Ivy? Can I call you Ivy?' Carter tried his caring smile that said: 'We're the good guys, help us out here.'

'Yes. Okay. Just take it gently.' She hesitated. 'When I got him undressed he had a lot of money on him.'

'How much?'

'Two hundred and fifty pounds and some change.'

Inside the room, there were so many connecting wires and tubes from machine to patient that it was difficult to get close to him. Carter walked round to the left-hand side and watched as Ivy checked the machines.

'Michael?' Carter said. Willis waited at the foot of the bed. 'Toffee? Is that your name?'

He nodded his response. Ivy leant in to speak to him.

'There are police officers in the room, Michael; they want to talk to you. Do you think you can?' His eyes fluttered, he looked at her, and then followed her gaze to Carter.

He nodded, cleared his throat as he said, 'Hope you aren't hurt?' to Carter. He struggled to talk, but when he did, he had the voice of a retired English teacher. Ivy fed a drinks tube into the side of his mouth to help with his dryness.

Carter shook his head. 'No, I'm not hurt. I'm just sorry I couldn't get you off the track in time. Are you the man who made the call about the dead woman, Toffee?'

'Excuse me?' Simon Smith opened the door and stepped inside. He looked annoyed to see Carter and Willis. He walked straight round to the opposite side of the bed to Carter and took Toffee's hand into his.

'Toffee? Is there anything I can do for you? Do you want the officers to leave?' Toffee shook his head.

'We need to talk to you about Olivia Grantham who, died on Parade Street,' Carter persisted, and Ivy flashed a concerned look at him as machines registered Toffee's heartbeat climb. 'You had Olivia's phone. Did you see what happened to her?'

Toffee turned away from Carter and sucked on the drinks tube again.

Toffee's eyes stayed on Simon, who held tightly to his hand. He was struggling to breathe.

'I tried to help her, I swear. It all went wrong.' He looked at Simon.

Simon nodded. 'It's okay, Toffee. You don't have to say anything.'

Toffee screwed up his face in pain as he tried to swallow. The nurse fed the drinks tube back into his mouth. She looked anxiously at Carter. Willis was watching the machines. Toffee's pulse was climbing fast. Carter leant nearer to him. Toffee kept his eyes fixed on Simon.

Carter spoke softly. 'Did you get paid to kill her, Toffee?'

Simon looked towards the nurse to stop the conversation. 'Don't talk any more, Toffee, rest. Nurse?'

Toffee shook his head, agitated.

'I tried to protect her but . . .' His voice rasped as he struggled to talk and breathe. He clutched at Simon's hand. 'Find Mason.' The machines around Toffee squealed out their alarms and flatlined. Ivy pressed the emergency buzzer. She pulled Simon out of the way and began resuscitating. Carter and Willis moved to the back of the room as the resusc team arrived and Ivy ushered the detectives and Simon outside.

'You have to wait in the corridor, I'm sorry.'

'Ivy – we need the clothes that he came in with,' said Carter.

She nodded. 'I'll get them for you. What about the rest of his belongings? The money?'

'We'll take those too, please.'

They were left alone in the corridor as they watched through the window at the frantic efforts to keep Toffee alive.

Carter turned to Simon. 'Mason, the lad with the dog? That's who he's talking about?'

Simon shook his head. 'I'm not sure.'

'He seemed to think you'd know. I hear Toffee is a father figure to some of the younger ones, Mason included. He asked you to look for him. He must think you have a chance of finding him. If it's the same lad we saw – he definitely needs help with the injuries to his face.'

'I don't know Mason or where he is. I wouldn't know where to look. But, I'll do what I can – talk to the regulars. I'll do my best.'

Carter wasn't having it.

'Did you ever see him with large amounts of money on him before?'

'No. Never.'

'So you'd be surprised to learn he came in here with two hundred and fifty quid?'

'It's a big surprise.'

'No idea where he got it?'

'No, I'm sorry.'

Someone must have an idea; one of his friends must know something. We need your cooperation with this.

They obviously talk to you. Someone's going to be wanting to get it off their chest – they might even be looking for the money. Find Spike for us. He must know Toffee's involvement. Tell them there's a reward for information. I'll pay fifty quid to the person who tells me something useful.'

They looked back through the window into Toffee's room.

The machines had come to life again.

Ivy brought Toffee's belongings and clothes in a bag for Carter. He signed for them.

A blonde-haired woman wearing the detective's unofficial uniform of black trousers and a dark jacket came towards them down the corridor.

'This is Detective Constable Zoe Blackman,' Carter said to Simon as she got near, before walking her back down the corridor to talk with her privately.

'We need samples: hair from all sites, DNA, finger-prints. As much as we can get. You'll be all right to stay the night?'

'Yes, sir.'

'That's our prime murder suspect in there.'

'Yes, sir.'

'And get friendly with Simon Smith. He's lying or at least he's not telling us everything he could. I want to know why.'

'Yes, sir.'

Sandy stood and stretched as she felt Mason move in his sleep. She was desperate to get up. She walked across to the other side of the arch, where she had once killed and eaten a rat and squatted and peed.

From there she could watch anyone approach. She began a low growl.

'Mason – it's Spike. Tell your dog to back off. Mason!'

Mason turned over.

'Sandy, come here, girl,' he called. She wagged her tail as she obeyed and sat next to him to wait, keeping an eye on Spike. 'Where's Toffee?' asked Mason.

'He's hurt. Train hit him. We saw the ambulance come. It was in a hurry so I suppose he's alive. Not sure for how long. Jesus, look at your face.'

'A train?'

'Yes, a train. The police chased him. We're all in a lot of trouble.'

Mason shook his head, confused. He couldn't take it in.

'He had this bag of stuff when it happened. He told me he was getting it for you.' Spike opened the carrier bag from the chemist's. 'I suppose I can try and clean you up if you want and you can owe me?' Mason didn't answer. Spike laid out the contents of the bag on the blue coat and tore open a packet of antiseptic wipes, opened a bottle of antiseptic. Mason flinched as Spike cleaned up the cuts and stuck strips across to hold them shut. The cut beneath Mason's eye opened up again immediately.

'There – that's the best I can do. I'll bring you some food later, if you've got money. Did Toffee give you any? I know he had some on him.' Mason didn't answer. He lay back and closed his eyes and breathed hard through the pain. 'Where is it?' Spike put his hand inside Mason's pocket; Sandy sprang forward and growled.

Spike got to his feet. 'All right, all right – you can fucking starve then. Have it your own way.'

After Spike left, the day grew dark and Sandy grew so hungry she couldn't settle, but she wouldn't leave Mason. She watched him as he slept. She sniffed Mason's face. She listened to him as he talked in his sleep and she lay close by to keep him warm.

Chapter 10

In the morning, Sandy opened an eye at the sound of the cars arriving to park for the day. She recognized the sounds of individual cars. She crept out to take a look and to watch the people. None of them ever took any notice of her or her master. She watched the young woman get out of her car. She did the same thing every day. She got out and put on her coat and then she reached back in for her backpack. It smelt of food.

At ten, Carter and Willis were back in Robbo's office with him and his staff. They had worked late into the night.

'Did you check her PC yet, Robbo?' Carter turned in his seat to ask.

'We're still doing it. It will take time.'

Carter picked up the sheets to read through Olivia Grantham's phone records.

'About one in five of these texts is sexually explicit,' said Hector. 'And they're from different men.'

'Did you have trouble getting into the phone?'

'No. I managed to bypass her code easily. It looks

like she gives several men the same surname: Naughties. So we have Peter Naughties, Mark Naughties, JJ Naughties. I Googled Naughties. It's a website for swinging Londoners.'

'I know it. Naughties is the one advertised on the Tube, isn't it?' asked Carter. 'The one with the woman with heavy eye make-up saying "Shhh" and the man stripping off in the background?'

'That's the one,' answered Robbo.

'Start phoning these men – the ones she's been texting,' said Carter, looking at Hector. 'No – on second thoughts, ring all of the male contacts you can find on her phone. We need to know if they met her, if they had sex with her and, if so, then we need the details. Check out where they were on Sunday evening. Tell them Olivia Grantham has been involved in an incident and we're trying to trace her contacts. Try not to give too much away. I want to know exactly who they are, what they do for a living, any previous for anything at all. We need to build up more of a picture of Olivia's life and we need to talk to her workmates again. Someone must know who she'd been seeing.'

'Do we need to be discreet?' asked Hector. 'They could be married.' He looked at Carter's expression. Carter had a face that read: 'Who cares?'

Carter shrugged. 'Okay. We'll be respectful ... for now.'

Robbo sat forward in his chair and pulled images up on his screen.

'You attended the post-mortem?'

Carter nodded. 'Yes. Dr Kahn, Harding's stand-in,

performed it. Have you got the post-mortem report yet?' he asked.

Robbo pressed the download button on the screen and Willis came round to his PC to view it.

He brought up the photos of Olivia Grantham's body on the mortuary table, then zoomed in and scanned down the photo of the first overall view of the body. Willis sat down in front of the screen.

'Three cracked ribs, broken humerus.' Robbo said, bringing up the X-ray. 'Several bite marks,' he added as he continued to study it. 'Kahn says here that she died from a brain injury caused by a head wound, but that there was internal bleeding and a ruptured spleen. Beaten to death, basically.'

They took a few minutes to look through the photos. Carter sat back.

'Mob frenzy that someone paid for.'

'Gang rape can't have been what she was looking for or buying in to?' said Robbo. He looked at the photo of Olivia that was on the Linkedin site. It was the profile of a family lawyer. 'She was headed for great things in her company: ambitious and bright. All the things you'd expect.'

'Except her sex life was lacking and she was look-ing to spice it up,' said Carter.

'You think of lawyers as cautious types,' said Pam. Her desk was neatly divided into piles of files. She was the senior researcher in the room. She spent her time trolling through details on websites and checking facts.

Carter shook his head. 'Not this one, Pam,' he said as he continued looking through transcripts of the texts. 'Her bucket list was getting longer by the minute.'

'She had plenty of sex equipment in her flat,' said Carter. 'She'd already tried more than the average person.' He looked Willis's way. She was quieter than he liked her to be. He wished she'd spend more time speaking her thoughts.

'Detective Willis?'

'Yes, guv?'

'The sex equipment in Olivia Grantham's flat. Is she a giver or a taker?'

'The hood with the mouthpiece was definitely a woman's. I think she must have been submissive.'

'Yeah ... submissive but not suicidal, huh?' said Carter, turning round to Robbo. 'I think she must have been still learning – she was pushing the boundaries of her sexual experiences ...'

'Any good photos of her on the phone, Hector?' asked Robbo. 'Anything we can give Intel, to try and spot her on CCTV in the area around? She may have checked out this place before she went there on Sunday evening.'

Hector smiled, embarrassed. 'Brings a whole new meaning to *selfies*. But yeah ... a few headshots, normal ones. I'll download her photo library and see who she's with in them.'

Carter leant back in his chair to think. 'Pam – your comment about her being a cautious type – you're right. It had to have been someone she trusted *enough*. She wouldn't have met someone in there that she didn't know, that she hadn't had sex with before. She was a bright woman – calculated-risk taker. How

far are you on the list of phone contacts, Hector?'
Carter looked across at him.

'I've phoned three so far. Haven't been able to get
hold of two others. Just about to try this one now.'

'Okay, I'll give it a go. Pass me over your list. I want
to ring the Mr Naughties myself.' Hector handed
Carter the sheet of names. 'Can you give me a line
that can't be traced?' Hector nodded. Carter read off
the first number on the sheet and rang from the phone
on the desk. He put it on speaker. The first two numbers went to voicemail. The third call was answered.

'Hello, is that Peter?'

'Yes.'

'Peter, this is the customer services department from
Naughties Dating for Consenting Adults.'

'What? Who?'

'Naughties website. You subscribe?'

'You shouldn't call me.' He hung up.

'Okay – give him thirty minutes then we'll try
again.' Carter rang the next number on the list.

'Hello?'

'Yes? JJ Ellerman speaking. Mermaid Yachts. How
can I help?' Pam and Hector stopped working.

Robbo had already started typing the name and the
company into Google. Willis kept her eyes on Carter
as she listened to the call. The reception wasn't brilliant on speakerphone.

'Hello, sir,' Carter said. 'Naughties Dating here –
London's favourite sexy adult encounters website.
This is customer services.'

'Pardon?' Ellerman sounded annoyed. 'I can't speak
now.' Robbo gave Carter a look that said: *Really?*

Followed by: *I want no part of it*. Hector grinned.
'This is supposed to be a discreet service. You should
not be ringing me.'

Carter winked at Robbo. Robbo shook his head
disapprovingly. But he hid a smile as he leant over his
PC, watching the seach results appear on screen.

'Don't worry, Mr Ellerman, your information is
secure. I just need to check we're giving the best service to you that we can. You put that you're looking
for encounters in the London area? Would you be
interested in extending your search countrywide?'

'Look, I don't have time now. I'm busy.' Ellerman
hung up.

'Unethical, but effective,' said Robbo. 'JJ Ellerman –
he's registered to an address in Richmond. He is the
MD of a boat-building company that builds luxury
yachts. Mermaid Yachts, as he said.' Robbo squinted
at the screen. 'Self-made, impressive.'

'Let's get the full picture of him and all the others
on her phone, Hector. Go back a year for me. Get all
the information on her you can. What type of men
does she go for? What does she look for? She must
have talked it through with someone. Talk to the girl-
friend she met on Saturday night. What about
Facebook, Pam?'

'She doesn't use it much. She uses Linkedin much
more but always professionally rather than socially.'

'She's got several dating-site aps on her phone,'
Hector said. 'Casualsex, Sparks, Adultfun. All of them
for sex rather than soulmates.'

'Try and get into her accounts.' Carter looked to see
if Robbo would react with his civil liberties chat but

he was still checking out JJ Ellerman's profile. Carter poured out the coffee. 'Was Olivia actually single?' Carter asked Hector. 'Do we know if she had a boyfriend?'

Robbo answered: 'So far as we know, she wasn't seeing anyone. Never been married. Bright, fast-tracked-in-her-career type. I think maybe relationships were an afterthought to her,' he added as he printed off a résumé on JJ Ellerman. 'Whereas, this guy, Mr John James Ellerman of Mermaid Yachts, has been married for twenty-one years. He's really big on relationships.'

Chapter 11

JJ Ellerman hung up and cranked up his classic rock CD as he hit the edges of Dartmoor. 'You're As Cold As Ice' came on. He sang along as his Range Rover thundered over the cattle grid.

As he rose up and over his first hill he slowed down to take in the view. Austere and wild, clouds' shadows raced across the stark moorland that was strewn with massive black-granite boulders toppling from dramatic peaks. The low winter sun gave a shimmering pink haze across the dried fern and yellow gorse.

He pulled over at the side of the road, where a mare and foal were grazing the sparse vegetation, and checked the coordinates on his satnav; then he reached back to pick up the printed directions from the back seat. Satisfied he knew where he was going, he picked up his phone and sent the same text to five people:

Miss you. Love JJ.

Ellerman skipped on to the next track in his rock anthems: 'Stairway to Heaven'.

He placed his phone on charge and then followed his directions and drove through a small village, past an ancient church with a cluster of crumbling graves, then a white-painted thatched inn. He turned off at the edge of the village and came to the end of a stony track – the wisp of woodsmoke circled above the roof of a smart-looking barn renovation.

Turning into the steep driveway his car finally came to a stop outside the long barn.

Megan opened the front door and stood watching him. He thought how she was just as beautiful as the first time they had met six months earlier. Her eyes stayed intensely fixed on him.

He switched off the engine, got out and reached in the back for his jacket. The icy wind blew through the fabric of his thin shirt and dried the layer of perspiration on his skin.

She stepped towards him. 'You were lucky you made it – the forecast is for snow. But you never know what you're going to get here – four seasons in a day sometimes. You found me okay?'

'Of course.' He gave her the look that he called his Bond look – it involved a lopsided smile and a raise of one eyebrow. A combination created to charm.

'Did it take you long?'

'About five hours.'

Ellerman closed the car door and took a step closer to her. 'It was a lovely drive. I was early so I even took a detour to see an art exhibition at a town on the way – in Ashburton.' She looked impressed as she tilted her head and smiled. All the time her eyes were watching him.

'I was wondering if your work would be there but I didn't see it.'

She smiled with her eyes. He thought how full of passion they were, so dark. Her skin was luminescent. Her hair was long and flowing around her shoulders in a mane of black and silver.

'I'm not exhibiting locally at the moment. My agent in London is taking everything I can produce. I can show you some of my canvases – works in progress.' She reached out a hand as he came near. 'I appreciate you coming all this way.'

He looked at her hands; they looked older than the rest of her – the years of oil painting had dried them.

'It's no trouble. I have an appointment in Exeter this evening, just finalizing a really big order for five yachts. But I couldn't wait to see you again – that's the truth. You left me wanting more.' He leant in to smell her as he kissed her neck. She smelt of roses and musk. She wore a velvet dress that came almost to the floor. Between her breasts was a silver pendant. He watched it rise and fall then traced it with his forefinger.

'A Claddagh pendant … Love, loyalty and friendship. Did you wear that especially for me?'

She gave a curious smile, her eyes shining. 'Perhaps.' She looked past him. 'Looks like the mist's following you. It wants to keep you here.'

Ellerman turned to see that all around was now obscured by white, and cold dampness filled the air.

She looked at him. 'I hope you don't intend trying to leave,' she said, laughing as she turned towards the house.

'No intention of it. One moment.' Ellerman turned back to his car, opened the passenger door and, reaching inside, he pulled out a box that had been on the floor. It contained six bottles of wine.

'I brought us something interesting to try. It's ideal for the Dartmoor weather. I hope you're keen on taking risks?'

'Absolutely.'

He followed her into the house and down some stone steps into a flagstone-floored kitchen with a large Aga, a sturdy oak table and hanging pots and pans. He came behind her and slipped his hands around her waist. The velvet of her dress was soft to the touch. He heard her intake of breath.

'But, are you ready for the first taste?' she said breathlessly.

'Yes.'

'Close your eyes.'

She stepped away from him and he heard the clink of glasses and the sound of liquid filling a glass. He smiled knowingly.

'Unmistakable.'

'Damn!' She laughed. 'I opened the bottle as you drove in. I hoped to be cunning. You heard the fizz as it hit the glass, didn't you?'

'Yes. Let me guess the vintage. Mmm. I can smell almond and cocoa and ... dried flowers.' He took a sip and held the liquid on his tongue for a few seconds before he swallowed and smiled and nodded appreciatively.

'Yes ... tactile, dark and chiselled, even. Dom Pérignon 2004?'

She laughed excitedly. He could feel her heat close to him.

He opened his eyes slowly. 'What a perfect choice to cement our friendship.'

She smiled, happy. 'When I read that on your profile – "my favourite thing of all is champagne" – then I knew you'd be romantic.'

'And you were right. I have a sensory nature: sensual, hedonistic – open to pleasure, sharing pleasure.' His eyes stayed on her and he took a step closer. 'I want to see where you paint. I want to know everything about you.'

'Then come with me.'

She picked up the champagne bottle and turned and led him through the kitchen to a room off the back of the house. It was high-ceilinged, with skylights, and one whole wall was glass set in stone. The smell of oil paint hit him. She was working on several paintings. Slashes of black and grey and yellow gorse covered her canvases. They were bleak, dark and full of movement and anger.

'Magnificent.'

'Thank you.'

She was watching him as he looked at her work; he went around the studio, pausing in front of each easel, each piece of art. He took his time. She had stopped by one she was currently working on: a whirl of blue spring sky above forbidding granite shelters. He walked over to her and stood behind her, pulling her closer to him, feeling her buttocks nestle into his hips.

'Your paintings are magnificent, beautiful, wild. They make me feel exhilarated. They overwhelm me with passion and excitement.'

She led him back through the kitchen, champagne bottle back in hand, and upstairs to her bedroom; he ducked to avoid the low beam. It was beautiful, minimal, with white-plastered walls and old beams.

Megan poured him another glass of champagne.

'It's been too long,' she said as she began undressing. Ellerman studied her. When she was standing naked, he walked across and pushed her back onto the bed. He placed his hands beneath her and cupped her buttocks, parted her thighs and sucked so violently on her sex that she writhed and squealed beneath his mouth. She tried to push his head away but he stayed until she orgasmed. He took a swig of champagne and looked at her as she lay in the foetal position, squeezing her hands between her thighs.

He refilled his glass.

She turned onto her back and brushed her hair from her eyes as she watched him walk naked round to the other side of the bed. He was semi-erect.

She crawled to the edge of the bed and went to touch him. He stopped her hand, gently but firmly.

'What do you want me to do?' she asked.

'I want you to be my slave.' He reached down as she knelt on the edge of the bed and touched her between her thighs: still wet, still swollen and still so sensitive. 'I want you to love me so completely. I want to be everything to you.' He held her and kissed her gently as he slowly made love to her.

He was just drifting off to sleep, feeling like he was floating in a warm, sex-scented bath, when Megan rolled onto her side and he felt her eyes studying him. He opened his eyes reluctantly and looked at her. Her eyes were narrowed, focused on his face. He smiled and closed his eyes again, hoping that she would get the hint as he reached out a warm heavy hand and laid it on her thigh.

'So tell me – if I fall for you, what am I letting myself in for?' she asked.

'As in?' he said on a sigh, trying not to sound irritated.

'As in – you are separated?'

'Yes, but it's complicated.'

She reached for her champagne. 'Go on.' She looked at him, waiting.

Ellerman breathed in deeply, resisted the urge to sound pissed off. He forced himself to sit up, rest back on the pillows.

'I have a son who needs me. My wife's unstable. I told you about it last time . . .'

'Unstable how? What has she got? She's bipolar, you said?'

'She's never been diagnosed with anything but she doesn't cope well with situations.'

'What kind of situations?'

'Anything really. If I want to talk about *us* – the relationship my wife and I have, or lack of it?' He looked across to gauge Megan's reaction. She was resting on an elbow, watching him intently. He could see his wife in her.

'How is that likely to change in the future?'

'Well . . . because my son is sixteen now. He's doing his GCSEs. He'll be going to uni when he's eighteen, then I can leave.'

'And you think that will realistically happen?'

'Yes. Absolutely. I will have fulfilled my side of the bargain then. I owe it to my son to stay and see him through this part of his life but then … when that's done, I'm one hundred per cent calling it a day. I'm already doing up the house in preparation. You know, I took on a wonderful old house that needs so much work and now, of course, I need to finish that work in order to get the best possible price for it when I sell it.'

'Does your wife know that you are dating?'

'Yes.'

'Really?'

'Of course. I expect her to be doing the same thing. We live in the same house but we are most definitely separated. We haven't had any intimacy for five years.'

'Really? You seem very practised at it, despite that.'

'Glad you think so. Must be beginner's luck. Maybe we're just good for each other. Who knows?' He pulled her to him and began kissing her, stroking her. She held his hand and halted him.

'It's not ideal.'

'No.' He looked into her eyes and gave her all the sincerity he could muster. 'But it's a good start,' he continued. 'And I feel we have a bond already. I feel … well … I don't want to rush things.' He sat up and got his champagne and sat back to sip it. 'After all – I don't know what you want from *me*? I have a lot at stake here too. You could do this kind of thing all the time – meet men from dating sites and lure them to your house in the country and then God knows what happens!' She laughed. He smiled. Grateful to see her mood lighten. Grateful to be let off the hook.

'I'll tell you what I want from you,' she said. 'I want

to see you when you can manage it. I won't look for anyone else. I mean, if you can make it down here once a week – at least once a fortnight – then I'll make sure it's worth your while. I won't ask for a lot – the one thing I will ask for is that I am not part of a harem.' She was watching him closely.

'Understood.'

Ellerman rested on his elbow, dipped his finger into the champagne, then traced the rise of her breast.

'Be honest, be loyal. I can wait – no problem. I understand you are still living with your wife. I accept that you can't leave her and I wouldn't want you to. It's noble and you've been honest with me and I respect that.'

He reached down and pulled her to him and turned her round – spooning her. His erect cock pressing into her back. He whispered into her ear.

'I'll keep this cock just for you. My mouth, my tongue, all yours. My hands ... fingers ...' He ran his fingertips over her. 'Trust me,' he said and then he felt her tense and draw away from him as she turned and rolled over on one side to look at him again.

'You have to accept my terms and conditions; you have to tick the "*I agree* box" – the one that says you agree to keep our relationship exclusive and that you will not have sex with another woman whilst you are sleeping with me.'

'Of course.'

'You have to swear it, JJ.'

Ellerman ejected one blast of laughter before he reached for more champagne. He handed her her glass.

'You going to make me sign an affidavit?'

Megan put her champagne down and took his glass and placed it on the side table. Then she rolled him onto his back and pinned him down by the shoulders as she straddled him.

'Yes. I'm going to make you write it in blood,' she growled.

He grinned. 'You're a wild woman.' Ellerman glanced towards his watch, next to the glass of champagne on the bedside table. It was ten minutes to three.

'Do you have to be somewhere?' Her eyes had turned cold as she pressed her weight into his lap.

'Of course not.' He reached out to run his hands up her thighs. 'We have plenty of time – till this evening for now, but after that? We have the rest of our lives.'

She leant forward and rested her head on his chest and then lifted her eyes to look at him. 'Can I trust you? Are you real?'

'Yes.' He hugged her tightly to him. 'This feels amazing. So special. I didn't think for one moment I would feel like this,' he said, his eyes filling with tears.

Her eyes stayed on his until she was sure he was sincere and then she lay back down, smiling, happy.

'Come on, let's go for a walk on the moors.' Ellerman rolled her off him and got out of bed, ducking to miss the low beam. He turned back to smile at her with a cheeky grin. 'You can't have it all your own way.'

'What do you mean?'

'Some things are worth waiting for. I'll decide when it's time for me to pleasure you again.'

She pretended to be annoyed. Then she laughed as she got up and opened a chest of drawers, pulling out a pair of jeans and a T-shirt.

'Okay. But I need to warn you – this is a tiny village,' she said as she found a jumper and pulled it over her head. 'And I'm already looked on as an outsider, so I don't want to be labelled a loose woman as well.'

'Okay – no problem. Let's drive somewhere.'

She turned to look at what he was wearing. 'I'd better find you a coat to wear. The weather can change in a second here.'

'Ah ... the famous Dartmoor mist again.'

'It's shifted now. It will be a clear sunset.'

'Lead on!'

They drove for ten minutes over the moors and parked below Hound Tor. Ellerman was watching the clouds race overhead. The banks of scrubby moorland fanned out around them; sharp and cold now. Trees grew bent and crooked. The sky was streaked with cold pale blue. They walked higher to get a good view. The bitter wind sliced into his face as he pulled the windproof jacket, fleecy-lined, around him and zipped it up.

'What a place.'

'Yes ... breathtaking. Too remote for you, I expect.' She glanced across at him. 'You're used to living in London.'

'I don't live in the middle. Anyway, what I want in life has changed. I used to want money, fast cars, big house, but then I got them and now I'm ready to give them up.'

'And would you trade your wine bars and cocktail

lounges for sitting next to a wood burner and listening to the sound of the birds outside?'

'In a heartbeat. By the way ... did I tell you I'm renovating a little bolt-hole in Spain. It's a beautiful old farmhouse. I'd love you to see it. Will you let me take you there when it's finished?

She nodded, happy. 'Sounds wonderful – I have a feeling I'm going to let you take me to heaven.'

Chapter 12

DC Zoe Blackman had been guarding Michael Hitchens – Toffee – all night. She'd get back in time to get the boys up and give them breakfast then drive them to school. Then she'd sleep. She was bad at sleeping in the day. For a fleeting, mad, sleep-deprived moment, she wondered if Simon Smith was the person she was guarding Toffee against.

She looked across at him and thought how odd he looked. He was thirty going on sixty, the way he dressed. Still, there was something old-fashioned and charming about his appearance: dishevelled posh boy. It seemed to her like he really cared about Toffee. It showed a basically good side to him. She stood up and went over to him.

'Fancy a coffee?'

He gave an exhausted smile. He was resting his elbows on his knees.

'I'd love one but do you think that's a good idea?'

'Yes. But you have to go and get it – my colleague went home for an hour, family stuff. I have to stay here and guard Toffee. It will give us a chance to compare notes. I'm white – no sugar.'

He stood and stretched, then smiled at her. She thought how his face was quite good-looking when he smiled. If she were into men who wore old-man sweaters with preppy stuck-up collars, then she might consider it, but she wasn't. Her husband had been the gym-animal type but always immaculate in his white T-shirt and perfect-fitting jeans. He took steroids. It made him aggressive in the end, or it had brought that side out in him – who knows? But she knew it would be a long time till she went down the relationship road again. Now she was a single parent who juggled a career she loved with the guilt-tripping of trying to give two boys everything and provide a future with money and options in it. Luckily, she had her mum to rely on.

'Okay,' Smith said, breaking into her thoughts, then walked off in the direction of the canteen. He came back ten minutes later, carrying two cups of coffee.

'No biscuits?'

'Of course. Just wouldn't have volunteered the info if you hadn't asked.' He smiled at her. 'Was hoping to eat the lot.' He handed her a coffee and then took two packets of custard creams out of his pocket.

'Good man.' Zoe took one and then sat down and put her coffee next to the leg of her chair. She opened her packet of biscuits.

'Do you mind if I ask you a few questions first?' Simon asked. 'Some things I wanted to better understand.'

'Sure. What do you want to know?' She prised the top off her coffee cup.

'What you think happened here?'

'Here – as in Toffee in here?' She gestured towards the window.

'Yes.'

'He had a run-in with a train.'

'Was he chased?'

'No. He wasn't chased. He was rescued by Detective Inspector Carter; otherwise, he would have died. He ran straight under the path of an oncoming train and just knelt there waiting to be hit.'

'He wasn't chased under it?'

'No. Absolutely not. According to the report, both DC Willis and DI Carter agree that they approached him with the intention of asking him some questions connected to the murder case, and he ran straight in front of the train. He even knelt down and wouldn't budge. If you believe otherwise then you need to make a complaint. I'm not here for that. I'm here to protect him. I'm also here to take a statement from him when he comes round. Our main priority is to get justice for the dead woman.'

'I want that too.' Simon sipped his coffee and sat back in his chair. 'It's a lot more than that. What about the dead woman? Do you know more about her?'

'I can't tell you a lot, only that she was forty, professional, single.'

'Why did she go in there? That's what I can't understand.'

'She probably went in there to meet someone she'd met on the Internet. That's what we think.'

'Ah.' Simon shook his head sadly. 'It's a shame people have to go to such extremes looking for love.'

'I think it was less love, more sex she was after.'

'Ah ... yes. Of course. The other side of the dating sites.'

'Have you ever tried them?'

'Dating sites? No. Well, maybe I had a look at one ... but I never signed up.'

'I've tried them. Disaster. I either had dates with men who were too shy to speak to me or men who wanted to kill their exes with their bare hands. ...' Zoe flashed an apologetic look. 'Not what I was looking for.

'Anyway, how did you come to be running the hostel – thought vicars just sang off-key and talked about things they'd never experienced?'

'I am pleased you have such a balanced view of us ...' Zoe held up her hands to apologize.

He shook his head and smiled. 'It's okay. Actually, I was homeless myself. I was one of those rebellious types who had everything but didn't want it. I ended up on heroin and living in a tent; that was until my girl-friend overdosed and died and I just woke up to what I was doing. My family never gave up on me, even when I stole from them. My sister and I are especially close and she looked after me. She nursed me through the rehab and she was there for me all the way, despite having plenty of her own problems. My parents offered me this chance to pay back a little to society – doing something that I understand. This was their project. They own the buildings behind here and they fund this hostel. I trained as a minister and here we are.'

'Bit harsh of your parents to make you deal with these problems every day when you've just finished dealing with your own – like a punishment?'

'Maybe it seems like that – but they think it's a gift

and so do I.' Zoe shrugged. She didn't look impressed. Simon smiled. 'I feel very lucky and very grateful and I will always help someone if they want to help themselves – only then.'

'Tough love.'

'Exactly. It's very satisfying work; yours must be too. You're a detective?'

'Yes. Just qualified. So chuffed. I've worked so hard to pass my exams.'

'Congratulations. Did you always want to be in the police force?'

'Always.'

'Do you have kids?'

'Yes. They're ten and seven – two boys. I'm a single parent.' Zoe didn't know why she told him that. It must be because he had one of those faces that said: 'Tell me your troubles.'

'So who's looking after them now?'

'My mum helps me loads. I try not to take advantage but she's my saviour.' As she said it, she looked at him and blushed. 'Not literally, of course.'

He laughed. 'Don't worry. I know what you mean.'

'My mum's religious – she goes to church – well, she did.'

'I understand. Everyone has busy lives.' He smiled.

'No – I mean, she hasn't since Dad died.'

'Oh, I see. That's a pity.'

'It's more than that for Mum – it's a devastation. It's a massive loss – her faith has just disappeared and exactly at the time when she needed it most.'

She stopped talking as a trolley went past with a patient on it and surrounded by medical staff.

'It's busy here – twenty-four-seven, isn't it?'

'Yes, organized chaos.'

'So what do you do every day?' she turned to ask Simon after the trolley had passed.

'I get up, shower.'

'No, you know what I mean. Work-wise. You must be really busy with the hostel. And sermons, I guess?'

'I have a few staff in the hostel who work really hard, mainly volunteers, who come in to cook, clean, wash up, teach IT, help with benefits applications, housing, health issues, that kind of thing – the skills related to being able to manage on your own.'

'Can people access the Internet in the hostel?'

'Yes. We have free WiFi for them to use. There are only three PCs, so they have to keep to twenty-minute slots and book it.'

'Did Toffee use the Internet?'

'Yes, my sister taught him. He's still at the basic stage though.'

'Often?'

'A few times. I could ask my staff. We can check how frequently he went on it. Why? You can't think Toffee was on a dating site?'

'You said he was a clever man. You also said that even you had looked at one now and again. There's no reason Toffee was any different. If he could use the Internet then he could access a dating site.'

'But he would have had to pay and that's impossible. He didn't have any money. He struggled to feed himself. He never had a bank card. It's laughable – plus, he's in love with my sister.' Simon laughed.

'Okay.' Zoe could see he was getting agitated but

pretending not to be. 'We can check what people were looking at. That will clear it up. We're working our way through her contacts.'

'Oh, yes. I see.' Simon became pensive. 'Toffee is basically a good man, you know. Most days he comes to chat to me after breakfast. He's articulate, clever. He follows world affairs. That is – until he starts drinking.'

'So, would you have expected him to have behaved in this way? We have to presume he had something to do with the woman's death. He was in that building when she died and he didn't come forward with the information – the opposite. He tried to kill himself rather than answer questions. He had her phone.'

Simon turned away. 'I am surprised and saddened if he did. I think he can't have been thinking straight to get into such a mess. Maybe he was misguided in his aims or lied to. Maybe' – he looked back at her – 'this was someone else's doing and he just happened to be in the wrong place at the wrong time. We have trouble from the gangs from Hannover Estate.'

'We're looking into that. We're trying to locate one of the leaders – Mahmet Balik. Do you know him?'

'I have heard that name – he's the light-skinned lad – about twenty. Charges were brought against him for the attack on Lolly, one of our regulars, but they were dropped – insufficient evidence.'

'When did you last see any of the gang members hanging about?'

'I had to tell them to get off church property. They were trying to break into the storage units we have behind the church.'

'Did they succeed?'

'No. Those buildings are burglar-proof. Doesn't stop them from trying of course. They will try and thieve just about anywhere and from anyone. They are responsible for nearly all the violent crime around here as well as the drug dealing.'

'Do you remember seeing anyone on Sunday evening when the woman was killed?'

He shook his head. 'But, I see them here a lot. Most days I see one or another of them. There's a hard core of about six lads. They hang around to intimidate people. In the evening they bring out their dogs – banned breed by the look of them – and they strut around the streets.'

'Did you ever see any contact between any of the gang members and Toffee?'

'No. Why would they have anything to do with him? He's just the kind of person they hate.'

'But he had money from somewhere. Have you any idea where he got it?'

'Maybe he won it. I just have no idea.' He shook his head. He looked exhausted. Zoe smiled, sympathetic – she could see he was struggling.

'Why are you here? You can't help him by getting exhausted. You should get back to the hostel.'

'I know, but I feel I owe it to him. He needs a friend and he counts me as one. I feel I should have been a better one and then maybe he wouldn't have got involved in all this.'

'What do you think he's involved in?'

'Well, somehow, he knew that the woman had been killed, he had her phone and he had money in his pocket.' He shook his head sadly. 'It doesn't look promising.'

'No, it doesn't. I hope he tells us the truth when he comes round.'

'Yes, I pray he does. Would you like me to see your mum?"

'Sorry?'

'I can see your mum. I'd like to help her. She had her faith knocked. I'd like to help her regain it.'

'Oh . . . thanks . . . I'll ask her.'

'I can come and see her or she can meet me for a coffee and we can talk. Just ask what she wants. I'm more than happy . . .'

'Yes . . . thank you. I'll tell her.'

'Great.'

'What about your family?'

'My family?'

'Yes. I don't want to take you away from them in your time off. Are you married? Kids?'

'No, my time is my own. My sister drives me mad and phones me most days; she comes and helps me in the hostel as often as she can. Apart from that, I take the services at the church sometimes but my main work is running the hostel.'

'Not much time left after you finish at the hostel, I expect?'

'No, you're right. I don't have a lot of time for hobbies. Although I would like to make time in the future.'

She smiled at him. 'What do you think about what happened on Parade Street, Simon?'

'I think it was something that was always going to happen. It was a bomb waiting to go off. If we have people living like that – like animals – then they behave like animals.'

'You think that someone was familiar with the area, with Parade Street and maybe your hostel?'

He shook his head. 'People in the hostel could be anyone – you or I – they've just run into trouble in their lives. There isn't a type. Almost ten per cent of our homeless are ex-armed forces. That's a shameful statistic – an indictment of the way we don't look after the people who serve us. Thirty per cent of people on the streets have mental-health issues – they shouldn't be there. Ten per cent have come out of care homes – they've already had it rough enough. Thirty-two per cent are out of prison – do we want them to be so desperate that they reoffend?'

Zoe was registering the passion mount in Simon's gestures and in his voice. He stopped talking and blushed, smiled, embarrassed. 'What I'm trying to say is … we are a very short-sighted society if we think that it works to turn a blind eye or to de-humanize the homeless.'

She realized she was concentrating on him and not on his words.

Spike stepped in front of the young woman who was wearing her shawl wrapped around her head. Her face was as pale as the moon – marked with craters from the ravages of a diet of drugs and hardship.

'Martine?' She stopped in front of him. 'Toffee's in hospital. He's hurt.'

'Will he be all right?' She clutched an old backpack in her hand; the strap was broken.

'Who knows? He would want me to keep an eye on you. You can bed down here with me.'

She looked from Spike to the bundle of rags and clothes in the doorway behind him. She tried to see who else was there in the gloom.

'Mason here?'

'No. Mason's lying low. I've helped him all I can. I'm not putting myself out for the ungrateful bastard.' Spike turned back towards the doorway. Martine turned and walked away. 'Don't go near him now. They'll come for him first. You're safer with me,' he called after her. 'Please yourself. If you see Lolly, tell her I have something for her.' Spike returned to his corner.

Martine knew where she'd find Mason. She called his name as she got inside the car park. Sandy came out from behind the arch and wagged her tail as she walked across to Martine. Martine ran her hand over the dog's back and thought how thin she felt. Sandy led her to where Mason was sleeping.

'Mason?' She sat beside him but he didn't answer.

Martine pulled out her sleeping bag and Sandy began snuffling inside the space it left in the backpack. Martine delved deep into the side pocket and produced half a torpedo roll salvaged from a bin. She gave it to the dog, who devoured it in one bite. She laid her bag out next to Mason and tucked her knees under her chin as she waited, listening in the dark. The train thundered overhead. She heard the scuttle of a rat and Sandy ran off in chase. Martine leant over Mason and tried to look at his face. He was lying on his side, his face half hidden in his woolly hat. He was lit by the street light nearby. She looked at the wounds on his face that had curled in on themselves.

'Mason, we need to get you to hospital.'

He groaned in his sleep. 'I'll be okay. Is Toffee coming back?' he said – his voice breathless. 'What are we supposed to do now?'

'I'll go and see him and find out – he can't just leave us with this.'

'Not now. Please, stay with me.'

Martine lay down and put her arms around Mason. Sandy returned and lay back down between them.

Chapter 13

Zoe phoned Carter as she was on her way home to get some rest.

'Does Smith think Toffee could have been clever, sober enough to fool Olivia Grantham into meeting him?' Carter asked her.

'I don't know. He's fond of Toffee and that must mean he can talk to him. He says Toffee's a clever man but off his face a lot of the time.'

'Could he have afforded the fees on a dating site?'

'That's what Smith said when I mentioned it. He said there was no way, but then ...'

'Someone else in the hostel might have paid for him?'

'Yes.'

'Does he have any more thoughts on the murder?'

'He thinks the gangs are responsible for all the trouble around that area.'

'It's true that they tend to know about it at least.'

'Have they managed to find Balik yet, sir?'

'No. We have increased patrols around the estate and neighbouring streets. It's time we picked a few people up and brought them in for questioning.

Smith must know where we can find Toffee's friends.'

'He says he hasn't seen them in a few days.'

'We need to get in there and talk to Sheila and Lyndsey, the volunteers. They know the people better than he does.'

'I'm working on getting someone inside the hostel for us.'

'Good. What about medical opinion on Toffee? What's the chance of him pulling through?' Carter asked.

'The doctors have put him in an induced coma – apparently there was some swelling on his brain. It will be a slow process – but there's hope.'

Carter came off the phone.

Willis was sitting on the chair opposite him. He studied her face. It looked like she hadn't slept for days and she had a drawn look that he didn't associate with her. She must have been the only person he knew who had lost weight over Christmas, not gained it. He wondered if she was pushing herself too hard and if the problems with her mother were getting to her.

'He's still unconscious,' he said, to interrupt her thoughts. 'They've put him in a coma. Damn ...' Carter stood and picked up his phone from the desktop. 'Let's see how far they've got with Olivia's PC. Then we'll grab a drink – talk things through over a beer.'

'Can we leave it tonight, guv? I'd rather go and see Olivia Grantham's body again. I want to get more of an idea of the attack on her and the kind of person we are looking for.'

Carter nodded. He was used to Willis's ways. He enjoyed working with her. They made a good team. If they were a jigsaw puzzle – then he was all the middle bits, whilst she was the edge pieces.

'No wonder you're single.' He smiled.

She shrugged and gave him a look that said: 'What can I say?'

'We'll have to find you a nice pathologist to hook up with. You could talk bodies way into the night.'

'Don't seem to be many of those that are the right side of forty,' she said as they walked along the corridor towards Robbo's office. Willis walked with her hands in the pockets of her black work trousers.

'Don't forget Mark.'

'Yeah ... don't think that will work. Mark doesn't know it yet but he's gay.' Willis smiled.

'Oh, Mark knows it; he's just keeping his options open.'

As they reached Robbo's office, Robbo was busy whizzing from one desk to the other on his expensive Italian blue-leather chair. Pam was sorting the papers on her desk – she was getting ready to leave for the night.

'Let's go through it again, Hector,' Robbo was saying as they walked in. 'Carter? Willis? Come in, have a seat. We're going through Olivia Grantham's last twenty-four hours.' Robbo began drawing a timeline on the board behind him. 'Olivia went out Saturday for the evening with one of her girlfriends – Marcia Adams. An old schoolfriend. We have her statement. She said she met Olivia for drinks at 8.30 in a wine bar in Covent Garden. They parted at eleven and, so far as she knew, Olivia went straight home. There was no mention of what Olivia intended to do the next day, beyond catch up on household chores at home. She didn't think Olivia was seeing anyone. She was aware that Olivia was on dating sites, but she didn't know which ones. She knew she met men from them sometimes.'

Robbo continued with his timeline: 'We know that at eleven o'clock Sunday morning, she took a call from an unknown number and that lasted thirty-two minutes. She made a call to the same number at three in the afternoon, which lasted only five minutes.'

Carter spoke: 'I would think that was the call that reassured her enough to go to Parade Street. Maybe she was having second thoughts before that. After the call she made at three, did she make any more, or did she get any?'

'None,' answered Hector.

'But she didn't put a name to this number – why was that?' said Willis.

'He could have been someone she knew well – he could have told her he was on a temporary number, told her his phone wasn't working – something like that?' Hector said. 'We know he's phoned her a couple of times on it. She must have thought it wasn't worth adding to a contact.'

'My feeling is she knew him.'

'Or . . .' Carter began, '. . . she might have been getting braver. This could have been a very convincing person on the other end of the phone – well-spoken, professional; maybe she thought: "How dangerous can it be?" Was she pushing her own boundaries?'

'Could it really have been Toffee?' Robbo asked.

'On the phone he could get away with it – he's articulate. He's definitely well-spoken. He might have been able to fool her,' Carter answered. He looked at what Hector was working on – Olivia's bank statements.

'Found anything interesting? asked Carter.

'Just looking into the sites she subscribed to.'

'Sign yourself up to all of the ones she was on, Hector. Ask Intel for a cover.' He turned to Robbo. 'Could it have been some gang-rites thing? If so, the rough sleepers must have been in on it. Toffee said it went wrong. What was the plan? To lure her in there, rape, kill. What did they steal from her? Toffee had her phone. I can't imagine she took her bag in there, but it's gone – probably from the car. No money was withdrawn from her bank account. Did they get paid to do it? Did someone pay Toffee to organize it?'

Carter nodded to Willis that he was ready if she was. She stood up and picked up her coat.

'We're going to take another look at Olivia Grantham's body and talk to Harding, if she's there.'

'Pam, have you got any photos of the men Hector's been phoning?' Carter asked before leaving.

'Yes ... some.' She pulled out a file from her desk and handed it to him.'

When they got outside, Willis went towards where the BMW was parked.

'Let's walk.' Carter started along the main road. She stayed where she was for a second. 'Yeah – I know, but I want to talk things through with you,' he added, then waited for her to walk alongside him.

'Any news about your mum? The lovely Bella Donna?'

Willis shook her head and looked at her feet. The pavement was saturated, but her new Chelsea boots, which her housemate Tina had got her for Christmas, were keeping her feet dry. The socks Carter gave her for her birthday were keeping them toasty warm. It was the kind of luxury that Willis could never have afforded herself. All her money went into savings accounts. She planned to buy a flat next year.

'I'll go tomorrow.'

'Is she still in bad shape?'

'She's still on a drip. Not sure what else. Have to see when I get there. They say she nearly bled to death.'

'Nearly, huh? Bad luck.'

'Yeah.' She smiled at the same time as she sighed heavily.

She carried on looking at the wet tarmac.

'You take as long as you need tomorrow, Eb. Get it done and then get back to the job – focus.' Willis looked across at him; she looked confused, hurt. 'You're just quiet, that's all. I need participation, verbal. I need you on the same planet as the rest of us.'

'Yes, guv.'

She looked away; he knew it was to hide her hurt. But a jolt back to the real world wouldn't hurt. Carter also knew that Willis was used to tough love and she knew he cared.

They reached the Whittington Hospital and rang the bell to let them into the mortuary. They were answered by Mark.

'The doctor's not here, I'm afraid.'

They stepped under the fluorescent striplights of the corridor.

'No problem. Can we take another look at Olivia Grantham?'

'Sure.' Mark led them through to the storage area and opened up the fridge. He wheeled out the body.

Carter stood back to observe as Willis walked around the body.

'Good job in making her look good for her family,' Carter said.

Mark nodded, pleased. 'Thanks. It took me ages to cover the bruises.'

'What was he like, the dad?'

'He didn't really speak much. He looked numb.'

'Did you take casts from these bites yet?' asked Willis.

'Not yet. We're waiting for the specialist to come over tomorrow and do it.'

Willis took the latex gloves now being offered to her by Mark as she examined the bite wounds on Olivia's breast.

She pressed the wounds with her hand, to see the depth of bite. 'These are from a dog. A dog first bites then tears.'

'Can you take a cast from a dog?' Carter looked at Mark for a reply.

'Yes, I don't see why not.'

'Balik's dog, maybe?' Carter said to Willis's back as she disposed of her gloves in the bin. 'Or that lad with the hat had a dog. We need to find him. He should be easy to spot with half his face hanging off. What happens if he doesn't get that fixed?'

'It will get infected,' Mark answered.

'And?'

'And it's serious – life-threatening. Infection kills people on the streets every day,' he added.

Harding walked in as they were finishing up and Mark was zipping the body bag back up.

'Evening, Dr Harding,' Carter greeted her.

She had on civvies: animal-print skirt tastefully stopping just on the knee, black boots stopping just below, a dark brown turtleneck sweater, and black-leather coat to mid-calf.

'Must be difficult,' Carter said, as he pointed to Olivia Grantham's body, more to see how she reacted than with sincerity.

'Not difficult. More strange than sad.'

'Can we have a word?'

'I suppose so.' They followed Harding into her office. She opened a bottle of wine. 'Pull up a chair. How's the investigation going? What's happened to the man you chased under a train, Carter?' She passed him a glass. Willis declined.

He smiled. 'Not quite how I remember it, Doctor. But he's now in an induced coma. His name is Michael Hitchens, aka Toffee – he's a former whizz kid in the City, now a homeless alcoholic. He's our only real lead so far. He said it went wrong with Olivia – I'm not so sure it did.'

'If he's in an induced coma, you can forget him for at least ten days. Plus, you have no idea whether there is permanent brain damage. He may never be able to answer your questions. What do you need from me? How can I help?'

'We need a little more background on Olivia Grantham, if we can.' Willis took out her notebook.

'I told you where she worked.'

Willis looked up from the notebook. 'If we tell you what we found when we went to Miss Grantham's flat, maybe you can think about the kind of info we are looking for,' Willis said. She was one of the few women who liked Harding. She had no husband or boyfriend to lose. They were alike in some ways – both used to being alone. Both found it difficult to relate to and trust others.

Willis opened her notebook.

'Not in a relationship – no couple photos. Corporate, neat – very tidy. Didn't get to know neighbours. The caretaker said she was polite, reserved.'

'That's right. I would say she was quiet, thoughtful. She wasn't a big party girl – she was private, discreet, boring really. Boringly average.'

'Average but with a dark side?' suggested Carter.

'There were a few specialist sex toys in her bedroom; not sure they are average,' Willis clarified, spoiling Carter's fun.

Harding tried not to smirk. 'Tell me.'

Willis read from her notebook: 'Bondage harnesses, an assortment of weapons: whips, spikes, hot-wax dispenser, clamps, needles.'

Harding raised an eyebrow. 'Not weapons, those are toys.'

'Does it ring a bell with you, Doctor?' asked Carter.

She fixed Carter with a look of contempt.

'Your point? What am I supposed to know about it?'

'Did you know that side of her life? The side that may have led to 22 Parade Street?'

'Okay. I will tell you what you seem so desperate to hear but none of it goes beyond this room. None of it gets written down,' she said, looking at Willis. Willis looked at Carter; he nodded. Willis closed her notebook. 'I tell you two and then it's forgotten.'

'We can't promise you that, Doctor,' said Willis. 'I may not write it down but I can't just forget it.'

Carter held up his hand.

'We understand. Carry on.' Willis was about to object again. Carter stopped her. 'If we use the information then it came from an informant who can't be named.' He looked at Willis. She nodded reluctantly.

Harding sighed and sat back in her seat.

'Don't get too excited, Carter. It isn't that sensational. I met her through an Internet site. I didn't set out to meet her. I met a man and he introduced me to her, one thing led to another.' She looked at Carter and waited for a reaction.

'Swingers?' Carter asked.

'Crudely put, yes; I suppose so. It's a website called Naughties.'

'We're looking into it,' answered Carter. 'We know Olivia Grantham had a subscription to it. It's a site for casual sex – is that it?' he added.

'Just a way of setting out your stall, that's all. It's an honest approach – no ties, no hang-ups. No harm done,' Harding said with a defensive, dismissive shrug of her shoulders.

'Sure ... Do you still have the number for the person who introduced you to Olivia?'

'No. It was just a man. We got on well – we met a few times after that.'

'For sex?'

Harding took a deep breath. She had fixed her eyes on Carter throughout the conversation.

'No, for tea ... what do you think?'

'What can you tell us about her?'

'Her life was mundane on a daily basis. So, she invented an alter-ego. That one enjoyed meeting strangers for sex.'

'Did you see her often?'

'Not often. She soon lost her appeal. There was a lot of bravado involved. She was quite the baby inside.' She paused. 'Anyway – it doesn't do to see the same person too often – you become overfamiliar with them. They start to mean something to you beyond a pleasure vehicle.'

Harding sat back in her chair.

'How does the site work? asked Willis.

'You pay and you get a service like everything else. You subscribe and get to study the profiles of other subscribers. What you do then is up to you. The site is a host. It's simple. I like sex with strangers. I like as many new partners as possible.'

'So if you like the look of someone you email them?' asked Willis.

'Yes. If I like someone on the site then we usually meet that same evening.'

'Where?'

'A hotel usually, their house or mine perhaps. A car park, anywhere you want. Whatever floats your boat.'

'Dangerous thing to do,' said Carter.

She shrugged. 'That's the point. If I met them in a bar, they would bore me within seconds. This way it lasts an evening – at least I've never had a problem.'

'What would have made Olivia go into that building on Parade Street? Do you know?'

'Because some risks are worth taking. What is it you want me to do? What do you think I can help with?'

'We need to see how it works first; will you show me?' Willis asked. 'We have two bogus profiles on there now – a man and a woman. We need to know how they look to the experienced eye. We have several hits already on the female.'

Harding took her laptop out of her bag and opened it up.

'You will have. Let me tell you – the women are few, the men are plenty,' she said as she put in her passcode. 'I'll log in and show you who's looking at who.' She looked across at Willis and paused, finger over the keyboard. Willis drew her chair nearer. Carter stayed where he was.

'Password. Okay – so once I'm in, I get onto my home page and see what activity there has been on it.'

'When was the last time you logged in?' asked Willis.

'Last night. I looked at Olivia Grantham's profile. She's still up on the site.' Harding turned and looked questioningly at Carter.

'I know, but it's not our business to inform them,' he said. 'We need to see if anyone has been looking at her profile.'

Harding turned back to her laptop. 'That would

mean you would have to admit to breaking into it – which you are obviously trying your hardest to do.'

Carter didn't answer.

Willis was leaning in to read what Harding had put on her profile. She stopped and looked at Harding. 'You're not worried about putting all this detail online?'

'No, because I go through a vetting process before I meet them and this site isn't cheap. It's thirty pounds a month – that puts it out of the ordinary weirdo's price bracket. No one can look at my profile unless they pay, and I am in control as to who sees what. If I "favourite" them then they can see more *intimate* pictures.'

Harding was about to click on the link to profile pictures that were hidden.

Willis stopped her.

'It's okay. I don't need to see.'

Harding shrugged. 'Please yourself. This section here shows the last twenty-four hours. I've had five views and I've got an email.' She clicked on the link to read it. 'Okay, well this is from a guy I've been talking to for a week or so. We've exchanged about three messages. I'll give him my mobile number now and we'll talk. If he sounds like someone I want to meet then we meet for a drink. If he passes that test then – bingo. It's not really that different from any other dating site. Some people vet scrupulously – some people never even talk on the phone, they just want to meet straight away.' She looked at Willis. 'Have you never tried Internet dating?'

'I look at it sometimes but I don't have the time for

it. Is anyone on there that you think Olivia Grantham might have been interested in?'

'Yes. I think I could pick out a few.'

Harding clicked on a profile of a man. His erect cock filled the screen.

'Hardly anyone shows their face. They are married or at least they are in a relationship that doesn't quite do it for them sexually and they think this way is cleaner, safer, no one gets hurt and it's free. Free sex is always a man's goal.'

'Do people who are one site tend to be on others?' Carter asked.

'Of course. Some people are on every single site.'

'Are you?'

'No, I find the right sort of people on this.'

Willis pointed to the cock onscreen. 'Do you know that man? Have you met him?'

Harding leant forward to look at the name on the account.

'No.'

'Are you willing to talk to us about any of the men you've met?' asked Willis.

'Yes. Bring me details of someone you're interested in and I'll tell you if I've had sex with them.'

'We have some photos to show you now,' Carter said.

'Shoot.' He took out the file Pam had given him.

'We're giving you all the info we have on them so far. These are the men who definitely contacted Olivia Grantham. They are from her phone. They have been given the surname Naughties by Olivia, which we presume means she knows them from there, so we're hoping you might recognize one or two.'

Carter handed Harding the first man's details.

'This is a man named Peter Hill; he lives in Kent but works in the City.'

She took the photo, studied it and shook her head.

'No. Don't know him.' She pushed the picture aside.

'This one is Malcolm Roberts – accountant.'

'No.'

'John James Ellerman – JJ – high-roller. He lives in—'

Harding held up her hand to stop Willis. 'Yes. Definitely.'

'When? With Olivia?'

'Once with her. I met him a few times on my own.'

'When was that?'

'Must be two years ago. But he still looks at my profile online. I still get the odd text from him. He's on this site all the time.'

'Why didn't you keep meeting him?' asked Willis.

'He didn't want to. I wasn't what he was looking for.'

'What were your impressions?'

'He was a bullshitter. He tried to impress with his car, his talk of going all over the world. I remember thinking: "Can we just cut the crap and get on with it?"'

Carter smiled.

'You think it's not just the sex with him?' he asked.

'That's right – he wanted to take me for dinner. He wanted to take me on holiday.'

'You weren't keen?' asked Carter.

'I made it plain I just wanted sex. That's what the site is for – not for relationships.'

'Of course ...' Willis said. 'Did you know he was married? Did he tell you?'

'Yes, he did, even though I wasn't interested in hearing it. He said he had a son, couldn't leave his wife — all that bullshit.'

'What do you want me to do?' asked Harding.

Carter answered: 'Nothing.'

'Okay, but I know it will take you weeks to get permission to access the dating site's private info. Let me help then.'

'How? We can't put you at risk.'

'I can go on the hunt if it's useful. I can contact him – it will be easy.'

'We appreciate it,' said Carter. 'Can we think about it, please?'

'Sure.'

Chapter 14

Ellerman drove to Exeter and parked up at the Quay. He put on his gold-rimmed aviators, got out and walked across to look out over the river. The low winter sun was shining in his eyes as it set. He breathed in deeply. He was always happiest when he was back near water. As man and boy he had been drawn to it. He looked at his phone. There were several missed calls and unread texts. The bank was chasing the mortgage payment again.

'Fucking vultures,' he said out loud.

He felt the cold air whip straight off the water and across the sweat that had come to his brow. The sky clouded over and turned slate grey and the river mirrored it. He shivered. He hurried back to the car and drove back along the main road into the city. He parked up and opened the boot of his car. Unzipping his bag, he swapped his dirty clothes for fresh and changed his smart shoes for suede loafers. He walked back along the street, stopped at number 35 and pressed the doorbell as he put his bag down. He smiled at the woman approaching from the other side of the bevelled glass door.

'Hello, darling,' she said as she opened the door and wrapped her arms around his neck before he'd had time to step inside. She had on a tight pencil skirt and a neat white blouse.

'Missed me?' Ellerman kissed her, squeezed her tightly as he stroked the side of her breast through the crisp white blouse. 'You've been to work today. I love it when you look so officious.'

She pulled him inside.

'Yes, I have. Come on, let's go to bed, it's been two weeks too long.'

He held back, grinning awkwardly. 'You'll have to feed me first. I've had a busy couple of days – difficult client. I need fuel. Then I'll ravish you.'

She pulled away, instantly annoyed.

'Where have you come from?'

'The wilds of Dartmoor.' He brought his bag further into the hallway and followed her through to the lounge.

'Not far then. It's just up the road.'

'Of course, it's a great place. We must go there for a night sometime. I'd forgotten how beautiful it is. The last time I saw it though I was on training exercises in preparation for Afghanistan. That was a rough experience.'

She smiled, tight-lipped. 'It must have been. You promised me you'd wear your uniform this time. I've never seen you in it.'

'Sorry, darling. I completely forgot to put it in the car. I'll wear it next time.' He held on to her and kissed her neck. He could feel the tension in her. Something wasn't right. He was trying to think what it could be. 'Wish I'd had you in Afghanistan. You'd have kept my morale up as well as something else. Now put the kettle on chop-chop and make me something to eat.' He smacked her hard on her bottom as he turned to pick up his bag from the doorway.

She gave a false laugh but didn't move.

'No. I really want to go out for dinner this evening. You said we would this week. I've been looking forward to it. Seeing someone every two weeks means you have to make a big effort when you do. Don't you think?'

'Of course. Thought we'd light the fire and get cosy.' He put his bag down in the hallway.

'You know what, JJ?' Gillian stood with her hands on her hips. 'I'm sick of staying in and waiting for you to come and then we do *nothing*. Absolutely nothing. I'm beginning to think you just use me as a stopover. Eighteen months we've been together and we've only been away once. It's not good enough. I can't even put photos of you on my Facebook. It's like I'm your dirty secret.'

Ellerman sighed. 'I'm sorry, darling. I'd love to announce our relationship to the world on Facebook but I was in the SAS, remember? Do you know how many people would love to get me? I put some serious terrorists out of business. I—'

Gillian didn't wait to hear him out; she turned and walked away into the kitchen.

'Did you bring any wine with you?'

'No. Sorry. I was in such a rush to get here.' Ellerman strained to listen to her response. Normally, she would have melted at that kind of a comment –

'couldn't wait to get here and rip your clothes off' kind of thing. But recently things had changed between them. Ellerman wondered whether their time was coming to an end. Christ knows, he was banking on her today. He was tired, hungry, a little hungover. He had been expected to really perform at Megan's. He'd thought he was in for an easy night at Gillian's. He hadn't anticipated this reception. He heard the fridge door open and heard the clink of bottles. 'I'll go and get some,' Ellerman called out as he jangled his keys.

'Don't bother ...' Gillian reappeared. She had stripped and was wearing a red corset. How Ellerman hated red lingerie. It reminded him of blood.

'It can wait. I've got some.' Gillian handed him a glass of cold white wine. He sipped it and tried not to grimace. *Eastern European.* He gave what he considered to be his deep seductive laugh – full of 007 promise, appreciative of what he saw in front of him and the beautiful figure that he was supposed to be delighting in, but in real terms he thought Gillian had become a little fat. He saw her as a little on the big side now and he wasn't a great lover of curvy women. He liked all his women to be petite, much smaller than him. He loved to be able to pick them up in his arms and carry them, but he was pretty sure that Gillian now weighed twelve stone and would take some lifting. She looked at him expectantly but he saw by the glint in her eyes that she was challenging him.

'Let's go upstairs.' She picked up the bottle. 'I want to work up an appetite for this meal that you're going to take me for.' Ellerman looked at her expression and thought how she had obviously been building up to this and he hadn't noticed. Whatever she had suppressed in the last few visits, it had certainly decided to surface now and he was feeling very deflated.

'I've booked a restaurant in town. It costs a lot but then I'm worth it, aren't I?'

She led the way up to her attic room.

He went across to look through the skylight at the evening. He could see the orange glow of car headlights going past on the road below; he could see streams of them in the distance on the motorway. He couldn't see his car from there – he always parked it further up the road, well away from any chance of it being knocked. But he knew it was waiting for him. He felt the urge to get back in it now and drive, put on his music, and hit the highway.

Coz, baby, we were born to run . . .

He turned back to the bed and saw that she was waiting, and said to himself: 'Get it over with . . .' He started his usual moves but today it wasn't working for him. He changed positions. Maybe if he thought of someone else – that would do it for him? But it didn't. He was having a difficult job staying hard, maintaining his interest. He stopped, sighed, smiled embarrassedly as he hovered over her.

'Sorry, darling – been a long day for me. I feel under pressure with you looking so damn sexy in your red corset. And . . .' He rolled away. 'My client really took it out of me.' He lay on his back, exhausted.

'You can't just give up – don't be so selfish. I thought you were Mr Stud?'

Forty minutes later, Ellerman was given the signal that enough was enough.

Gillian rolled over and looked at her phone on the floor beside the bed. 'Just in time – we have forty-five minutes to get to the restaurant. And God, I'm hungry. I hear this place is Michelin-starred – a hundred pounds a head. But then . . .' She turned and looked defiantly at him as she opened the attic-bedroom door and went out on the landing to have a shower in the bathroom next door. 'You owe me – all the meals and the bottles of wine you've had here in the last eighteen months and, to be honest, I'm beginning to think you're mean with money . . .' Ellerman turned over in bed and lifted his head in protest but didn't speak. 'Yeah . . .' said Gillian. 'Prove me wrong.'

Ellerman got dressed whilst he heard the shower running. He gathered up his things and stepped down the stairs from the attic bedroom. He was thinking it through. He'd lost his hard-on halfway and had to spend half an hour on his knees pleasuring Gillian and now he was going to have to pay two hundred quid for a meal he couldn't afford. Enough was enough. Ellerman went downstairs and into the lounge and was just contemplating what would be the best plan of escape when Gillian hurried down the stairs wearing a white towelling robe, as if she knew what he was thinking.

'You going somewhere, darling?' she asked in a child's petulant voice as she pulled the robe tight around her. Her eyes were set hard. He could see that she was still in the mood she'd been in before they'd had sex, despite his exhaustive efforts.

'I'm so sorry, babe. Just had a call. I need to go.'

'What about the restaurant, *babe*?'

'I can't this time, *darling*. I am truly sorry. I have to

drive up North straight away. I've got a six-hour car drive ahead of me.' Gillian shook her head in mock sympathy as she glared at him. He reached for her and rubbed her arms as if she were a needy relative. 'Oh, bugger it – you're so much more important to me than you realize. I'll stay here but let's relax, get cosy, get drunk together. I wanted to talk to you about the Spanish house. I wanted to give you an update. You know ... I am so looking forward to us moving out there, darling.'

'Really? All the money I've put into it these last eighteen months, I would have thought you could have built a fucking mansion by now.'

'Yes ... well ... I wish.' He pulled back to look at her. 'It's so nearly there, darling. You just need to keep the faith. It's within our grasp and then we'll be flying out there and living a life of luxury – lying in the sun – just you and me.' He could see by her face that she'd been waiting for the chance to explode. The time was now. He braced himself. But then he saw a tiny chink of light. Her face was softening, her eyes melting. Was she going to relent? He knew why – she didn't want to be on her own. She had missed the boat for having kids and had banked on a career that had not come through for her. Now she was lonely and brittle and too old to compromise.

He smiled as his eyes searched hers and he did his best dejected look.

'I'm so sorry, darling – you know I wouldn't let you down for the world but I'm finding it so hard at the moment with cash-flow problems. The architect in Spain needs paying or he's threatening to stop working on the site and we don't want that, do we?' She shook her head. 'Look – I can't lie to you. I'm not mean – God forbid! But, you're right, I haven't had any money recently. It's all tied up in building boats. I'm so pissed off I can't take you to a fancy restaurant like I know I should. You deserve that and so much more and you will have it, I promise.'

She sighed. 'Okay. But I wonder if you're ever going to leave your wife.'

'I promise you when Craig goes to uni in two years' time, I will start divorce proceedings. Once I know that my son is away from home and old enough to make up his own mind. It's not safe to leave my wife with him.'

'You said – many times.'

'She has bouts of depression. She hardly leaves the house. She is paranoid.'

'Why don't you put her on medication?'

'I don't want to have to stay and look after her. I need a life. I need you.'

He tried to kiss her but she turned her face from him.

'I can't wait for ever and I've seen you back on the dating site.'

He shook his head. 'You know what the sites are like. I'm not paying a subscription. They get hold of your photo and then suddenly you're on every site. I'll get hold of Love Uniform Dating and I'll demand that they delete my profile.'

'I didn't see it on there, I saw it on Single Parents Looking For Love.'

'There, that proves my point. Why is my photo on that, for Christ's sake? It makes me really angry.'

Gillian stared at him coldly.

'My friend is on it and she sent you a message. You answered.'

'Can't have been me. Must have been a scam. You should tell your friend to be careful. All sorts of shady characters on the net. Anyway, darling, what were you doing on there? If you saw a photo of me then you must have been looking for men.'

'Yeah, I had a look.' Gillian stood, shoulders raised, eyes glaring. 'I even had a drink with a policeman last week but he wasn't right for me.'

'I promise to come down more often. I'll book us a weekend in Spain and we can see how the house is getting on. That's if it hasn't been repossessed. Is that what you want? Will that do?'

'Don't sound so enthusiastic! It better not have been repossessed. I've put a lot of money into it.' Ellerman was seething as he watched her face turning the colour of her lingerie. 'That's another thing ... I want some of it back now. You said it was just a loan. Otherwise I want it in writing that I own part of that house. I've put in twenty thousand. That would probably mean I'm entitled to a share of it, like a timeshare.'

Ellerman was beginning to feel like he was about to explode. He felt his phone vibrate in his pocket – telling him he had received a message. He thought about the bank again. If he could get Gillian to transfer more money over via the Internet then he might just be able to swing it. Gillian handed him an official-looking letter.

He looked at it. 'What's this?'

'I need some guarantee. I asked a girlfriend of mine

who works in a solicitors' office to help me draw up something.'

'This is not for real?' He read it through. 'You want a share of the house – is that really it? Christ, you've really been waiting to spring this on me, haven't you?'

'Yes, I have actually. I've been waiting and hoping that you would give back the money but you don't seem to have any intention of doing that voluntarily.'

'It was a loan between friends, for God's sake.'

'Then why do I feel less and less like a friend and more like someone who's been conned? Added to that – you can't even get it up. So what do I have left? I should charge you bed-and-breakfast rates. Sign that or I'm going to the police to see about bringing fraud charges against you.'

'I haven't done anything wrong.'

'You took my money.'

'You gave it to me.'

'No, I didn't. I lent it to you to do up the Spanish house and now I want proof that the Spanish house exists and that I own part of it.'

'I can't give you that. It's too complicated.'

'Doesn't seem complicated to me. You sign it or I'm going to your house to see your wife and tell her that I own part of a house that her husband is renovating in Spain. I'm sure she'd like to know that you intend to leave her.'

'She knows I intend to leave her. She's got to be given time to deal with it. She's unbalanced. I told you. Now promise me you won't go near her. You will put my son at risk if you do.'

'Then sign it.'

'I can't. You know I can't. It's not as easy as that. It would be stupid . . .'

'So now you're calling me stupid.'

'No. Of course not. But naïve maybe?'

'Naïve? Does that mean you conned me and I didn't notice?'

'Look, I've had enough. I'm leaving. We'll talk later. Hopefully, you'll have seen sense by then.' Ellerman picked up his bag and coat and started walking towards the door.

'I know where you live. I traced you. Say hello to your wife and tell her I'll be up to see her soon.'

Ellerman turned round when he got to the front door.

'Gillian – I'm warning you – don't go near my family. Just think about it. We've had good times. They may be a bit thin on the ground at the moment but they'll come back. When I get this contract for the yachts done and dusted, I'll give you your money back and much more besides. Don't blow it now. Don't throw what we have away. I am very fond of you.' Ellerman pinched the bridge of his nose and his eyes began to sting with tears. 'I'll phone you later.'

Ellerman pulled up at a services outside Exeter. He went in and bought a sandwich and a drink and came back to sit in the car park with the lorries that were there for the night. He hadn't yet decided where he was going to go for the night. He had intended to stay at Gillian's, before she kicked off. He looked at the message he'd just received from her.

'Jesus Christ. Why does it have to be so hard?' he said out loud as he reread her text demanding that he give her back her money in the next twenty-four hours or it was over and she'd go to the police and she'd be paying his wife a visit as well. He knew she was capable. Ellerman scrolled down his list of recent messages and thought about where he could get some help with paying off Gillian. It was too soon to ask Megan – he hadn't reeled her in far enough yet – but he needed to speak to her.

'Have you had a good day, darling? I've done nothing but think of you,' he asked as soon as Megan answered the phone. 'I'm in a service station in God knows where and I wish I could be back in your bedroom, holding you close. I can still smell you.' He knew she would be smiling. He heard her sigh contentedly.

'I must admit I half-expected you to be tucked up with someone else by now,' she said.

'Really?' He laughed. 'You must be joking. You wore me out.'

She giggled. 'Yeah. I had to sit down to paint earlier. For some reason my legs were wobbly.'

'Good. I hope I always have that effect on you.'

Ellerman ended the call and looked at Gillian's message again. He switched his music on as he sat in the dusk and thought what he should do. Nothing mattered now but the end prize. He turned his music up loud. Alice Cooper was belting out 'Fire'. He sent a text to his wife:

I'm coming home tonight.

*

After Carter and Willis left, Harding stayed logged on to the Naughties website. She watched Mark washing down the dissecting tables. She could see him through the window in her office. She loved the way his hands moved. They were a ballet to watch; they were beautiful: light, soft, gentle. She turned back to the screen. But they weren't what she needed, even if he was interested, which he wasn't. She looked at her messages. Ellerman had viewed her profile. She looked at his. She smiled to herself – tempting . . .

A message came up on her phone:

Want to play? Sorry it's taken me so long to get back to you – decided to keep you waiting. I know what you like. You like to be controlled. You like to be made to submit.

Who is this? She didn't have a name against the number. She looked for previous messages – there weren't any.

You gave me your number a few weeks ago. You don't remember? I remember what you said – you like people to watch. You like living dangerously. Ever tried dogging?

Interesting.

Meet me next to the lorry park in Shadwell – in the adjoining car park. See you there at eleven.

Harding looked at her watch – it was seven. She poured herself another glass of wine and contemplated what to do. Another text came through:

I'll be waiting.

Chapter 15

At seven o'clock, Gillian put three ice cubes in her vodka and tonic and climbed the stairs up to her bedroom. She plonked herself down onto her bed and rested the glass on her chest and lay looking at the ceiling. She thought it through. She didn't regret the text. She didn't regret finishing it and she meant it – but then, if that was true, why did she feel so sad? She sat up and opened her laptop and logged onto Love Uniform Dating. She scanned through the men – nobody new, nobody worth looking at. There was the policeman again. There were all the same men that had been on there the last two years. She gave a heavy sigh and lay back on the bed that still smelt of Ellerman's aftershave. Maybe she should ring him and give him another ultimatum and try to force him along a bit? She wished he'd come back and she could talk it through with him. She'd been hasty maybe. Gillian regretted it now. She'd got into such a state about things. Two weeks of waiting for him to turn up, missing him like mad. She had too much time on her own to stew over things and some things just didn't add up. But she didn't want to finish it. She hadn't meant to get so angry. Now she was lying here on her own; that was not what she wanted. She heard the squeak of her letterbox and waited for the sound of junk mail landing on the mat – it didn't come; she picked up her drink as she sat up on the bed. It was then she smelt smoke.

She scrambled off the bed and ran to the loft stair-well. Between her and the front door was a wall of fire. She closed the door and grabbed her duvet – jam-ming it at the bottom of the door. She was crying, her hands were shaking as she found her phone and dialled 999.

'Help me – I'm on fire – my house is on fire!'

Gillian ran back and forth from the locked window to the door with the phone in her hand as she waited for the sound of the fire engine. She felt the heat build-ing in the room as she coughed and choked on the thin smoky air. She stared at the door and prayed as she lis-tened to the roar from the other side. Then she heard the fire engine and ran back to the window and started to bang on the glass ... She slammed her hand against it as she saw the firemen running towards her house.

'Help me ... help ...'

She looked back towards the door. It was starting to blacken and smoulder and smoke was beginning to pour through.

The heat was burning her lungs. She felt dizzy.

She screamed as she banged on the window. The front of the house was on fire now. She tried to open the window and her hand stuck to the metal handle. In that second all the holes in the burning door joined up and it exploded inwards.

Chapter 16

At just before eleven, Lolly made her way towards the lorry park in Shadwell. Her legs were so weary that she could hardly move them. Her backpack felt as if it contained rocks instead of her few possessions. The day had taken its toll on her as she hid from the cold, and the last few nights had been all about staying warm. She had nowhere to go. She'd been kicked out of all the hostels because, as hard as she tried, she couldn't stop taking heroin. The heroin helped her to forget the happy life she'd once had. It was five years ago that her boss discovered she was sleeping in the offices he employed her to clean at nights; that was after she lost her home, after her husband left her with nothing but debts and memories that were too painful. The heroin helped.

Now she knew she had to lie down somewhere before she fell down.

She saw the flicker of a television in the cab as she approached the lorry. She saw the man inside shovelling pot noodles into his mouth as he watched television. She tapped on his window. He opened his door.

'Suck and fuck?'

He looked at her, disgusted. 'Wouldn't give you a pound for it.'

'Not asking for a pound. Just need a bed for the night.'

'All night?'

'Yeah. We can do it again in the morning.'

The driver stuck his head out and made sure none of the other lorry drivers were watching. Then he looked back at Lolly, looked her up and down and nodded as he slid across to open the passenger door.

'Get in quick.'

She heaved herself up into the cab as the driver turned his attention to a car driving into the adjoining car park. It was an Audi TT, a convertible. He watched it circle and then stop.

Harding drove round to the entrance to the car park and paused as she took stock of the lorries in the adjoining park. She saw the cars to her right. As she drove in one of the lorries flashed its headlights and she was about to make her way towards it when she felt the car begin to rock. Faces grinned at her through the windows – including a mixed-race lad with a nasty-looking dog – and hands yanked at the door handles and started smashing at her window. One of them jumped onto her bonnet and onto her roof. His boot tearing into the fabric. She felt a hand grab at her as an arm came through the hole in her driver's window and reached in to open the door. She slammed the car into reverse and hit the accelerator hard as they ran after her. She slammed on the brakes and skidded on a frozen corner of the car park as she turned, pulled and locked her door shut, and sped off down the road.

It was midnight when JJ Ellerman crept up the stairs to his bedroom. He tried to be as quiet as possible, as light as a feather on his feet. He didn't do it because he was kind and didn't want to wake her. He did it in the hope of catching her out. He hoped to see a moment that revealed what was in her heart, her soul, her bed. He longed to know his wife again.

Chapter 17

The next morning, whilst Willis went to see her mother, Carter went to catch up with Sandford, who was working on Olivia Grantham's car. The Fiat was just a shell now.

Carter put on his protective suit and walked in past the drying cabinet and saw the seat covers hanging inside.

'Was there much on those?' he asked, stopping in front of the glass.

Sandford answered from inside the car; he talked through the gap where the windscreen had been.

'There was. But most of it isn't any good. Matching to the samples taken from her flat – there were at least two other people in this car after Olivia got out. Their prints are over hers. But they wore gloves. Of course there was a dog in there as well. Its paw-prints were pretty distinct.'

Sandford carried on working on the inside of the car. He was looking slightly irritated at Carter's presence.

Carter knew it and it didn't bother him. 'Care to elaborate?' The sooner Sandford stopped resisting, the sooner it would be over.

Sandford stood, and bent backwards to ease his aching back. He was a tall man to fit into a small car.

'The dog had blood on its paws when it made contact with several sites on the upholstery and the door frames,' he said as he pulled off his gloves and put them into a waste bin. He motioned to Carter to follow him as he walked across to his desk and the PC. He brought up the images of the car examination.

'There are traces of it on the driver's door.' He showed Carter a diagram of the evidence recovered and where it was in and on the car. The 3D image rotated as Sandford tapped the keyboard.

'There were things taken from the car – the first-aid kit was ripped open. The spare-wheel kit is also missing. Not that you get much in these new cars – a spare tyre and a few tools. But they're gone. I've asked for a full list of what the car should have had in it, from Fiat. Here, highlighted, you have all the sites in the car that I've matched to the two different glove-prints and the dog's paws.'

Carter sat down to study the screen better. He counted the sites.

'I count twelve places. They got around in that car. Can you get a print from the glove?'

'I'm working on it. I also found traces of blue cashmere. It's got to be hers.'

'The blue coat the caretaker said she was wearing.'

'Were there any fibres that match that at the crime scene?'

'Not so far. Round up some suspects and I'll match them to the traces left in this car. Have you done that yet?'

Carter let the question pass him by.

'Have you had a look at Toffee's clothes?' he asked. 'We got them back from the hospital.'

'Yes, I did. There are traces of Olivia's blood on them. Were there any swabs taken from his genitalia?' asked Sandford.

'No. He'd been washed by the time we got to him. He went straight down for an operation before we could take any samples.'

'Shame.'

'Yeah.'

'You still might get something.'

'No. We tried, believe me, but we have bite marks on Olivia Grantham's body; it's a dog – but you never know, we might be able to tie in all this information and get the owner, especially with what you've found. We also have skin particles beneath her fingernails. There are several sites of bruising on her body – we might be able to pull off a fingerprint or two.'

'Do we know why she went in there?' asked Sandford.

'She was on sex sites. She went in there to have sex. Toffee says something went wrong – something he was involved in. But he also said he tried to save her. He is guilty of something and he is our key witness to what happened to her. He had several small cuts and bruises on his face. It could have been from the train but it looked like someone had punched him in the face a few times.'

'Can we get a knuckle imprint from the bruises on his face?'

'Listen, to be honest, if he was dead we could get

anything we wanted, but right now the hospital aren't too keen on us taking samples from him. I'll get what else I can.'

'Are you facing an enquiry?'

'For what?'

'For his injuries?'

'No, I hope not. Willis was there. There are witnesses.'

'Good luck.'

Chapter 18

Ellerman awoke not knowing where he was for a few seconds. He was in no-man's land between wake and sleep, where his eyes had opened but his dreams continued and the room was dark. The curtains had folds that seemed to him like a tidal wave of water in front of him. It was so near he raised his hand in the air to see if he could touch it. His hand passed through the ghost of the wave.

He closed his eyes and slept again.

When he awoke next time, morning had come to bang on his head like rapping knuckles. He reached for his phone and saw it was nearly nine o'clock. His own bed was the only place he ever slept so late. He would have been up and gone at anyone else's house.

He turned to look at the empty space next to him. The pillow smelt of his wife. He listened hard and heard the sound of movement downstairs. He heard the scrape of the chair on the kitchen floor as she stood and he heard the click of a switch, the kettle boiling. He lay there thinking, his hands spread out along the sheets, and he ran through the events of the last few days. He thought of Megan again and he smiled to himself. She excited him. Maybe she was the one to change his life, to turn it round and give him back some luck. She had money. She wanted him. He could tap into that. Would it be enough for him to leave Dee? How many times had he thought that before, with every new woman? He didn't like to consider it. He looked at his phone again and at his text messages. He had four already this morning. The women had all missed their morning text from him because he had overslept; he normally sent a round of texts as he left in the morning – always by eight anyway. He'd have to answer them soon, before they started calling him. He'd send one text to them all now to keep them happy. He sent a text to Paula in Reading and one to Lisa in Brighton, Emily in Taunton and finally to Megan on Dartmoor.

Morning, my beautiful wild woman – miss you.
xx

He showered and went downstairs. Dee looked up at him and smiled mechanically. There was no happiness in her eyes. Her smile tugged at the corners of her mouth.

Nothing has changed, thought Ellerman. She is the same. He could almost feel her flinch as he passed. He strode across to the kettle and made as much noise as he could. He stood with his back to her as he waited for the kettle to boil. He looked out at the garden.

'The bank keep ringing,' she said, in her quiet voice; it had an apologetic but at the same time accusing tone.

'Yes, I know. I'm dealing with it.' He could sense that she would love to say more, that if he turned round now and asked her what she really felt, she would open her mouth and the truth would explode in an eruption of volcanic hate that nothing would stem. She blamed him for everything.

'Why did you come back early this week?' she asked.

'I'm not staying. I just came to pick up some papers I left behind. I'll be off again this morning, just as soon as I'm packed. I'll see you Friday as usual.'

'Would you like lunch before you go?'

'No, sorry – can't hang about – people to see, money to make. Someone's got to dig us out of this hole, after all.' Ellerman made himself coffee then took it into his office and closed the door. He sat at his desk and rested his head in his hands, closed his eyes as he thought things through. A text came from the bank – he needed to put some money in by the end of the day. He scrolled through his emails for any sign of good news. He found none. *Christ's sake – could something go right for him for once!*

He looked around at the office and the photos on the wall. They were from holidays. There was a photo of him and Craig fishing in Florida. There was one of the three of them in Disneyland, when Craig was eight. There was Ellerman's favourite photo of his wife. Dee was standing looking happy – her face flushed with the sun. She was laughing at him. He remembered taking the photo. That was just before they bought this house. It was after they'd secured their first big sale. It was before it all went wrong.

He sent a text to Paula:

On my way.

Chapter 19

Willis was half watching the news, or rather reading the subtitles, when her mother's case psychiatrist, Dr Lydia Reese, entered the waiting room.

'Thanks for meeting me here.' She extended her hand in a fingers-only handshake. Her hand swallowed by Willis's own. The doctor managed to look perfect even after working a seventy-hour week. Her auburn hair was clipped back from her pretty face in several clasps. She had no make-up. Her face had a fresh, scrubbed look. 'Your mother should be sent back to Rampton soon. She's been brought here to this general hospital whilst her injuries heal.'

'Are you sure she can't escape?'

There was a pause as the doctor seemed to gauge her response. She smiled but her light blue eyes pierced.

'That's not a concern at the moment.'

'But she is handcuffed?'

'Yes ... Ebony, I understand you have a less than perfect relationship with your mother ... Annabelle, but ... I am slightly disappointed that you seemed so reluctant to come in and see her. It's been a fortnight since Christmas. A fortnight since we called you. It's such a shame that this happened because she was responding so well to her new treatment. I had hopes that we could get it under control.

'She's on a drip still; she is taking a small amount of food now but she still talks about wanting to die. She really inflicted a lot of damage with the razor. She needed over seventy stitches.'

'Where?'

'What do you mean? Where was she when she tried to kill herself?'

'No. Where on herself did she cut?'

The doctor looked at Willis as if she were asking something unsavoury.

'On her arms mainly.'

'Where did she get the razor?'

'We think she became a little too close to one of the members of staff and she stole it.'

'What happened to him?' Willis hid a smile.

The doctor didn't answer but she couldn't hide her surprised expression at Willis guessing it was a male.

'The nurse in question has been transferred to another hospital.'

'Why did she say she did it?'

'Suicide attempts are quite common from someone serving life; they reach a point a year or two into the sentence when they would rather die than serve it.'

'She can never come out.' The doctor's expression showed that she wasn't sure how to repond. 'I mean this self-harming – it isn't gaining her anything, is it?' Willis added.

'No. If anything, it lessens her chance of ever being

transferred to a normal prison and therefore qualifying for parole. I'm sorry but if she's suicidal it shows she's still mentally unstable. Follow me, she is in a side ward with another patient from Rampton.'

As they entered the ward, Willis saw her mother with her shock of platinum-blonde hair glowing like a halo in the sunlight.

She looks like an angel, she thought. Her mother used to say: *Bella is a fairy – she is a captured ballerina in a jewellery box – open the box and watch her dance*. She remembered how her mother would get up and dance, turning circles on her tiptoes – dancing around the room, laughing and twirling until she'd collapse onto a chair, laughing. Willis remembered watching her mother dance and feeling her happiness. Once she had tried to join in, but her mother had snapped at her: '*Sit down, Ebony, you look ridiculous.*'

As they walked in, a male nurse passed them. He had *Jamey* written on his name badge. Willis felt the swish of air, the smell of something on him – sex. By the time she looked back up her mother was watching her approach. For a second, Willis felt her feet stop – stop dead. She looked at the pregnant woman in the bed across from her mother. The woman was handcuffed to the rails of her bed. She seemed so still that she looked dead. Until she jerked upright in her bed, snatching at her handcuffs, and screamed obscenities at Willis. The ward was filled with screaming.

'Don't bother about her.' Bella glared across at the pregnant woman. 'She can't hurt us. Big fat ugly lump.'

Willis stopped a few feet away from her mother's bed. 'Hello, Bella.' Her mother was as beautiful as ever – she had the look of a 1960s French film star: chiselled cheekbones and deep ocean-blue eyes.

Annabelle was looking past her, watching the nurse until he was out of sight. Then she sighed deeply.

'Why didn't you come and see me on Christmas Day? I know they rang you. They must have told you I was injured. I was in such pain. I wanted you to come here so badly. I thought I was dying. I wanted to tell you something. I was frightened it was too late.'

'You were never fond of Christmas.'

'Ah.' Her mother lost any residual smile and her face became the flip side that Willis knew well. 'I lost a lot of blood, you know – I could have died.'

'You did it to yourself.' Willis took off her coat and draped it over the back of the chair before sitting down.

Bella laughed drily. 'Not really, darling. I was upset. I was a little angry, perhaps. I ... I saw the razor and I thought: *You are worthless, Bella – you are a monster. You've failed the very person you love more than anyone else in the world. You've failed your baby.*' She threw herself back onto her pillow and seemed to be gasping for breath. She turned her head and kept her eyes on Willis. 'That's you, Ebony, darling. You've been my reason for living, my raison d'être. Everything we went through in life we did together.' Willis started shaking her head; she turned away. 'What? What? I know I was a terrible mother. I didn't get diagnosed early enough with my medical problems. No one helped me. No one but you, my little baby girl. You were my world. Remember how you used to ask me to dance. We used to twirl round

the room together. Ahhhh, Ebony, my little girl ...
you kept me safe all those years. It was only when
you left that ...'

'I didn't leave – I was taken away for my own protection.'

'They didn't understand how much I needed you.
You were the very thing that kept me under control,
kept my illness from spiralling out of control.'

'I spent my childhood waiting for you to explode.'

'I know – I know – that's exactly what you did. You
were so steady, so quiet. You were always watching
with those big brown eyes of yours – always looking
after your mummy. Weren't you, darling? You were a
very special child. My child. My flesh and blood. Born
from my womb, brought into the world by my will
and desire. Mine ...'

'You can't use a child like that. I was your daughter, not your nurse. Not your possession. It wasn't
right to make me responsible for you. What do you
want from me?'

'It's only now that I've been having so much ther-
apy, after I tried to kill myself.' She looked at Willis
as if waiting to be contradicted. 'They tell me I have
all sorts of conflicting feelings towards you.' Willis
couldn't hide her smile. 'What? Why is that funny? I
don't want to feel anger towards you – you are all I
have in this world. I need to make my peace with
you. Because I do take responsibility for the way my
life has gone – to a certain extent. And I do know
that you are the most important person in my life
and I haven't always been as fair as I could have
been.'

Willis looked at her mother. She would only need to wait. She knew her mother better than any psychiatrist or doctor.

'That's why I attacked myself with the razor – I thought: *You don't deserve to live.* You know I adore you. You were a tiny baby, I loved you so. I held you in my arms and we danced and danced and people said to me – what a good baby, she sleeps, never cries, but she doesn't smile, does she?'

'Bitch ...!' the pregnant woman screamed across at them.

She was leaning towards them as far as her handcuffed arm would allow.

'Shut up, you worthless piece of pregnant scum,' Bella hissed across at her. She turned back to Willis. 'You think that I want to be out of that place, that I want to move to an open prison and show how much I've learnt about growing vegetables, and you think I want to earn my freedom?'

'It had crossed my mind.'

Bella laughed. It was a laugh that was high and false.

She turned a sweetened face back to Willis and reached out her hand. 'You're no "catch", you know.' Willis resisted the urge to recoil.

'I swear your father was a good-looking man. The best-looking black guy I was ever with. And yet ...' She reached out again and pushed Willis's hair back from her face. Willis held still. 'I do believe you are growing into a kind of beauty – unique. Yes – I can see it now.'

Her mother's smile slowly eased.

'Do you have any memories of your father?'

'There were so many men in my childhood. Not sure if he was one of them.'

'What do you mean? I wasn't some slut who bedded men left, right and centre.'

'Maybe not, but you loved a fair few.' The pregnant woman choked with laughter.

'Well, you can judge me any way you want but I am asking for us to go forward with a new relationship now; put the past behind us. It's not as if I can do any more harm stuck in there.'

Willis smiled. 'We both know that's not true. What about the member of staff who you stole the razor from?'

She shrugged. 'He was a stupid boy who fell for the oldest trick in the book. He deserved everything he got.'

'I bet you didn't share that thought with your therapist?'

Bella didn't answer. She yawned.

'You know what? You've tired me out – such a shame you are not softening. It would reflect in your face more if you could find that inner peace. Inner beauty.'

'I'll go.' Willis stood and picked up her coat.

'Yes, go, but come again in two days. I didn't get a chance to tell you something important. I wanted to show you something, to explain something.'

'I'm listening.'

'Don't talk to me like that – with such disdain. That's what you've always done. You forget, I gave birth to you. You came out of my vagina. You were the result of passion and wild sex and fun. Does that mean anything, Miss Sourface?'

Willis turned to go.

'I'm sorry.' Bella started crying. 'I'm so sorry. Please come back and see me. I want to tell you all about your father. I have photos to show you. You could find him if you wanted. I'd like to see him again before I die.'

Willis stared at her mother. She didn't know whether to believe her or not. But she knew that behind every lie of her mother's there was a grain of truth and a whole heap of mischief.

Chapter 20

The last few lorry drivers were getting their vehicles ready to hit the road in the morning. In their silent routines they walked around, checking their load was secure. Their quiet concentration was interrupted by the noise of traffic on the roads nearby and by the primary school when the children were let out for morning break, bursting into the playground in a joyful mass scream. Dominik, with white goods from Poland on his lorry, went to empty his rubbish in the bins at the corner of the car park. He came out of his cab with three carrier bags full and walked across to the bins. It felt good to stretch his legs before he started his long day's drive to the North. As he approached the waste bins he saw the bare legs of a woman poking out from behind the bottle bank.

Dominik had been allowed to leave by the time Carter got there. The patrol officers had stayed at the scene to protect it.

'We often see her – her name is Lolly. She hangs about here and offers sex to the lorry drivers. We've had to move her on sometimes when she gets to be a nuisance. But she never meant any harm – she just needed her fix too much – only a matter of time, I suppose.'

Carter knelt down beside her.

'This is hers . . .' The patrol officer handed Carter Lolly's purse. Inside, he found her library card and a card for the needle exchange. *Lorraine Chance.*

'It could have been an overdose, I suppose?' one of the officers commented.

'Could also have been hypothermia, if she tried to spend the night out here,' added Carter. 'Anyone see anything?'

The officer shook his head.

'Most of the lorries had gone by the time we got here. There were only three left and we've taken the details for them but this park will have been pretty full last night. At least half are foreign drivers.'

'We'll be a long time trying to trace the lorries.'

Carter squatted beside her as he looked her over.

'She's been interfered with,' he said, as he lifted her layers of clothing. He looked up at the officer nearest. 'Could she have been servicing a customer out here?'

'Not likely. He would have been a lorry driver. She didn't charge them – she just wanted some warmth and a place to sleep usually. No way would they do it outside in freezing temperatures when they could do it in their warm cab.'

Carter stood and looked around him. 'Hard to tell if she was dumped here or she was sheltering. Have you made a scout of the rest of the car park to see if there's anything?'

'Yes, sir. There's broken glass in the car park side of here, the other side of the recycling centre, but no evidence of blood.'

'Okay – let's get her taken to the mortuary.'

Chapter 21

'Are you okay, JJ?'

'Yes, of course, babe. I'm good now I'm here.' He stepped out from the shower and swung his head, spraying Paula with water. She giggled but her eyes were still watching him, concerned. He wrapped the small towel around his waist. He was proud of his physique. He kept himself trim and he played tennis whenever he could. He did fifty press-ups every day, a hundred sit-ups. He liked to look slim rather than big-muscled. He stopped drying his hair and looked at her appreciatively.

'You look lovely. You've done something different with your hair?'

'It took me ages.' She looked at her reflection. Her long black hair was piled up on her head in a large doughnut shape. 'I'm practising for a wedding I have to do this weekend. The rest of the girls in the salon are all busy and it's good money.'

Ellerman looked up from drying. 'That's good. You clever little thing, you.'

'I'm going to put it in the bank, I'm saving for the salon.' She was still looking at him, waiting for his response. 'For when we move to Spain and I get my salon.'

'Good idea.' Ellerman kissed her forehead as he passed her on his way to the bedroom to get some clean clothes out of his bag. 'Are the kids okay?' he called out as he replaced his neatly folded clothes and zipped up the bag.

Paula came to stand in the doorway of the room and watch him get dressed.

'Yeah, the girls are great, asking about you. What about Craig – what's he up to? Has he got a girl-friend?'

Ellerman pulled a T-shirt over his head as he answered. 'No, not yet. Or maybe he has and I don't know. He doesn't tell me anything. You know what teenagers are like. If he does talk it's because he wants something. They always just want money. I see less and less of him now as he stays in his room on his laptop.' Ellerman grinned. 'We know what that's about.'

'Yuck. Glad I haven't got boys. Filthy creatures.'

Ellerman made a lunge for her and wouldn't let her go. She screamed with delight.

'You love it when I get dirty, you know you do.' He smacked her on her bottom and she giggled. He let her go and went back into the bathroom and closed the door this time.

'Come on, babe. What you doing in there?' Paula called outside the bathroom door ten minutes later.

'Yeah – won't be a minute.'

He'd had another text from Dee. He knew what she would want to know – had he sorted the bank? He checked his emails on his phone. If only the contract he'd been chasing for two years now would just happen, for Christ's sake! He'd poured so much money into courting the potential buyers, a conglomerate of Middle Eastern businessmen, that he had no more money to risk. Still they kept him waiting, with more questions about supplying this or that, tweaking and customizing and basically screwing him down until he was too far under their thumb to work himself loose.

He opened the door to find her standing there waiting for him. 'I heard you texting. Is it work?'

'No, babe. It was Craig. He likes to text me when I'm away.'

'Ah. He sounds lovely. What are you going to do with him this weekend?'

'I promised him I'd take him out on the speedboat.' He could see Paula melt. She loved any discussion of wealth and the trappings that went with it.

'When am I going to meet Craig? You've met my girls. They talk about you a lot. Ever since we came back from those few days in Disneyland Paris – it's all they keep asking – when is JJ going to take us away again? I still feel guilty that we didn't take Craig.'

'Craig would have hated it with us. Believe me.' Ellerman came out of the bathroom, looking perfectly groomed and with his blond hair neatly brushed. 'I need a haircut if you have time.'

Paula nodded. 'Sure, babe.'

She followed him downstairs into the lounge.

He looked at his phone again when yet another text came through. It was another from his wife that he wasn't going to read. He switched it off and looked at Paula and her anxious face. She was watching him intently. 'Nothing to worry about – it's all taken care of. I'm not going to be bothered by clients right now. Now, what have we got to eat here? I'm starving.'

'I thought we could get a takeaway?'

Ellerman made his disappointed face.

'And there's me thinking you'd have a lovely meal waiting for me like you usually do.'

Paula shrugged. 'No time – sorry. I had to get the kids over to my mum's, to give us some peace. You said you have some photos of our house in Spain to show me?'

'I do. They're on my phone. I'll show you in the morning. I don't want to turn it on again – I'll just have to talk to clients. More stress I don't need.'

'Let's go down the pub then. I told my friends you were coming and they're waiting there for us. I thought we could pick up a takeaway on the way back. Come on, JJ, it'll be fun. I want to show you off – my sugar-daddy boyfriend.' She reached out and ran her hand around his waistline.

Ellerman looked at her and felt real affection for her. She was simple and sweet, uncomplicated and for-giving. When she had contacted him on the Sugar Daddies dating site, she was looking for a secure future for her and her girls. She was willing to wait for him. She was the easiest of all the women and, in a way, he was drawn to her; he was fond of her trusting, simple nature. She reminded him of the way Dee used to look at him; look up to him; idolize him. He enjoyed taking Paula and her girls away. They were grateful and they were proud of him. But even Paula had begun to notice that the presents had dried up. If they went out this evening, she'd expect him to buy several rounds of drinks for her mates. He didn't see how he could. He might just be able to get a few quid out of the new credit card. He hadn't used it yet. He was trying not to – the rate of interest per annum was sky high. He'd try to make her pay first.

She pouted at him. He laughed. She was like a small child when she made her petulant, pissed-off face. She went to move away in a huff and he grabbed her and tickled her so that she screeched with laughter, and he guided her back into the bedroom.

An hour later, she gave up trying to keep him hard. He lay back on the bed and sighed. She cuddled into him.

'What's the matter, babe? Are you all right?'

'Sorry.'

Christ – it was coming to something when he had to say sorry to these women. What the fuck was the matter with him? He sat up in bed and pulled his jeans on.

'What's the matter? Aren't we going to try again?'

'We'll have all night. You're right, let's go out, darling. Let's go and get drunk and then I'll come back here and screw you senseless.'

'*Darling?* You've never called me that before.'

'Well, it's because that's how dear you are to me – my little darling.'

'Give me an hour to get ready.'

'No, I'm not waiting an hour. I want to go out now. You look perfect as you are.'

She made the face again. He didn't laugh this time and she got off the bed and went into the bathroom.

'Okay then, but I only want you to be proud of me. A girl's got to look her best.'

Ellerman went downstairs and into Paula's kitchen, where he knew she kept a stash of spirits. He passed the television on the way – the news was on. He didn't stop to look at the house fire in Exeter that had claimed a woman's life – he found the brandy and poured himself a large one.

Chapter 22

'Which one are you?' Carter asked, looking over Hector's shoulder at his screen.

'I'm a male doctor named Lawrence,' said Hector. 'I'm also Sharon Thomas, a teacher. They list their jobs as teachers, politicians, civil servants, policemen.'

'Well, you pay to get a better class of person, apparently,' said Carter.

'You have to go into a lot of detail about what you will and won't do. You're encouraged to lay it on the line – make it absolutely clear. For instance, this woman I'm looking at here, can't see her face but she likes bondage, submission and to be dominated. She says she's not too keen on pain but mild spanking is great. Humiliation and exhibitionism boxes? Yep – tick, tick – she likes those a lot.'

'I'm sure I recognize that woman's mole on her left buttock,' Carter said, watching as Hector flicked through the profiles onscreen. 'It's a good job we can't see faces. Could be half of the Met's vice squad on here.' Pam giggled in the background.

'Have you managed to get hold of most of Olivia Grantham's contacts yet?' Carter asked Robbo.

'Yes. We're starting interviews tomorrow morning – bringing them in one by one.'

'What else do we know about any of them now?'

'I've been looking at JJ Ellerman's story,' answered Pam. 'He's from Portsmouth. He's forty-five now. Left school at fifteen. He served an apprenticeship in a boat builders' in his home town and worked his way up the ladder until he became a partner. He married a local Portsmouth-born hairdresser, Dee Thompkinson – she's five years younger than him – and then they moved to London.'

'What was his background?' asked Carter.

'He's done a few interviews about his tough upbringing. He seems to have lived alone with his father. His dad died when he was seventeen. Cause of death: liver failure brought on by alcohol abuse.'

'No sign of the mother?'

'No. They were already divorced at the time of his dad's death.'

'He was their only kid?'

'Yes.'

'So he worked his way up the ladder. Determined type. Admirable. Can't have been easy living with a father who drank himself to death,' said Carter.

'He bought out the other partner in Mermaid Yachts at the end of the '90s and Ellerman and his wife bought a big house in Richmond. It looks like things started to go down for Ellerman after that,' said Pam. 'The company accounts show a sharp decline in profit.'

'How does he afford to stay in the house in Richmond?' asked Robbo.

'He has another business. He's the director of a company renovating houses in Spain,' answered Pam. 'He looks like he draws a salary from that.' Pam's azure-blue eyes flicked back on Carter.

'Can we see some of these houses?' Carter asked as he helped himself to coffee.

'I've had a look for a website – it's amateur at best. It's more of a one-page advert than an interactive website. There are a couple of pages of photos of houses, that's it. There doesn't seem to be anything else about it online. The company's called Hacienda Developments; it's based in Spain although registered here.'

'If he makes money from it, he must advertise it somewhere.'

'You'd think so,' said Robbo. 'Everything's online these days.'

'Unless he's doing one bespoke project at a time,' said Hector. 'I saw something like that on one of those building TV programmes. This one was for a wealthy Brit and it cost a million. If you were in charge of that project, you could expect a fair whack.'

'So – we think he's got two high-profile businesses going on? Restoring expensive Spanish homes and selling just as expensive yachts?'

'The yachts haven't been doing well for a while,' said Pam as she looked at the screen over her glasses. They were glam ones – leopard-print with winged sides.

Carter turned to Hector.

'Did you ask him where he was on Sunday after-noon and evening?'

'At home.'

'When was the last time he had contact with Olivia?'

'They texted one another a lot, said Hector. 'Last time looks like a week ago. They sent a text to one another first and then there were a few phone calls between them. The last one we have is one from Olivia to him saying: "Great to chat, looking forward to putting plan into action. Very exciting!!!"'

'She seemed to like him,' said Carter.

'Yeah, there are a lot of calls between them, long ones, sometimes lasting more than an hour,' Hector replied, looking at the lists of phone records. 'There is also a six-month period a year ago when Ellerman was texting her every day; looks like a basic, round-robin text – he says the same thing every time: "Hello, gorgeous, how's things? I'm so hot for you right now. Miss you, love you . . . " That kind of thing. They must have felt a connection—'

'I'll interview him myself when we bring him in,' said Carter.

'Won't he recognize your voice from the call about Naughties?' asked Robbo, who was opening another pack of Haribo. He was trying to get down to one a day. He took out five sweets and folded over the packet top, jammed it under the stapler.

'I'll let Willis do most of the talking. I'll sit in on it – I don't think he'll remember my voice – he was too busy panicking at the time.'

'Where is she?'

'Personal stuff. She should be back by now.' He checked his phone and rang her number.

'I'll be there in two minutes, guv. I'm just parking the car.'

'Go straight to the Whittington – I'll see you there.'

Hector began tapping on his keyboard frantically. 'I'm into Olivia's profile now.'

'You got past her password?' asked Carter.

'Wasn't so hard in the end – she put it in the reminder section on her phone.'

They crowded round to have a look at Hector's screen.

'This is not strictly legal,' Robbo said as he scrolled down the images of the men she had messaged. 'But well done.'

'Good job,' said Carter.

'I can only look at the past thirty messages on this and that just takes us back a month. We'll need to get permission to look further. It will mean bringing in the companies' computers. It's not going to be easy. It looks like she surfed the net most evenings. Some people have noticed her absence. There are a few "where are you?" messages.'

'We have to wait to get permission to use the information from the website. It's an infringement of these men's human rights,' said Robbo.

Carter opened the file on the desk and looked at Ellerman's photos. He was posing by yachts, his company logo and emblem emblazoned all over his T-shirt: blue sky and a golden mermaid figure in the middle. *Miranda* was written in the circle around the mermaid. Carter stood and took his coat from the hanger behind the door.

'Has Ellerman tried to get in touch with Olivia?'

'Yes,' answered Hector.

'Smug git,' Carter said as he turned to leave.

Carter drove down to the Whittington and parked in one of the spaces allotted to the mortuary.

'You okay? How did it go?' he asked Willis as she joined him, carrying her coat. Carter thought she looked slightly different. She'd worn a colourful blouse to see her mother. It looked too big for her. He wondered if she'd borrowed it from Tina. Still the same black work trousers though; but she had made an effort – she couldn't help herself. She nodded.

'Fine. But have you seen Dr Harding's car?' Carter shook his head. 'I just parked up next to it. You want to see it – it's a mess.'

'Jesus Christ,' said Carter as he examined the damage. 'The driver's window is smashed.' He walked around the car. 'Also looks like there were several attempts at smashing the passenger window too. The tear in the roof alone will cost a fortune. She must have seriously pissed someone off. This is going to cost five hundred quid to put right.'

He rang the bell and spoke into the intercom:

'It's Detective Inspector Carter and DC Willis. Is Dr Harding free? We need a word.'

They found Harding in her office. Mark was sitting at the other desk. He got up to leave as they came in.

Harding indicated for Carter to pull up the chair Mark had just vacated. Willis perched on the side of Mark's desk.

'First things first – what happened to your car?' asked Carter.

Harding looked a little 'caught out'.

'Just parked it in the wrong place, that's all.'

'What, and someone did that?'

'Obviously.'

'Did you report it?'

'No. I didn't see what happened.'

'There could be CCTV in the area. Are you claiming on the insurance?'

'No. It's not as bad as it looks.'

'Seriously? You want to get a crime number, that's a few hundred quids' worth of damage. Thank God you weren't in it at the time – they were obviously trying to get in. Where did it happen?'

'I don't remember exactly. I was visiting a friend.'

'Where?'

'In the East End. Look, I don't really want to discuss it, if you don't mind. I can't remember exactly where and when my car got damaged. It's just one of those things.'

Carter looked at Willis and raised an eyebrow as Harding turned back to her desk and clicked on an image of Olivia Grantham's post-mortem test results.

'Drugs tests came back negative. She was clean and sober when she walked into that place. I presume that's what you want to see me about?'

'Yes, and I wanted to ask if the bite cast worked out.'

'Seems so. They didn't come back to me to say that they couldn't make an impression. I'll chase it.' She looked up her notes. 'And I'll let you know when I do. Stomach contents show she hadn't eaten in the last five hours.'

'This wasn't a dinner date then. This was definitely for the sex. Here's a few more names we've lifted from Olivia's contacts for you to have a look at. We start interviewing them tomorrow.' He handed Harding the list of names. She looked them over. 'Recognize any of them?'

'No, sorry.'

'Please keep this list and check if any of the phone numbers on it match contacts you have. Someone could be under a different name.'

'Yes. Okay.'

'When are you performing the post-mortem on the homeless woman, Lorraine Chance?'

'As soon as I have a slot free. I'll let you know what I find.'

Outside, Carter and Willis walked back across to Harding's car to take another look.

'Guv? I didn't know we had a new case? Lorraine Chance?'

'Known as Lolly. She was found in the lorry park at Shadwell. She works that area. She's well known to the patrols. It looked to me as if she'd accidentally overdosed. Coroner's ordered an enquiry into how she died.'

'She's the woman from the Faith and Light hostel?'

'Yes. I presume so.'

He shone his torch on the damage. There were large deep punctures on the driver's door.

'She didn't seem to think this was anything, did she? Why didn't she want to do anything about it? This is serious damage to property.'

'She seemed a little shaken up by it. Most of the damage is on the driver's side.'

'Unless she knows who did it and she doesn't want to say. She didn't make a comment when you said thank God she wasn't in the car when it happened, did she?' said Willis.

'You think she was?' Carter asked as he took photos of Harding's car with his phone.

'To me, it looks like someone's tried to get at her through the window. She said she was visiting a friend; could be she doesn't want their name mentioned?'

'But, this is too bad to just ignore it. If this was my car, would you tell me to ignore it? No. Exactly!' said Carter. Willis didn't answer. Carter looked at her expression and shrugged. 'You're right – it's none of my business, I suppose. Come on – I'll buy you a drink at the tavern.'

They drove down Holloway Road and parked outside the Shamrock Pub.

Willis ordered a Coke. Carter had a bottle of lager. They sat in a booth. Cricket from the other side of the world was on a screen at the other end of the pub.

'What do you think about Harding?' Carter asked.

'There's an honesty in her admitting about the sex sites but I'm still surprised she does it. I never thought she had trouble with getting one-night stands.'

'It's a case of the more the better, I think. Plus, she obviously likes the anonymity of it all. And she could be useful to us. She could talk to some of the men from the Naughties site that we're interested in; we're not looking for anyone new to the site. If the killer was in touch with Olivia, it's very likely he's tried his luck with Harding at one time.'

'I think it's dangerous to use her in that way. Plus, it'd be embarrassing for her if it comes out. I don't know how we can promise her anonymity.'

'We can't.'

'But you did.'

'And she knows I was lying. She just wanted me to say it; she didn't expect me to mean it. In reality, she doesn't give a toss.'

'Maybe. It's hard to know with her.'

'If we find out anything through her then "confidential sources" will have to do.'

He paused, looking at Willis. He thought how tired she looked. She hadn't been right since the case that ended just before Christmas. He made a mental note to go and see Tina in the canteen. She was Willis's housemate and she might tell him if he was missing something. He was so busy worrying about his own father, who had throat cancer. The love he had for his dad was a million miles away from Willis's feelings for her mother.

'So how was Mommie Dearest?' Carter took a drink, rubbed his hands together as the cold from the bottle hit them. He searched Willis's face.

'She hasn't changed.'

'What's she after? She knows that trying to commit suicide means messing up any chance she might have of transferring to a jail.'

'She's bored and she wanted my attention.'

'You think that's it?'

'Yes. She managed to find herself a man in the

hospital, a male nurse, and I'm not convinced he's the only one – they shouldn't put men anywhere near her. She got tired of him so she self-harmed. My mother is a bright woman. She knew exactly where to cut. If she wanted to hit an artery – she would have. But she didn't. She just made a nasty mess of her arms. She wanted attention. She wanted me to rush to her bed-side.' Willis sighed. 'She wants to have a say in my life.'

'How can she hope to have that from where she is?'

Willis shook her head.

'She says if I visit her she'll tell me about my father.' Willis looked up from her lap. 'She has photos.'

'Don't you know anything about him?'

She shrugged. 'I know he was from Jamaica … and I know he was much younger than her – a young ath-lete over in the UK for some sponsorship promotions. They met in a bar. He never knew about me. They lasted a few weeks and then he went home. She didn't put him on the birth certificate and she never con-tacted him again.'

'If she gives you a name then he should be easy to trace.'

'I know – that's what I was thinking.'

It was the most animated Carter had seen her for a while. There was an enthusiasm in her now, a spark of excitement. She saw Carter studying her.

'I know it shouldn't mean a lot to me, but it does. I would love to know him. He would be in his forties now.'

'I understand – we'd all feel the same way. But you must be prepared for the fact that this could just be a lie.'

She nodded.

'I know, but equally the lie could have been told at the very beginning. Maybe he always knew about me, always wondered. Maybe they had something more than a few weeks together. I want to see the photos.'

Carter nodded. He understood that the risk was worth taking for Willis. He also understood that her mother had played a clever hand.

Zoe Blackman called as they were coming out of the pub.

'How's it going?' asked Carter as he took her call. 'How's Toffee?'

'He looks worse to me but they say it's natural for his face to swell up. I've left guard duty now but I'm going to call in for an update once a day.'

'Make sure no one gets in there.'

'Yes, sir. Someone is guarding him twenty-four hours a day. He's safe.'

'Has Smith been around? Are you getting anywhere with him?'

'He has been in. He's opening up a little but he cherry-picks the parts he tells you. He used to be in a mess and his parents bought him the hostel to run. Doesn't make perfect sense to me. Can't see how running the hostel is going to provide a good career move for an ex-junkie – I think it's asking for trouble.'

'I'll get Pam to look into the family backgrouind. They must be über-wealthy if they are using the hostel as a tax write-off.'

'I'm not sure you'd see the whole picture unless

you're inside that hostel. I'm trying to work my way in there somehow, or at least get my mum in there.'

'If she succeeds – we need her to get on best terms with the volunteers and find out the relationship between Smith and Toffee.'

'If she succeeds she'll do what comes naturally and find out all that and more.

'There was a young woman asking for Toffee. She called herself Martine, said she knew him from the Faith and Light hostel. I tried to talk to her but all she really wanted to do was see Toffee and she wasn't allowed. She scarpered before I could grab her.'

'We heard about a Martine when we went to the hostel – we need to find her – she's one of Toffee's protégés. She could be just scared without Toffee but instinct tells me she must have something to hide if she scarpered.'

Chapter 23

The next morning Zoe made sure she was called when Simon came into the hospital. She was there within twenty minutes. Simon looked up at her and smiled as she approached.

'Fancy a home-made brownie?'

Simon stood and picked up his jacket. 'Lead the way. You said the magic word: brownie.'

Zoe quickly tidied up the front seat of the Corsa and got rid of the crumbs on the seat.

'Sorry, I never meant to let the kids eat in the car but there we go – rules, huh?'

'I know – to be broken. Please don't worry,' Simon said as he got in and buckled up.

'Okay. Hold tight ... only kidding.' She smiled across at him and thought how, out of the hospital environment, he looked so much more calm.

'Your mum won't mind us invading her like this?'

'No, she needs something to do in the day when the kids are at school. I'm always telling her she should get a job or do some charity work or something.'

A ten-minute drive and they were outside Zoe's

house. Her mum walked past the window and saw her car pull up. She waved. Zoe could see her eyes go towards the passenger seat, checking Simon out.

At the front door she made the introductions: 'Simon, this is my mum, Diane. Mum, I've been bragging about your brownies.'

'They'd better be good then.' Diane held the door open to let them in. 'Come in and I'll get some tea on. Tea or coffee, Simon?'

'Has to be tea with brownies.'

'Absolutely, I agree.' Diane watched him walk past and then smiled at her daughter. Zoe gave her mum a look that said: 'Don't be silly – don't even think it. I am not becoming a vicar's wife.'

'Please, Simon, have a seat.' Diane put the kettle on as she watched Simon looking around the kitchen. 'Do you mind sitting in here? It's the warmest room.'

'Of course not. Thanks so much for inviting me.'

'You run the Faith and Light hostel, Zoe tells me.'

'I do, yes. I don't cook unless I have to but I'm a mean washer-upper.'

'And you take the services at the multi-denominational church there?'

'I do, sometimes. Do you go to the church near here?'

'Yes. Or rather I did. I haven't been for a few weeks.'

'Months,' corrected Zoe as she walked around the kitchen, folding her son's clothes from the drying rail.

Diane looked embarrassed.

'Zoe told me that your husband passed away. I'm sorry to hear that.'

'Yes. Thank you.' Diane poured the tea and took a plate of brownies across to the kitchen table. 'Please help yourself, Simon.'

'Will you join me?'

Diane went back across to the sink. 'Yes. Of course.' She glanced at Zoe.

'Mum – I'm going to check on the kids' rooms while I'm here. Josh is missing some of his sports kit.'

'Okay, love. As long as Simon doesn't mind you deserting him.'

'Not at all,' he said. 'I'm looking forward to chatting with you, Diane – can I call you Diane?'

'Please do.'

Zoe took the piles of clothes and walked up the stairs with them.

'Can I see a photo of your husband, Diane?'

'Of course.' She went into the front room and came back with a shot of them together.

'This was before he got ill. On holiday in Palma. We used to go away often. Always tended to go back to the same places but you know what you're getting then, don't you?'

'Absolutely.' He held the photo in his hands. 'You look a lovely couple. You obviously made one another very happy. That's a precious thing in this world.'

'Yes. It's even more difficult then, isn't it? To lose your soulmate?'

'Not lost. Still with you in spirit.'

'I feel he's lost. I worry that I've been living a lie and that we will never be reunited in any form. I try not to think like that. I've tried very hard to keep believing but something's missing in me now.'

'Have you got new challenges in your life? We all need daily challenges.'

'I think I have enough. I come here most days and help so that Zoe can pursue her career. I am always busy.'

'Because if you felt you had any time, just whenever you could – we could always do with a hand in the hostel.'

'I don't know what use I'd be ...'

'You're kidding! You'd be a godsend. You could teach the clients to cook basic food for themselves. You could listen to their troubles, sit and talk to them. It's that I wish I had more time to do things ... and you could make us brownies as good as these.'

'Okay.' She brightened up. 'I will certainly think about it.'

'And Diane – I understand how you must be angry. It never seems fair. I can promise you, you will find your faith again. Don't punish yourself, don't go to church if you don't want to, but don't block your faith out. It's okay to question. We all have our faith tested now and again.'

Chapter 24

'Mr Ellerman?' Willis walked in first, followed by Carter. 'I am Detective Constable Willis and this is Detective Inspector Carter.'

'I've been sitting here for half an hour. I understood this was just an informal interview?' He was irritated.

'It is, Mr Ellerman,' answered Willis. 'We thought you'd want to keep this as discreet and private as possible. So, in here is the best place to take a statement from you. We won't keep you longer than necessary.'

Ellerman shifted in his seat, impatient. Carter stayed quiet.

'Okay, well let's get on with it. What do you want to ask me? The officer who asked me to come in said it concerned Olivia Grantham.'

'Yes – I'm sorry to inform you that Olivia Grantham was killed – we think she was murdered.'

'No ... how terrible ... How did it happen?'

'We don't know why but she walked into a derelict building in Shadwell, where she was attacked. Where were you last Sunday evening?'

'Sunday? I already told the officer on the phone; I

was at home in Richmond. Poor Olivia.' He rubbed his forehead with his fingertips.

'Have you got someone who can verify your where-abouts?'

'Yes. My wife; but I'd rather not involve her.'

'Were you close to Olivia?' asked Willis.

'I wouldn't say we were close.'

'How long had you known her?'

'We met a few months ago, I think it was. Maybe even as much as twelve months. We didn't see one another often.'

'When was the last time?'

'Probably three weeks ago.'

'And how was that?'

He shrugged. 'Fine. She seemed okay – same as usual.'

'Usual?'

'Yes.'

'What was usual for her?'

'Well – you know ... maybe a little obsessed with work, but not depressed or anything.'

'Where did you meet that last time?'

'I think it was at her flat.'

'Which is where?'

'Brockley. I think.'

'What was your relationship with Olivia, Mr Ellerman?'

'We were friends. I told you.'

'Was it a platonic freindship?'

'We had a physical friendship.'

'You were lovers?'

'On a casual basis, I suppose so.'

'How did you meet?'

'We met online.'

'Where online?'

'An adult-friend-finder service called Naughties. It's a site for finding sexual partners. It's an honest way of hooking up with a stranger for sex.'

He looked across at Carter. Carter sat opposite him and smiled politely but still said nothing.

'Would you say your relationship with Olivia was just sexual?' asked Willis.

'Yes.'

'You never went to dinner? You didn't spend time with one another? You didn't ring her for a chat – ask her how her day was?'

'We may have had dinner. We liked the friendship we had. It was enough.'

'Is that unusual for someone meeting on this type of site, to have dinner, to form a relationship? To become friends outside the bedroom? Isn't it dangerous to become attached? I thought the whole idea was that you meet, have sex and then walk away without forming a bond.'

'No, not necessarily. It's a starting point sometimes.'

'So you formed a bond with Olivia?' Willis asked.

'I didn't say that.'

'I want you to think clearly, Mr Ellerman,' she continued. 'We have phone records of Olivia's dating back five years. Your messages appear on them in the last two years ...' She opened the file on the table and took out the page so that Ellerman could see the heading: *Messages sent and received between Olivia Grantham and JJ Ellerman.*

'There are many times that it appears you met one

another. You talked to one another for nearly an hour sometimes. And you know what strikes me, Mr Ellerman? There seems to be a proper relationship between you.'

'Nonsense. It was just phone sex.'

'In one text message she mentions her investment. What does she mean by that?'

'No idea.'

'Could it have something to do with your Spanish company – Hacienda Renovations?' asked Carter, speaking for the first time.

Ellerman looked from one detective to the other. He watched Carter turn the page in the file and pull out the printout from Companies House.

'Am I under investigation? I was told this was an informal interview. I want a lawyer here if you persist in cross-examining me.'

'We only want to build up a better idea of her life, Mr Ellerman. I'm sure you will want to find out what happened to Olivia,' Willis said. 'After all, she was a friend at least, wasn't she?'

'I told you, she was just someone I met for sex.'

'Did you tell her about your Spanish renovations company?' asked Carter.

'I might have done.'

Ellerman shifted in his seat. He was sweating. A bead had begun to trickle down his temple.

'Did she invest in any of your businesses?'

'I can't remember. I don't think so. What does that matter, anyway?'

'Everything matters, Mr Ellerman. Everything helps us to build a picture of her life.'

'Did Olivia know you were married?' asked Willis.

'Yes, of course. I don't lie about things like that. Look, I have absolutely had enough. I demand to be allowed to leave now. You've had quite enough from me and I feel very threatened by your line of questioning.'

'I understand,' said Carter. He looked up at Ellerman and smiled politely.

'We're really hoping that we don't have to ask you to come in again, so we are being as thorough as we can be this time.' He turned to Willis: 'Detective Willis, is there anything else you'd like to ask Mr Ellerman before we thank him for his cooperation and send him on his way?'

'There is one more question.' She scanned down her notes. 'Did Olivia mention that she was seeing someone else or had just begun a new *friendship*?'

'No.'

'Have you any idea who she might have been meeting on Sunday evening?'

'No. I've said – I don't have any idea. Can I go?'

Ellerman got up. Willis was scanning through the phone records again; she stopped halfway down the second page.

'Sit down, please. Do you have another mobile number that you use?'

'No, I don't.'

'Not even a back-up one that you keep for emergencies?'

Ellerman shook his head, annoyed. 'I said – no.' He sat back down heavily in his chair. 'I've told you all I want to say.' He stared straight ahead, his arms folded across his chest.

'Okay. Thank you for your cooperation,' Willis said, closing the file. 'I have to ask you not to leave the country and to be available for us to talk to you again if necessary. Is this the best number to get you on?' Willis read the number from the sheet pinned to the file.

'Yes. I don't want my wife bothered.'

'I am sure you don't,' said Carter.

'It's not like that – it's just that she has been depressed. I want some reassurance from you that she won't be bothered.'

'No guarantee – as Detective Willis said, Mr Ellerman, please keep yourself available and make sure that we can locate you easily enough and then that shouldn't be a problem.'

After the first set of interviews, Willis and Carter headed back to the Dark Side.

Robbo was at his desk, engrossed in sorting the images from the crime scene. Pam was at hers. Hector was out of the office. 'How did the interviews go?' Robbo looked back and forth between Carter and Willis for an answer.

'We interviewed four men who had some kind of encounter with Olivia Grantham. Only JJ Ellerman is of serious interest. The other three have watertight alibis. They only saw her once each.'

Willis went to sign in to Hector's empty workstation.

'What was Ellerman like?' asked Robbo. Pam stopped her work to listen to the reply.

'He's a smart-looking man.' Carter looked towards Willis to confirm.

'Yes,' she agreed. 'He cares a lot about his appearance. He keeps himself in good shape but he looks frayed around the edges. He sweats a lot. He is arrogant and thinks he's cleverer than he actually is.'

Carter smiled.

'Exactly – couldn't have put it better myself. He looks down his nose at the world. He is Mr In Control. Selfish, self-absorbed and ruthless.'

'Nice guy then; can see you two warmed to him.' Robbo smiled. 'What did he say about his relationship with Olivia Grantham?'

'He said as little as he could get away with,' answered Carter. 'He definitely didn't want to talk about the fact that he might have been fond of her. But he admits they went to dinner, they had a friendship besides just sex. But he didn't seem to really care that she was dead. He certainly wasn't that shocked by it. Do we know any more about him, Pam?'

'I think I've found him on seven dating sites so far,' said Pam. 'On three of them he has his photograph; it's a version of the photo on his website, taken at the same time by the look of it. He describes himself as someone slightly different each time – his age is always between forty and fifty. His height varies, interests always include classic cars and his income is always huge. That seems to be the key for him – he is how much he earns. He wants everyone to know. In each of the adverts, he uses the same line: self-made man, used to luxury.'

'Except he doesn't earn it any more,' said Carter. 'What about the classic cars?'

'He still has those. He has four altogether. A

Porsche is amongst them. That's been SORNed as has a Ferrari. Two cars are taxed and on the road. They are registered to his address. He must keep the Porsche and Ferrari somewhere else.'

'It costs a lot of money to keep a car in perfect condition,' said Robbo.

'What about the Spanish Hacienda company, Pam?' asked Carter. 'Have you found anything else on it?'

'Not yet. Do you want me to contact the Spanish police in the area?'

'Hold fire with that. I think we'll follow up the interview with a home visit, just to keep the pressure on Mr Ellerman.'

Chapter 25

Dee Ellerman stared down onto the garden below her. The gardener was tidying up after the storm the previous week. She wondered that he didn't feel the cold. He had just a T-shirt on and the temperature had dropped to below freezing.

She opened the window. 'Mike, do you want tea?'

He stopped on his way towards his van, dragging a large fallen branch behind him.

'Lovely.' He smiled.

'Come in for it.'

'Okay. I'll just put this in the van and I'll be there.'

He came back and hovered in the doorway, afraid to step into the clean kitchen. 'I'd be better off outside. I'm going to drop bits all over your floor.'

'It's okay. It doesn't matter.'

He started unstrapping his boots. He didn't like to appear rude and his hands were blocks of ice, even though he'd managed to work up a sweat moving all the wood.

'Biscuit?'

He sat where she pulled out a chair for him at the table. 'Never say no to one of those.'

She opened a new packet of chocolate digestives, having been out to buy them that morning.

She placed a plate with biscuits down in front of him and sat opposite.

He took a slurp of tea and it burnt his mouth but he didn't want to show it. 'That hits the spot.' He snapped a biscuit in half and put one half in his mouth. He looked around the kitchen, trying to think of something to say. He saw her open laptop on the worktop.

'You studying? How's your car-maintenance classes going?'

'Good, thanks.'

'And what are the other classes you're taking?'

'Spanish and IT, website design.'

'God, I could do with that – I'm rubbish at creating a website.'

'I could help you.'

'That's kind but I think you'd soon realize you'd have your work cut out. I'm next to useless. You must be quite good.'

She nodded towards the laptop. 'I enjoy it.'

'You used to be a hairdresser, didn't you? I remember your husband mentioning it once.'

'Yes. When I was young.'

'You're not old now.' He smiled.

'You know what I mean.'

'You could start it up again.'

'Maybe – I'd have to retrain – everything's moved on since I learnt. What about you? How's the gardening business?'

'It's good. It's difficult to work through the winter but I manage. I need to find something else to do really. I've lost my way a bit, I think. I used to be good at building stuff; loved designing things. I might give that a go again one day. It's hard sometimes to get yourself moving, isn't it? I was thinking of asking Mr Ellerman if he might have any work for me in Spain – you know, on the houses he mentioned to me?' He looked up at Dee, hopefully.

Dee smiled and nodded. 'You'll have to ask him. You have children, don't you Mike?'

'I have two, yes. I get to see them every weekend.' He looked across the table and held her gaze. 'My wife and I are separated.'

She looked down at her tea and held the mug with both hands. 'How lovely for you to spend time with your kids.'

'Yes, I wish it was more. I wish they could live with me but – you know how it is – there's no way you can make a break-up any different than it is. It's a painful process for everyone involved.'

'Yes.'

'Mrs Ellerman – if you don't mind me asking – are you okay? You seem a little upset today.'

'Thank you for asking, Mike, but I've just got a lot on my mind.'

'Mr Ellerman's away a lot, isn't he? It's a big house to be rattling around in all week on your own.'

'Yes. But I don't mind. You get used to being on your own, don't you? Sometimes it's much harder being with someone than being alone.'

'I know all about that. I never thought I could live alone – but you get so used to it. I think I'd have a hard job finding someone now.'

'You don't have a girlfriend?'

'No. I have the occasional date. You know – I'm on a couple of dating sites.'

'Meet anyone nice?'

'Yes, but I've also met a lot of women who scare me.'

Dee laughed. The sound even surprised her. She hadn't heard it for so long.

He finished his tea and stood. 'Better get back to work.'

Dee tidied up and then went upstairs armed with clean washing to put away. She went to stand at the window overlooking the front of the house.

Mike was putting on his protective helmet and doing up the strap beneath his chin. He stopped and looked up to the bedroom window; he smiled at her and then his eyes went towards the driveway. She knew who it was by the way Mike reacted. But today was only Thursday: JJ usually made his way home on Friday.

Dee heard her husband's key in the front door.

'Dee?' Ellerman closed the door and threw his keys on the table in the hall. He went to see if she was in the kitchen.

'Dee?' He climbed the stairs, then stood watching her from the doorway. She was staring down towards the garden still. Mike was busy slicing through a fallen trunk with his chainsaw.

'We should sort this room out.' Ellerman walked in and stood behind her, breathed in her smell. Her long dark hair was plaited down her back; from behind she still looked like the schoolgirl he'd met. From the front she was just the ghost of her. 'We can't keep it as a shrine to Craig. Dee? Come on, let's go down-stairs.'

'I like being in here.'

'I can see it's upsetting you.'

'It's not being in here that upsets me. Being close to Craig could never make me cry. Only missing him every day does that.'

Ellerman went down the stairs and out to talk with Mike outside. He looked up, to see Dee watching them from the bedroom window. She had one of Craig's T-shirts in her hand. She lifted it to her face and he saw her breathe in the smell of their son. Then she was gone from the window and Ellerman talked through the plans for the garden with Mike for ten minutes whilst he packed up. Dee opened the front door and came out of the house, pulling her hat down over her ears. Mike stopped talking as she walked towards them; he was packing his tools away in his van.

'Which class is it today then?' he asked.

Dee smiled at him and Ellerman thought how she seemed coy; she and the gardener seemed to know one another on a personal level. They must have chatted before, properly chatted.

'Car maintenance.'

'Can you have a look at my van for me – there's a funny sound coming from the engine.' He grinned.

Dee smiled. 'I'm not that good yet.'

'Where are you going?' Ellerman asked, feeling like the stranger.

'I always go to my car-maintenance class on a Thursday.'

'What are you going to be doing today?' asked Mike. 'Is it an oil change again?'

'No. The teacher is taking us to a working garage to show us how to do a full service.'

Mike looked impressed. Ellerman looked bemused.

'Your wife will be able to save you a fortune, Mr Ellerman.'

'You must be kidding – she's not going near my cars. See you later, darling . . .' Ellerman turned back to Mike, who was still busy packing up his van. 'How much do I owe you?'

'It's three weeks – so that's three hundred.'

'What about the logs?'

Mike stopped loading his van and turned to face Ellerman. 'Sorry – I don't get what you mean?'

'Can't you take them and sell them? Take it off the money I owe you?'

'Uh, no. They're not seasoned, I'm not sure who'd want them.'

'It doesn't matter – I just hate waste, that's all. I'll have to pay you next time. I'm sorry, I don't have any cash on me.'

'You still have my Internet banking details? Can you put some money over as soon as possible, Mr Ellerman?'

'Run out of beer money, have you?'

'I don't drink.' Mike continued loading his tools.

Ellerman opened the boot of his car and took out his bag. Then he went back into the house and into the utility room, past the kitchen. As he emptied his bag on the floor something dropped out. Ellerman stared at the sprig of Dartmoor gorse in his hand; its bright yellow flowers seemed garish now and out of place in the stark white of the utility room. He turned it over in his hand. It meant Megan liked him, he supposed. He wasn't sure what it meant. She was showing that she was already feeling an attachment to him – he hadn't lost his touch – that was reassuring. He still had the charm and the wherewithal down the business end to hold his women's attention. He didn't know why he worried so much. Sure, he had good and bad days. Sure, he had problems maintaining interest and an erection sometimes, but basically – yeah … basically, they all wanted something that he could promise.

He placed the sprig of gorse on the shelf next to the washing powder. He might think about giving it to Dee as a present. He put the first load of his clothes into the machine, before picking up the empty bag and taking it upstairs. As he went into the bedroom he ran his finger along the top of the door and looked at the thin layer of dust on it. He mumbled to himself as he threw his bag on the bed. Was it too much to ask to keep the fucking house clean, for fuck's sake? He kicked his shoes across the floor and walked into Craig's room. Dee had left the door open as she always did. He knew why – she wanted Craig to be with them all the time, part of their every day. He wanted to let go.

He picked up the photo of Craig from the desk and held it in his hands. The room, the house, Dee, it all served to show him what a failure he was and he couldn't bear it. He looked at his text messages. He had heard nothing from Paula. Lisa had texted him from the gym. It was her third text this morning. She wanted him to phone her. He texted her back:

Sorry, honey – on the way to a client's. Will ring you later.

The reply came straight back:

Don't forget – you promised you'd come to my friend's party tomorrow eve.

Shit ... Ellerman hadn't so much forgotten it as chosen not to remember it. He had intended to cry off at the last moment. Tomorrow was the start of the weekend, for Christ's sake. Weekends were sacred. They were the time when reality kicked in, when Dee became his focus, when his struggle to make it financially through another week ended, for good or bad. He wanted to take Dee out somewhere nice this weekend. He wanted to force her to sit opposite him in a restaurant and to look into his eyes. He wanted to tell her she had the power to change everything. Only she could make things right. They'd drink wine and laugh and flirt and then they'd come back to this bed and make love like they used to. No other woman felt like she did. All the others were pale imitations of her. He sighed as he lay down on their bed and closed his eyes and his hands clenched the bedspread; he twisted it in his fists. The bed had become a place of torment to him – so close to her but so far away. He wanted to feel her body next to his whilst they slept but she seemed to manage to take up the smallest space, furthest away, and he heard her get up every night after she thought he'd fallen asleep. He heard her moving around. He was sure she slept in Craig's room.

Lisa came back with another message:

Never mind. I don't feel that well. I'm not going. But I just need to see you, please.

He replied, relieved:

Yes, I feel the same, honey. I'll ring you later, I promise. Love you. xx

Chapter 26

Willis looked at the address she had in her hand for Ellerman.

'Satnav says it's on this street. I've got a name, not a number, guv. The house is called The Cherry Orchard.'

'Must be extremely posh not to get a number. Look at the size of these houses.'

'There it is, guv . . .'

Willis pointed across the road to a high hedge and a collection of storm-damaged trees behind. There was evidence of some recent tree surgery.

'Someone's been tidying up,' Carter said.

'We passed a van up the road.'

'Yeah, could be – chances are, if they do one house they do a lot on the same street. We'll go and talk to him after we talk to Ellerman. There's one of the cars in the drive, Eb.' Carter wound down his window to get a better look at the Range Rover. 'Bet that costs a lot in fuel.'

'Need to keep up appearances, I suppose, guv.'

'Yeah, how much did Pam say Ellerman bought this house for?'

'Four million, ten years ago.'

'He bought right in the boom. *Boom . . . bust . . .* So he must have a fair mortgage on it.'

'He remortgaged it three years ago.'

'The car, the house, it all belongs to the time he had money – it shows he's living off past glories.'

'And investments in Spanish renovations.'

'Let's call his bluff.' They got out of the car and walked across the road and opened the gates to the house.

Carter looked up to see Ellerman at the window. He was on the phone. He was smiling when Carter first looked but his face soured when he saw them. Carter waved. Ellerman's face disappeared and he had answered the door before they reached it.

'Sorry to bother you, Mr Ellerman, we just need to ask you some further questions and wanted to save you a trip to the station,' Carter said as they stepped inside.

'Very considerate.' Ellerman led the way into the kitchen.

Willis looked around. It was immaculate. It looked so spartan and clean it was as if they were waiting to move in.

'Hope we're not disturbing you and Mrs Ellerman? I can imagine you don't get much time to spend together,' Carter said.

'She's not here.' Ellerman held Carter's gaze. Carter nodded thoughtfully.

'Maybe that's best. We don't want to upset her unnecessarily. But then you said she know about your affairs, Mr Ellerman?'

'That's none of your business.'

'It could be looked on as very much our business when one of them is murdered and it turns out she lent you money.'

Ellerman was looking flustered. His face was reddening.

'We wondered if you could show us any more details about the company you own called Hacienda Renovations?'

'Of course. Like what?'

'Like a brochure. We'd love to see the kind of houses you find to renovate – before and after. That kind of thing. I'm really interested, might even be looking to invest, you never know.'

'Okay. I can probably find something to show you. Wait here a minute.'

He left them in the kitchen and walked across the hall and into a room that Carter could see was super neat and tidy. Nothing was left out.

Ellerman reappeared with a few pages of house details from an estate agent and some architect plans.

'I am working on this one at the moment.'

'Very nice.' Carter took the plans and spread them out on the pristine worktop. 'Mind if I take a detailed look at the floor plan? It's always interested me – renovating, building my own place. So these are the plans for this house here in the picture, is that right?' Ellerman nodded. Carter looked at the original specifications on the estate agent's blurb. It was written in Spanish. Carter was half-Italian. He could just about read the Spanish.

'It says that you have a well, a bore-hole, that, by

the look of it, you're planning to cover with your dining room.' Carter looked up. Ellerman was irritated. He gave a dismissive shrug with his shoulders and changed his mind about looking over Carter's shoulder at the floor plan on the worktop.

'This may not actually be the exact floor plan for this exact house. But I don't keep the current plans here.'

'Do you have an office outside here?'

'No, I tend to work on my laptop anywhere I am.'

'And that is all around the UK?'

Ellerman looked instantly caught out.

'Yes, I travel to see clients. I wouldn't say it's all around the UK.'

'South? North? This is when you're selling your yachts, is it? Or is it when you're asking for donations for your Hacienda fund?'

'Okay, I've had enough of your questioning. I find that extremely rude.'

'No problem. We'll send a squad car round to pick you up and take you up to Archway for an interview.'

'What is it you want to know? I don't understand what you're accusing me of.'

'We believe you took money from Olivia Grantham to invest in a company that, as far as we can see, and judging from what you've shown us, doesn't really do a lot. You can't show me one completed project.'

'I certainly can.'

'Do it then.'

Ellerman gave a one-shouldered shrug and started packing up the floor plan from the worktop. 'I don't have the photos here.'

'Show me what you showed Olivia Grantham to make her invest ten thousand pounds in your business. You – a man that she supposedly meets just for sex. You must have charmed her to make her do that. She wasn't a stupid woman. She was a partner in a legal firm. Did she draw up an agreement for the loan?'

'I'm not sure.' Ellerman looked like a drowning man.

'Did she say when she wanted you to pay it back?'

'We hadn't discussed that.'

'I find that hard to believe. Every lawyer I've ever met wanted everything written down and signed for and they want to charge you an arm and a leg. Was she charging you interest?'

'She may have wanted interest.' Ellerman had become quite still. He stood motionless, hardly daring to breathe. 'You obviously haven't found any written contract between us otherwise you'd have the answers to these questions.'

'We are going through her paperwork and her PC. I don't doubt that we'll find it. So now you don't have to pay it back. Olivia is dead and you get to keep the money.'

'Is that what you think my motive would be? A mere ten thousand pounds? That's ridiculous.'

'Maybe, but whoever set her up to go in that building may not have expected her to get killed. They may have aimed to just teach her a lesson, or give her the kind of thrill they thought she wanted – after all, she was a thrill seeker. Who's to say someone didn't just take it a step too far?'

'Not me.'

'Not your style, derelict buildings?'

'No.'

Carter paused. The kitchen was still. 'Where did you usually meet?'

'We met in many places. I told you that before.'

'No, you told me you'd only met her a few times. "We met in many places" sounds like more than a few.'

'We met at her flat. We sometimes went away.'

'Have you many investors in your Hacienda company, Mr Ellerman?'

'A few.'

'Women that you meet?'

He didn't answer at first then he bristled. 'You know I've been racking my brains to think where I've heard your voice before, Inspector, and I am pretty sure it was you who phoned me pretending to be from Naughties customer services. If that's so – I'm not an expert in law but I know someone who is – and that is unethical to say the least.'

'Was it a man with a cockney accent?'

'Yes.'

'Sorry, Mr Ellerman – you lost me there. That's the trouble with the cockney accent – we all sound the same. Okay, thank you, Mr Ellerman. Have a good day.'

Carter turned on his heels and Willis followed. They reached the car and got in. Carter didn't start the engine. He sat looking at Ellerman's house.

'I want to know every deal Ellerman has ever done.'

'Yes, guv. But ...'

'What?' He turned to Willis.

'Is it because he's a tosser or is it because he might have murdered Olivia Grantham?'

'Point taken. I will not let my dislike of Mr Ryanair Jetsetter get in my way. Olivia Grantham must have drawn up some legal paperwork about the money she invested. We'll find something.'

'Hector has gone through her paperwork from her flat. There was nothing about Ellerman or Hacienda Renovations.'

'Then we need to go into her office and see if she left it there somewhere.'

Willis's phone rang. She looked at the caller number on her screen and declined the call.

'Your mum?' Carter looked across at her.

'Yes. It's the hospital again.'

Chapter 27

After they'd gone, Ellerman paced around the kitchen, thinking what he should do. He had to keep focused, positive. He went into his office, sat at his desk and logged on to his Internet bank account, bringing up his statements. He had to see exactly how much more he needed to cover expenses at home and abroad this month and then he would be able to make a plan to find the money from somewhere. He spent the next hour moving money around and jotting figures down – no matter how hard he tried, it didn't add up. He spent the evening watching television with Dee. They ate pasta with a bought sauce. Ellerman picked at his. Neither of them spoke. Dee went to bed early. The next day they hardly saw one another: Ellerman worked in his office and Dee worked in the garden or watched television by herself. By Sunday they had begun to row. Dee had cried herself to sleep and Ellerman had drunk almost a whole bottle of brandy.

On Monday morning, Dee went out without telling him where. He got up, made himself some coffee and then paced about the kitchen.

He picked up his phone and wrote a text and sent it to several contacts:

Remember I love you.

And then he wrote another to Megan:

Coming down today. Be with you at three.

He knew what he should do now. He'd go to Megan's first and charm her, push the idea of Spain again and show her the photos. Then he'd go and see Emily and get her to transfer ten thousand and that would see him through the next ten days and by that time he might have some results from the yacht deals.

He went and repacked his bag hastily, then he went into the bathroom and looked at his wife's shelves and saw the bottles of perfume he'd brought her back from his travels abroad. Some of the bottles were still in their boxes, cellophane on. He slipped his hand into the back of the shelf and pulled out Angel. He particularly liked that smell but his wife never wore it. He also picked up a bottle of Chanel No. 5. He put his bag in the boot of the Range Rover, then headed out of London and took the scenic view down on the A303 towards Devon. The further he got from London the better he felt. He sang along to his music. By the time he turned into Megan's courtyard he was in a great mood. He switched off Santana's 'Black Magic Woman' and stretched as he got out of the car. The sun was glorious. The cold air – reviving.

Megan met him at the door. He kissed her.

'Close your eyes and hold out your hands,' he said as he placed the Chanel No. 5 in her outstretched palms.

'How kind.' She looked at it and he knew she

would never wear it. Come to think about it – he would have been better off if he'd given that to Paula and chosen a book for Megan, one of those arty photography ones. *Damn* – he should have thought about that.

'Fancy a picnic?' she asked, putting the perfume on the kitchen table.

'Lovely.'

They walked up through the field she owned at the back of her property. Bramble, a pure-bred Dartmoor pony, was grazing there. Megan stopped to stroke her.

'She won't bite.' She laughed at Ellerman's reluctance to come close.

'Best place for a horse is in a burger.'

'Don't listen to him, Bramble.'

She stroked the pony's mane as it nuzzled into her and nudged her with its head.

As they walked through the gate at the top of the field the moor took hold: waterlogged tufts of dead fern squelched beneath their feet.

After skirting the village they came out on the main road. Haytor stood dark and solid, stark on the horizon. They crossed to follow the old granite tramline that ran up and round to the right of Haytor, and walked for ten minutes in silence as they climbed steeply until they reached a place where the last of the cut granite was piled ready for transportation that never came.

'On a fine day you can see the sea,' Megan said, smiling, happy, as they stopped to get their breath.

'Lovely.'

He could see that it would take a lot to shift her from this place. If he ever married her he would make her move up to town.

They skirted round to the right of the discarded granite, and around the back of the largest of the three quarries. The way into the quarry was a narrow path, flanked by high hedges and built into the hillside. It was a pathway that led straight into the base of the quarry and to the edge of the lakes there.

Ellerman looked back across the crater. The lakes in the basin were beginning to freeze. Snow was still white and unsullied on the stems of grasses blown into the quarry and surviving in the stillness.

'It's so still here – what an eerie place.'

'Yes – but beautiful. Things grow here that wouldn't survive on the top. Welcome to my secret world.'

Ellerman picked up a stone and threw it into the centre of the deepest pool.

'Won't be long before it's completely frozen. The water is as grey as all this granite.' Ellerman looked around him. 'Do you come here very often?'

'Every day. It's the inspiration behind a lot of my work. I see it change through the seasons. I love the way the light reflects on the water and illuminates the walls of the quarry, creating depth in the shadow. I love the way the trees have taken root between the slabs of cut rock. I love the way . . .'

He kissed her. 'And I love the way you feed me. I'm starving.'

'Of course. Let's eat. Follow me – I have just the table for us.'

He followed her past the lakes and up into a sheltered place where the granite had been cut and left in slabs and blocks. Megan unpacked her picnic and laid it on top of the slabs.

Ellerman couldn't wait to get away from the quarry. The more he sat there, hemmed in by a hundred feet of jagged rock, three freezing lakes between him and the path out, the more he felt the knuckles back rapping on the top of his head.

'Are you okay?' Megan looked at him, concerned.

'Yes. Just a little headache after the drive, that's all. Have you got any wine in that backpack?'

She smiled. 'Of course.'

She took out a bottle of Spanish Rioja and showed it to him.

'I thought we could have a toast to us – to good times ahead, holidays in Spain in your farmhouse there.'

Ellerman brightened. He turned his back on the chill breeze that had come to swirl around the basin and send ripples across the centre of the lakes where the ice had yet to reach. 'Perfect choice. You clever little thing.'

For a moment, Megan looked at him, puzzled by his choice of words, but then she smiled and let it pass. She opened the wine and poured and handed him a glass then raised hers to a toast. Ellerman had half finished his already.

'To us.' She felt a flash of annoyance at his rudeness but she recovered quickly whilst he finished his glass.

Chapter 28

Monday was Diane's first day helping at the Faith and Light hostel. It went so well that she stayed on for the evening service. They were short-staffed for cooking dinner. Zoe was having the evening off to spend with her boys. Diane had been looking forward to it. It felt different to working. Everyone was grateful and took time to explain things to her. Simon helped to cook the dinner. Diane found herself peeling spuds for the mash and packing sausages on trays. She met some interesting people and they treated her as a person in her own right, not a widow, not a grandmother or mother. She was Diane, the volunteer. Sheila and Lyndsey were very friendly.

The time flew by; it was so busy. When they had finished serving dinner there was the tidying and washing up and then the preparation for breakfast. Diane sat down for a cup of tea with Lyndsey and Sheila.

It was ten o'clock when she went to find Simon to say goodnight. She knocked on the door of his office.

He opened the door and Diane could see he had company: a woman who quickly hid her face in a handkerchief. She looked upset.

'Oh, sorry, I didn't mean to disturb you.'

Simon smiled, embarrassed.

'Thanks for your help, Diane. Can I ring you tomorrow and we can catch up on how things went?'

'Of course.'

Diane dropped in on Zoe on her way home and heard the wonderful peaceful sound that meant the kids were asleep. She knew she'd find Zoe sitting at the kitchen table on her laptop.

'How did it go?'

'It was great, love. So many interesting people. You wouldn't believe people's stories – how they end up on the street. Just bad luck, most of them.'

'Keep an eye on your purse.'

'Tut-tut. That's not a good attitude. You're becoming a very cynical young lady.'

'Yeah, well, I'm really glad it will work out, Mum. Tea?' Zoe got up to put the kettle on. 'Did you see much of Simon?'

'Yes, I did. He's quite the chef in the kitchen. Except he doesn't shout at anyone.'

'I should hope not.'

'There were lots of people asking what would be happening now about someone called Lolly.'

'I saw that on the board at work. She was left in the lorry park at Shadwell.'

'What's going to happen now?'

'Well, we'll do our best. We'll investigate it like we do all unexplained deaths but the truth is, we don't hold out a lot of hope of solving it. She was always vulnerable.'

'Yes, but they say this is the second time someone has tried to kill her. The first time the gang from the estate tried to set her on fire whilst she was sleeping.'

'We will investigate it, Mum. I'll have a look into it myself, see if I can find out what's happening for you.'

'Yes, because, after all, these people are her family. They are the only people she had left in the world. They deserve to know what happened.'

'Yes, I know, Mum. I will do it, I promise. Did you get any gossip on Simon?'

'I didn't ask. I'm not going to be a spy for you. I would hate them to think I was.'

'They won't, Mum. I'm just interested, that's all.'

'Mmm, not falling for that, but anyway – he's difficult to work out. No one mentioned a girlfriend to me.'

'Did you learn anything about him at all? Was there talk about Toffee – the man in hospital?'

'The other volunteers can understand why he's spending so much time at the hospital. According to Sheila and Lyndsey, Simon and Toffee spent a lot of time in his office and they seem to have a special bond.'

'Did you meet any of the other regulars to the hostel? Did you meet a young woman called Martine?'

'I heard her name mentioned.'

'If you get the chance to talk to the people who come in – just listen out for anything that seems worth remembering.'

'I told you, I'm not spying for you.'

'Just helping people, that's all. Not spying.'

'There is something – nothing really but when I left there I went to say goodbye and there was a woman in his office.'

'Who was it?'

'I didn't ask. But she wasn't one of the clients in the hostel. She was smartly dressed. She was crying her eyes out when I went in there and he clearly didn't want to talk to me. She hid her face in a hanky.'

'When are you going back in, Mum?'

'I was thinking of going in tomorrow, to help out in the day, if they need me; I can make tea, talk to people. I think that's what I'll enjoy doing the most, just listening. But Simon is going to ring me first.'

'Be good to go in as much as possible.'

'Trying to get rid of me?'

Zoe smiled. 'When you've finished your duties here, that is.'

'Simon can't be intending to go into the hospital tonight, can he? Maybe he knows that you're not going in.'

'I wouldn't get your hopes up of having a vicar as a son-in-law, Mum. I don't think we're suited, do you?'

'Who knows? But you couldn't help out at the hostel – you'd probably have everyone strip-searched just to get a cup of tea. And you certainly wouldn't believe anything they said to you – you'd be like, why did you say you did that but then you said the other . . .?'

'I'm not that bad.'

'Mmm. You don't notice it. I saw you interrogating

the postman the other day. What made you leave your trolley outside number 36 while you delivered letters to 44?'

'Now you're exaggerating.' Zoe laughed.

Chapter 29

The next morning, Willis got up at six and went for a shower before breakfast. It was dark in the house. She put the light on in the kitchen and the windows were black. She walked around with a bowl of cereal in her hands. She drank tea. She stood for minutes just staring out of the kitchen window at nothing and mentally preparing for the day. Normally, the scene from the window was a mash-up of lit bathroom windows with bevelled glass, back doors – today it was a snow-capped scene.

She picked up her bag and slipped out of the house at 7.15. She walked across to her sky-blue Polo. It had a hat of snow and she slid her hand across it, breaking it off in chunks. The snow was not going to stay, according to the weather forecast. It was almost too cold for it.

Willis didn't often drive. She didn't enjoy it; but today she was pleased to be warm and dry inside her car. She had arranged to meet her mother's doctor in charge of her treatment. She headed north on the A1 to Nottinghamshire. She hit the edge of the town and followed the signs for the hospital.

*

Dr Lydia Reese was waiting for her in the sitting area outside her mother's ward.

'Sorry, am I late?'

'Not at all – you just caught me catching up on some work. Please have a seat. Or we could grab a coffee, if you like?'

'Yes, that would be great.'

'I'll show you where the café is.'

They walked back towards the entrance of the hospital and turned into the café area.

'I'll get it – what would you like?' Dr Reese offered.

'Hot chocolate, thanks very much.'

Willis went to find a table. The place was recovering from breakfast going by the tables littered with plates. Willis cleared a table for them. Dr Reese approached and set the tray of drinks down, before sitting opposite her.

'Thanks for agreeing to see me, Doctor. I need to talk to you about something Bella wants from me, before I go in and see her. I need to know if it's something you would recommend me doing or not.'

'Of course, I appreciate you running it by me. I will give you my professional opinion.'

'Bella says she has photos of my natural father to show me. She wants me to find him. There can only be one reason. She is up to something and she must think it will help her get out of prison in some way. I don't know whether I should even try to find him or leave him well alone. I don't think it's fair to involve him.'

'If you do find him, will you tell him everything?'

Willis sighed, staring at her cup. 'If I do – I think I

have no chance of ever meeting him. Who is going to want to know either of us?'

'What your mother did should not reflect on you.'

'Oh, but it does – tarred with the same brush.'

'You were there when it happened?'

'And I arrested her at the scene.' Willis played with her cup as she talked. She steeled herself; she'd been building up to telling Dr Reese her side of the story for a while – now seemed the right time to do it. She wouldn't have told her unless she had to. She never told anyone exactly how it felt that day. But, if there was one person who should know it was Dr Reese.

Dr Reese put her hand on Willis's and for some reason it brought a lump to Willis's throat. She smiled at the doctor and removed her hand from the table.

'Take your time,' Dr Reese said. 'Tell me what happened that day.'

'I'd just joined the police force. She wanted to see me. I didn't see her often. I agreed to go to her flat. She lived in a housing association flat. Bella never managed to hold down a job, never managed to accept her family's generosity and do something good with the money. She gave wild parties, she took drugs. She wrecked marriages and lives. She always has done – she goes through life like a tornado. Everything spins around her. She feels nothing for anyone else unless it will achieve her aims. She uses us all.

'When I got there the door was open. I called out my mother's name and I heard the softest voice reply. It wasn't a word, it was a breath.

'I saw the blood as soon as I stepped inside. There were handprints in the hallway, smears all over the walls, smudges of blood and flesh where someone had fallen against the wall and struggled forward, trying to get away. The blood led towards the kitchen. I called her name. She hated me calling her Mother. I called out to her: *"Bella?"* I heard a whimpering, someone else trying to breathe coming from in front of me, from the kitchen. I walked forward and I saw the man's legs first. He was sitting on the floor. His blood was pooled around him. He looked at me for help. His breathing was coming out in squeals. He clutched his chest and bright red blood pumped over his hand. His eyes flicked to the other side of the door. Bella was standing with a big kitchen knife in her hand; she was drenched in blood. She was shaking violently. She was looking at me with the eyes of someone who believes they can do whatever they like and there will be no consequences. There was a look of triumph in her eyes as she lunged forward and planted the knife into his chest. I tried to save him but he was dead in seconds.'

'Who was he?'

'He was a twenty-one-year-old. He was studying medicine. He was planning to go back to his home in Somalia and help his community when he qualified.'

'Your mother was very sick at the time.'

'Yeah, I know. I've heard people say that many times.' Willis shook her head. 'Bella has a long-term plan to get out. She needs motivation.' She took a drink of her hot chocolate. She couldn't make eye contact with the doctor for a minute.

'Then it seems you are the one to make all the

choices,' Dr Reese said, and, for the first time, Willis saw a softness in her eyes. 'I know that your mother has had a terrible effect on you. I can see it in you. I know that Bella is manipulative and dangerous. I cannot say to you that she has no hope of ever getting out of Rampton because there are systems in place that would allow her to, if she was judged not to be a risk to herself or others. But ... if it was me ... I might take this chance of a new relationship with your father and I might choose not to share it. If, however, you do and he intends to visit your mother then I am very happy to work with him and you towards the best treatment for her.'

Willis nodded; she cupped her hands around the hot chocolate and stared straight ahead.

'Now we have to go and see your mother.' Dr Reese stood. 'I'll leave it to you to decide what you want to do.'

Bella seemed to be asleep as Willis opened the door to the side ward. There were just the two beds. The pregnant woman was still opposite – she spoke as Willis got level with her.

'Please, I'm begging you – I can't take it any more – *Shut that bitch up*. She keeps saying my baby is rotting inside me. She keeps telling me it's dying. Make her shut up.'

Bella smiled as she lifted her head to laugh at the pregnant woman.

'You'll die in labour.'

'Evil BITCH ...' the pregnant woman screamed across.

Bella laughed softly. She looked up as Willis approached.

'Morning, Ebony, my baby.'

'What is all that about?' Willis gestured towards the woman opposite, who had turned her back to them and started crying. 'Leave that woman alone to mind her own business, Bella; otherwise you will be in trouble.'

'Don't you dare side with her. You have no idea what she says to me when no one is listening. She's not fit to be a mother.'

'Bella. That's enough.'

'Sorry, Ebony. You are all I have in the world. It isn't fair. It is you who have committed a terrible crime. I feel such a weight of remorse for leaving you in foster homes, in care homes for your childhood while they sorted out my medication. I feel such a sense of loss that it's unbearable. You can make it right between us.'

'The care homes were wonderful. My time in foster care was one of the best childhood memories I have. To have someone look after me for a change, to have unconditional love, warmth, respect even. To have people tell you that you are in charge of your own destiny – I look back at those times with such gratitude.'

'But not the times with me?'

'No.'

'No happy memories?'

'Not many.'

'Any?'

'There was always a price for those times. There were the highs followed by lows.'

'That's my illness.'

'An illness that you managed to disguise very well when you wanted something.'

'I did not.'

'When you wanted me back, when you wanted a new flat to live in, a new start.'

'I loved you.'

'No, Bella, your love is all centred on yourself.' Bella was breathing hard. 'Do you want me to get the nurse?'

'What for? You want me dead.'

'I don't, Bella, but I want you somewhere where you can be looked after. You wanted to show me a photo of my dad?'

'Go around to my locker now – there's a large brown envelope. Get it out. You will see – we can be a family again. You find him, you tell him I always loved him and no one else and you bring him home, Ebony.' She didn't speak as Willis did as she was told. Willis opened the top of the envelope and peeked inside. There were three photos.

'Bring them round here.'

Willis went around the bottom of the bed.

There was movement opposite them and Willis looked across at the pregnant woman. She was trying to sit up, straining to see what she had in her hand.

'Ignore her . . .' Bella hissed. 'Ugly fat bitch.' She looked at the envelope in Willis's hands. 'Open it. I want to see your face.'

Willis slid them out and stood looking at the photo of a good-looking young man with his arm over Bella's shoulder. Ebony had to admit that they were a beautiful couple. His vest shirt was pure '80s. Her mother had short spiky hair, heavily made-up eyes. She had on a hessian crop top and MC Hammer trousers.

'Why did you get pregnant?'

'I didn't mean to. Complete accident. I forgot to take my Pill. Funny that – I seem to have my whole life dictated to me by whether I remember to take medication or not.'

'Did he ever see me?'

'No. I left him as soon as I found out and decided to keep you. I didn't want to be with anyone.'

'Why *did* you keep me?' she asked.

'I thought it would make me happy.'

'Did you ever consider my feelings?'

'Of course. I thought about you all the time. I had to change my whole life to look after you and you were not worth it. You scared away the only decent men I could meet. You never smiled at anyone.'

'Sorry I was a disappointment.'

'Yes, you were. I thought you would be a girly girl but you didn't have hair I could do anything with. You didn't have a face that could be prettied up,' said Bella.

Willis almost smiled as she shook her head sadly. Her mother's brutal honesty was finally being unleashed. All the years, Willis had known that her mother thought it, and now she had said it – Ebony hadn't been worth the effort.

'No, Ebony, please, you know I don't mean that. I regretted leaving you with the social workers. I should never have let them take you from me.'

'Those were my happiest times.'

'When?'

'When I was with foster parents. In the kids' home. I felt safe. I felt loved. I didn't feel judged on my looks.'

Willis had heard enough. She was anxious to leave.

'*Will* you trace him for me?' Bella asked.

'I'll try. But he may not even be alive. He may want nothing to do with either of us.'

'Yes, but if we don't ask we'll never know. There you go again, always Miss Negative.'

'What are you really hoping to gain by this, Bella?' asked Willis.

She watched her mother's expressions change as Bella thought about the answer she wanted to give – as she thought through the consequences of speaking her thoughts out loud.

'I told you I want to see him before I die.'

'Yeah, I might believe that one, except you're not dying and you are rubbish at making a good job of suicide.'

'I will die some day and I want to make peace,' Bella said.

'No. That's not it. Try again.'

'I want to see if there's any spark left.'

'Getting warmer. What good would it do?'

'It would give me hope. It would mean I would try my hardest to be a model patient and get out.'

'No, Bella. You are better off like this. I won't help you with that.'

'I would accept any treatment they wanted to give me if it meant I was cured. You could make sure of it.'

'Don't get your hopes up – you were convicted of

murder and sentenced to stay here indefinitely,' Willis reminded her.

'But – there are court cases coming up, challenging that ruling. The European Parliament. They might order a review of that.'

'Not likely to change anything for you.'

'I'm just saying I need hope, Ebony, for Christ's sake. I am a human being and I need hope. Don't you understand that, in all the books you've read, all the studying you've done, don't you understand the most basic of human values and emotions?' asked Bella.

'I understand that you don't really know the impact you have on people. You are manipulative and ruthless and you only think about yourself. Yes – I accept you're sick but don't accept that you didn't know what you were doing when you killed your lover. I will never help you get out.'

'So you won't even help your own mother?'

'I am helping you by leaving you to get the treatment you need and serve the punishment you deserve.'

'You cold fish, Ebony Willis. I gave birth to a lump of ice.'

Willis picked up her coat and the envelope containing her father's photo and details.

'Cold-hearted bitch,' Bella said. 'That's what you are. Ebony?'

Willis turned and walked away from her mother's bed.

Her mother screamed at her. 'Ebony, I'm sorry! I'm so sorry! Ebony – please. Please don't write me off. Tell your father that I will always love him.'

Willis stopped and turned to face her mother. 'That's the trouble, mum, you destroy the things you love. I'm not sure I'm ready to see that again.'

On her way out, Willis stopped at the nurses' station and asked to see the sister-in-charge.

'Miss Willis, how can I help?'

'Something's going on in there with my mother and the pregnant woman.'

'It's no concern of yours, or ours – merely interplay between your mother and the woman opposite. They seem to have a fair amount of animosity between them.'

'No.' Willis held up her hand for the sister to take a breath. 'Let me tell you – my mother is a pressure cooker and she's set to burst. You need to move that woman opposite.'

The sister was irritated. 'We don't have any more private wards available. They will have to share. When high-security patients come into us from Rampton, they just have to accept what we have to offer. We can't be giving your mother her own private suite.'

'Then move the pregnant woman to a maternity ward.'

'She isn't due to give birth yet. She has a month to go. She has come in with high blood pressure. When it goes down, she will go back to Rampton. I would appreciate it if you would let us deal with things. We are used to patients from Rampton.'

'But you haven't met my mother before, have you?'

Chapter 30

Emily finished unloading her carrier bags and put the steak in a black-pepper marinade. She made the salad and went into her kitchen cupboard to choose some wine for the evening. She belonged to a wine club and she got it by the case. She knew she drank a little too much wine, especially when Ellerman was staying. They seemed to bring out the worst in each other – that was why it worked between them. That was one of the reasons she knew they were meant for one another. No one else had ever freed her to be herself. No one had made her feel so passionate, so alive.

Ellerman arrived at three. He rang her to make sure she was in.

'Come on up.'

He carried his bag up the sweeping staircase to her flat on the first floor. Emily lived in Taunton town centre. Her parents had bought the house for her after her first husband was paid off, after her breakdown. After the school had agreed to give her a job because she used to be a pupil and her parents had paid for the new library.

She clung to him as he got inside the door.

'Lucky you were home,' Ellerman said, stepping inside.

'I should get you a key, then you can come whenever you like.' She held on to him.

'Yes. Good idea. What's for dinner?'

'The usual: steak and a lovely bottle of wine; I hope that's okay?'

'Marvellous. I look forward to it.'

'Did you like the case I gave you last time?'

'Wonderful. Much appreciated.' He kissed her forehead. It was the case of wine he'd taken to Megan's last week. 'And I have something for you.'

He brought out the bottle of Angel perfume and gave it to her.

She kissed him, unwrapped it straight away and daintily dotted it behind her ears. She was happy. Ellerman was pleased with himself.

Emily opened a bottle of French white and gave him a glass.

Ellerman took it from her and sat down in one of the tapestry-covered armchairs; he leant his weary head back onto the chair as he closed his eyes and drank the cool crisp Sauvignon Blanc. He loved staying at Emily's. There was a reliability about it all. Even her house was just as he knew it would be – every time. Emily had traditional taste in furnishings. The house was neat. The rooms were high-celinged with original Edwardian features: dado rails and architraves. There were heavy-framed portraits of moody-faced children and hunting scenes on the walls. It suited Emily because she looked like she belonged in a period drama. She was small-mouthed and large-eyed. Wiry and tall with a quiet elegance and strength.

'Ah, it's good to be here,' he said.

She sat down opposite him. 'I've gone part-time at work now.'

'Don't the school object?'

'I've given in my notice anyway. My parents have offered me a chance to set up something for myself.'

'Doing what?'

She shrugged. 'I was hoping you might have some ideas.'

'Me?'

'Yes. Something we can do together, maybe? Craig will be leaving for uni and we can move on to the next phase in our relationship. That was always the plan, wasn't it?'

'Yes. Absolutely. A business together? That would be great. Let me think about it. Meanwhile, I'm really stuck for cash at the moment in Spain. The architect miscalculated something major. The idiot. He put the dining room over a bore-hole – stupid. That all needs sorting.'

'How much do you need?'

'Ten? Would that be possible?'

'Ten thousand?'

'Yes. Think of it as a loan.'

'Or I could become your business partner?'

'I'm not sure the Spanish business is the one to start with.'

'Why not? I have put quite a lot of money into it

already. My book-keeping skills could come in handy. Maybe it's time you let me handle the financial side of it?'

'People have different ways of doing things, don't they? I'm not sure you'd approve of mine.'

'What do you mean?'

'Well, I might do things differently than you. I'm self-taught – I do things my way. It may be too difficult to come in on the Spanish business, that's all I'm saying.'

'Nonsense! Good business sense exists or it doesn't. It starts with good housekeeping. I think you could benefit enormously from my help. Cash-flow problems seem to plague you.'

Ellerman shook his head and sighed irritably. 'It's all so much more complicated than you think.'

'I can make it simple for you.' She smiled.

He reached out and squeezed her hand. 'Thank you, darling.'

Mason woke intermittently and called for Sandy. She was never far away. She came back from her scavenging and wagged her tail as she sniffed Mason's face. She whined and nudged him with her head. He knew what the nudge meant. It meant she was hungry and she needed him to get food for her. She had found water in the puddles in the car park but no food. It had been days since she'd had proper food and she was frantic. Mason drifted back to sleep; Sandy was uneasy.

In the evening she sniffed the air as she heard the sound of people passing on the road that ran beneath the adjacent arch. She smelt takeaway kebab. Laughter echoed beneath the arch.

Sandy stood upright and walked nearer – she peered through the fence. Sandy never went near people without Mason. The streets had taught her to trust only those that Mason trusted and even then to be cautious. Her face pressed against the fence as she watched them pass. The smell of food made her whimper, her mouth drool. She looked back at her master and her loyalty was tested. She needed food to live. One of the three lads picked up a stone and aimed it at her. She yelped as it rattled across the fence and hit her on the nose. She backed away, whimpering.

'Sandy?'

Mason tried to move. He forced himself to sit upright but he could not stand. He slumped down again, he was too tired. She went back to him and lay down next to him. She smelt the infection rising in his body. She couldn't sleep from hunger.

In the morning she heard cars come into the car park. She heard the car door slam and she knew it would be the woman who put on her coat and had food in her bag. She crawled out and watched the woman. She saw the woman open her bag and look at Sandy. She smelt food so strongly now that she began to whine.

The woman threw half a sandwich across to Sandy before she walked quickly away across the car park.

Sandy picked up the sandwich in her mouth and took it back to Mason. She placed it next to him on the blue coat. She nudged his head. He stirred at the smell of food. He reached out a hand and she licked his palm. Mason took a bite of the sandwich as Sandy watched him and then he placed it in front of her and nodded; she finished it.

Chapter 31

Ellerman awoke to see Emily getting dressed. It was Wednesday morning and a school day for her.

The room was so dark that he could only just make out what she was doing, reaching behind, zipping up her skirt. He heard the slide of her underskirt against her legs.

'You should have woken me, what time is it?' he asked.

'It's seven. We're going to have an archery tournament today. I can't afford to be late.'

'But you're a maths teacher—'

'Not according to my head of department – now I'm apparently the archery expert. Especially since we have an Open Day coming up.'

'Come back to bed; I have something I need your help with.' She giggled but it was a polite giggle rather than a heartfelt one.

'Have to be a one-man job, sorry; they will be beginning breakfast in a min and then my duties start.'

'Come on, miss. What about your duty to me? I need you to demonstrate square roots and top-heavy fractions to me again.'

She smiled as she came across to the side of the bed. He reached out and pulled her down on it and wrapped her in the duvet as he held her tightly and snuggled into her.

'Same time next week?'

She didn't answer straight away. She tried to move but he held her tightly and she relaxed again in his arms.

'What is it, Emily? Are we okay?'

'Yes, but ... I like being with you. I like the fact that we both share a Christian faith. I don't like the fact that you are still living in the family home when you told me that was just a formality. Sometimes I feel like you're not really with me. You're always looking at your phone, checking your texts. You're always leaving the next morning. You could stay around, you know?'

'I will next time – I promise. You're busy anyway – Miss Archery Expert.' He gave her a squeeze and tried to see past her curly hair to kiss her cheek but he couldn't quite make it. 'I'd stay but you're working anyway.'

'I'm only working three days a week now.'

'I know. Well, I promise to make a special effort from now on and come and see you more.'

'Saturday evening. You could come Saturday. We could meet some of my friends maybe – to make it worthwhile – then we could go out for a drink and grab something to eat. As much as I like seeing you, we always seem to do the same thing. I cook and we go to bed.'

'You're right, as always. You're right and I'm sorry.

I've been so bogged down with work that I just haven't given you enough consideration; but I will, I promise. Just bear with me. This winter is tough for me. It's the worst time to try and sell yachts and the weather is interfering with the Spanish renovations. You know I really love you, Emily. I will try to keep you happy, I promise. When the spring comes, we'll fly over to Spain and lie in the sun. You tell me the dates of your holidays and I'll work it all out.'

'I gave them to you already.'

'Are you sure you did? Well, just give them to me again and I'll get straight on it.'

She slipped out of his reach and stood to smooth her skirt down and make herself presentable. She reached down and kissed him.

'You wouldn't hurt me, would you, JJ?'

'No. Never.'

'You know I will never let you down? I know we were meant for one another. I would do anything for you. I just want it to work between us. I want us to live happily ever after, just us. I've been waiting for so long now.'

He sat up in bed and held on to her hands.

'And that's what I want too. Have faith in me, in us. I promise you it will all be okay. You mean the world to me. You know me better than I know myself.'

'Yes – perhaps that's the trouble.'

Emily left for work and Ellerman looked for his phone. He reached down and patted the carpet, looking for it. He usually kept it next to him whilst he slept. He couldn't feel it. He had been so tired the previous evening he didn't remember coming to bed. Too many brandies had left him making mistakes. He reprimanded himself. That was sloppy. And it wasn't the first time recently that he'd put his phone down and forgotten where.

He got out of bed and put the light on, looked through the pockets in his jeans, his jacket; he couldn't find it. He looked under the bed, in case he had kicked it there by accident. He went out into the hallway and into the lounge and he saw it on the coffee table. He picked it up and looked at it. Across the cover was an alert that he had three messages and one missed call. He was running things through his brain – what could she have seen? Anything? He was reassured. *Nothing*. There was nothing she could have seen. If she had read his messages he would know, unless she'd marked them as unread. Not likely. She was a technophobe. She could barely use her own phone. That's what she always said.

He put in his code. He must alter it again. He couldn't be too careful. He smiled, curious, when he saw a new message from Jo Harding:

Hello, stranger.

He made himself a coffee and sat down at the kitchen table to text her back:

If I remember rightly you're an early riser; and if you remember – so am I. Fancy meeting up? Why don't I just come straight to you? I still have your address in my satnav.

Her text came back:

Tempting, but I'm just leaving for work. Call me later and we'll discuss.

Ellerman didn't reply. Today it was only

Wednesday. He had two more days before he'd be heading home for the weekend. The thought didn't fill him with joy. He preferred it on the road now. He liked to hit the floor running.

Ellerman put his phone down on the kitchen table, turning the phone over and over as he thought about the texts. He had always seen Harding as out of his league. She was more merciless than he was and she had a sex drive that far surpassed his own. Maybe when he had enjoyed life at a more relaxed pace, she would have been a good match for him but, right now, he needed to keep it simple. He needed to find himself a woman of simple character with a lot of money. He needed to up his game and forget the ten thousand here, five there. He needed to find women who didn't question everything he did, who were grateful and kind and loaded. Harding had money. It might be worth another go. She had a brittle side to her that he might just be able to tap into. Did she know about Olivia? Was that why she was back in touch? Ellerman began to feel the heat coming to his face. He felt the sweat start to trickle down his back. What if that was it? A trick. Harding worked for the police pathology department. Was she trying to trap him? He needed to stay calm. He needed to use his wits. He logged on to his emails. He had several new messages from dating sites. He didn't put his photo up, or if he did it was one he really couldn't be recognized in. On one site he had a full-length shot of him standing by a river, one foot up on a rock, in shorts, backpack, hiking mode. His shoulders side-on to the camera. There was another of him skiing, his face partially obscured by goggles, wearing a hat. He stood tall and strong, ski poles in hand, squinting in the Alpine sun as he grinned into the camera. A third was an action shot of him racing down rapids in a canoe. None of the images could be made any bigger before they turned too grainy. They had served him well – Mr Action-packed. Mr Hunter-gatherer. *I can afford to ski every year.* He was anything between thirty-eight and forty-eight. His height ranged from five ten to six one. His preference for red wine over white stayed constant. His like of action thrillers sometimes gave way to romcoms and documentaries. He was loyal and charming and as faithful as a Labrador puppy. He always had an Aston Martin.

Chapter 32

Harding looked at her schedule for the day – she had taken her car into the Audi body-repair garage but they had said it would take two more days: they had to order a new roof from Germany. They weren't even starting the body work until that came. That was annoying. She was sick of waiting. But it meant that she could get more work done if she didn't have to pick up her car.

She looked at her list and Lorraine Chance's name was top. She opened the door to her office and went to find Mark, who was preparing Olivia Grantham's brain for further dissection – cutting it into centimetre slices – the task made easier now that it had hardened.

'Mark – I want to reschedule Lorraine Chance. Let's do it now whilst we have a few hours. Ready in ten?'

'Yes.' Mark smiled at her enthusiasm. He knew that the study of how the homeless die on UK streets was something that Harding had written a paper about.

Harding went back into her office to create a new file. Mark stopped what he was doing and went to prepare the tools for the post-mortem, which were laid out on table four, second to last in the row of six steel dissecting tables. Mark then went to Hardy's office, entering as she was printing off new body diagrams for her to use. She brought up Lolly's details onscreen.

'We have her medical records and her file from Social Services. She attended a rehab clinic in 2010 and she stayed clean and on methadone for a few months. During that time she stayed in two hostels, where she is thought to have lapsed into heroin abuse again. Twelve convicitons for theft. All of them are related to her heroin addiction. Okay – let's get her out.' Harding stayed in her office to finish downloading the files on Lolly, whilst Mark went out to finish preparing.

Harding finished up and went to get suited before joining Mark.

'Okay, checklist: coroner's consent form, identity ... Yes or no?' she said as she came out of the changing room.

'Yes, Lorraine Chance, known as Lolly. Age forty. Height five foot five. Weight eight stone one.'

'We're here to establish the cause of death and whether it was natural. No particular risks. We know Lolly worked as a prostitute and was a heroin user. Normal precautions with an HIV-positive patient.'

Harding began her dictation as she approached the body.

'Lorraine Chance was homeless; she slept outside due to her addiction to heroin and lack of suitable residential care for her. The average age of deaths in women who sleep rough is forty-three. Outward inspection of Lorraine Chance shows a large amount of surface lesions and bruising. Patient has needle marks in her arms and feet. She has abscesses on the left inner elbow. The lividity has mottled her skin; hard to establish if she was moved after death. There are multiple swellings and abrasions on her body – I'd say that Lorraine suffered a beating before her death. I would say bruising around the genitals indicates more than one partner just prior to death.'

'She worked as a part-time prostitute; she was known in the lorry park.' Harding looked up at Mark.

'Was that where she was found?'

'Yes, behind the bins in the corner of the lorry park in Shadwell. It's where the lorries stay overnight.'

'I am aware what a lorry park is, thank you.' Harding looked back at Lolly with this new knowledge. 'We need swabs taken here. She was definitely raped.'

Harding finished up and went into her office to think. She phoned Carter.

'I've just completed the post-mortem on Lorraine Chance and she was severely bruised and looks like she was raped.'

'Okay.' Carter sighed. 'We'll do our best to find the CCTV footage of the lorry park. We need to see if we can find the lorry driver she was with that night; it's a task next to hopeless. You know as well as I do that she would have been a target. She slept on the streets and she was addicted to heroin; sold her body to feed that addiction. Is there anything else, Doctor?' Carter asked in the pause that followed.

'No.'

Harding got off the phone and sat in her chair, distracted. She reached for her bag and took out the mail that had arrived at home before she left for work. More bills. She sighed, still thinking about the dilemma she faced with Lolly. She put the mail on her desk, pushing the letters aside, unopened, when a thick cream-coloured envelope from London caught her eye. She'd been waiting for an invite to a seminar on advances in victim identification. She opened the envelope and unfolded three pages of names, addresses and telephone numbers.

To all the women who know JJ Ellerman . . .

Megan went for a walk that morning and to check on Bramble. She went across to break the ice in the water trough. The mare followed her. Its sweet, fermented grass-breath was warm on Megan's face as the horse nuzzled into her, whilst Megan cracked the ice with the heel of her boot. Megan looked up at the sky. It was tinged with green, more snow on the way.

'You know what, Bramble . . . ?' She stroked the thick soft fur on the horse's neck. 'I could never be with someone who looked at you and saw a burger, even if it was a joke. He's a townie, isn't he, Bramble? He's just pretending that he loves it here – really, he would be overwhelmed by it all. He'd be as vulnerable as a newborn baby out here on his own.'

She left the pony watching her as she walked back down to the house, and got there just as the postman's van was in her drive. She took the mail from him and looked at it as she turned and went back inside. There were the usual bills, a package she'd ordered, and a letter from London in a thick cream-coloured envelope.

Paula dropped the girls at school and came back to tidy up the house before getting ready to go to the salon. She didn't have a client until twelve that day. As she got in she picked up the mail from the doormat and looked at the usual round of bills and junk mail, and then she saw a thick letter from London in a cream-coloured envelope.

Emily went home to do some marking during the second period of the day. She picked up her mail as she opened the door and walked up the sweep of stairs. She opened the door to her apartment and walked through, putting her books on the study table. She placed the children's work that needed marking in a neat pile. She opened a thick cream-coloured envelope from London. She unfolded the sheets of A4 paper, neatly folded in half, and she read the first page:

To all the women who know JJ Ellerman.
Ellerman is a liar and a cheat. He has so many women hanging on and waiting ... for what? They all think they're going to get a piece of him. Ellerman is a washed-up has-been. He's pathetic. Do you want to be just another woman on his long list? If you've given money towards the Spanish house company in the hope that you'll one day be living there with JJ then think

again – so have many other women. You've been
conned.

   And – are you waiting for Craig to go to
university before JJ leaves his wife and runs to
Spain with you? Craig was killed five years ago.
You've been conned. Ring the other women if
you don't believe me.

Megan dialled a number. Paula answered. She was
sitting at her kitchen table, with the letter in her
hand. She was working backwards in her mind, going
through all the times she should have known he was
lying.

   'Hello, you don't know me but we have something
in common – JJ Ellerman. I'm also on his list. I think
we should meet.'

Chapter 33

Harding was waiting in Carter's office when he came back from a meeting about the Hannover Gang. She handed the letter across to him.

'Jesus. Someone's in big trouble,' he said as he looked through the contents of the letter. He phoned Willis, to get her in from the Investigation Team Office, where she worked with the bulk of the murder squad.

Willis was handed the letter when she joined them.

'When did this arrive, Doctor?' she asked.

'This morning. It's a bit worrying that someone has gone to this much trouble and gone into his contacts on his phone and found my address.'

'The person who sent this letter must have done a lot of snooping to be able to get this much info from his phone,' said Willis.

'But I think he has the kind of arrogance not to put a password on his phone or, if he does, then it's one of those swipe ones – I had one like that. If you watch someone closely, or enough times, you can see what they're swiping with their finger.' Harding sat back in her chair. 'He drinks a fair bit,' she said. 'He's not likely to even know where he is some nights. When I met him, he seemed to spend just one night somewhere and then he moved on.'

'One night, one woman,' said Carter. 'A woman in every town. It must save on the bed-and-breakfast bills.'

'And it seems it creates income for his schemes,' added Willis.

'It's not signed.' Willis turned the pages over in her hand. 'But Olivia Grantham's name is here,' said Willis as she handed Carter back the letter.

'You know, I got back in touch with him,' Harding said as she offered Willis a seat. 'I was contemplating meeting up with him.'

'Did he ask you to?'

'Yes. He was keen to come and see me but it seemed like it had to be right then and I couldn't. He was on the road. He lives a very strange life, travelling all week, literally on the road – coming home just at weekends. Did you interview him yet?'

'Yes.'

'What did you think?'

'I thought he looked like he drank too much,' said Willis. 'He was puffy and red-faced. He was sweating buckets.' Carter nodded his agreement. 'His clothes were immaculate: expensive shirts, shoes; he didn't have a hair out of place but, behind the façade, he looked frazzled.'

'Really? When I met him, he was very slick, very ice-cool and in control. He was great in bed. Just needy outside it, I thought. Of course, if I'd known what I know now about him, I might have enjoyed stringing him along for a bit longer. Just to see how far he would go to con me out of money for his Spanish home.'

'Money gained by fraudulent means,' said Carter. 'We need some concrete evidence of that.'

Willis was looking at the names on the letter again.

'I can't believe that these women will part with money that easily.'

'I can,' said Harding. 'You fall in love with a man who seems like Prince Charming and you lose your grip on reality. That's the reality, Ebony: if he seems too good, he probably is.' Harding laughed.

'He's been lying about everything,' said Carter. 'His life hangs on a lie – he told you he had a son, didn't he?'

'Yes. He even spoke about his son going to university.'

'Five years ago, he was killed in a car crash,' Willis said, looking at the letter. 'Our files show it was a car crash. Ellerman was driving the car he was killed in.'

'Strange. Why would he bullshit about that? Especially to someone like me, who's not interested?'

'He has created a world for himself,' said Willis. 'He has to keep control of it. He has to be sure to always tell the same lie to everyone, otherwise it's too hard to remember.'

'So does someone hate him enough to want to set him up? Is it about the money or the other women?' Carter asked.

'What about his wife, Doctor?' asked Willis. 'Did he give anything away about his wife?'

'No, but if she was anything like me, she wouldn't

have stayed with him. She can't possibly stay after this.' She tapped the letter with her forefinger. Harding had the remnants of burgundy nail polish on her nails.

'Unless she already knows and she doesn't care,' said Willis.

'I think we need to go to his house and have a chat with her,' Carter said.

'I'd love to be a fly on the wall.' Harding laughed. 'Strangely enough, his discomfort is doing something for me. I can still meet him if you like.'

'I think it would serve no purpose, Doctor ... but thank you,' Willis said – she could see that Harding would love to push it. 'It will smell of entrapment if we aren't careful.'

'Okay.' She smiled. 'Spoilsport. But what if one of these women rings me?'

'Find out as much as you can but tell her that you only met him the once,' answered Carter. 'Don't give anything away.'

'Can I take a copy of this now?' He held up the letter.

'Be my guest.'

Carter copied it on the photocopier in his office.

'It did make me laugh.' Harding took back the original letter from Carter. 'It's a hell of a list. Even for Ellerman – he'd have to be superhuman to get round all these women. God bless the great God, Viagra.'

Chapter 34

'Who are the women on his list and what kind of women are they, Pam?' Harding had returned to the Whittington, and Carter and Willis were now in Robbo's office.

'Here's one of his ladies: Lisa Tompkins, she runs a gym in Brighton,' Pam answered Carter. 'Here's another: Emily Porter,' Pam read from her notes. Willis and Carter came round to her desk, to look at her screen. 'She's a schoolteacher in a private school in Taunton.' Pam brought up the cover photo from the school's brochure and pointed to a photo of a tall, slim, smiling woman in a tracksuit, standing erect, hands at her sides; she was flanked either side by a class of teenage girls with archery bows. 'That's her.'

'Have you managed to get hold of her?' asked Robbo.

'I've left a message on her phone for her to call me but I'll try again this evening.'

'We mustn't panic these women. Keep it casual in your questions when you ring.'

Pam brought up a photo on her PC of a hair salon

from an article in a newspaper about the owner and her staff.

'I traced a number to this salon, True Colours, and the hairdresser, called Paula Seymour. I think that's her, third from the left. She met him on the site Sugar Daddies. The photo's from the local paper from when they opened True Colours three years ago.'

'Pretty-looking woman,' said Robbo, looking at Pam's screen.

'She wasn't in today,' said Pam, 'and I tried her home number. I didn't leave a message. I'll keep trying her. I did get through to a woman in the West Country. She's quite a well-known artist who lives on Dartmoor. Her name is Megan Penarth. She paints atmospheric land-scapes.' Pam read from her notes: 'It says on the letter that she met him through a wine-lovers' dating site.'

'You know . . .' Carter spoke his thoughts out loud. 'That's one thing you can't accuse Ellerman of – being lazy in this. He hunts women. I wonder what his end goal is? Is it just financial?'

'Must be. If he is actually looking for a relationship with women, why does he stay in his marriage at all?' answered Pam as she typed in the name of the company the next woman on the list, Gillian Forth, worked for: Dreamcars.

'Maybe he doesn't leave his wife because he thinks she'll take what he has left,' said Willis.

'Does the wife have money?' asked Robbo.

'I've looked into her,' Pam replied. 'She was a hair-dresser when they married. It looks like she worked the first few years but then she gave up when Ellerman started to make big money.'

'How's Toffee doing?' asked Robbo suddenly, as they stood around Pam's screen, waiting for the information to load.

'Zoe is keeping us up to date,' replied Willis. 'She said that Simon Smith has been around a lot. She's talking to him, trying to get him to tell us more about Toffee's friends. We're still looking for Mahmet Balik, who seems to have gone to ground.'

Pam brought up a photo from the Dreamcars website.

'This was taken when the London Olympics were on,' she said as she zoomed in on the image.

'Nice car,' said Robbo. A woman was posing with two men in front of a red Ferrari.

Pam read the details: 'It's a photo of clients with the sales manager Gillian Forth. I'll see what else I can find on her.'

Pam Googled the name Gillian Forth and read out from the screen: 'Gillian Forth was named as the woman who died in an arson attack on her home in Exeter last week.'

Chapter 35

Megan looked across the table at the three women opposite. They were sitting in a café close to Paula's salon in Reading. They had chosen the most convenient location for Paula because she had Fifi and Esme to pick up from school later.

Paula, Lisa and Emily had all arrived within a ten-minute period of one another. They sipped their drinks nervously, watching one another. Megan took charge.

'Okay, well if it's all right with everyone then I'll chair this meeting.'

'Go ahead,' Lisa said. She was the last to arrive and she had taken a seat at the end of the table. 'Although I'm not really sure what we can hope to achieve.'

'We can at least find out what's what,' said Emily. She'd managed to get cover for her lessons today. She'd set all her pupils mock exam papers and someone just had to make sure no one cheated.

'Yeah.' Paula had made a special effort with her make-up today. She looked like a young Priscilla Presley. Her black hair back-combed; her eyeliner thick black and her lips pale pink. 'We need to know the truth.'

'The truth is that he's a bastard ...' Lisa was shaking with anger. 'And an ungrateful twat.'

The rest fell silent. Paula bowed her head as she skimmed the chocolate off her cappuccino.

'Okay ...' Emily got out a pad of paper and double-clicked the top of her ballpoint pen. 'I'll take the minutes.'

Megan smiled at her.

'Let's talk facts then,' Megan started. 'Is anyone here going to admit to writing this letter?' She held it up.

'Wasn't me ...' went around the table as each of the women shook her head.

'Okay, well, if it was me, I'd own up and be proud. This is a lot of work. And it looks like it's long overdue,' Megan said, putting it in the centre of the table.

'Won't the person who wrote this get in a lot of trouble with the police?' asked Paula. 'What about spying? What about all this information about other people – isn't that illegal?'

'What would the police charge you with?' said Lisa. 'Slander isn't going to stick. These are plain facts, most of them.'

'Oh, God ...' said Paula, shaking her head. 'It's such a mess.' She stared wide-eyed at the other women. 'We are never going to get our money back.'

Megan held up her hand for silence.

'Who, around this table, has put money into his

scheme and how much?' Megan glanced towards Emily to be ready to record the amounts.

They looked at one another, reluctant to answer.

'Okay, I'll kick off,' said Lisa. 'I'm down twenty thousand.'

'It's fifteen thousand for me,' said Emily.

'And you, Paula?' asked Megan.

'Twelve. It's all my savings. I really thought we were going to have somewhere together in Spain. The girls, *my* girls, they're very fond of him. It's so hard – so sad.'

'I know.' Megan reached out and put her hand over Paula's.

'Will the police take our money if they find out it all comes down to fraud? Will we lose it?' Paula looked for an answer around the table.

'I don't know, but in my heart I think the answer's yes,' replied Megan. 'Yes, you will lose everything if they throw Ellerman in prison. So we'd better be careful what we say to the police if they ask.' Megan lowered her voice for the last part.

'I agree,' said Lisa. 'Just until we get him to sign an agreement. I don't want to lose my investment. Christ – look at us! How can we all have been so stupid? We're none of us dumb ... but we certainly fell for it.'

'I know what you're saying,' said Paula. 'I have had such a struggle to build up my business and look after my girls but I fell for his schemes. I can't believe I wasted all this time believing in him.'

'That's because he's a liar and a scammer,' said Lisa. 'We shouldn't blame ourselves for trusting.'

'How much do you think his wife knows about JJ's life?' asked Paula, looking at them one at a time.

Megan shrugged, Lisa shook her head. Emily looked back blankly.

'Then I think that's something we should find out.' Megan went on. 'We need to know what and who we're up against.'

'As far as I'm concerned, she needs to understand that she's been conned just like us,' said Lisa. 'She is at the heart of all this. She seems to be the one person he really cares about.'

'I don't believe that,' Paula said, averting her eyes as the anger around the table turned to sadness. 'But I do think she must have a lot more in common with us,' she said as she played with her coffee spoon.

'We also need her if we are going to get the money back,' said Megan in a voice that showed she wasn't going to allow the group to descend into self-pity. 'It will be easier if she's on our side. I'll talk to her.'

'How do you know JJ won't be there?' asked Paula.

'Because we must carry on as normally as we can. If we're not careful and clever, he'll run if we let him. He'll move on to greener, fresher pastures. There's still a lot of the UK for him to cover. What we do is – we pretend we don't believe it or we *do* believe it but we forgive him. Whatever we choose it has to be believable.'

Lisa was shaking her head. 'I'll try and act like I can carry on with the relationship but I can't guarantee anything.'

'Well, that's okay. Whatever works for you. It would seem odd to him if none of us reacted to the letter. You do what you think's best.'

'I can do it,' said Paula. 'I can pretend like I'm hurt but I'm willing to see both sides.'

'Um ... so can I,' Emily said.

Lisa swung her head back and forth in disbelief.

'Don't tell me, deep down, you're all okay with what he's done?' She gestured towards the letter. 'Don't tell me you're just going to bend over and take it?'

'No. Of course not. I wouldn't be here otherwise, would I?' said Paula.

'I don't know. You could be here to check us all out. You could have written the letter and maybe there is a place in Spain and you're the one who's going to be living in it.'

'Please.' Megan called for calm. 'I know we are all upset about this but we need to keep to the facts. Paula is fond of JJ; we all are, *were*. I understand this is going to be very difficult for a lot of women. But we are here to teach him a lesson, not to upset one another. And we are here to come out of this with some justice. It's a good thing that Paula is still talking to Ellerman, we can use it. What about you, Emily?'

'I haven't contacted him since the letter arrived. I just want my money back. I thought he loved me. I feel so stupid. I feel humiliated for all of us.'

'You mustn't beat yourselves up about falling for it.' Megan reached out her hands across the table to the other three. 'I may not have parted with any money *yet* – but I can see how it happened to all of you. Maybe I would have before long, who knows? I know he was beginning to try and push me in that direction. I am hurting like the rest of you, I thought I had a future with JJ. I will do everything to help you get your money back. I've been pretending to him that I don't know about any letter. I am going to keep that a secret from him. I would be grateful if you all remember that if he phones you. Don't mention my name. I think the best thing is to lure him down to Dartmoor and we can all confront him there. We can make him sign a contract about the money and investments. We can hand over power to the investors, you. We will all witness it. We'll be in this together. How does that sound?'

'Sounds good,' Lisa said. 'Safety in numbers. Plus, we can force him into action. We might even make the Spanish scheme work. We can make him sign a properly worded contract.'

'I can help with that,'said Emily. 'I have access to legal representatives through the school.'

'Okay, then we all need to set out exactly what we were promised and what we want from it. Let's do that now, round this table, and then Emily can make a start.' Megan looked at each woman around the table. 'Shall we decide what our aims are here?' They nodded.

Lisa answered: 'It's to fuck him over and get our money back.'

'And to be in control of the Spanish investment,' said Paula. 'Say we will go to the police if he doesn't sign.'

'I think it's to get justice, to make him realize he's been wrong and so terribly unfair,' said Emily.

'And I want to make sure he's too scared to ever contemplate doing this kind of thing again,' said Megan.

Chapter 36

Willis and Carter arrived mid-afternoon and parked in the police-station car park at Middlemoor Regional Headquarters on the outskirts of Exeter.

A tall, slim, dark-haired man in jeans and a blue-and-black-check shirt called to them as they were on the way into the station.

'Hello, Dan.'

'Scott – how's things? Good to see you.' They gave one another a man-hug.

Carter turned back to introduce Willis.

'This is my partner – DC Ebony Willis.'

'Nice to meet you.' Scott shook her hand. 'Did you get your passport stamped coming this far south?' he said, smiling at her.

'I did think about it.'

'How's Cabrina, Dan?'

'Good, thanks, mate.'

'What happened to your stag do, Dan? Croatia, Barcelona? Which is it to be – vodka shots or tequila?'

'Not there yet, mate. We had a kid first. Have to wait for the right time.'

Scott looked at Willis and gave a nod Carter's way.

'Is he still planning what he's going to wear?' She laughed.

Carter looked at Willis. It was nice to hear her laugh again.

'Yeah – don't think so, mate, no time.' Carter grinned. 'Too busy with proper crime up in the big city; it's not all about who stole all the cabbages.'

Scott laughed and rolled his eyes.

'That's right, I forgot, it's a bad world north of *Brizztol*.' He laughed. Carter winked at Willis. 'We can talk in the car.' He led them over to the blue estate. 'I'll take you to see Gillian Forth's body first.'

'What kind of a woman was she? Any enemies?' asked Willis as they drove out of the car park.

'She was thirty-eight,' Tucker answered. 'She worked in the sales department of a car-parts firm. She'd lived in Exeter all her life. She was a divorcee but her husband kept in touch – no animosity there. She never had kids. She was quite highly strung. If pushed she could fly off the handle. But nice most of the time – her workmates liked her. She was kind and fun to be with, they said.'

'Boyfriend?' asked Willis.

'Her workmates said they thought there might be, but they weren't absolutely sure. There are only two other women working at the company, the rest are blokes. Not sure how much she would have told them. We've spoken to friends outside her work and they say they've never met him but have heard about a man who visits once a fortnight.'

Carter flashed Willis a look.

'Interesting.'

'She didn't elaborate though.'

'Did they get a name for him?'

'John. No surname.'

Carter looked at Willis expectantly. She didn't look his way; she was staring at Scott's profile. She didn't seem to have heard what he just said.

'This man JJ Ellerman you're looking into – what's the connection? Could he be the boyfriend, John? Is that what you're thinking?'

'It's possible,' Carter told him. Willis took the letter from her bag and handed it to Carter.

'We got this about him. Two of the women from this list are now dead. Gillian Forth's name is on it and so is Olivia Grantham's, the lawyer.'

'This is a helluva list,' Tucker said as Carter showed him the three pages of names. 'Who are all these women?'

'These are his conquests,' answered Willis. 'He travels all over the country, trying to flog luxury yachts and he meets women from dating sites.'

'Yeah … he has a novel way of finding a bed for the night,' said Carter. 'A woman in every town. Whilst he's there, we also think he cons them out of money. He got Olivia Grantham to invest ten grand. That was made by a bank transfer to his Spanish Hacienda company – a renovations company based in Spain but seeming to do no advertising.'

'She didn't die the same way as Gillian, did she?'

'No, she was murdered by a third party, or several of them. She was lured into a building thinking that she was meeting a man for sex. Instead, she was set up to be raped and beaten by a gang of homeless drunks or gang members, take your pick – who were given large amounts of drugs and drink to get them in the party mood.'

Scott shook his head. 'You can't get Ellerman for her murder then.'

'Could be conspiracy to murder – he could have paid to have it done. We're going to try and get him for fraud at least – we don't know if he missold the investments to these women. We're still trying to find some paperwork but we're hopeful – Olivia Grantham was a lawyer, she must have written something down. The other women need to press charges. We're contacting all the women on the list.'

'What were Gillian Forth's finances like?' asked Willis.

'She didn't earn a lot of money; friends say she was careful. She had a small mortgage – fifteen grand, thereabouts. Up to six months ago she had twenty grand savings in the bank, then she withdrew the lot. Could be your man Ellerman but equally ...'

'House improvements?' Carter asked. 'Did she do the attic conversion with it?'

Tucker shook his head. 'My first thought too but no ... that was done two years ago. She withdrew it all in cash – twenty thousand – and it didn't turn up again. She may have accounts elsewhere that we haven't found yet.'

'What about this boyfriend of hers?' asked Carter. 'Neighbours never saw him?'

'No. He must have been an infrequent visitor if he existed at all. We'll have to wait for the phone records.'

'Meanwhile, we can ask Ellerman if he knew her,' said Carter. 'We can ask to see his phone records, save time. We'll see if that twenty thousand turns up in Ellerman's bank statements. '

'He's not likely to give us permission, guv.'

'Yeah, I know, but we'll try,' said Carter, then turned to Tucker. 'Did you ask her work if they'd ever heard of Ellerman?'

'I did,' answered Tucker. 'They said he was down as one of their clients. He's used them for parts for his cars.'

They drove to the mortuary and Tucker introduced them to the technician in charge. He wheeled out the body and began removing it from the bag.

'This is Gillian Forth.'

The charred remains were shrunken into a boxer's pose: knees up, arms ready to punch.

'It's okay.' Carter held up his hand. 'I don't think we need to get the body out – we can see it fine, thanks.'

'Okay, call me when you're done.'

'Thanks.' Tucker had the post-mortem report in his hands.

Willis peeled back the bag away from the zip.

'If there's one thing that I hate it's barbecued corpse,' said Carter, standing back.

'Yeah, nasty,' agreed Tucker. He opened the post-mortem report on the trolley and rested it on the end of the body bag. There was also a diagram of the house and where she was found.

Willis was taking a closer look at the body.

'Her skin is blistered where her clothes were,' she said, matching up the page of the report to the body. 'Which means she had begun to try and defend herself against the burning.'

'She didn't die from smoke inhalation then?' asked Carter.

'She had no chance in hell of getting out,' said Tucker. 'She was found here, beneath the window.' He indicated the spot on the diagram of Gillian Forth's bedroom. 'There was one way up to her bedroom in the attic and it was completely impassable as soon as the fire started.'

'They're saying now that it didn't have the necessary planning permission. Is that right?' asked Carter. He was holding the plan of the house in his hand.

'Yes. It's true.'

'What was found in the room with her?' asked Carter.

'Usual bedroom furniture: bed, chest of drawers, mirror on the wall, photo … of what? We don't know. There was also a tablet computer, glass from more than one drinking glass and her phone.'

'It was too early for her to be in bed,' said Willis. 'Was there any evidence that someone else was there, Scott?'

'In the 999 call she made, she said there was no one else in the house with her. Are we done here?' asked Tucker. Willis nodded. Tucker called the technician in.

'Do we know how it started? asked Carter as they walked back to Tucker's car.

'It started at the front door. We haven't found out what was used yet – some kind of inflammable liquid was poured through the letterbox.'

'Can we go and see Gillian Forth's house now? And it would be good to talk to anyone we can about her boyfriend,' said Carter.

'No problem. It's not far.' Tucker started the car. 'Where are you two staying tonight?' Tucker looked from one to the other; his eyes settled on Willis. Willis shrugged. 'Let me take you out and show you some of the sights of Exeter. You can stay in the accommodation at Headquarters.'

Carter grinned. 'Woo-hoo. Not sure if we can take the excitement, hey, Eb? He turned round to wink at her. Carter could swear she was blushing.

They drove to the cordon surrounding Gillian's house and parked up.

'That's a nasty sight,' said Carter as they got out of the car; the house had a blackened front to it. The windows were intact on the ground floor. The skylight and part of the roof was burnt out, a gaping black wound in the roof's structure. 'You have to seriously hate someone to want them to die like that.'

'Yeah – the intention to kill was there from the start.'

'This road is on the way out of the city, isn't it? Does it get much traffic coming through?' asked Willis.

'Only during work hours. It's not a short cut. Most people go on the bypass. It's quiet in the evenings. There's no trouble with parking on this street.'

'Any recent reports of trouble that might lead up to this kind of thing? Anti-social behaviour? When was the last arson attack you had in the city?'

'Last summer we had a school set on fire,' replied Tucker. 'We have a couple of kids for that. We've looked into her company – no court cases pending, no customer complaints, mainly praise for the company.'

'So, this is personal then,' said Carter as they stood outside the front of the house. They could see the white of the SOCO forensic team moving past a window upstairs. The blackened stairwell was in front of them as they looked through the open door.

'Can we talk to the neighbours again?' asked Carter.

'Be my guest.'

They knocked on the door to the right of Gillian's house. It was answered by a man in his late seventies.

'Hello, Mr Tiller, it's Detective Sergeant Tucker again. Sorry to bother you. These are two detectives from London who are helping to investigate what happened next door.'

'Terrible. Terrible shame.'

'Did you know Gillian well, Mr Tiller?' asked Carter.

'Well enough. I've only been here a couple of years. If she saw me then we would stop to speak. She was a nice woman. Kept herself to herself.' He shook his head sadly. 'Terrible shame.'

'Did you ever see anyone visiting Gillian, Mr Tiller?' asked Willis.

'Like friends, you mean?'

'Anyone really. What about in the last week?'

'I don't see much at all. The weather's been so bad I haven't ventured far.'

'Do you have a car?' asked Willis.

'No, dear – not any more.'

'Do you know the people who have cars on the street?'

'Yes, I suppose so. When I go down the Spar shop at the end of the road I see the same cars. One of them belonged to Gillian; that's the blue one over there.' He pointed to a Polo.

'Do you know anyone else's?'

'That white one down there, with the dog sticker on the window, that belongs to a man and his friend, they live at number 85, that's three doors the other way. Then there's the lady in 89 – she has a green hatch-back, three-door.'

'You have a good eye for cars, Mr Tiller.' Tucker picked up the thread of the conversation.

'Is there any car you see sometimes and don't know who it belongs to?' asked Willis.

Tiller thought about the question and nodded.

'Yeah. Someone further down the street has a visitor sometimes. He drives a very fancy car. Beautiful-looking machine. Aston Martin.'

'Have you seen the person driving it?' she asked.

'Once I saw a man getting in it and driving off.'

'Would you recognize him again, Mr Tiller?' asked Carter.

He shook his head. 'I only saw the back of him as he got in the car.'

'Did you see which house he came from?' Carter stood back to look up and down the street.

'He had his back to me so he must have come from this end of the street. I'm sorry, I can't remember more than that. I wish I could help.'

'Okay, thanks – you have been a help.' Tucker smiled. Tiller turned back towards his front door.

'What are you thinking?' asked Carter as Tiller went back inside.

'Just that there's no residents' parking here. Someone might park here to go to work or commute,' said Tucker.

'But are you too far away from town to think that someone would park here for the station?' asked Willis.

'Yes, I think so. There's free parking nearer than this. I think anyone who parks here is visiting someone on the street. I'll double-check the statements from neighbours when we get back. Mr Tiller was pretty sure on the make of car.'

'There are only so many registered Aston Martin owners in the UK,' said Carter.

Tucker nodded. 'We'll get searching.'

In the evening, Carter went to the men's room in the pub in the centre of town – the Fat Pig was warm and cosy and served great food. They were waiting for their food to arrive. Willis fiddled with her cutlery – she was starving and trying not to show it.

'You worked with Dan long?' Tucker asked, whilst drinking a bottle of real ale.

'Just over a year.'

'He's a great bloke. You're lucky – there's a lot you can learn from him. Great detective.'

'Yes, he is.'

'I was made up when I heard he'd got promoted. It was too long coming.'

'I know. He definitely deserved it.'

'And some. Took him long enough.'

'Yes. How do you know one another?'

Tucker took a few seconds as he waited for the waiter to finish setting down the condiments.

'I used to work in the Met.'

'Really?'

'Yes. We worked together. I went undercover on a job, a paedophile operation. It was messy. Kids traded for favours in the drug world. Kids taken out of children's homes just to entertain dignitaries. We uncovered someone really high up. I was told to lose files, to shut up. I was told I didn't see what I know I did. I was told to make a false statement. Ultimately, I was told to resign or face dismissal. I went to Dan. He was my superior. He was my sergeant. Dan took it as far as it could go and he took me off undercover. I decided to resign but Dan said we should fight it. We did and it was a five-year battle; in the end, I took what was offered to me – a job with no hope of promotion. I came back here to my roots and have worked here ever since.'

'Any regrets?' Willis asked as she looked at his face. He had the look of an angry man, disappointed in himself.

'Yes.' He gave a half-smile. 'A few. I wish I'd taken it further – it never felt like justice. I never cleared my name.'

'But if you'd been dismissed you would have messed up any career you tried to have after the force.'

'Yes, and I love my job. I just wish I'd played ball.'

'You're not serious? You wish you'd falsified information? You acted really honourably.'

'Yeah – and where did it get me? Perhaps I could
have done so much more if I'd stayed in.'

'Are the men still serving who you were on the team
with?'

'Oh, yes. Those are the fuckers I said were as guilty
as shit … sorry …'

'Don't be.'

Carter returned. The food arrived at the same time.

'Was thinking …' said Carter. 'Could Ellerman
really be that clever?'

Chapter 37

Wednesday early evening, Ellerman arrived to find Lisa outside the front of her place, putting out the rubbish; she lived on one of the roads near the station in a tiny one-bedroom terraced house with a dark lounge and a minuscule kitchen.

She stopped and watched him park. She kept an eye on him as he opened his boot and took out his bag.

'Trainers?' she called out. 'Hope you remembered them.'

Ellerman bent to look inside the boot. He moved his arms around and pretended to rummage. The cold air made him shiver. He longed to get in somewhere cosy and warm. For a few seconds he contemplated closing the boot and getting back in the car and cranking up his music and his heater and driving away, anywhere. Then he ran through the list of possibilities and decided this was probably the best option for now.

'Damn and blast.' He emerged from the boot and shook his head, disappointed. 'I could have sworn I put them in there. Sorry, honey. I don't mind waiting here while you go out for a run.'

'No, it's okay, the weather is closing in anyway. I'm not keen on getting soaking wet.'

'Really?' He slipped his hands around her waist from behind and pulled her hard to him. She laughed.

'Yeah, you're right – better than a gym workout. Come on then.' She took him by the hand up her front steps.

'Whoa . . .' Ellerman pulled back and stayed on the first step.

'What? You used to rip my clothes off in the hallway. What happened? Thought you'd be gagging for it, seeing as you haven't had it for over a week.'

'I am, of course, honey, it's just I'm feeling a bit coldy.' He sniffed.

'Then why did you come?'

'I thought you said you weren't feeling all that well. I thought I'd come and we could have a duvet day and snuggle under it and watch films and drink bottles of wine.'

'I don't feel so bad now. I think it was inactivity.' She screwed up her nose in disgust. 'The last thing I need is to get drunk.'

'Oh. Well, maybe I should go?'

'It's up to you. I know you explained about the letter but it doesn't make me feel any better.'

'Honey . . .' Ellerman pulled her back down to him from the step above. 'I'm sorry if someone's upset you with that pack of lies. I don't even know most of the women on that list, I've never even met them.'

'Where were you all week? You didn't answer your phone. It's impossible to get hold of you in the evenings. Your phone goes straight to voicemail.'

'I have to switch it off, honey, I'm with clients.' She sighed. 'If you want me to go, honey, I will,' he said, looking pathetic.

'No. You're here now. Let's walk down to the seafront and get some fresh air. We can grab a drink on the way back and buy something for dinner. Unless you want to eat out?'

'Well ... perhaps.'

'I thought not.'

The Brighton seafront was bracing. As Ellerman walked along he turned his face from the bitter wind, and wondered if he really was getting a cold. He didn't feel well. His stomach was churning, his head pounding. He felt shivery. He reached out for Lisa's hand. She was striding along as usual. She had to win at everything. She had to be the best. She wanted a kiss. She stopped and held him back. She looked up at him and frowned.

'Are you feeling okay? Your eyes are watery.'

'It's the cold.'

'Athletes use it to recover all the time.'

'Not sure I need a cryochamber at the mo. Probably prefer a hot toddy.'

'You poor old thing. You're falling apart on me!'

'Not quite. I need to fly off to Spain, I think. I need to warm my bones.' He turned to her. 'You do believe the house exists, don't you, honey?'

She didn't answer. 'Let's go and eat somewhere and get out of this cold,' she said.

'Okay.'

She steered him to a pub that they'd eaten in a few

times. She wanted to sit under the patio heater outside but he ignored that.

'Open a tab,' he said to the barman as he ordered a large single malt and a large glass of white wine for Lisa. He didn't ask her if she wanted it; he was hoping she'd soften a bit with alcohol. He took the menu from the counter.

'Let's sit over here.' He picked up his coat and headed for a table that a group had just left. It was nearest to the fire. Lisa got there first and doubled up athletically as she slid behind the long oak table and into the corner of the old church pew, the fire to her side and the rest of the pub to her front.

'You okay? Come on, Granddad.' She laughed. Her voice came out squeaky and sharp in the soft ambience of the pub.

Ellerman didn't answer. He stood tall by the side of the pew and slid the scarf from around his neck, then carefully placed his gloves on it before folding his coat on the top.

'There ...' He pulled out a chair for himself, a little way from the fire, and smoothed back his hair as he settled down to take his first sip of the deep amber liquid. He was aware she was watching him. She knew she'd overstepped the mark. She'd been rude.

'Cheers,' he said. 'Here's to ... us?'

Even as he faltered, hesitated, he knew by the look she shot him that she wasn't thinking along those lines.

'What are you having to eat?' he asked her. He'd already looked at the menu. He was having a man-sized portion of something stodgy that she would hate. No salad tonight. He needed potatoes or pastry and lumps of red meat. She would opt for the lentil pie, the beetroot salad. She wouldn't have pudding. She wouldn't have cheese. They ate their dinner in silence. They glanced at the others in the pub. They smiled at one another occasionally. Lisa didn't want another glass of wine. It made her tired, grumpy. Ellerman was flying after three large whiskies. He finally felt ready to flirt. He didn't want to go home. The thought of going back out into the bitter cold made him miserable. Lisa had become Lisa Long-face. She yawned and fiddled with her glass and she still wasn't talking.

They trudged back to her cold house and went to bed. Ellerman lay awake, listening to the sounds of people passing outside. The orange from the street lamp made the room light. They hadn't had sex. She hadn't reached for him in bed. He was grateful. He hadn't the stamina or the interest. She slipped out of bed in the morning and he sank into a deep sleep. He woke up in a panic, throwing himself out of a deep sleep that had become a nightmare. He was trapped, he was in danger. He was about to be killed – someone was strangling him. He sat up and shook his head to dispel the dream's remnants. He pulled on his tracksuit bottoms and his socks and T-shirt and walked down the stairs. He could hear her in the kitchen.

'Sorry – I was sleeping so soundly,' he said as he poured himself a mug of coffee from the filter machine.

'You were snoring constantly from two o'clock on.'

'Must be the cold. I'm sorry.'

'It's over.'

He looked at Lisa and shook his head. He was just setting his coffee down on the table in the kitchen, just about to help himself to some cereal.

'Sorry?' He paused on the way to the cupboard. 'You mean us? Our relationship?

'Yes.'

She turned away from him and began tidying her breakfast things away.

'Can I ask why?'

'Do I need a reason?'

'Well, I think you owe me one. We've been together for a while.'

She turned back from the sink. 'Yes, and look how far we've progressed,' she said sarcastically, her voice high-pitched. 'Two years and we've got nowhere.'

He hated it when her voice took on a shrieky edge to it.

They stared at one another for almost a minute before he shook his head, turned back to the table and picked up his coffee.

'I thought you understood the situation – the fact that I can't leave my wife just yet but I fully intend to ... and then there's the house in Spain ...' He pulled out a chair to sit at the kitchen table. He was trying to stay calm. In truth, he was reeling a bit. He hadn't expected it.

'Yes.' She went and picked up her trainers from their place beside the back door and sat down opposite him. 'Let's talk about that.'

'Okay. Of course. What is it you want to talk about?'

'When? I want to talk about *when*.'

'As in?' He swung his head from side to side and his expression screwed into an awkward smile.

'There must be a timeline, a timescale? You? Me? This house I've invested in? When – *when*, for fuck's sake?'

'The internal walls are being plastered; the garden is being landscaped. The pool is in the process of being dug. It's all happening now.'

'You said that last time.' She slipped her feet into her trainers and fastened them up.

'I will ring my builder right now if you like and I can ask him what he's working on today.'

'You're a master at sarcasm, JJ, but you are getting tangled in your own lies.'

He looked at her face. He had not seen this side of her. Where had his sweet little gym bunny gone? Where was the girl whose girlish looks, whose large black eyes were always filled with a sweet dark passion, always anxious to please him, to see that he was happy? She looked demented today. She looked angry enough to kill him, but at the same time she looked terribly sad. When had he seen that look before? So many times. Dee. It was Dee's disappointment all over again.

'I'm so sorry I've upset you, my darling. You mean the world to me. I can't bear to lose you. Let's not fall out. I promise you – absolutely *promise* you – that it won't be long. Can you wait for me, darling, please?' He reached out a hand and covered hers. She snatched it away.

'It's too late. I was waiting to see what you'd do

when you arrived yesterday. I know you've been seeing someone else. You've lied about everything.'

'I promise you, darling . . .'

'Don't bother. I'm sick of your promises. They don't mean jack. I'm going for a run and I want you to leave while I'm out. I don't want anything of yours here when I get back.'

He watched her open the back door and she turned to look at him.

'I actually feel sorry for you. You're a sad fuck-up. You're too old for me. You've got old since we met. Or maybe I never noticed it like I do now.'

Lisa rested her back against the door frame and looked at him with pity. She couldn't do what had been asked. She hated him enough but her hot head got the better of her.

'Give me my money back, JJ, and I'll chalk it up to experience. I'll know better next time. We had some good times but you're a liar and a bad one. Money back in my account by the end of the week or I am going to take legal action and I'm not alone.'

Chapter 38

Carter and Willis were on the way back from Exeter to London. They stopped at Gordano Services outside Bristol and grabbed a Costa coffee to go.

'What did you think of Scott?' Carter asked as they walked back towards the car. 'Not bad-looking? You could do worse?' He winked her way and grinned.

She shook her head. Turned away, smiling. 'You never give up, do you?'

'Come on – I could see you liked him.'

'He's a nice man.'

'Yes, nice. Single – tick. Doesn't have a train set in his attic – double tick.'

'I told you that in secret. Darren's train set was high-speed.'

'Look – I'm only saying your past boyfriends have been a little dull. I don't think I've ever seen you so interested in someone. Give it a go.'

She didn't answer. She played with the lid of her coffee cup.

'Eb, listen to me – I think sometimes you worry too much about your past – about your mum. She isn't part of who you are. She is mentally ill. You're not.

You seem to date nerdy normal guys as if you're saying: "Look, this is me – normal!" But you don't realize there is no such thing. You should use what you have to bring to the table. Don't fight it. Nothing will make you "normal", thank God! Now take a chance on life and stop being so scared.'

They reached the car and Carter rested his cup on the roof as he found the keys. He looked across at her. He could see she was mulling it over. She always got that sad expression that he understood was just a look that meant she was in thinking mode. Carter unlocked the car, picked up his coffee.

'He's one of the good guys,' he said as he got inside and opened the cup holder, placed his coffee in it to cool down.

'He told me how you helped him.' Willis looked across at him.

'Yeah – I tried, maybe not enough.'

'He thinks he was a scapegoat. Is that true?'

'Yeah, definitely. We worked for a year solid on it. We were really getting somewhere. That was the trouble. We came across so many "no-go" areas that we were shut down.'

'It sounds bad.'

'It was. We weren't allowed to investigate some avenues so we could do our job. We came out with more questions than we went in with.'

'He said people incriminated went right to the top.'

'Yes, they did. We weren't allowed to haul them in – national security and all that bullshit. The top brass pulled rank over us and that was that.'

'Were some senior policemen involved?'

'Yes. Sometimes not directly, but they were best buddies with ones who were. They included politicians and judges. We couldn't touch them so the whole thing became a mockery. Nobody came out of it satisfied but most people accepted that. I didn't and neither did Scott. Difference was that I was Scott's boss and a sergeant. I would have stuck with him through it all but he decided to take what they offered in the end – get out or go away. He went back to Devon. I don't blame him.'

'No. Neither do I.'

'You risked your own career to help him, even though it didn't work out?'

He nodded. 'I did it willingly. It held me back, of course, let's be honest. I was labelled as a troublemaker, a maverick – definitely not a team player. I was posted out as a woody to the other end of Hertfordshire for a few years and I had to fight to work my way back. It's worth it. You have to be in the system to change it. You know, Eb, my dad taught me the ethics of hard work and doing right by people. He has respect for folks. He listens to people in his cab and he knows about humanity. He taught me some invaluable lessons. But maybe the biggest lesson I learnt was not one he ever meant to teach me – never settle for less than you set your dreams on. Never let life grind you down, there's no such thing as bad luck – even when you're dealt a shit hand, come back smiling. That's what Scott did in the end – he just has to practise the smile a bit more.'

'I'm not sure he should have stayed in the police force,' said Willis. 'He's never going to get promoted.'

Carter glanced over at her. 'Is that all it's about for you, Eb?'

'No, of course it's not, but my career is massive to me and I expect that in someone ... in someone ... I think is worthy of more.'

'Someone you fancy? Say it!' he teased. 'Say that you might like to have his babies.'

'Don't be ridiculous.' They finished their coffee and Carter began driving.

'What's ridiculous?' He laughed as they drove past the petrol station and rejoined the motorway. 'Cabrina said it would happen one day and so did Jeanie. I didn't believe it until I saw you with Scott – perfect match.' He glanced over and smiled as he accelerated into the fast lane.

'No, we're not,' she said indignantly.

'In what way aren't you?'

'In every way – I will never leave the Met. I know where I belong and it's not in Devon and he doesn't belong anywhere else.'

'One of those long-distance relationships then,' Carter teased.

'No, because in the end, one of us would have to give up something really important and it would have to be me because he's never coming back to London and he's never making it higher than a DS.'

'For someone who's adamant she doesn't fancy Scott, you've really thought this through.'

She didn't answer; she looked out of the window and watched the scenery change. Carter rang Robbo.

'Can you also run a check on all the owners of

Aston Martins in the UK, Robbo? One was seen regularly outside Gillian Forth's house,' Carter said.

'Okay, will get on it. Did she definitely die in the fire? She wasn't killed first?'

'No. She had no chance of escape. She was in an attic room when the fire started. It went straight from the front door up the stairs – chimney effect. She fried, basically.'

Carter came off the phone to Robbo.

'Eb – ring Ellerman for me. I want to talk to him. '

He could hear rock music in the background as Ellerman answered the call.

Jump ... Jump for your love ...

'Mr Ellerman? Detective Inspector Carter here.'

'Yes?'

The music disappeared.

'Sorry if this is a difficult time to call. You seem to be always working away somewhere.'

'What can I help you with, Inspector?'

'Have you heard of the name Gillian Forth?'

'Who? Sorry?'

'Gillian Forth?'

'No ... I don't think so. Should I?'

'You might have seen something about her on the news. She lived in Exeter. She was killed in an arson attack on her home a week last Tuesday.'

'No, I didn't see it, sorry. How awful.'

'She worked for a company called Dreamcars – you're one of its clients.'

'Oh, really? Never heard of them. I can't help you then, sorry. I have no idea who she was.'

'You sound distracted.'

'I'm driving, that's all.'

'Hands-free phone?'

'Yes. Of course.'

'You seem strangely connected to the death of two women. I need to know where you were on that Tuesday evening.'

'I was with a friend.'

'I need the friend's address and I need to talk to her or *him* to confirm it ... and, Mr Ellerman ... just to let you know – we will be applying for Gillian Forth's phone records and we will be analysing all her computer data. If I find that your name crops up, I'm going to request *your* phone records and I am going to go through your life with a fine-tooth comb.' Carter hung up. 'Slippery fuck – that's what he's been called and that's what he is.

'I need to write up my report on today, guv,' Willis said as they drove past the road to Fletcher House.

'Yeah, but it's ten o'clock and I want to make sure we get in early tomorrow for a meeting at eight.'

'I'll be there, no problem.'

'I know, but I need you to come in two hours before that. We'll check things through then and write up today.'

'Okay,' she said reluctantly.

'What do you think about Harding getting involved?' Carter asked.

'I think she needs reining in. She'll be surfing all the dating sites and she'll have joined half a dozen looking for Ellerman to hook in further. Dr Harding strikes me as unpredictable in her emotional affairs.'

'Bunny boiler, you mean?'

'Yeah, I do. She's tough on men even in the work-place. Let alone ones that cross her in bedroom affairs.'

'I know, but she already knows Ellerman and she knew Olivia Grantham. She seems to have something that Ellerman wanted – *still wants*.'

'Not the sex then,' said Willis. 'Is it all about the money now for him – the money for his investments?'

'We'll pay a visit to his wife tomorrow. I want to talk to her on her own. We need to decide if she's complicit in any of this – after all, she stays with him for a reason.'

Carter dropped Willis off outside her house.

Willis opened her front door and picked up her post from the shelf just inside and carried it up to her room on the top floor. She stopped to listen at Tina's door, heard nothing so went on up to her room.

The room temperature was only just above freezing. She flicked on the halogen fire, got undressed in front of it and into pyjamas and her onesie that Tina had given her for Christmas. She checked her mail and discarded it and then tapped her password into her laptop. She had a friend request from Skype. She looked at the name

Scott Tucker wanted her to add him. He was online.

She logged on to Skype and added him. She saw his face appear. She squinted at the screen to try to make out what was around him. It wasn't the station she could see, it looked like a lounge. He seemed to be sitting on a dark-coloured sofa. Behind him was a wall with a large black-and-white poster of a wooden pier. She heard the sound of a television .

'Hang on a minute,' he said and the TV sound stopped. 'That's better – can't hear myself think.'

Willis smiled. 'What were you watching?'

'Um, not sure really – some thriller from some place that looked even colder than here. Wait a mo – I can't see you.'

'My camera is disabled.'

'I don't know – you politically correct gurus ... only in London could you buy one of those.'

She smiled again. She also wondered if he'd had a glass or two. 'Any more luck with neighbours seeing the Aston Martin or any other unusual car activity?'

'Yes, two more sets of neighbours have seen it sometimes, in the week, parked overnight. There have been some other sightings of cars that may not be common on this street – a Range Rover has also been seen a few times but it's possible that belongs to a relative of someone on the street.'

'Any CCTV to look at for the Tuesday evening when she died?'

'We are looking at the motorway cameras but it's not a small job. There is no CCTV in the immediate area around Station Road. I'm still waiting for Gillian Forth's phone records but – a traffic cop I know told me he met her recently on the dating site she used to meet Ellerman, according to the letter, called Love Uniform Dating. He met her once. I've had a look at it. There are a lot of military types down here. That's what she was after, he said. She told him she wanted someone high-ranking – who spent a lot of his time away.'

'I suppose that counts Ellerman out – he isn't military.'

'No ... it doesn't count him out of anything. Everyone tells a few lies on the dating sites. You know: he says, I'm six foot two and he turns out to be two foot six. Or I'm a size twelve and she turns out to be a size twenty-two. Plus, he could say he was retired.'

'Did you find him on there?'

'No, but he could have hidden his profile till it all calms down. We'll keep looking.'

She smiled to herself as she thought about what he said about the dating sites and the way people lied. Tina said she did it all the time. She said sometimes you turned up and the person looked nothing like the man in the photos. But then, Tina also said she could speak several languages and Willis knew she was barely proficient in one.

'You sound like you know a lot about it?' Willis asked.

'Me? I've only just come out of a long-term relationship so I don't need any more trouble for a while. But it's just one more way of hooking up, I guess.'

'Okay ...' Willis didn't know what to say. She was glad he couldn't see her face. She felt awkward. Her heart missed a beat when he said he'd been in a relationship. 'Well, I'll keep you informed if anything to do with Gillian Forth turns up this end. We are looking into all of Ellerman's movements and I'll let you know if anything turns up there too.'

'Okay – you off to bed now?'

'Yes. Night.' She went to switch off Skype but he leant into the camera.

'So you're not sitting in your pyjamas and that's why you don't want me to see you?'

She smiled. 'Might be.'

'Okay, Detective Willis. This is Detective Scott Tucker signing off for now. Night. You are the weakest link – goodbye!'

'Night.'

Willis stared at the screen. Scott's face loomed into the camera as she pressed the *end call* button and logged out. She could see he was still logged on to Skype after he'd ended the call with her. She wondered if he'd be doing the rounds of friends now. He was lonely, just out of a relationship, he said. He hadn't really had anything to say to her. He'd just wanted some contact with the outside world. Willis didn't really get that. Everything she wanted was inside the room. She didn't want contact outside it.

Harding put the bag of takeaway containers into the bin and opened another bottle of wine as she settled down to surf the sites. She sat at her kitchen table but didn't open her laptop. She knew there was something she had to do, something she'd put off. She phoned Carter. He'd just got into bed beside Cabrina when his phone rattled on the bedside cabinet. He slipped out of bed to take it.

'Dr Harding?'

'Sorry – I know it's late but there is something else I need to tell you about Lorraine Chance. Are you having any luck with tracing the lorry drivers?'

'No, not so far.' Carter slipped out of the bedroom, wearing just his boxers. Cabrina sighed as she watched him go. He walked quickly down the stairs so as not to wake Archie. Once inside the kitchen, he closed the door.

'What's on your mind?'

'My car.'

'The damage, you mean?'

'Yes. It happened the same night as she was killed.'

'Okay. That's unfortunate. But is it connected?' Carter was beginning to think that Harding was drinking and dialling.'

'It happened in the adjacent car park to the lorry park. I was going to meet someone there. He didn't show up, or I'll never know if he did or not – the minute I circled the car park I saw a light come on in a lorry's cab and I thought that perhaps my date had made some other arrangement ... I thought – as we were meeting for a dogging liaison – it was just possible that the lorry driver was going to watch. But, I was just about to make my way towards the lorries when the car was surrounded by youths in hoodies. They just started attacking it – well, you saw the damage.'

'Substantial. You should have told me sooner. They tried to get in the car by the look of it.'

'Yes, sorry, that was their intention. I don't know what they would have done then but I'm pretty sure it wouldn't have gone my way.'

'Who was the person you were meeting?'

'He sent me a text message. He said he'd contacted me before. He had my number so I thought he must have, even though I didn't have any previous messages from him. But he seemed to know what I wanted so I thought, "okay . . ."'

'You have no idea where you met him before?'

'None. It could have been in a bar – it could have been on a dating site.'

'Have you messaged him at all since that evening?'

'No. I was debating what to do.'

'He didn't give you a name?'

'No, I'm sending you the message he sent me. You can see for yourself.'

Whilst he waited for it to come through, Carter went to get his laptop from the sitting room. He fired it up and got into the file on Olivia Grantham.

The message came through from Harding:

I'll be waiting.

Carter scrolled down until he found what he was looking for – it was the last message Olivia ever received.

I'll be waiting.

'It's our guy, Doctor; it's the same man who set Olivia Grantham up, I'm sure of it. What do you remember about the people in the car park who trashed your car?'

'Just a bunch of youths.'

'You didn't notice any distinctive dress – gang insignia? Any bandannas?'

'I didn't look that closely at what they were wearing, I was trying to stop them dragging me out of the car.'

'Anyone you'd recognize again?'

'One face pressed against the window – mixed race,

Middle Eastern-looking – Kurdish – that area of the world. He had a dog. The dog was being held back. Having seen what it did to Olivia's body, I'm feeling grateful now.'

'Where is your car now, Doctor?'

'It's waiting at the Audi garage for a new roof to come from Germany. It's due in the workshop tomorrow.'

'Call them first thing and cancel, please, and I'll alert Sandford and get him to look at the car. You really should have mentioned this before. Tomorrow, we'll need to see if we can persuade the Dogger to answer a new message from you. Until then, Doctor, can I please suggest you don't meet anyone else for now. We've just come back from looking at the body of another of Ellerman's women from the list. Please be vigilant and please stay safe. I'll see you in the morning.'

As she was going to bed, Harding got a text:

I'm still waiting.

Chapter 39

DC Zoe Blackman parked up in the Faith and Light hostel car park and checked her watch – she had ten minutes to wait till ten o'clock, when her mum, Diane, was due to finish her shift. Zoe's boys were staying with friends tonight and she didn't want Diane to have to get a taxi or a bus home from an area she didn't know well, even though she'd said she'd be fine. Zoe was going to surprise her and take her home. She was just about to get out of the car and go in when she saw Simon Smith. She sat back in the shadows and watched him cross the car park, then she saw him stop and look back ... Mahmet Balik walked up behind him, leading his dog on a chain. Blackman stayed where she was. She looked at Smith and wondered how he would handle it. She couldn't hear the conversation. She was trying to work out how she was going to disarm Balik and not get mauled by the dog. She was also praying that Diane would not walk out just at that moment. Zoe watched and waited. Simon seemed to be in control. The dog stayed where it was and Balik's arm gesturing didn't seem to bother it. It stayed calm. Simon was nodding. Zoe watched as he took something out of his pocket and handed it across to Balik. Zoe didn't dare breathe or move. Then the hostel door opened and her mum, Lyndsey and Sheila walked out, chatting.

Shit!

Now she had no choice but to get out of the car.

'Mahmet Balik?'

He stood his ground as she walked towards him.

'Correct.'

The dog growled at her.

'You're wanted for questioning at Archway Police Station about a death that happened on Parade Street.'

'Yeah, sure.' He started walking. Zoe shouted for him to stop. He stopped with his back to her. She stood a few feet from him and the dog, which had resumed its snarling. Balik slowly turned to face her.

'What's the problem, Officer?'

'I already told you. You need to present yourself at Archway Police Station for questioning. What is your current address?'

She got out her notebook.

'My current address is no-man's land. I'm every-where you won't find me.'

'Mahmet Balik, I am placing you under arrest.' Zoe took out her handcuffs and took a step towards him but stopped immediately as five other youths appeared in the car park and one of them stepped up and blocked her way. She pushed him hard.

'Get out of my face. Stand back.' She held a pepper spray where he could see it.

One of the lads opened his jacket, to show her he was carrying a knife.

'You spray that – you will take one of us out but then you'll be dead,' said Mahmet. 'After you, then I'm going to cut these people. No one's going to leave here unless you back off.' Zoe held up her hands. 'And tell Toffee and his mates we will find them.'

They turned and walked out of the car park. Zoe called on her phone for back-up.

'They've got to be stopped,' said Lyndsey. 'Can anyone stop them?' The three women were visibly shocked by the confrontation.

'We will.' Blackman was just very angry. She didn't like having to back down. 'I'll make sure that something's done about it.'

'They've been coming around here, intimidating people, for long enough,' said Sheila. 'That dog will kill, sooner or later: he can't control it—'

Simon interrupted: 'We're bound to get it, living this close to an estate like the Hannover.'

'So this isn't the first time he's been round here?' Blackman turned to Sheila and Lyndsey.

Simon turned to go past the women and walk inside.

'It's since the murder – it's got worse,' Sheila said.

Simon held up his hand to silence Sheila.

'Let's not get carried away with this. He's a mindless thug, that's all.'

'Sheila – what have the clients said to you?'

'Martine, Mason, Spike, they're all too scared to come here. They saw something that night. People are staying away – too scared to come here for food.

Shameful the way they behave, these gangs. It's a disgrace.'

'Sheila – it's okay,' said Simon.' I'm going to be keeping an eye on things tonight. Any trouble and I won't hesitate to call the police.'

'Has anyone seen Toffee's friends?' asked Zoe. They shook their heads.

'But Lolly's been killed and they definitely did it,' said Sheila.

'We don't know that, Sheila,' said Simon.

'Yes, we do. They were bragging about it to Lyndsey when they stopped her the other day; weren't they?'

Lyndsey nodded. 'They said they raped her and then injected her with corrupted heroin just for a laugh. She died in agony.'

Zoe was keeping one eye on Simon as Sheila talked. She wanted to ask him what he gave to Balik but decided she'd bide her time and talk to Carter first.

'I can get extra protection here. I will make sure the search for Balik is stepped up,' she said. 'Okay, Mum, you ready?'

'Thank you, Diane. You're a great help,' Simon said as they walked towards Zoe's car.

'I'll be back tomorrow,' Diane said. Simon looked surprised. 'Well, you'll need me, I'm sure.'

'We certainly do,' Sheila called out. 'We need all the good help we can get. Thank you, Diane.'

Zoe waited until the patrol car had come and then dropped her mother home – she was too adrenalin-fuelled to go home herself and sleep.

*

Martine was waiting at the station ticket office, to see if her friend would be working there tonight. She pulled her shawl up over her head, against the bitter wind.

'Spare some change,' she asked a man walking through the station.

'No, sorry.'

She was waiting for Larry to appear on the other side of the ticket barrier and let her in, but there was a new face.

'Where's Larry?'

'Not working here this week. You got me instead. What do you want?'

'Larry lets me sleep in here, in the toilets. Please can you let me in?'

'Wish I could, love; but it's more than my job's worth.'

'Please. Larry does. I need somewhere safe tonight.'

'I understand you got troubles but I can't help. You need to be on your way now. Larry will be back next week.'

'Please.'

'There's no one can help you here. Go on now.'

She turned back out into the cold. She thought about where to get warm and thought of Mason; he would keep her warm and she could cuddle Sandy like a hot-water bottle.

Sandy listened to the sound of boots on gravel and began to pant. She looked at Mason and knew that she couldn't go anywhere. The enemy was coming to them and they were already backed into a corner.

Sandy licked Mason's face in her anxiety. He stirred but he didn't wake; she kept one eye on the edge of the fencing and waited, knowing that every instinct she had was to run but knowing too that she couldn't.

Balik moved through the car park with the swagger of one who knows his prey is cornered and there's just enough competition to make a fight interesting. He scraped a stick along the walls of the railway arches as he walked with his five deputies towards the far corner, like he usually did, where the fence met the road and where Mason and Sandy were hiding.

Martine came as far as the car park and hid behind a parked car when she heard the swagger chant of the Hannover Boys. The last time she had heard that, she'd watched a woman being killed. Now Martine hugged her knees as she hid by the wheel arch of the car and listened to the chanting as they moved across the car park, flushing out their prey. Everything inside her told her she must run. Survival was a solitary ambition. Now she must only care about herself. Martine picked up her bag and ran.

Zoe was still angry – her anger was legendary. No one – but no one – talked to her like that and got away with it. It was one of the reasons she'd been so grateful for passing the detective exams and keeping her head. She knew it was in her – the same anger that, made someone a criminal and made her a cop. But anger was frowned upon now in the modern force. Handling others with kid gloves didn't come naturally to her and had been bad news when it came to role-playing in the cadet training school. But, luckily for her, her common sense had won the day and she had passed. Detective Inspector Dan Carter was her mentor. She had to learn from him and he watched over her. She phoned him now.

'Sir, sorry to disturb you.'

'That's okay – shoot.' Carter had just come off the phone to Harding and he was sitting in his kitchen, going through Olivia Grantham's last text messages.

'Something happened tonight at the hostel – Mahmet Balik turned up when I was waiting to give my mum a lift home.'

'Did you call for back-up? You didn't approach him on your own?'

'It was a difficult decision, sir. He didn't see me; I was in my car. He approached Smith. I saw Smith give him something. Then the volunteers, along with my mum, came out and I had to act, so I tried to arrest him but it turned out he wasn't alone.'

'Sure you okay?'

'Yes, just too angry to go to bed right now, so I'm seeing if I can find any of Toffee's friends. Sheila, who helps at the hostel, says that Balik has been looking for them. He threatened them all as he left.'

'He might think one of them has the money that Toffee was carrying. What did Smith give him?'

'Something compact, from his closed hand. Could have been money. I'm pretty sure he knows I saw it but he didn't volunteer any information about it.'

'We need to look into Smith a little deeper. We need to get hold of Toffee's friends fast before Balik does, bring them in for questioning and offer them some safety to testify. Could be our chance to get a gang member off the street. Where are you now?'

'Down by the railway arches in Shadwell. There used to be a car park here that homeless people slept in at one time.'

'Keep me posted.'

Zoe slowed down and reached the road that ran beneath the railway arches in Shadwell. As her car turned the corner, she saw the dog's eyes caught in her headlights and youths running away across the car park. She drove round to the other side, to see if she could get a better look – she was pretty sure that it was Balik and his gang. They had gone.

Martine ran back to the parade of shops where she knew Spike slept. She found him by the shop door. He didn't move as she approached. She knelt beside him and shook him but he didn't wake.

Mason turned onto his side to vomit as the burning flashes of grinding pain in his gut caused him to heave. He reached for Sandy. The blood was pouring into his eyes and he couldn't see. He couldn't hear her. He panicked as his hand reached into darkness and touched just the gravel of the car park and the wet of blood. He found the softness of her ear and traced his fingers to her muzzle. Her face was torn. Her eye smashed. No movement, no breath. He called her name again. He felt down her head to her neck and the injuries there, the bites that had ripped her flesh.

Her shoulder had a large open wound there. His hand reached around her ribs to her heart. For a few seconds he felt nothing beneath his hand but then the faintest beat touched his palm.

Chapter 40

In the morning, Willis caught the bus up to Archway. It was dark, an hour before rush hour started. The streets had a post-sales scruffiness to them now that the Christmas decorations were down and the sales were finished. January depression had set in on the high street as hatches were battened down against the economic climate.

Willis closed her phone and stood to get off the bus as it pulled in at Archway Station. The cold smacked her in the face as she stepped down from the bus.

She entered the code at the door and took the lift up to the third floor in Fletcher House and went straight to see Carter, who was on the phone to Harding.

'I got a text from the Dogger last night,' Harding said.

'What did he say?'

'Just that he was still waiting.'

'What did you take that to mean?

'I messaged him on Naughties and said I'd be in touch but I haven't yet. Could be that.'

'Then send a message now, please – we may catch him before he starts work. Ask him if he's all right and tell him you're sorry for not making it but you were attacked by persons unknown in the car park. Let me know what you get in response. Did you ring the Audi garage yet about your car?'

'Yes. I said someone will be along to pick it up.'

'I'll get that organized now with Sandford. Keep me informed and I'll do the same. I will need to look into your Naughties account, if that's okay? I'll make sure it's just me and Willis.'

'Yes, okay. When you looked at the Naughties website, did you see my profile?' she asked.

'Hard to tell.' Carter was lying. He had looked for it and he had found it. He knew Harding's body very well. He'd been near it many times. He'd imagined her naked more than once. But when it came down to it, it had been her hands that had given her away. He'd watched them work countless times. She had old hands for her age. She had short fingernails, except when she had acrylics put on for something special, and this had been such a time. Harding always went for the same colour on her nails: dark burgundy. Yeah, the hands had definitely given her away, even when they were parting her labia for the camera.

'That means, yes – then, okay. I have nothing left to hide, as it were. It doesn't bother me anyway – I just don't want to see T-shirts with photos of my bits on the front.'

'Of course.'

'I mean it, Carter – I'm holding you personally responsible.'

'Can we have your laptop?'

'No, you can't. Don't push your luck.'

'Do you always send messages from your laptop? Carter asked.

'Yes, I do.'

'If we send a message and he checks the IP address, he's going to know it's not you.'

'Then I'm going to have to do this with you. I'm not having technicians dismantle the hard drive in my laptop.'

'Okay, I understand. Go online at your usual times and reply to any messages you have. We'll be over to see you later. Did you reply to the Dogger?'

'Not yet.'

'When you do, keep it interested but vague.'

He finished up his conversation and stood and picked up his coat.

'Don't get comfortable, Willis – we're off to talk to Mrs Ellerman.'

They parked up and walked across the road to the house. Carter was watching the movement at the kitchen window. A shadow passed there. They stood and waited after ringing the bell. Dee Ellerman was dressed in black leggings and a dark tunic top. Her dark hair was scraped back into a ponytail. She had large dark eyes that looked tired and slightly dazed as she came to the door. Carter wondered if she was on medication.

'Sorry to bother you. Mrs Ellerman?'

'Yes?'

They showed their warrant cards. 'Can we come in for a chat?'

She looked from one to the other, before stepping back into the house.

'My husband isn't home.'

'It's you we'd like to speak to.'

They followed her as her slippered feet shuffled across the parquet floor and into the living room. The parquet floor gave way to green-flecked carpet.

'Would you like us to take off our shoes?' He could see by her face that she wanted to say yes but instead, her eyes flicked towards the kitchen entrance. 'We're happy to sit in the kitchen, if that suits you better?'

She led them into the kitchen, which was L-shaped with a living area at one end.

'Would you like a drink?' she asked.

'No, thanks.' Willis couldn't risk spilling anything. She was clumsy to the extreme.

'Love a coffee, please,' said Carter. 'We won't keep you long, Mrs Ellerman. Thank you ...' he said when she handed him a cup. He took a sip of the coffee and tried not to grimace. 'We wanted to have a chat with you about your husband. He seems to have got himself in a spot of trouble with complications in his life.'

'The letter, you mean?' She sat opposite Carter and Willis.

'Yes. You've seen it?'

'Yes.'

'Did your husband show it to you?'

'God, no! I got a copy in the post.'

'What did you make of it?'

She sat with her elbows on the table, her hands clasped. She stared at her hands. 'I was expecting it.'

'How do you mean?' asked Carter.

'It's not the first time women have got in touch with me.' She glanced up at them both.

'This has happened often?' Carter said, smiling sympathetically.

'It has increased in the last five years.'

'Since your son died?' asked Willis.

'Yes.' She looked from Willis to Carter. 'Craig. My son was called Craig. My husband was responsible for his death.'

'Is that what you believe?' asked Carter.

'That's what happened. He was showing off in his car. He skidded taking a corner too fast and he hit a tree. Craig died two weeks later when the life-support machine was switched off.'

'We are so sorry, Mrs Ellerman. I know it must still be very raw for you.' Carter leant forward, to put his hand on her shoulder.

She bowed her head, composing herself. 'Yes.'

'It must be very difficult for you, especially when you're alone here. Mr Ellerman is away from home a lot, isn't he?' Carter asked.

'All the time. He comes home at weekends but he doesn't always stay. This place reminds him too much of Craig. We remind each other of Craig.'

'Yes, I understand; it must be so difficult. Would you like to speak to someone in our victim-support unit, Mrs Ellerman?' Carter asked. 'It's always helped people in the past.'

'No ... thank you.' She looked at the clock on the kitchen wall.

Carter glanced at Willis; she took out her notebook.

'Okay, well, we'll get on with some questions, then we'll be out of your way,' said Carter as he drank the rest of his coffee. Willis took out a copy of the letter and handed it to Carter. He took it from her and opened it up, turned it round to face Dee Ellerman.

'When you got this letter, what did you think?'

She shrugged. 'Not a lot. Nothing surprises me any more. I perhaps wondered at the amount of women on the list. That's a lot of lies, even for my husband.'

'Excuse me for asking, Mrs Ellerman, but why do you stay with him?' asked Willis.

Dee Ellerman turned to her.

'I don't know. I stay because we have all this together, maybe.' She looked around. 'Maybe because he is my connection to Craig. I couldn't bear to leave this place, to leave Craig.'

'I understand,' said Carter. 'But, financially, it must be a struggle. Do you have a large mortgage?'

'I don't know. I don't handle that side of things. JJ doesn't want me to worry about that.'

'So what do you know about *his* finances? Do you take an interest in his business at all?' asked Willis.

'I listen to his plans sometimes but I don't know the ins and outs. I never look at his bank statements.'

'Did you know that he was in financial difficulties?'

'Yes. The bank keeps ringing.'

'That must be difficult, stressful for you?'

'JJ says to ignore them. He usually manages to find some money from somewhere every month.'

'The women on the list seem to have parted with a lot of money,' Carter said, glancing at the letter.

'More fool them.'

'Mr Ellerman never mentioned his fund-raising to you?' asked Willis.

'No.'

'So what do you feel about the women on this list?' asked Carter. 'Do you feel anger? Shame? Sadness? Do you feel sorry for them in any way?'

She shook her head. 'They knew what they were getting into. They knew he was married. They shouldn't have done it ... got involved with a married man.'

'But he promised them he would leave you,' Willis said, her eyes fixed on Dee.

'Lies come naturally to him.' Dee looked at Willis and glared. Her sadness had been replaced by anger. 'He will promise anything to get what he wants,' Dee continued. 'He never had any intention of living with any of them.' She rolled her eyes, as if she couldn't care, but her hands were shaking.

'What about you, Mrs Ellerman? Will you stay with him now?' asked Carter.

She didn't answer for a few seconds and then she shook her head sadly.

'I don't see how I can.'

'Mrs Ellerman, what do you know about the Spanish properties?'

'I don't know much about them. He's always talking about us living out there. It's been his goal for several years now but the business always seems to keep us here; there's always a crisis.'

'Do you have any paperwork that we can see for these properties?' Carter asked.

She hesitated and then stood. 'Of course. It's in his office.'

'Would it be easier if I came with you, to help?'

'Yes, perhaps it would.'

Carter looked back at Willis and smiled.

Lisa's gym was packed with people – it always was in January. They'd all be gone by March. New Year's good intentions were hard to sustain. She managed to get away and phone Megan during her lunchbreak.

'I failed to keep calm about it all. I just couldn't do it. I realized when I looked at him that I really fucking hated him for what he's done. I couldn't be that two-faced, even though I tried. Sorry.'

'Not to worry. It will work out, I'm sure. I'll phone Paula and Emily and tell them that it's important they keep on his good side.'

'The thing is, Megan. I'm really thinking that we should go to the police about it all.'

'I appreciate that you're angry but we need to stick to our plan. As soon as the police get involved and charges are brought against him, the money becomes ring-fenced. You stand a good chance of losing it.'

'I'm not sure if I care any more. My hate for him outweighs the desire to get my money back.'

'Please, Lisa, just let the scheme play out. Give us a chance, all of us. We agreed we'd do this together, didn't we?'

'Okay, but I can't promise.'

Megan came off the phone to Lisa and called Paula.

'You have to keep him sweet, Paula, give him hope. Lisa is out of the equation.'

Chapter 41

Esme and Fifi were finishing their turn when Ellerman stuck his head around the door of the ballet class. Paula didn't think she'd manage it, but she did – her eyes said it all – she was glad to see him but she was hurt.

She took her coat and bag from the seat next to her and waved him in. He walked in, grinning apologetically to the teacher, who smiled and looked as if she were delighted to see a dad in the ballet class. Esme and Fifi skipped over to say hello before being ushered back.

They sat in silence, watching the girls for five minutes, before Ellerman reached out a tentative hand and placed it on Paula's. She gently removed it whilst still smiling at the girls. Ellerman leant forward in his seat and watched intently as the two girls hopped and skipped and pretended to be trees opening in spring and then, when the class was finished, they ran over, excited.

'Come on, let's go for pizza.' Ellerman looked at Paula for approval. The girls shrieked with excitement. He knew there was no way that she could refuse now.

'Okay then.'

She stood and picked up her belongings and sent the girls off to pick up theirs.

When they got outside they looked for his car.

'I am driving that Kia four-by-four, the white one,' said Ellerman.

'New car?' Paula asked.

'Thought I could do with a change. Family car, really. Now I can fit the girls in the back. And I know it's Saturday but I hoped you wouldn't mind if I called in.'

The girls got in, thrilled.

Paula looked at him.

'Did you get this car for us?'

Ellerman didn't answer. He just smiled and looked pleased with himself. He'd been loaned the car whilst the Range Rover was in for a service.

After the pizza they went home. The girls were read a story and put to bed by Ellerman, and Paula stood awkwardly in the kitchen, pouring herself a glass of white wine. Ellerman came up behind her; he knew he'd done the best job he could possibly do at remaining credible in her eyes. He stood behind her, not touching, just being close.

'The girls were so sweet today. Like little fairies, jumping around.'

'Yeah – they love their ballet.'

'We should take them to see *The Nutcracker*, or *Swan Lake*. They'd love it.'

'Yeah, maybe.'

'We could make a weekend of it in London.'

'Yeah, perhaps.'

'Paula – I want you to know that I really do love you and the girls. I wouldn't spoil that for the world. You know that, don't you?'

'Talk is cheap.'

'But not for me ... I mean every word. I wouldn't hurt you for the world.'

She turned round, her glass of wine in her hand.

'I know that. I know you care about me – about the girls. But ... I also know that I might not be all you want. I know I'm not the most intellectual person on earth. I don't have a lot to say about certain subjects but I do my best and I feel a lot for you. I didn't realize how much until I got the letter.'

'That fucking letter.'

'Yeah.' She turned away and began tidying the kitchen. 'It was a massive shock. At first, I thought it must be some kind of scam and then I saw my name, my address, all my numbers written on that sheet of paper.'

He reached out for her and she didn't resist this time. 'I cannot tell you how sorry I am, baby.' He kissed her forehead. 'I love you more than you know. I promise you that's true. Paula, I thought I explained to you – I can't say it any more clearly – I love you and someone has been trying to split us up. You mean the world to me.'

'And all those women on the list?'

'It's all a pack of lies. I have no idea who most of them are.'

'Really?'

'Well, some of them I recognize – they are past

girlfriends – *well* in the past – they were work colleagues or friends, friends' wives even! It's like someone has gone through all my contacts and picked out the women and decided that I'm having a relationship with them all. It's absolute nonsense.'

'I want to understand this, JJ. I know I contacted you on the Sugar Daddies site but I've always been honest with you. I am willing to give up a lot for you. I have turned down a lot of dates with other men for you.'

'I know. I understand.'

She swung round, angry. 'Yeah, but I don't think you do. I have put up with so much – I can't see you weekends, I can't visit you in your home. I can't even meet your son ...'

'Now you know why that is. It's Craig.'

She laughed sarcastically. 'I thought I did. The letter even said that he had died.'

'You must understand: in my position there will always be jealous people. There will always be people who want to see you fail. One of those people has got hold of my personal information and has decided to stir up trouble. I am not what they have accused me of. I am not a philanderer – I promise – I swear – I love you, babe.'

She turned from him and shook her head.

'I want to believe you.'

'Then do. You should support me now, Paula. I think I've always been good to you and the girls. I've taken you on holiday, I've paid for the girls to do things they wanted to; I've always bought them presents. Don't let some nutty woman come between us. Don't let her spoil what we have – what we've built up between us.'

'Not this Christmas, you didn't.'

'Didn't what?'

'You didn't buy anything for the girls.'

'It's been a hard year for me. You know that. I told you, I've had a difficult time of it money-wise.'

'The thing is, JJ, that's not the only thing that's been thin on the ground this year. You seem to have gone off me a bit, even in the bedroom. Every time I talk about a future with us, you change the subject.'

Ellerman's phone rang. He tried to ignore it.

'You'd better answer that.' Paula turned and walked from the kitchen, sighing. 'On your way out.' She looked back at him and shook her head sadly. 'I need more from you, JJ.'

'Paula, I need you to have faith in me, that's all.'

'You can't stay tonight, JJ. I still love you but I'm hurt. Come and see me again soon and we'll talk properly.'

'Okay – I understand. I will always want what's best for us. I'll go but I'll be back soon, baby.'

He went across and held her and kissed her forehead. Her eyes welled up. She hated the deception but, right at that moment, she hated him more.

Ellerman got outside and took a deep breath before he looked at who was calling him. It was Emily. He declined the call and sent her a text message, telling her he'd phone her later. He had a text from Megan:

Hope you're having a good day. Ring me when you get time for a chat. Miss you. M

Lisa had sent a text, saying that she was going to the police.

'*Bitch!*' he said out loud, and felt his anger ignite when he got back into the car.

Ellerman sat in a lay-by in his car and pulled his collar up. The temperature outside had dropped to freezing. Dee wasn't answering the phone. Ellerman sat back in his seat and listened to the whoosh and spray of the passing traffic. He clenched and unclenched his hands on the steering wheel. He closed his eyes and sighed deeply from his diaphragm. He was boiling over with the feeling of injustice. How dare someone expose him in this way? His first thought was Lisa. She could have easily looked at his phone. He had been lax a few times now. He'd drunk a bit too much some evenings and didn't remember the latter part of them. Not just with Lisa, with all of them. He could have left it unlocked. If one of them had got into his phone they could have also seen all his emails, transferred lots of data whilst he was asleep. Whoever did this, hated him. They wanted his blood. They wanted to ruin his life. It was all about the end gain. Nothing mattered but winning. When he was sitting in his Spanish home with Dee; when they were happy again and when money was coming in – after all, the deal for three yachts was so nearly signed – then all this would have been worth it. He needed to find more women with more money. The truth was that he couldn't juggle all of them successfully without losing a few along the way. The ones that fell were casualties to the cause. It would all blow over and then he could regroup. If he lost some women along the way, then okay. But the money worried him. Lisa had been particularly vocal in her venom. Did the police know it all by now? He opened the glove compartment and took out his list. He crossed through Olivia's and Gillian's details. He circled Lisa and turned to the next page, ran his pen down the list until he came to Harding.

His phone rang.

'JJ Ellerman speaking.'

'Mr Ellerman, Inspector Carter here. I need you to come back into Archway Police Station again – we need to clarify a few things.'

'Next week.'

'Tomorrow morning, Mr Ellerman, at nine o' clock. You know where to come. You'll need to bring your lawyer with you this time, Mr Ellerman, and I want to see all your company accounts.'

Ellerman got out of the car and vomited. He held his stomach, tried to press in his guts as they heaved. He felt like he was vomiting up his insides. It took him three minutes to stop retching. He wiped his mouth as the traffic whizzed past and then he leant against the passenger side of the car as he took deep breaths and tried to calm himself. He opened his lungs, stuck out his chest and breathed in deeply through his nose.

Ellerman looked into the passenger footwell for some water and couldn't find any. He rummaged round in the boot and found a plastic bottle half full of water. He drank it a few gulps at a time.

Back in the car he rang Lisa.

'I just wanted to say I'm sorry for the way things have turned out.'

'I don't believe you. You're a liar through and through.'

'Well, if that's the way you feel about things then there's no altering it. I am sorry that you prefer to believe the words of a malicious trouble-maker instead of someone who has supported and loved you for the last year and a half, but I cannot stop you believing what you will.'

'Give me my money back now.'

'Yeah – that's right – stick the knife in, why don't you? You're a petulant bitch. You can go and whistle for your fucking money. You bore me stupid anyway.' He hung up.

Lisa took a few deep breaths. She felt so angry she badly needed to calm down. The letter shook in her hand. She picked it up and put it down several times before settling down to read the list of names again. When she was ready she picked up the phone.

'Who is this?'

Dee Ellerman was in the kitchen when she answered the phone. She was watching the gardener pick up the rest of the debris he hadn't been able to fit in his van the week before.

'My name is Lisa.' Lisa's words stuck on her tongue. 'Look … I just wanted to say that I've been seeing your husband but he told me that you knew all about it and that you were cool about it – you had your own life … hello?'

'Yes, I'm listening.'

'Look – I just rang to say I'm sorry. It's not my style – married men. He told me he was separated, just stuck living in the same house as you. And he told me he had to stay because of your son.'

'He's dead.'

'Yes. I heard. I'm truly sorry.'

'Thanks for calling. Goodbye.'

'No, please, please wait just a minute. I need JJ to give me back the money I gave him for the Spanish house we were supposed to be going to live in.'

'I think you've lost your money.'

'No, well, I'm sorry and all that, but that's where you're wrong, because I will take him to court if he doesn't give me it back.'

'How much is it?'

'Twenty thousand.'

'Why did you give him such a lot of money?'

'I didn't give it to him. It was a loan. He said the house needed urgent work before the winter; he said he'd pay me back and then it became an investment in our future.'

'I can't help you.'

'Look – I don't like to cause you more problems but I need you to impress upon him that he either pays me or I'm going to sue him and you, *both* of you. I'm sorry.'

'Do what you must.'

Chapter 42

Later that day, Lisa was sick of thinking about nothing but JJ Ellerman. She needed a run. She needed to think about everything and decide what to do. She headed out of the house, back out through the alleyway. The weekend traffic was noisy as it drove over the wet road, the swish of tyres on Marine Drive – the coastal road that ran over the top of the cliffs from Black Rock to Saltdean. The cliffs shone luminescent as the last rays of sun fell across the Channel.

She got into a good pace and ran for further than she thought she would. It was dark when she doubled back along the top of the cliffs. As she ran she heard her own breath, her lungs beginning to burn with the cold air. Her legs were tiring on the homeward stretch and her sweat cooled ice cold on her skin as the air temperature plummeted. She glanced behind at the sound of another runner. The thud of trainer on tarmac. She felt reassured. She never liked running late and it was already gone nine. To her left the ocean was now a vast expanse of pitch-black. To her right a lonely stretch of road now, with just the odd car passing. In the darkness she was aware of the other runner gaining on her. Lisa sprinted a little. The coastal road was a long one. Her legs were already weary. She didn't have a lot left in the tank. The other runner was now just a step behind her but just out of her vision. Lisa thought about stopping, pretending to have stitch, letting the other runner pass her, but they were alone on the road and beside them was the long cliff drop. Lisa put on another spurt. The runner caught up. Lisa turned to look again and she saw that the runner's face was hidden beneath a hood. They were coming close now and matching her speed. Now the runner's arm was brushing hers as her arm moved with the running motion. Now their breath was on her neck and she felt herself panic. She stifled a scream as she tried to run faster but the runner pressed even closer. She went to turn away but she felt her legs buckle and a pain in her shins as she fell over something hard and rolled towards the cliff edge. She was lifted and pushed and, screaming, she felt her body twist in the air as she fell.

Chapter 43

The next morning, Willis parked up in the car park at Fletcher House and, instead of taking the lift up to the third floor and MIT 17, she walked across to the staff entrance of Archway Police Station. She found Carter waiting for her outside an interview room on the ground floor.

'Everything okay?' He asked, watching her walk towards him along the corridor. She nodded.

'Good. Right then, let's go.'

Carter opened the door to the interview suite. JJ Ellerman was sitting next to his lawyer Petron, deep in conversation. They stopped talking and waited whilst Carter and Willis sat opposite. Carter switched on the recorder and introduced himself and everyone in the room.

'This is Detective Inspector Carter showing exhibit number 312, a typewritten letter three pages in length. Have you seen this, Mr Ellerman?' Carter asked.

Ellerman glanced at it. His eyes flitted around the room. Panic registered on his face as his eyelids fluttered, his breathing quickened.

'Yes, I've seen it. Where did you get it?' Petron

glanced his client's way. Ellerman didn't react to him.

Carter watched Ellerman play-act at being Mr In Control of the Situation, on top of his game. But Ellerman had a bloom of perspiration on his blanched face. He didn't look well, thought Carter. There were bags under his eyes. Life was catching up with him. Carter could see Ellerman's mind turning over. He would be working through the list of women, to figure out how Carter could have got the letter. He might come to Harding. That was a risk they knew they would have to take.

'Did you receive it in the post?' Carter asked, keeping his voice soft, taking his time, watching Ellerman all the time.

'No. Someone showed it to me. I don't understand what business it is of yours? This is a purely private matter.'

Carter tapped his forefinger on the letter. 'It's not private when two of the women on this list have been murdered.'

'May I?' Petron picked up the letter and looked it over. 'I need a copy of this. This should have been shown to me first. I want to register my complaint.'

'Registered,' said Carter.

'Where did you get this?' asked Petron.

'We are not prepared to disclose that information at this time. Does it matter where we got it?'

'Yes, because you are confronting me with a document that I can't defend against or advise my client about.'

Carter turned back to Ellerman 'Two women are

dead, Mr Ellerman. Olivia Grantham and Gillian Forth. Now would you like to comment on that?'

'It's a terrible tragedy.'

'And so surprising that they both were in a relationship with you.'

'I was not in a relationship with either woman.'

'But you did know them both. You had had sexual relations with them both?'

'Yes.'

'When I first asked you about Gillian Forth, you denied knowing her. Why was that?'

'I wasn't sure who you meant at first.'

'Why did you feel it necessary to lie about it?'

Ellerman stared coldly at Carter and sat back in his chair, tight-lipped, then said, 'I didn't lie – I just told you.'

'And when you realized you were mistaken – you still didn't contact me to say that you did actually know Gillian?'

'I thought I was being adversely judged by my choice of lifestyle.'

'Your choice of lifestyle is what? What does that mean?'

'I am referring to my relationship status.'

'Your relationship status with these women listed in the three pages of this letter, you mean?'

'I am not having a relationship with any of these women. This letter was written by a malicious individual who I would certainly sue for slander if I knew who she was.'

'Do you have any idea?'

'No, I don't.'

'One of the women on this list, you think?'

'Yes, I would think so. It stands to reason.' Ellerman looked curiously at Carter, as if it had set him thinking.

'Do you recognize all the names on this list?' Carter asked, watching Ellerman, who was scanning the list of names as if looking to see who might be missing.

Petron answered first: 'I think my client needs time to look through this list thoroughly. He can't be expected to make a snap decision.'

'Sure. Okay. He can do that. For now, let's go back to Gillian Forth, the woman you said you didn't know, but then changed your mind. The woman you say you weren't in a relationship with.' Carter tapped his finger on the third page of the letter. 'It says here that you were seeing her for eighteen months and you met on a dating site called Love Uniform Dating. Is that correct?'

'It could be. I can't remember exactly. I haven't seen her in a while. I told you.'

'When was the last time you saw her?'

'I think it was about six months ago, last summer. I called in when I was working in the area.'

'So, you haven't seen her in six months? You're sure about that?'

'To the best of my knowledge. I might be slightly out. It's been a while anyway.'

'Did you keep in touch in any way? Did you phone or email her?'

'No.'

'So when I look at Gillian's phone records, I won't find any recent activity between the two of you?'

'We phone each other sometimes. We text "hello". We exchange the odd message, that's all.'

'What kind of messages were sent between you?'

He shrugged. 'The usual.'

'And that is?'

'Sometimes just a hello, how are you? Other times a bit more racy.'

'Racy? What kind of thing would you say in your message?'

'I don't know, for God's sake! Things like: "I'm feeling horny, would love to be shagging you right now." That kind of thing. The type of sex messaging that everyone sends these days.'

'Do they? I don't. Do you, DC Willis?'

'No, sir,' she answered.

'Okay, well, I'm sorry your lives are so dull.' Ellerman kept his eyes on Willis as he answered, sitting back in his chair and smiling sarcastically. 'But other people besides Met officers then.'

'Would you send sexually explicit messages to women you had never had sex with?'

'Probably not.'

'Yes or no?'

'I would if I anticipated having sex with them but I wouldn't just message a stranger with something explicit.'

'So you knew Gillian Forth in a sexual way, an intimate way.'

'I told you I did.'

'No, you said it wasn't intimate.'

'It was physically intimate, not emotionally. I've already told you – it wasn't a serious relationship. I am a married man who enjoys the company of women besides my wife. It isn't a crime.'

'It was serious enough for you to text her every day.'

'I didn't text her every day. I told you, it was a casual relationship. She knew it was never going to go anywhere.'

'Not according to her friends; she felt she was in a relationship that would definitely lead somewhere.' Ellerman shook his head. He didn't answer. 'What can you tell me about Gillian, Mr Ellerman?'

'She was just a normal sort. Not a lot more I can tell you really.'

'A normal sort? Normal for you? Did she typify the women you go for?' Ellerman didn't answer. He shrugged.

'She was professional, hard-working, career-minded. She was a strong character just like Olivia Grantham. Is that your type?'

'I don't have a type.'

'Yes, you do – they have to be willing to part with a lot of money.'

'I resent that accusation. I am always truthful.'

Carter could see that the lawyer was about to step in and stop the interview. Carter smiled and offered Ellerman something to drink.

'How often did you see Gillian, do you think?' Carter resumed his questioning.

'Sometimes once a week, sometimes not for a fortnight. Whenever I had business down her way.'

'Eighteen months is a long time to maintain a relationship.'

'It is easier when you don't see someone often. It was a casual relationship, as I said.'

'And you think she viewed it that way?'

'Yes, I think she did.'

'Can I just stress, Mr Ellerman, we have ordered Gillian Forth's phone records and we will see the truth.'

'I have nothing to hide.'

'So you told her all about the other women?'

'No. That is my business.'

'She didn't know about the other women?'

'No, not as far as I know.'

'None of these women knew about each other until they got this letter, is that right?'

'I can't answer that.'

'But they weren't supposed to know about one another?'

'No, obviously not.'

'So that's the kind of truth that you were talking about, is it? That's your interpretation of the truth? Must be difficult for you to know which one wrote the letter? One of them has *obviously* done her homework.'

'Illegally gained access to private information.'

'You say your relationship was a casual one with Gillian Forth, but was it also a financial one?'

'What do you mean?'

'We know that Olivia Grantham invested in your Hacienda Renovations company – did Gillian Forth also?'

He didn't want to answer; he mumbled.

Petron looked at him. 'You don't have to answer.'

'No. But I have nothing to hide. Yes, I believe Gillian did invest a sum of money in my company.'

'That will be … in the company that …' Carter picked up the page where Ellerman's bogus company was exposed. 'The company that it says in the letter doesn't exist.'

'It does exist.'

'Well, we know it's a registered company. It has accounts that show a non-profit. It's worth a nominal amount of one hundred pounds. Where does all the money invested go?'

'It goes into restoring Spanish properties. I have some accounts I can show you.'

'I don't need to see them. We are conducting our own searches. If necessary, we will send officers out to Spain to hunt down the truth. We won't stop now, Mr Ellerman. We're very grateful to whoever sent this letter. We intend contacting each of the women and asking them all about their relationship with you. You had better prepare your wife for some unpleasant surprises. One more question, Mr Ellerman – have you ever heard of a hostel for the homeless called Faith and Light?'

'No, I haven't.'

Ellerman drove home after the interview, but first, his lawyer took him for a drink. They had a lot to talk through.

'Okay – well, thanks for going through the list of these women with me,' said Petron. 'I will hopefully not need to contact them. We have to see what the police come up with. I can tell that they are just fishing at the moment. They don't have enough to charge you with anything. They're hoping the Spanish company, the women's investments, will lead them to something. They don't want to spend money getting sidetracked with going to Spain unless they can connect it with the murders. Just sit tight and don't answer any more questions. Do you have alibis for the nights the women were murdered?'

'I was either on the road or I was with a woman. I can call on them if I have to but I'd rather not.'

'How many of those women are you actually involved with?'

'I probably see five women regularly, another eight when I can. I haven't seen the rest of them on that list for over a year.'

'Jesus … if you don't mind me saying so, that's a lot of work to maintain that many relationships at once.'

'Normally, it works like clockwork. As long as you do the same things at the same time every day then you can keep control of it. Nothing can be left to chance.'

'It doesn't feel … difficult? You don't feel like you're being a bastard?'

'I'm giving the women a part of me. I'm giving them what they want. I don't go into it thinking that it won't work out. All of the women have meant something to me.'

'But you just can't finish it, or what?'

'I don't want to finish it.'

'Do you have any idea who could have written the letter?'

'I think it must be one of the five that I see almost

every week. Some of the women on the list I call in at for lunch, for the afternoon; they just wouldn't have a chance to look at my phone. It has to be a woman who I spend the night with. Is someone trying to frame me for the murders?'

'Perhaps.'

'I didn't do it.'

'I don't think they're seriously thinking that you were anywhere near, but they obviously suspect you of having organized them. It's about the money. It's all about the women giving you money and ending up dead. I want you to go home and stay home. No more going around the country visiting women.'

'I have work to do. I won't give in to this bullshit. The women's deaths have nothing to do with me. It's up to the police to prove it.'

'Well, believe me, they are going to try. These were completely innocent victims in all this, John. I won't lie – you don't come out of this smelling so good.'

'I don't know what you're implying. I've done nothing wrong.'

'Technically, maybe not. Morally? That's a different question. I think most people would consider it wrong to go round the country using women as you go. You told me yourself that some of them are single parents, one of them has been with you for five years. I mean – I like the odd fling, but all these women, really? And the money that they've parted with – in good faith?'

'Absolutely in good faith and I resent the implication that they've been conned out of money. They knew what they were getting into.'

'Yeah, that's the bit that I can see Detective

Inspector Carter is not buying. The women must have been promised something in exchange for the money. What they obviously got is nothing. Added to that, two have ended up dead.'

Chapter 44

Carter and Willis returned to the Dark Side after the interview was over. Carter was bristling.

'What did you think? Was he telling the truth?' They talked as they walked back down the corridor and caught the lift back up to the third floor.

'No, guv. He was as shifty as it's possible to be. He is arrogant enough to think he can get away with anything. You could see his mind churning, trying to decide what to admit to and what not to. It's a good job we didn't tell him we had the letter before the interview.'

'Yeah. The letter was a surprise and a half. We are going to get some flak for that. Petron will lodge a complaint. He's a difficult lawyer to work with. He knows how we think; he likes to try and be a step ahead.'

'Do you think we should make it a priority to find out who sent it, guv? If Ellerman is a killer then he'll go after them. Harding could be at risk.'

'Warn her to be vigilant. But I think he'd have to be very sure first and we know it's not Harding. Plus, she hasn't invested any money in his company.'

'Do we know it wasn't Harding who wrote the letter, guv?'

He looked at her and shook his head incredulously. 'Willis – you have to start trusting someone. You can't live your whole life thinking that everyone is a liar. What happened when you went back to see your mum?'

'I have my dad's name and his picture. I know a bit about him but not a lot.'

'Enough to trace him though, I expect.'

'Maybe.'

'What, you haven't started yet?'

'No. I'm thinking about it. Plus, it's a busy time here at work.'

'It's always a busy time. And you know – you should think about taking that holiday. Make it to the Caribbean and go and find him.'

'He may be over here.'

'Exactly. Start looking.'

'I'm not sure I want to feed my mother the hope that she's looking for.'

'She has a plan?'

'Oh, yes, and she must be getting careless because she told me it. She thinks that if she wanted, if she *really* wanted it, then she could get out of there. My father is just to feed her ego. Give her hope, as she calls it. She hopes to use him, the same way as she uses everyone. It's still all about her. She shows no remorse for anything she's done.'

They walked into Robbo's office.

'Robbo? I got your message; what's up?'

'Has Harding had a reply from the message she sent the Dogger?'

'No, not yet.'

'We checked the messages she's exchanged over the last year. The ones where the words "I'll be waiting" were used is basically the Dogger and one other. We're still tracing that one other. By the way – Toffee's friends and protégés? We found Spike – dead in a doorway. Martine was seen at the railway station but she's not been seen again. Mason still hasn't been seen since his encounter with Willis in the garage. And Lolly, we know, is dead.'

'What happened to Spike?'

'Stabbed.'

'Any witnesses?'

'None. What do you want to do about the letter and the list of women? My feeling is that we might be getting sidetracked, concentrating too much on them?'

'I don't believe we are,' replied Carter. 'Harding was attacked; she's on the list.'

'But Gillian Forth was also murdered in a completely different manner and she lives over a hundred miles from the hostel.'

'But, Ellerman connects them all,' said Carter. 'We need to check out his alibis more thoroughly now. We still need to talk to the core of women he sees regularly.'

Carter turned back to Willis, who was signing in to a spare PC on Hector's desk. 'Ring Scott, Willis, and get him to go and see Megan Penarth – that's his neck of the woods – and we'll go and see Lisa Tompkins, the gym manager in Brighton.'

Chapter 45

'Megan Penarth?'

'Yes, come in.'

Tucker could feel himself being looked over as he walked past her.

She closed the door behind him.

'Sorry to disturb you,' he said, wiping his feet thoroughly on the doormat.

'That's okay. I like being disturbed. Otherwise my day is only punctuated by the postman coming and the rising and setting of the sun, the noise when the wind changes direction.'

He looked at her with slight wonderment. Her looks were distinctive. Now as she reached her mid-fifties her hair was streaked with a seam of silver in a black mane. He wasn't sure whether he found her beautiful or strange.

'You can tell you're a landscape artist. This is a great place to hide away.'

'Yes, it is. Come in, I've just made some coffee.' She indicated that he should sit at the kitchen table and brought over a cafetière.

'How can I help you? Our phone conversation

seemed a little odd.' She poured him a coffee and pushed the sugar and cream towards him.

'Thanks very much. Yes, sorry I was a bit brief. I didn't want to talk about things over the phone. I need to talk to you about a personal matter. Do you know a man named JJ Ellerman?'

She nodded. 'Is he okay?'

Tucker answered with a nod and took out the copy of Harding's letter that Willis had emailed him.

'Have you seen this letter before?' he asked, handing Megan the three sheets.

She glanced at it and nodded. 'Yes, I got one in the post.'

Tucker looked at her and had the feeling he was part of a stage play. Enter stage left, assume look of surprise. She knew what he had come about.

'You were expecting me?'

'I was expecting one of these women on this list but I presume you're not in drag?'

He smiled and shook his head. 'Not a drag day for me. So you have had contact with the other women on this list?'

'No, not yet, but I intend to start phoning, once I hear what you have to say.'

He took out his notebook. 'Can I ask you a few questions about your relationship with Ellerman?'

'Of course.'

'How do you know him?'

'I met him on a dating site for wine lovers. We got on. He was working all over the country and I like to get out of here when I can, so we arranged to meet at venues around the country. Once in Harrogate, another time in London, then in Bristol. We had met three times before he came here.'

'How long have you known him altogether?'

'From the first time we talked on the phone? It's got to be nine months.'

'It must have been quite a shock to get the letter?'

'It was a disappointment.'

'Did you have any idea he was seeing other women?'

'I had made it quite clear to him that I wouldn't accept that. I suppose I thought that maybe he was too good to be true.'

'What kind of person is he? He seems to be very attractive to the opposite sex?'

'Yes. I suppose it's a sad fact that he made it his job to be attractive to us. What's the old saying: if it seems too good – it probably is?'

Tucker smiled. He was staring at her again. She could feel his scrutiny. She realized how bizarre it must seem to anyone from the outside.

'I'm sorry,' he said. 'It's a pity that that's so true.'

'But, luckily, I hadn't yet invested much of my time in the relationship. It suited me while it lasted.'

'You talk about investing – did you invest any money in his company, Hacienda Renovations?'

'No.'

'Did he try and sell you anything?'

'No, not yet. He showed me photos of properties, some finished, an old farmhouse he was working on. He said the other projects were all going towards funding this one farmhouse that he intended to keep for himself – and me of course. Ha ... it would have been a bit crowded in there with all these other women.'

'Yes . . .' Tucker grinned. 'He might have had a hard job introducing everyone. So, when you looked at this list of women, did you recognize anyone you knew?'

'No. Why? Should I?'

'No, I was thinking along the lines of whether he'd ever mentioned any of these names.'

She looked at the letter again and ran her eyes down the list.

'No. What's the problem?'

'We're investigating some issues around this list. Some issues concerning two of the women. I can't say any more than that. What do you intend to do about Ellerman now? Has he been in touch in the last week?'

She shook her head. 'I guess he's lying low.'

But what will you do?'

'Ummm . . .` I haven't decided. Is this a criminal matter? Can you get him for being a multiple philanderer, for breaking hearts, lying?' She smiled but he could see how sad she was. There was also more than a hint of anger in her eyes.

'I can tell you that he in under investigation, but only in a broad sense of the word.' Tucker shook his head apologetically. 'I'm sorry, all I can suggest to you is that you don't allow him to come and visit you at the moment, until we clear these matters up.'

'What are you saying? Is he dangerous?'

He held her gaze. 'I'd just feel happier if you do what I recommend.'

Chapter 46

After Tucker had left, Megan rang Ellerman's home number. On her second attempt she got an answer. Megan was intrigued to hear Dee's voice. It was hesitant, cautious. She had a slight Portsmouth accent.

'Hello?'

'Hello, is that Dee?'

'Yes. Who is this?'

'My name is Paula Seymour,' she lied. 'I'm one of the women on the list, on the letter?'

'What do you want? My husband has gone out.'

'I want to talk to you. I'm really sorry to involve you in all this but you are already and I thought I'd better keep you updated. I have met with some of the women on the list ... we decided to meet and discuss what we should do. I know it must seem really weird to you but a lot of the women had thought they were in a committed relationship with your husband. For many of them this is a massive blow. I wanted to phone you to involve you in what we have decided. I know that Lisa talked to you. She said, in her opinion, you were not going to get involved. I hate to state the obvious, but you are involved ... Your husband has defrauded several women out of money and they want it back. For them, the way they see it, they have lost everything.'

'They shouldn't have got involved with a married man.'

'No, of course, and they didn't. They got involved with a man who said his wife knew all about his life as a single man, that she even had the same arrangement going.'

'I don't.'

'No, well, I can hear what you're saying but JJ is a very convincing liar and we all fell for it. I wanted to talk to you to clarify things. Can I ask you – did you know that we all existed?'

'No.'

'So JJ has never admitted to having affairs? You've never discovered anything?'

'Yes. Years ago. I found out he'd had an affair.'

'And what? You thought that was the end of it?'

'No. I thought that I would let him get enough rope to hang himself.'

'I'm sorry – this isn't a criticism, but why didn't you leave him, if you feel that way?'

'Because I don't want to.'

'How can you want to stay with someone like that? I'm sorry, I don't mean to upset you. I know that JJ told me that as well as other women you have had problems with depression. Well, I can help you get some help with that. We can support you now. I'd like to. I think you must have gone through some awful times.'

'Yes.'

'Would you like me to visit you, Dee? I come to London often. It's no problem.'

'I don't think so, but thank you for the offer.'

'Do you know what you want to happen from all of this? I don't think you can go back to the way it was. I have had a visit from the police. I think they are investigating JJ because of the Spanish company.'

'Did you give him money?'

'No, not me, but I seem to be in the minority. Everyone else has been taken for a lot of money.'

'They can't have it back.'

'Dee, I understand how you must feel and I know this must be scary, but they will take you both to court.'

'As you said, I talked to a woman named Lisa and she said she would. What about the others?' asked Dee.

'I don't know. Some of them are too heartbroken to think it through at the moment.'

'What do you want from me?'

'I want to ask you to join us, be united with us. Stand together and we will help you to get out of this marriage. Will you join us?'

'No. I can't, I'm sorry.'

Megan came off the phone to Dee and phoned Lisa but she got no reply. She phoned Emily and left a message:

The police are coming your way.

Chapter 47

In Brighton, morning dog walkers were out before work on the undercliff path, making the most of the lull in the bad weather. The sun had just risen. It was crisp and cold but there was a milky-blue sky.

Andrew the accountant was out walking his two miniature poodles Pompom and Lulu. He called to them to be quiet as they stopped on the path ahead of him and yapped excitedly. He reached them and looked upwards. Hanging above his head a woman was impaled on the metal cage used to collect falling stones. Her twisted body was bathed in frost. She was frozen solid. Her eyes were shining as they reflected the rising sun. Her blood was a dark stain on the white cliff face where it had run out.

It was 7 a.m. Willis hadn't slept more than a few hours when she switched off her alarm clock before it rang. The business of finding her father had turned out to be relatively easy once she had his name and photo. But once she started it was hard to stop looking for things written about him. Eddie Francis hadn't been able to make it as a sprinter, in the end. But he'd coached many good ones over the years and was still involved with the Jamaican athletics team. He'd never married but he had two sons. Willis wondered why her mother had never bothered to find him before. She hadn't needed him before now, Willis supposed. Or maybe she had contacted him but not got the response she wanted. Willis needed to talk to Dr Reese again. Bella's normal accommodation was a twelve-patient ward for people with personality disorders who were deemed to be both a risk to themselves and the public, but a ward was a collection of rooms. Bella was diagnosed as having paranoid schizophrenia. The hospital allowed her mother Internet access, along with a swimming pool, her own TV and a garden to tend. But it was still a maximum-security hospital and every movement she made was meant to be on camera or watched over – maybe they had decided it wasn't going to help her to contact Eddie Francis.

Willis printed off a couple of clear photos she had of Eddie and then she took one downstairs when she heard Tina getting up for work. They met in the kitchen.

'What do you think, Teen? He's an athletics coach.'

Tina took the photo from Willis and gave it straight back.

'He's all right but he's a bit old for you.'

'No, I don't mean as a potential boyfriend. I mean as a dad.'

Tina stopped buttering her toast and looked wide-eyed at Willis.

'Excuse me?'

'This is *him*. Or he could be. We don't really have any proof except what my mother said and she's—'

'STOP ... stop right there. Let me see this photo again.' She took it from Willis and looked at it closely.

'OMG. Yes ... for feck's sake – he's not going to be able to deny it. Look at you both – two peas in a pod!'

'Well, it's early days yet, Teen. I mean, we only have my mum's word and that's not worth a lot.'

'Oh, for goodness' sake. Christ, Eb ... is this where I think it is? Is this in Jamaica?' she said, scanning the background to the photo. Willis nodded. 'Book us flights. We are going out there to confront him. I mean, who wouldn't want a dad in Jamaica?'

'No confrontation ...' Willis smiled as she shook her head. Tina's enthusiasm was infectious. 'We don't want to scare him off.'

'What's to scare? Who wouldn't be proud of a daughter like you? Look at all you've achieved. Look at who you are.'

'Thanks, Teen.'

'I mean it.' Tina picked up her toast and munched double-speed. 'Eb – you know what this means?' Willis shook her head – hardly daring to ask. 'We have holiday opportunities *off* the scale.'

Willis got a call from Scott Tucker as she was getting off the bus at Archway.

'Just thought I'd catch up.'

'What did you think of Megan Penarth?' she asked.

'Interesting woman – lives on Dartmoor in a barn conversion. She seemed to be quite sorted. She doesn't seem to be finished with JJ Ellerman yet – seems to me like she was planning to have her say before walking away.'

'Did she give him any money?'

'She says not. How are you getting on with the other women on the list?'

'I'm just about to attend a meeting now. I'll send you a report when we're done. After that, we're planning to head to Brighton to talk to Lisa Tompkins, the gym manager.'

'A phone call will do. I mean, I know you're busy. We could Skype again and you can let me know later.'

'Yeah. Okay, thanks a lot for the call. I'll keep you informed. Actually, you should come and meet us when we go to Brighton. I'll text you when we're leaving. How long will it take you?'

'Four hours. I'd better start now. When are you going?'

'After this meeting – in a couple of hours.'

'Okay – see you there.'

'Can you spare the time?'

'Absolutely.'

Willis ended the call and went straight to Robbo's office, ready for the meeting. Carter was already there.

'What did we find out about the women's history, Pam?' Willis asked as she hung her coat on the hook.

'Paula Seymour has a conviction for ...' Pam opened and read the file on her desk. 'Shoplifting and assault. The first offence came after several warnings. Seems she was known to the police as a teenager. The assault charge was when she was nineteen – she glassed another woman in a club. She's not had anything since.'

'Bored teenager syndrome,' said Hector from his desk.

'Not many people are capable of glassing someone,' Carter remarked.

'Drink was involved,' said Pam, as she continued reading from the email. 'Paula Seymour always denied it was her but a jury convicted her. She was pregnant at the time; she did community service. She's been clean since.'

Carter sat quietly. He leant back in his chair as he stared out into space.

'Ellerman could have killed Gillian Forth,' he said after a few moments' contemplatation. 'He had time that evening, to get from Exeter to Reading; three hours max. Fire started at seven. He would have got to Paula at ten.'

'It's possible – she seemed vague on the phone; we need to pinpoint his arrival time.'

Carter sat up in his seat.

'But then we know that whoever set Olivia up is able to manipulate or pay for someone else to do the job,' he said. 'Could someone have been paid to set fire to Gillian Forth's house?'

'We looked into the possibility of a hired killer coming to do it,' answered Robbo. 'Truth is, it would cost a lot more than the money Ellerman took from her. I can't see that being worth it.'

'He could have paid one of Toffee's crew to come and do it. That would have cost him, what? A few grand, tops. Or Balik – he might be up for a change of scenery. We need to look at CCTV of trains to Exeter, see if we can spot any of them waiting to board.'

'I think,' said Willis, 'that if he paid someone, he might even have to drive them there. They're all off their faces. How could you be sure they would do the job?'

'No, I reckon you could go through the route with one of them. You could show them exactly what, where and how and they could do it. We need to get the computers taken out of the hostel and we need to look at them – that's the most likely place any planning would have been done. Toffee's got to come out of this coma with a name for us of who paid him. Someone must have seen him talking to a stranger. We need to ring Detective Blackman now and ask her if there's any news on Toffee.'

Willis rang Blackman and put her on speakerphone.

'What's the latest on Toffee?' asked Carter.

'I'm at the hospital now, sir. He's stable, and there's talk of starting the process of bringing him round. The swelling on his brain is reduced. They're not sure how much it will affect his memory or speech at the moment.'

'Is Simon Smith still there?'

'Most days he calls in. Sometimes he stays a few hours, sometimes it's a flying visit.'

'We're having the PCs picked up from the hostel. What about your mum in there? Does everything seem okay in there to her? Is there any more talk of the murder?'

'There's plenty of talk about it. Apparently, Balik is bragging about how he murdered Olivia Grantham. There's talk that he kept a souvenir from the attack. He's saying he got paid by Simon. The Hannover Boys continue to come over and intimidate the residents. I think we need to have a show of force on the estate.'

'Why is it so hard to find Balik?'

'I don't know, sir. We have patrols out looking for him. I think the only hope is through his grandfather.'

'Well, keep looking, Blackman. We need Balik in for questioning.' They fininshed the call to her as Sandford joined them.

'I've prepared a report on Harding's car.'

'That was quick,' said Robbo.

'Yes, well, it didn't have to be examined on the inside. We're just looking for matches on the outside to Olivia Grantham's car and to the crime scenes.'

He came across to Robbo's desk, put his case on the floor and opened the file, spreading the photos and diagrams in a line across the desk.

'There are twelve sites which are of interest on Hardings's car. We have dog hair of a similar light colour to that found in Olivia's car. We have two sets of hand and fingerprints that match to her car also. Here, on the roof, where someone's stamped on the roof and a boot has torn the fabric. There is a match to the heel imprint and the boot print around Olivia's body.'

'That's not going to convict anyone,' said Carter.

'No, but this along with evidence might do.' Sandford brushed aside Carter's negativity. He had saved his best piece of information till last. He pulled out another set of photos from the file and held them in his hand.

'I contacted Fiat and they sent me a replacement first-aid kit because someone had ripped hers open.

They also sent me a replacement spare-wheel kit.' He took the kit out of his case and unfolded it. 'This ...' He held up the foot-long piece of metal piping with a square end for undoing the wheel nuts. 'Is an exact match to the puncture wounds on Harding's car.' He spread out the photos he had in his hand. 'And the same diameter as the ...' He looked at Willis.

'The blow that killed Olivia, the one that punctured her skull.'

'Exactly.' He smiled at her.

After she finished talking to Carter, Zoe picked up her car keys and drove to Hannover Estate. She sat there, watching the activity. There was no sign of Balik. She regretted not arresting him outside the hostel. She thought it reflected badly on her. She hadn't handled it as well as she could have. She thought about Balik's dog and rang an old boyfriend – a police-dog handler.

'Griff, I'm not good with dogs; what should I know if one attacks me?'

'It will lunge, teeth bared. You kind of know it's going to do it. Before it attacks, don't make eye contact, don't wave your arms around. Stay still. Don't front it, turn to the side so that it doesn't think you're aggressive – a threat. Don't scream unless it starts biting you and then scream as loud as you can to get help. Throw anything at it to give it something to chew on besides you – a bag, shoe, book, anything, then get away, walk. Don't run, it will see you as prey.'

'What if that doesn't work?'

'When the dog bites, it is trying to bring you down. Stay on your feet. If it bites your arm or leg, don't move. If you move then the dog bite tears into your flesh, causing maximum damage. If it gets you onto the floor and starts biting you then roll into a ball and make fists with your hands and protect your neck, your head, face. Wait until it loses interest in you then walk away.'

'What if it doesn't? How will it try and kill me?'

'Rip out your throat. Anyway, how are the kids? How are you? Fancy a drink some time?'

'I'll let you know – thanks for the advice.'

She parked up, got out of the car, and walked across to the tower block. On the sixteenth floor, she listened hard at Balik's grandfather's flat. She could hear the sound of the dog moving. It was walking up and down behind the door, pacing back and forth. She knocked. The dog went ballistic; it hurled itself at the door.

'Mr Balik, can you hear me?' There was no reply.

Inside the flat, Mr Balik was dead. His throat had been ripped out but not before he had been bitten one hundred and seventy-three times.

Chapter 48

'We came here expecting to talk to Lisa about her connection to a murder in London and another in Exeter,' Carter said to the crime-scene manager, Jesse Arnold, who was standing with them at the cliff edge. A tent had been erected around the point where Lisa fell.

'We didn't treat it as suspicious at first. We get suicides all the time on this stretch of the coastline, but we had a report of a driver seeing what looked like a scuffle and he saw the woman being lifted over the fence here. One of the officers recognized her from the gym he goes to. When you contacted us about your enquiry, we knew it was her.'

'Who was the driver?'

'A local man, name of Mendrik-Sutton. We have his statement.'

'What made him come forward?'

'He drove past here this morning and saw the police activity – he thought he should come forward.'

'Can we talk to him?'

'Yes. He works from home – a web designer.'

Tucker parked his car and walked across to them. He had driven straight up from Exeter.

They looked over the railings. Beneath them were three SOCOs. The body was shielded from view by a makeshift screen to either side and suspended across the front. 'The doctor said she had probably died from a broken neck. She'd been dead about twelve hours when she was found at eight this morning.'

'Who found her?'

'A man walking his dogs. We don't know what injuries are on the body yet but there are signs of a struggle here at the cliff edge. Several sets of footprints here at the edge and leading to this spot. The grass is so wet there are some slide marks here and over there, where the area has been ringed for casts to be taken.'

Carter and Willis walked across to take a look. Willis squatted at the edge of the disturbed patch of grass.

'It's going to be difficult to get a clean print. Looks like someone's been stamping on this ground.'

'Our best bet is what's on her body. It hasn't rained overnight. We might be lucky. We haven't been able to get her off the cage; it's going to take a crane.'

The officer in charge looked up at them.

'We're going to be able to get her down soon. If you want to take a look at her from this angle you'd better hurry up.'

'Coming,' Carter said.

Tucker led the way back down the road and down some steps that led to the walkway beneath the cliffs.

Lisa Tompkins's body was caught on the metal cage. There was a scattering of stones on the path beneath it.

'Anything fall with her?'

'We haven't found anything so far. We might dislodge something when we move her,' the officer said.

They watched as the recovery of the body began. It was extracted from the cage and lowered to the walkway beneath.

Willis stooped forward to take a better look at the body as she donned protective gloves. It was frozen solid in a twisted position.

'She has wounds where she was impaled on the cage,' Willis said as she stretched the fabric on Lisa's running top and jagged puncture wounds became visible. The T-shirt beneath was saturated and crisp with blood. 'And she lost a lot of blood.'

'She didn't die from a broken neck?'

Willis stood, shook her head, as the rain started. Large icy drops settled in her hair.

'She was alive long enough to bleed out.'

'Mr Mendrik-Sutton?'

A slim, tall man, wearing thick black trendy glasses and dressed in a T-shirt and expensive jeans, opened his front door to the three detectives.

'Yes.' He smiled.

Carter showed his badge. Willis and Tucker did likewise.

'We phoned earlier. Can we come in?'

'Please, do.' He stepped aside and held open the front door for them to walk through to his lounge/office. It was an uncluttered space with more PCs than sofas.

'We'd like to run through what you saw on Saturday evening when you were driving along the coast road.'

'Yes, sure. Please sit down.'

All three detectives sat on the red 1960s sofa, which was more chic than comfortable. Willis perched on the edge of the seat and took out her notebook. Mendrik-Sutton sat in the only other seat – an orange armchair.

'Can you just tell us what you saw.'

'Um, well, it was just after nine. I'd been to dinner with a friend and was driving home when I saw two runners.'

'Male or female?'

'I'm not sure. I saw them out of the corner of my eye. One had a hoodie on. I remember thinking that it was a very cold night. The road was freezing. I had to watch out for black ice. I thought that I wouldn't have been running so late in the evening.'

'Did they look like they were running together?'

'No, not at first. One was a few paces away from the other. The next time I looked they seemed to be alongside one another and then something caught my eye and I nearly crashed as I saw what seemed to be a fight between them. There was a car passing me and I took my eyes from them for a split second and then I looked back and they were both gone. When I drove by this morning and saw the police activity, I thought I should say something. I hope it helps.'

'Yes, many thanks and we'll get back to you if we need anything further.'

*

After they left Mendrik-Sutton's they drove to Lisa Tompkins's house. They parked at the end of the road. The house had an officer outside. The team of SOCOs were finishing up. The man in charge of them – Penny – stopped to talk to Carter.

'Any sign of anything untoward going on here?' Carter asked him.

Penny was a slight man. The white suit ballooned around him.

'No,' Penny answered. 'No signs of any disturbance. Just what you'd expect to find.'

'Would it be okay if we bring our team down here? This could be connected to another investigation. This woman was on a list of women involved with a man we're looking into. Three of the women are now dead. All died in different circumstances.'

'Let us know what you need and we'll oblige,' said Penny.

'Can we have a look round now?'

'Be my guest.'

They stepped inside the front door and walked straight into the lounge.

'You can't swing a cat in here,' Tucker said as he stood in the middle of the room, looking around.

'No, you don't get a lot for your money. Location, location, location,' said Carter as he moved through to the kitchen. 'This is a bit better. At least you can sit down in here. There's a table and chairs.' Carter began opening the drawers. Willis opened the back door and stepped out into a lean-to.

'Nice bike,' she said. A racing bike was leaning against the wall there. Tucker joined her and took a step past her, down into the lean-to and then to the tiny patio beyond. He walked to a back gate and opened it.

'This is the way she must come in and out with the bike.'

'Where does it lead? Do we know?' asked Willis as she rejoined him.

'My guess is it comes out at the end of the houses, towards the station. Useful little short cut.'

'Yes, she would probably use it most days. Maybe just hide the key somewhere while she's out running. It's a nuisance to run with a bunch of keys.'

'Do you run?' He turned to look at her.

Willis felt herself blush. 'Yes, but not every day.'

'Fast?'

'As the wind.' She smiled and almost added, 'it's in my blood', but decided not to.

'Ha-ha. You'll have to give me a head start then because I've got a war wound. One leg is longer than the other.'

'Which is it – a war wound or uneven legs?'

'Both. I can't dance like I used to.'

'What kind of dance?'

'Salsa, ceroc, jive, you name it . . .'

She looked at him. 'I'm always suspicious of single men who go to those classes.'

'Okay. Right. Just as well I'm lying then.'

'I'm even more suspicious of men who lie.'

'Of course. Sure. Well, that's it then.' He grinned at her back as he followed her into the kitchen, and found Carter still looking through Lisa Tompkins's kitchen drawers.

'Found anything?'

'Actually, yes, I have. Follow me.'

He walked back into the lounge and stood in front of a landscape painting of moorland and windswept trees.

Willis took a closer look.

'Recognize the signature?' Carter asked them.

Tucker stepped in beside Willis.

'I do. That's one by Megan Penarth. The artist I went to talk to. From one woman on the list to another.'

'We need to talk to all the women now,' said Carter.

'I'll ring Robbo to see how far they've got with compiling a route for us.' Willis made the call then came off the phone. 'Pam's emailing it to me now. We head north-west. Our first stop is Reading.'

Chapter 49

Ellerman was on his way home. He left his date in bed; she was someone he'd met in a bar the night before. He'd already thrown up in the middle of the night. He wasn't even sure whether they'd had sex or not – all he knew was that it probably wasn't protected. Now, he couldn't wait to go – he dressed and got into his car before the sun was up. He had delayed going home since the letter arrived but now was the time to deal with it all. He arrived at eleven. Dee's green Mini Cooper wasn't in the driveway; he was relieved. It would give him time to settle in before she got back. He needed a shower and a shave. He was still sweating from the hangover. Sitting in the car, he splashed himself with aftershave and washed down an Alka-Seltzer with some bottled water.

After he got out of the car he stood looking at the garden and the clearing that had been going on and he remembered he hadn't paid Mike. *He can wait.* He slammed his door shut and went round to the boot to get his bag out.

Once inside the house, he put his bag down in the hallway and stood listening to the silence in the house.

It killed him. It wasn't peace, it was oppression. It was not a home, it was a fancy obelisk erected to his failings. A white elephant. He picked up his bag and took it into the utility room and put on the first wash. He zipped the bag back up and went into the kitchen. He sat at the kitchen table and opened his laptop, logged on to the home network. He heard the key in the lock.

'Dee?'

'Yes.'

He heard her moving around the hallway. She didn't immediately come in. He closed his laptop.

'Where have you been?' He kept his voice light and breezy and completely opposite to the way he felt.

She stood in the doorway.

'Class.'

'Oh, yes? Which one?'

'Spanish.' She held his gaze; he returned it and then smiled. He surreptitiously wiped the bead of sweat that had formed at his temple.

'How are things?'

'Okay.'

She turned and went out into the lounge. He was relieved that she hadn't mentioned the letter but at the same time he was worried. There was no way he was going to bring it up. If she wanted to bury it under the floorboards, or sweep it under the carpet, then that suited him just fine.

Ellerman moved into his office to work. There were some calls to make regarding the yacht order. By lunchtime he was ready for a break. He'd been feeling better all the time as he forced himself to settle back into the house, to own it. He heard Dee periodically but she was otherwise quiet. He realized, the last time he came home, that she was using Craig's room as an office. Her whole life seemed to be wrapped up in Craig's. He looked at the history on the printer. She'd printed out articles about Spanish building companies and about property for sale.

Ellerman walked up the stairs. He found her where he knew he would – in Craig's room.

'What are you up to?' he asked.

She hadn't glanced his way when he entered the room but her fingers froze on the keyboard. She sat at Craig's desk, overlooking the front garden.

'Anything interesting?'

'My car-maintenance course.'

'Is it time for lunch?'

'I don't want anything. You go ahead.'

'What is there to eat?'

'Not a lot.'

'You know I expect a bit more than that. You could at least have some bread in the house.'

'I wasn't expecting you home.'

'No ... well, change of plan.'

'The letter, you mean. The women, the lies, the money?' She kept looking down at the garden.

He stood in the doorway. 'I explained that to you.'

'No you didn't. You told me your version of the truth. That's not the same thing.'

'It has nothing to do with you, Dee. I will handle it like I always do. Don't worry, it will all go away soon; it's all a pack of lies.' She turned and looked at him with loathing. 'Okay, I admit to having the odd affair but we don't have a sex life any more. We hardly even rub shoulders, let alone anything else! I have needs. I am a man, after all.' She held him with her gaze and he felt her contempt. 'Bottom line, Dee – everything I do is for you, for *us* ... Every decision I take, it's for the best for *us*. I want you to be happy again. I am very close to clinching this yacht deal with the Middle Eastern men. They've jerked me around for long enough but they want these boats. Once that happens, I'll pay off these whingeing women and you and I will relocate. Put everything behind us – start again.'

Downstairs, the house phone started ringing. Dee walked past him into the bedroom to answer it.

'It's the bank.'

Ellerman was seething as he took the phone from her. He listened to the bank manager telling him how much trouble he was in, as if he didn't know. Then he spent twenty minutes pointing out the history that he had with the bank. Pointing out the good times that had once been very good indeed. Where was the loyalty? He concluded by saying that the deal for five yachts was almost in the bag but the manager on the other end of the phone wasn't interested in promises. By the time Ellerman came off the phone, his face was blanched and he didn't want to talk to Dee. He went into his office, closed the door, and pulled out the list of women from his laptop bag where he kept it. He sat in his chair and went through them. The bank were about to call in the loans. If they did that then Mermaid Yachts would go bankrupt and be forced to close. All he needed was to hang on for the deal with the Arabs. If they smelt an opportunity to pick up the yachts at cost price they would take it. He had to keep up the appearance that he was a buoyant money-making company director.

He felt his stomach start churning again. He rested his head back on the chair and took some deep breaths. The bile was rising in his mouth. He was forced to keep swallowing, breathing deeply to try to stave off the nausea.

He called out to Dee in the other room: 'You know if I go down – you do too. We are a fine fucking pair, we two. I may have conned women out of money, Dee, but you were always the reason in my mind. If I am to blame so are you. You have persecuted me ever since Craig died in the accident. Everything I've done, I've done for you, to make amends. All I've ever wanted was to make you happy. This house, this precious shrine to Craig, all goes if I go under and then reality hits. You have to face things, just like me. You can't keep blaming me, Dee. Are you listening?' He heard nothing but silence but he knew she'd heard.

Chapter 50

Paula was blow-drying a client's hair when she heard the chime of the salon door opening. She knew instantly that the two men and a woman were police officers. She also knew they had come to see her even before Jill the receptionist glanced across at her and pointed. The man at the front, the good-looking, black-haired, stocky one, smiled at her and gave her a nod that said: 'We need a word.'

'Ella, can you finish off for me, please?' Paula called the young stylist over whilst she excused herself and walked up to the reception desk. She gave her professional smile.

'Can I help?'

'Paula Seymour?'

'Yes.'

Carter showed his badge. 'Hello, I'm Detective Inspector Dan Carter, and this is Detective Sergeant Scott Tucker and Detective Constable Ebony Willis. We just need a few minutes of your time. Is there somewhere we can talk?'

'Yes. I suppose the café next door is the best place.'

She turned to the young stylist. 'I'll be back in a few minutes, Ella. Okay?'

Paula picked up her coat from behind reception and led the way out and into the coffee house.

Willis went to buy the coffees whilst the others found a private spot to talk. Carter distributed them when she brought them over and then he waited for her to sit down before he took out the letter. Willis took out her notebook. Tucker observed.

'Thanks for sparing us some time, Paula,' Carter said. Willis was thinking that Paula Seymour was definitely expecting them. She hadn't been the least surprised.

'What's it about?'

'Have you seen this letter before?' She nodded. 'Did you write it?'

'No.'

'But you got one?'

'Yes. A few days ago.'

Carter stirred his coffee. 'Were you expecting us to visit you, Paula? You didn't seem surprised when you saw us.'

Willis was watching her. To gauge her mannerisms – to form a benchmark of normality. She had a habit of curling in her lips like a child when she was nervous. She looked upwards as she considered her answer. 'I thought you might. One of the other women on the list told me you'd been in touch with her.'

'You've talked to some of these women?' Carter spread the three pages of the letter out on the café table. Willis took notes. Robbo and Hector had given them a list of questions that they should work into the talk. Some facts that had to be established.

'I've talked to a few. We met up.' All three detectives looked at her.

'Oh, really? Must have been quite a get-together. Who did you meet?'

'Megan, Lisa and Emily.'

Carter looked at the list.

'Is that Megan Penarth?' She nodded. 'And Lisa Tompkins, Emily Porter?'

'Yes.'

'When was that?'

'Last Wednesday.'

'Where did you meet them?'

'Here in Reading. Here in this coffee shop. We sat over there . . .' She gestured to a window table.

'Just the four of you?'

'Yes.'

'Whose idea was the meeting?'

'Megan called it. It was to decide what we should do about JJ.'

'And, if you don't mind me asking, what did you all decide?'

'We didn't really. It ended up more of a chance for some people to just say how angry they were. People just wanted to let off steam.'

'That must have been awkward,' said Tucker. Carter smiled encouragement at Paula.

'Yeah, it was. A bit.'

'It says you've been in a relationship with JJ Ellerman for eighteen months. Is that correct?' Carter asked, looking at the letter.

'Yes. It must be about that.'

'Can I just ask you ... when you received this letter, was it a shock, Paula?' he continued.

'Yeah, I guess it was. I mean, I had kept an open mind about things. But we were supposed to be starting a hairdressing salon in Spain.'

'Did he promise you that?' asked Tucker.

'Yes.'

'And did you give him money?'

'Yes. We were saving together.'

'How much money?'

'Altogether, I'm not sure ...' Paula looked nervous. 'I can't remember the details.'

'Tuesday the seventh of January. Can you remember what happened that evening?'

'JJ came. The girls went to stay with my mum.'

'Tuesday? Is that a night he usually spends with you?'

'Yes.'

'What was he like when he appeared? And what time was that?'

'He turned up in the middle of the evening, about nine. No – it was quite late really, maybe half past.'

'How did he seem?'

'He was okay. He seemed harassed. He'd got cash-flow problems.' She rolled her eyes. 'As usual.'

'And, if you could think back to a few days before that, Sunday the fifth? Where were you that day?'

'I was here. I can remember. Doing things with the kids. We had a party to go to in the afternoon.'

'Was there ever a time with Ellerman that you felt threatened at all?'

'No.'

'Would you be willing to press charges against JJ Ellerman for defrauding you out of money?'

'No. I don't want to do that.'

'Why, can I ask?'

She shook her head. She looked cornered, flustered.

'I don't really want to. I know he's been a bastard but he's also been good to me and the kids.'

'Have you seen JJ Ellerman since you got this letter?'

Paula looked down at her coffee. She nodded. 'Just briefly.'

'Have you talked to him on the phone?' asked Carter.

'We haven't talked a lot. I think he's hoping everything will calm down.'

'Do you think it will?'

She shook her head. 'Who knows?'

'Am I right in thinking that you would be willing to continue this relationship with Ellerman?' asked Carter. 'I realize you've invested a lot in it.'

'No. I can't see it – can you?'

She looked at them in turn and was obviously panicking. The more she shook her head at the thought of it, the more it became obvious that she had no intention of giving Ellerman up.

Carter sat, leaning forward, his elbows resting on the table, as he smiled at Paula. Tucker sat right back; Willis wrote her notes.

'I want to ask you to do something for me, Paula.' Carter decided they'd waited long enough. 'I want you to resist contacting Ellerman. Don't answer his calls, or if you do, don't say anything about meeting us or the other women. Get off the phone and call us if you are at all worried about anything.' Carter handed her his card.

'What's the matter?'

Carter picked up the letter and turned to show her three names.

'Olivia Grantham, Gillian Forth and now Lisa Tompkins, all women from this list and now all of them now dead.'

Paula knocked her coffee cup as she brought her hand to her mouth in shock at the news.

'Not Lisa, who I met?'

'Yes, she died the night before last whilst she was out running. She fell off the edge of a cliff. We don't know if she was pushed or whether she fell, but she is dead and there will be an investigation into her death.

After Paula went back to work, she phoned Megan from the back room; Megan was out – she phoned Emily. Emily was between lessons.

'They say three of the women on the list are dead – including Lisa. She died Saturday night – possibly murdered. They say to stay away from JJ and they asked me if I wanted to press charges. I don't know what to think. I'm worried I'm in danger.'

'They're just trying to scare you into pressing charges against him. They want to get him for fraud, I expect. They need us to do that. Don't tell them anything. They are out to get him. Let's get our money back first. There's an awful lot of women on that list – three dead is not a lot.'

'Poor Lisa.'

'Yes, poor Lisa. We need to stick together, Paula.'

'Are we still going to meet at Megan's house?'

'Yes, as soon as we can – we need to get it over with.'

Chapter 51

The police officers drove back to London in two cars and Ebony left Carter and Tucker at Carter's flat. Tucker was staying the night there. Cabrina opened the door and invited her in for some supper. Willis declined. It was late.

'I'll see you tomorrow.'

Carter and Tucker talked deep into the night as they finished off a bottle of whisky. Carter was suffering the most when they walked into Robbo's office the next morning.

'Come in, Tucker. How does it feel to be back?' Robbo stood and shook Tucker's hand as he walked into the office.

'It feels ... interesting.' Tucker smiled. He shook hands with Pam and Hector. He smiled at Willis, who was already in the office.

'Okay, well, let's get this meeting started,' said Carter. 'Robbo, can you talk us through the timeline of events?'

He drew up a chair for Tucker and one for himself. Hector stopped working at his PC, to join in the meeting.

Robbo wheeled his whiteboard forward, took a marker and drew three circles, each linked to the other, then put a name in each:

OLIVIA ... GILLIAN ... LISA ...

'All three women were having a sexual relationship with JJ Ellerman. All killed in different ways. So far, the only lead we have is the homeless man, Toffee, who is currently in an induced coma. We know Toffee had money on him and we know he witnessed the attack on Olivia Grantham because he said so.'

'So do we think Ellerman has a connection to Toffee? Why did he choose him for the mission?' asked Tucker.

'We've looked into Toffee's past. He was a high-flyer but he has no connection to Ellerman's past or the people in it.'

'Someone was watching him, watching 22 Parade Street, and singled Toffee out as someone they could do business with,' said Carter.

'They must have talked to him first. They must have trusted him,' Tucker added.

'Or known his weakness. Drink is what he lives for,' said Willis.

'But he liked to be seen as something of an intellectual in his lucid moments,' said Carter. 'He knew he was brighter than your average rough sleeper. If I had to choose someone to lure Olivia Grantham to her death, I'd probably have chosen someone trustworthy, someone who sounded right for the job.'

'So did someone pick him specifically? Does the

area count then? They could have had a connection to the area,' said Tucker. 'Or to the hostel ... Faith and Light? What do we know about it?'

'Run by a man called Simon Smith.'

'What do we know about him?'

'Rich kid, who went off the rails and whose parents are stinking wealthy but like to throw the odd charitable crust the peasants' way – they seem to be using their son as a kind of experiment. He comes out of rehab and, instead of giving him a cushy number running one of their many other businesses like holiday complexes in Sardinia or glamping holidays in Italy, they make him run a homeless shelter in the East End. Can a parent really want to set their own kid up to fail?' Instinctively, Carter looked across at Willis.

'Does Simon Smith have any connection to Olivia Grantham or JJ Ellerman?' asked Tucker.

'I'm looking into it now,' answered Pam. 'But not so far.'

'If Ellerman has paid someone or is our murderer, what is the motive?' asked Tucker.

'Money,' answered Carter. 'He has claimed to be buying Spanish property for renovation and he gets the women to invest. They wise up and ask for their money back.' He passed Tucker a photo of Ellerman with a yacht behind him. 'Why do these women find Ellerman so attractive? I don't get it.' Carter shook his head. 'These women could do so much better than him – he's just an ageing bullshitter who likes to flash the cash and sponges off women when it dries up.'

'So far, the only thing we know for certain that these women have in common is JJ Ellerman,' said Robbo.

'We don't know if they knew one another.'

'No. But it's unlikely,' said Carter. 'Pam?'

'Yes. I have talked to all of the women now and, out of every one on the list, only Dr Harding says she knew one of the others and that was Olivia Grantham. None of the others were on that sex site. I can't see how they would have met.'

'Unless through Ellerman,' said Tucker.

'We have requested phone records for the dead women. They should be through to us soon and then we'll be able to answer that,' replied Robbo.

'I still don't understand how Ellerman manages to con all these women,' said Carter.

'Because he's good at giving them what they want,' said Tucker. 'He researches them before he meets them. After all, he knows exactly what they're looking for from the dating sites. He just becomes that.'

'Plus, he keeps them hanging on,' Pam chipped in. 'If your whole relationship is based on a once-a-week meeting, of course it can last for a year or more because you're never going to get to the point where it's boring or where it's confrontational.' Tucker studied the photos of Ellerman.

Pam continued: 'He makes it clear from the start that he is married, so none of the women can complain about that.'

'And he uses his son as a con,' said Tucker. 'His dead son.'

'Yeah ...' said Carter. 'That's macabre. To keep your son alive just so that you can cheat women into bed and out of money.'

'Ruthless, inhuman and a life built on lies – not easy to juggle so many balls in the air without dropping the lot,' said Tucker.

'I agree. It's an indication of someone who can step outside social and moral normalities without flinching,' said Robbo. 'We know he's an accomplished liar. He's a dangerous man. It's hard to know what would mean anything to him.'

'His wife,' said Carter. 'Whatever bubble he exists in, she's in the same one. All this is for her as well as him. Keeping up appearances, maintaining that massive house for just the two of them. If they sold that, they could start again somewhere, but that would signal a defeat, a failure.'

'Plus,' added Pam, 'the mortgage, the remortgage – they won't come out with a lot. But what kind of woman stays in that situation, knowing that her husband is a complete charlatan?'

'Willis and I went to see her and she seemed almost numb, depressed. She is one of those people who's built a wall around herself.' Willis nodded her agreement.

'Is she on a lot of medication?' asked Tucker.

'My thoughts exactly. Her pupils were black pinpoints, she was puffy around the eyes. She must be on some doctor's repeat prescription list,' Carter said.

'If she's gone too far down the medication road, she will find it hard to change her circumstances or leave.'

'They have just the threads of a relationship left. They're like a rotten tooth hanging on by the roots,' Carter said.

'So, it's all about the money.' Robbo went over to Pam – she handed him a folder. Robbo spread the content out on the desk.

'Here we have the only three properties that we think Ellerman has purchased. We have some deeds that Carter found in Ellerman's office.'

'Good work.' Tucker winked. 'Is "found" a loose term?'

'His wife left us alone in there – we took photos,' said Willis. 'But we needed more time to go through it all.'

'Two of these properties are located in the centre of a large town and the other is on its outskirts. Bearing in mind that Ellerman is supposed to specialize in renovating rural farmhouses, these purchased buildings are nothing like that. One is a commercial property right in the middle of Málaga, the second is a flat in a block on the beach and the third is a large property in a touristy area towards Marbella. As far as I can see, there is no renovation to be done.'

'You said there were texts to Olivia and Harding from a number without a contact name?' said Tucker. 'When you were in Ellerman's office, did you see any evidence of spare phones?'

'No, but he could have a wallet full of SIM cards, couldn't he?'

'Pam, you have the list of women narrowed down now?'

'Yes; if we start with these then widen the net. These are the women he sees regularly. The list is getting smaller now. It did include Olivia, Gillian and Lisa. Now I have added Dr Harding because she has

come back into it. Or rather, she is in both camps –
the ones he sees once in a blue moon and the ones
who are of interest now. We still don't know who
wrote the letter but it's being analysed for typeface
and printer-ink type. We're waiting for the results. We
have an expert looking at the language used, the
length of sentences and so on. They have asked us to
get a voice recording of all the women who it could
possibly be, as much as we can, and then they will
compare the language.'

'Yeah – I've made a start on that,' said Willis.

'Have you dug anything up on any of the women?'
asked Tucker.

'Yes,' answered Pam. 'Paula has some convictions
in her past. There is some interesting history on
Megan Penarth. You went to see her, didn't you?'

'Yes. She looks a lot like she stepped out of the cast
of a King Arthur film – masses of black and silver hair.
I made some enquiries at the local pub after I left her
that afternoon. You know – how great it must be to
have an artist living in their village, that kind of thing.
They didn't seem too keen on her. They liked her husband better, by the sound of it. He died of cancer. It
was a long battle, I think. There was talk of assisted
suicide.'

'We need to go back to the village and find out more,'
said Carter. 'We'll go and talk to her again, and the
other women. Pam, keep looking into all their pasts.'

'I still don't get why the killer chose the hostel to
pick Toffee from. It's got to be an area he knows well.
People would have noticed a stranger hanging around,
talking to the men there. He must be someone they see

all the time. Did you confiscate the PCs from the hostel?'

'Yes, they're being examined now.'

'When does Toffee come round?' asked Tucker.

'It will take a few more days, the doctors say,' answered Carter.

'Better double the guard on his room,' said Robbo. 'The gang are becoming a real problem now. Ever since the dog chewed up Balik's grandfather.'

When they finished their meeting with Robbo and the team, Tucker, Carter and Willis headed to the canteen to get some lunch.

'You know, Tucker, this woman can eat me and you under the table,' Carter said as they walked.

She shook her head. 'It's not true.'

'You must burn it off,' said Tucker. 'There's nothing on you.'

'Athletic genes,' she answered, and Carter looked at her and then raised an eyebrow, stopped walking. She shook her head.

'We'll get some lunch then hit the road,' said Carter. 'We have Emily Porter to see first, in Taunton, then we'll head down to see what Megan Penarth has to say and come back up to Reading for Paula Seymour again.'

'Can we do it all in a day?' asked Tucker.

'No, we'll grab a razor and a toothbrush from somewhere on the way and we'll get a Travelodge tonight. Is that a problem?'

'No, absolutely not. I'll leave the car here, pick it up next time.'

*

After lunch, they took Carter's car and drove through central London. It took an hour before they joined the M4 headed towards the South West.

Two and a half hours later, at 4 p.m., the three detectives parked up in the visitors' car park at Prince's School in Taunton and headed into the reception area. They waited there whilst a sixth-former went to fetch Emily Porter, whose classes were just coming to an end for the day.

Carter introduced himself discreetly.

He thought that whilst Emily didn't look surprised to see the detectives, Willis couldn't help but compare the women on Ellerman's list – she saw Emily like Harding: athletic and wiry, guarded and aloof.

'Do you have a room we can use to have a chat?' Carter asked. Emily looked towards the receptionist for approval. She nodded.

'Um ... Yes. We have a room next door we can use,' Emily said, trying to smile, but it didn't quite come off. 'Tea?'

'Yes, please.'

Emily asked the receptionist to bring tea and they went into a study to have some privacy. It was a light room, sparsely furnished, and felt like a doctor's waiting room. Outside, it was already dark. Emily went across to pull the curtains on the two bay windows.

She strode over and sat down, bolt upright, legs to one side, slightly uncomfortable-looking in her tweed pencil skirt. Willis looked at her shoes – they were shiny court shoes – highly polished.

Willis surreptitiously switched on her recorder and placed it on the table, out of sight. She was hoping

Emily would think it was her phone and not ask. They needed a sample of her voice, to see if they could match its style to the person who wrote the letter. Willis was working Emily Porter out. She was studying the way Emily held herself, the way she answered questions. Carter would start by asking her the basics so that Willis could establish a baseline of behaviour.

'Thanks for sparing us some time, we just have a few questions for you.'

'Yes, okay . . . um. Please take a seat. Tea will be coming in a few minutes.'

'This is a great-looking school,' said Carter. 'Have you worked here long?'

'Ten years.'

'It must be very rewarding.'

'Yes, it is.'

'Do you have children of your own?'

'Um . . . No, I don't.'

'I bet it puts you off when you've got so many here to look after. This is a boarding school, isn't it?'

'It's both a day school and term-time boarding.'

'You're known as Mrs Porter here? Were you married at one time?'

'Yes, I was. Um . . . I kept my married name. I got used to it and they already knew me as that here. I didn't see the point in changing it back.'

'And do you live near here in the grounds?'

'I live in a house in the middle of Taunton.'

'How does that work out for you? Is Taunton a lively place in the evenings?'

She smiled. 'Lively enough for me.'

Carter looked at Willis. She held his gaze for a

second, which told him she had established a normal baseline for Emily Porter. Some things would be difficult to gauge. *Emily has a habit of pushing her glasses back up her nose as she talks and when she pushes them she scrunches up her face. She is nervy and abrupt and has the annoying habit of ending or beginning many of her sentences with an 'um'. Her body is still, upright. Her legs are still. They don't move. When she's answering Carter she keeps her head vertical, her movements small. She reminds me of a puppet.* Now Carter would see how Emily behaved when she was under stress.

He took out the letter.

'Did you get one of these?' He held it up for her to see.

'Um . . . Yes.' *Legs clenched, knees clamped. She holds her hands tightly until she pushes up her glasses, this time adding a small grooming movement with her hand as she pushes her hair back from her face.*

'When did it arrive?'

'Um . . .' *She looks up to the left.* 'I got it on the Wednesday morning when I went home to finish some marking at coffee time. I had two free periods so I went home and checked my mail.'

'Was it a shock?'

'Um . . .' *She pauses.* She was thinking what she should say. 'I would have to say – not really.' *She stares straight ahead. Her legs relax a little.*

'Did you already know about the existence of the list?'

'Did I write it, you mean? No, I didn't.' *Her shoulders rise a little. Could be anxiety, could be lying.*

'How long have you known JJ Ellerman, Mrs Porter?'

'Um . . . About five years now.'

'How did you meet?'

'On a dating site for Christians.'

'You are divorced?'

'Um . . . Yes. My marriage only lasted two years, unfortunately. I've been with JJ since it ended.'

'Five years is a long time.'

Emily's eyes went to Willis. Willis didn't react. She was taking notes.

'Yes . . . Um.' Emily glanced briefly at Tucker, who smiled, and then she turned back to Carter. 'I suppose it is, um . . . but I wasn't in a hurry to settle down with someone else. One marriage is enough.' She smiled but it didn't reach her eyes.

Willis wrote in her notes: *Demeanour changed. Eyes looking up to the right. Face colouring. Hands restless in lap. Body language not corresponding to words.*

'So you never wanted anything more from Ellerman? You never thought: "This isn't going anywhere?" Not even now, five years down the line?'

'No. It suited us both.'

She's lying – beginning to perspire, breathing rate increasing, fidgeting.

'So you will be happy to continue your relationship with him?'

'Absolutely not. Of course I can't.' *More lies.*

'I'm sorry if this is an indelicate question, but have you invested money in any of his business schemes?'

'Um . . . I'd rather not tell you about my financial

arrangements, if you don't mind. Not unless it's absolutely necessary. Please tell me what this is about first. Is he under investigation? Surely, it isn't illegal to do what he's done?'

'It's not illegal to date several women at the same time but three of the women on this list are dead, under suspicious circumstances. And there's the possibility of Ellerman having defrauded these dead women out of their money.'

'Dead? Women from this list?' *Her demeanour changed slightly. She seemed more guarded, aware that she was being watched. She seemed to be able to control her reactions.*

'Yes. Um ... I'm sorry to have to tell you that these women died under suspicious circumstances and we are conducting murder investigations,' Carter said.

Willis watched Emily intently.

'So ... um ... what has that got to do with JJ?' Emily looked up from her lap, composed, her breathing rate returning to normal. 'It seems that ... um ... all that the women had in common is knowing him. We know that he knows a lot of women. I understand that he has a dubious past.'

'We think you might have met one of the women who died – Lisa Tompkins?'

'Um ... yes. I did. Once, um ... just briefly. I didn't know her before that day.' Emily sat, covering her eyes and her forehead with one hand. 'Why are you here today? Have you come to warn me?'

'Yes, partly, and also to ask for your help. We would urge you not to see JJ Ellerman again, until these enquiries are resolved.'

'When you say their deaths were *suspicious*, that means you are not sure they were murdered?'

'Olivia Grantham was. She's on the third page of the letter. Gillian Forth was – definitely, she's on the second page. Lisa, we have yet to solve her death. Did you ever meet either of the other two women?'

'No. Just Lisa. Once, as I told you, in the presence of the other women: Paula and Megan. Did you talk to them?'

'Yes, and we will be doing so again, and many of the other women on this list.' Emily pushed her glasses up on her nose several times in succession. 'Just so that we can create an accurate picture of the events, we need to know where you were on the dates that these women died. They are Sunday the fifth, Tuesday the seventh and Saturday the eighteenth.'

'Um . . . I was here in my cottage. I was here and so was JJ. He was with me.'

Carter waited. Willis paused in her note-taking.

'You know, Mrs Porter, we will have to check out these facts and this is not a time to make hasty statements without being sure of the facts. I appreciate that you are fond of JJ Ellerman, but you do him no, or youself any favours by lying on his behalf.'

'Maybe it's the other women who are lying, not me. Um . . .'

'When you met up with them, what was the outcome of the meeting?'

'We talked about general things. We wanted to support one another.'

'That wasn't at all awkward?'

'No.'

'How did you leave it with the other women? What were your parting words?'

'I can't remember exactly.'

'See you again? I don't ever want to see you again?'

'More like – we'll wait and see what happens.'

'What could happen?'

'Um . . . I'm not sure.'

'Let's hope what can happen is not another murder, Mrs Porter. Our aim here is not to get anyone into trouble unnecessarily or to cause embarrassment or to expose you in any way. But serious crimes have been committed and JJ Ellerman seems to be in the middle of it all. Would you mind if I ask you what you intend to do now?'

'What do you mean?'

'Will you be carrying on your relationship with Ellerman?'

'No, of course not.' Carter looked across at Willis. She was watching Emily Porter intently and she knew she was lying.

Chapter 52

Bella had been waiting too long for Ebony to call. She'd chewed all the scenarios over in her head and she hadn't slept for days.

She looked across at the pregnant woman, who stared back uneasily.

'Let's stop all this,' said Bella. 'We're both in here for the same reasons.'

'I'm not a murderer like you,' the pregnant woman, Jolene, replied.

'Maybe not, but you were sectioned, weren't you?'

'For my own protection.'

'Okay, well I accept that we don't have masses in common but we are here together and we may as well make the most of it. I have a present for you, to say sorry for the way I've behaved towards you.'

'What present?'

'Chocolate. I got my daughter to bring it in.'

'I didn't see her bring anything.'

'No, come to think about it, you're right. I asked the nurse to buy it from the hospital shop. I've had a couple out of the box but I don't want to get fat sat in here doing nothing all day. It's all right for you, you can eat what you like.'

'That nurse? Is it the young lad? The fit one? What's his name? Jamey.'

Bella chuckled.

'Yeah – you're full of shit,' Jolene hissed. 'He's not going to be interested in a pregnant woman or a killer.'

'Believe me, he has exotic tastes. I have come to know him quite well when I've been on my exercise break. Why do you think I've been taking so long?'

'I thought you must be having tests, to see if you are actually human or not.'

'Yes – you're right, I was testing Jamey and he passed with flying colours. He's coming back in a minute. He's on the night shift.'

Jolene sat up in bed, waiting.

The door opened and Jamey walked in.

'Hello, ladies. Just come to make sure you have everything you need.'

'I need to take a shower. Would you be able to help me with that?'

He looked back towards the door of the ward. 'Yes, we're not too busy. I can help you, no problem. I'll go and request your key.'

'Told you...' Bella smirked.

Jolene grinned at her and shook her head. 'Lucky bitch.'

Jamey came back a few minutes later and unlocked Bella's cuffs. She picked up her towel and wash bag and the box of chocolates, which she handed over to Jolene.

'You can have the rest.'

Half an hour later, when they returned to the ward, Jolene was sleeping deeply. Bella caught hold of Jamey and pulled him towards her for a kiss.

'Pull the curtains,' she whispered.

Jamey shook his head. 'I'll get the sack; anyway, Jolene might wake up.'

'She won't. She's snoring her head off like a pig.'

'I've got some work to do – when it all settles down for the night, I'll come back.' He kissed her. Bella held on to him as he tried to leave – her arm beside the bed as if she was handcuffed, as if he'd remembered to handcuff her back up. She watched him leave the ward then she slipped out of bed and felt beneath the back of her cupboard. She felt along, until she found what she was looking for, and picked the corner, stripping off the sticking plaster that held it in place. She walked across to Jolene and looked at the empty box of chocolates beside her bed. The sleepless nights that Bella had endured, the sleeping tablets she'd stashed would all be worth it now. She peeled back the bed cover and exposed Jolene's stomach. She whispered, 'Come to Mummy.'

Jamey could hear her singing. He walked towards the door of the side ward and paused outside, to listen. He heard the sounds of a lullaby.

As Jamey opened the door, Bella had her back to him. She was dancing around the room, twirling on her toes, but, in the gloom, she turned and saw him, and danced her way towards him, laughing. He could see her nightdress was covered in blood and in her arms was a baby.

Chapter 53

After they left Emily Porter, the three detectives walked back to their car in the visitors' car park in Prince's School.

'Are we going to make it down to see Megan Penarth tonight, guv?'

'How far is it now, Tucker?'

'It's at least three hours to Exeter and then half an hour on from there.'

'Is there anywhere to stay there?'

'Yes. There's a really good pub that does rooms.'

'Ring ahead and get us fixed up with some accommodation there and then we'll visit Megan Penarth as well. We have to stay somewhere tonight, after all. If nothing else, we can find out a bit more about her from the locals.'

Tucker got the number and phoned through to the Boulder Inn.

'All done. Three rooms, breakfast included. They have a restaurant there for dinner.'

'Sounds great,' said Willis.

Carter glanced across at her and grinned. 'Must be getting hungry again by now.'

'Starving.'

'Yeah, and me,' Tucker spoke up from the back seat.

'Jesus ...' Carter started up the engine and put on the headlights. The place was suddenly swarming with noisy children, loading into home-time coaches in the car park.

'Let's get out of here – where we can hear ourselves think.'

They hit a heavy stream of traffic making its way towards the motorway. It was rush hour. They were stuck in a queue before they'd managed to get a mile.

'We may as well get some work done ... impressions of Emily Porter? '

'Interesting to hear that she thought all the women were lying,' said Willis.' She was definitely having trouble sticking to the script – she'd expected us and rehearsed it. She has a lot she's covering up.'

'Covering up about what?' Tucker asked. He'd found some chewing gum in his pocket. He passed the packet forward to the two in the front. Willis took it from him and unwrapped a piece of gum for Carter and handed it to him.

'I tell you something that I know she's lied about,' Tucker added. 'She sure as hell lied about her lack of expectations for the future for her and Ellerman. No one invests five years of their life and their savings with someone and says it's still just a casual thing.'

'She was straight out of a failed a marriage,' said Willis. 'If she met Ellerman on the rebound, does that make a difference to the way she sees him? Is he more of a friend that helped her through a bad time?'

'No, I don't think it does. She would have gone through a lot of emotions in those five years. Maybe her expectations would have changed from the start, when maybe she just saw it as flattering that he would come and see her once a week. After all, he comes across as a good catch. It would have helped to rebuild her bruised ego, but, by now? By now, she's got to want something permanent. She may have known there were others but she's got to have thought she'd come out the winner in the end.'

'Maybe she still does,' said Carter. 'She didn't want to tell us how much money she's given him.'

'I think it's a case of think of a number and double it,' said Tucker. 'She's not going to let Ellerman get into trouble if she can help it. It's her and him and she doesn't seem to see the others.'

'You have to take your hat off to him, how he's managed to inspire loyalty,' Carter said. 'I suppose we have to look at it from her point of view. She needed a friend, she needed to feel attractive, and he didn't promise her that anything would happen fast; so, in her opinion, he hasn't really lied – that much.'

'Yeah – I've got a horrible feeling you're right,' said Tucker.

'What did Megan Penarth seem like when you met her?' Willis turned to ask.

'She seemed very bright, very independent, confident, used to doing things her own way.'

'Olivia was the same type – driven, confident; quite a loner at work. Gillian too. Lisa was a boss at a gym,' said Carter. 'Emily seems independent, quirky, strong.'

'Megan Penarth organized the meeting between the women,' said Tucker. 'We need to know, did she contact others who were going to come and couldn't make it or were these women the only ones interested?' Carter turned.

'These are his regulars,' said Willis.

'A fast-diminishing group,' Tucker said.

'Do you think Emily will see Ellerman again?' asked Carter.

Willis replied: 'Yes. Definitely.'

At just before eight they arrived at the Boulder Inn. They parked up, signed in and went straight to the bar and restaurant with their room keys in their pockets. They sat in the restaurant of the old mid-eighteenth-century coaching inn. Willis switched her phone on to vibrate only. She had texted Tina, to tell her that she wouldn't be home tonight; having previously promised that, if she was back in time, they'd meet for a hot chocolate and a catch-up.

Carter ordered a pint of the local beer and Tucker had the local cider. Willis ordered a Coke. They sat in the restaurant and spent an hour making meaningless chitchat in a room without background noise and with too few people for them to talk privately without being overheard. At the end of the dinner they went back to the bar.

Tucker pulled out a brochure of Megan Penarth's work from his briefcase.

He put it on show on the bar. 'She definitely lives

very near here,' he said, within earshot of the land-lady – Rachel Goody, a woman who had run a bar in Chelsea before buying the inn seven years ago. 'I wonder how far it is to her studio?'

'It's not far.' Rachel, glancing at the brochure, commented as she pulled a pint. 'But you have to make an appointment – she doesn't welcome people to her house. You could try and catch her tomorrow morning. She's a bit odd like that – you'd think she would be grateful for the work and walk-in trade, but apparently not.'

'Do you know her personally?'

'Oh, yes. We all know her. She's down here complaining about the noise or the light pollution. Her husband was a practising Wiccan.'

'What's that?' Carter asked.

'One of those "would-be" witches. But, he was a good bloke – he brought in a lot of custom here. He was all about the area – bringing tourism in and making sure he contributed to the area, but she doesn't do any of that.'

'She's not well liked then?'

'No, not just by me – I'm also a newcomer. But I don't feel she makes any effort with the locals. She behaves oddly; we see light sometimes, coming from the old quarry. People say it's her carrying on with her husband's pagan ceremonies – but I don't know – all a load of nonsense what people say when they get talking.'

They said goodnight and Willis was so excited to get inside her room, or rather to stand outside the door and put the key in the lock. She had never stayed in a hotel until she first went on holiday as an adult and that was with Tina. They'd gone to Ireland and stayed with Tina's family but, besides that, they'd spent three nights in a hotel in Dublin and it had been the best fun Willis had ever had. Now she felt enormous excitement and pleasure at turning the key in the lock and pushing the heavy door open to her room. She almost laughed out loud as she walked into a beautiful beamed room with a large kingsize bed with scatter cushions. She walked around the room, looking at the place with delight. Her phone vibrated in her pocket.

'Miss Willis?'

She answered: 'Yes?'

'This is Dr Lydia Reese. I'm afraid we've had some problems with your mother.'

Carter and Willis met up on the way down to breakfast.

'They've had something serious happen with my mother.'

'We'll drop Tucker off on the way and then we'll head back as soon as we've seen Megan Penarth, Eb.'

'Please, guv, it's okay. As far as I could tell there's nothing I can do. They're merely informing me that my mother has committed an act of violence against another inmate; they've given no further details. I am not rushing to her side. I wouldn't be any help. We have work to do today and I don't intend to dwell on my mother. Whatever her reasons, whatever the scheme behind them, I can't keep trying to work it out.'

'Okay. I respect that, Eb, but if you change your

mind, or you hear something to the contrary, let me know and you can get a train back up or hire a car and go.'

They went into the breakfast room, which had been the restaurant the previous evening, and were shown to their table by the window. It was the first time they had seen it in the light and they looked out on clouds racing across the moors. Ponies were grazing in the hedge opposite their window. Tucker was last to appear. By the time he did, Carter had finished. Willis was on her second plate of English breakfast from the buffet.

'What a place.' Tucker joined them at the table. 'I could live out here, no problem. Couldn't you?'

'No,' Carter answered.

Carter looked at Willis and tried hard to suppress a smile.

After breakfast they walked down through the village and up the lane to Megan Penarth's house. They knocked at the door but she was out. They walked back up to the pub. The landlady, Rachel, was clearing away breakfast.

'We were hoping to catch Megan Penarth in but there's no answer. There's a car in the driveway. Do you know where she could be?'

'She's up at the quarry most days. If you've got walking boots, you just need to cross over at the top of this hill and you'll be on the moors; you'll see Haytor in front of you, right at the top. Instead of walking straight up towards it, take a detour right and you'll see the quarry. The front entrance is there through a gate behind the granite pile.'

'Thanks. Great help.'

'Have we got wellingtons?' asked Tucker. They looked at one another.

'Straight answer – no,' said Carter. 'We'll just have to prepare to get muddy.'

They set off up the hill and crossed the road. They kept to the tufts of grass between the bog areas frosted with ice as they walked up towards the Tor and then veered right. They found the entrance to the quarry and opened the gate. Saplings had rooted on the sides of the cliff face. Beyond them was a sheer drop.

'Christ, that's a long way down,' said Carter as he stepped closer to the edge.

'You'd think you wouldn't be allowed to have something so dangerous without a railing in front of it,' said Willis, recoiling from the edge.

'Willis – you're such a townie!' Tucker laughed at her. 'It's not all about sanitizing. This isn't Disneyworld.'

'Point taken – but you've got to have deaths off here?'

'Suicides, yes, tragically, and the odd dog falls off, or sheep.'

'Clever sheep to open the gate,' said Carter.

'There's another way to get in here from the back,' said Tucker.

Willis looked down at the frozen water. 'How deep is it?'

'Fathomless.' Tucker turned back and smiled at her. He was enjoying exposing the Londoners to a bit of ridicule. 'Legend has it – it has no bottom to it and it calls for a new victim to be sacrificed to it every year.'

'Cut the crap, Tucker.' Carter stopped walking and listened – the icy wind had dropped as they descended into the quarry. There was an oppressive stillness. As they walked further down and wound their way around the outside of the first of the three lakes, they saw a figure standing at the far side, in a sharp cut-out in the granite rock. The figure turned and studied them.

Megan Penarth came down from her place and walked towards them. In her hand were bunches of bright yellow gorse; she was watching the three people but she kept her eyes mainly on Tucker. When she was within hearing distance, she said, 'Strangers in the quarry – always a bad idea in civilian clothes.' She smiled. 'Detective Tucker, I presume?'

'Morning, Megan. I've brought a couple of Londoners down to talk to you.'

'Great – fresh meat.' She came level with them and smiled at Carter. 'Only joking.' Her eyes were red-rimmed from the cold. Willis waited her turn. Megan glanced round to acknowledge her and there was a peculiar softness in her eyes. She reached out to touch Willis on the hand. 'You're freezing.'

Willis felt no warmth coming from Megan's hand – it was a block of ice. Willis shivered.

'This is an eerie place,' Tucker said, looking about him.

'Yes, the place of legends.'

Willis was distracted, looking at a bunch of roses drying on a rock. Her eyes went upwards to the top of the cliff directly above.

'It's a sad place sometimes, did you hear about the

tragedy of the suicide a couple of months ago?' asked Megan.

'I saw it on the news. It was here?'

'Yes.'

'It would be awful to come here for that; such a lonely-feeling place,' said Willis.

'Ideal then.' Megan smiled at her. 'It's not that lonely for me. I am surrounded by friends here.'

'I was telling them about the legends here. The water claims another person each year,' Tucker said.

'You're thinking of the legend about the River Dart crying when it wants to claim a new heart. They say it's a meteorological fact that it makes the sound like crying when the weather is getting bad, gales are coming and the river is swelling. I suppose in the old days when people had to cross it, there were many lives lost. It must have seemed like a curse. But here in this quarry, the water doesn't ever disappear. It's very deep. Surprising it freezes as often as it does.'

'You love it here?' asked Willis, looking around at the granite rockface.

'Yes, I do. My husband loved it here. He came here every day. He was a Wiccan. A Wiccan believes in the power of nature's spirits.'

'What about you?' asked Carter.

'Yes – I guess I believe in it too. I believe in two gods – the Moon Goddess and the Horned God.' She smiled at the expression that was creeping across his face. 'It's just the male and female sides of the universe, equal and necessary to one another. Yin and yang.'

'You're a witch too?' asked Carter.

'Not really. I just believe in the power of certain things: moon, stars, earth, sun.'

Her dark eyes were watching him intently – they were bright in the gloom.

'What is it about this quarry that makes it special to you?' asked Carter. 'The landlady at the pub says you come up here most days.'

She shook her head. 'Just a world of its own in here. Its own climate; its own life. I feel connected here. It gives me inspiration for my work. There – I've made you think I'm a complete nutter. Do you want to follow me back to my coven for a witch's brew, otherwise known as a coffee?'

'Sounds perfect.' Carter smiled.

'Come with me.'

She led them back and up out of the quarry.

Halfway up, Willis stopped.

'Megan, do you mind me asking? What happens to Wiccans when they die?'

Megan stopped and turned and smiled at Willis.

'You feel their presence here, don't you?'

'Just curious.'

'Decomposition should happen as fast as possible. No casket, just a cloth and then laid in the ground, or left in the air, placed in the water, so that you can nourish other life quickly.'

'Are there places you can bury someone like that?'

'Yes.'

She turned and led them away from the quarry.

'Please come in, sit down. Make yourselves comfortable.' They took their muddy shoes off at the door and stepped inside the warm kitchen as Megan stood on a stool and hung the gorse up to dry from the hooks above the dresser. She got down and slid the kettle across onto the top of the Aga.

'What can I help you with? You have questions you'd like answers to?'

'Since the last time I saw you, have you had any calls from the women on the list or contact with Ellerman?' asked Tucker. 'I understand you went to meet some of the other women.'

'Yes . . . I did . . . last Wednesday. I went to Reading, to meet them in a coffee shop.'

'Who did you meet exactly?'

'I met Paula, Emily and Lisa. I can't believe Lisa is dead.'

'Who told you?' asked Carter.

'Paula – she was very upset – we all are.'

'Do you and Paula talk often?'

She laughed. 'We have a lot in common.'

'How did the meeting go?' asked Carter. Willis was already taping Megan Penarth's voice but it hadn't escaped her notice.

'It went fine.' She smiled curiously at Willis.

'Who called the meeting?'

'Me.'

'Why? What reason did you have to do it?'

'I called the meeting because I felt we all had a lot to discuss – after all, I was the newcomer in terms of knowing JJ but some of these women had known him for years. I felt they needed support. I mean, how difficult must it be to find out something like that?'

'Something like what?'

'Like the fact you're part of a harem.'

'How did you part that day?'

'As friends, I hope.'

'How did you leave it? Were there any decisions made about going forward?'

'Going forward?' Megan asked. Willis wrote in her notebook: *She repeats question – giving her time to think of an answer.*

'We left it in the air – we decided to support one another as best we could.'

'Did you stay in London that evening?'

'Yes. I had things to do.'

'Busy time?'

'I spent the evening with my agent.'

'From what time was that?'

'From seven. I left the other women and I walked to the station with Lisa. Emily was going the other way, Paula was just next door, working. I left Lisa at the station and then went to do some shopping and met up with my agent at about nine.'

'That's quite a long time to go shopping.'

'Of course it isn't.'

'But the shops close normal time now – that's half five.'

'Okay, so you're right – I spent my time drinking in various bars, until I met my agent. I don't get into town much so I like to enjoy myself. I was staying the night at my agent's, so I could afford to let my hair down.'

'Did you drive up to town?'

'Yes. It's just too much of a nuisance sometimes to leave the car at Plymouth Airport or at Exeter St

David's to catch the train. By the time I do that I could be halfway there. Then there's all the disruption to the track because of the storms. Look – I'm sorry but I don't get your line of questioning. Have I done something wrong?'

'We would urge that you don't entertain the idea of having JJ Ellerman to stay here until we solve these deaths.'

'I can't believe he is capable of anything like that.'

'You never saw any flares in his temper, or any behaviour that worried you?'

'I've seen the normal stuff associated with a man who is used to being Mr Big. He loves the sound of his own voice. He is short-tempered, but I wouldn't say his temper is a major problem.'

'When we went into Lisa's house, we found something that we think belongs to you.' Tucker took out his phone and showed Megan a photo of her painting. 'We found this on Lisa's lounge wall.'

Megan shook her head. 'Figures. JJ often came down with random gifts. I expect we've all got things that belong to others. It sums him up, doesn't it? We're all part of a chain, aren't we? Interlinked.'

'Can I ask you again what you and the other women decided to do about your "interlinked" relationships and financial dealings with JJ Ellerman? I am trying to persuade the women who have invested in his so-called business ventures to consider pressing charges. It will give us the ability to thoroughly investigate him.'

'Personally? I didn't invest money and I will chalk it all up to experience. I can't speak for the other

women. I intend to have my say with JJ Ellerman,
then walk away for ever.'

After the detectives had left, Megan phoned Emily and
left a message for her to return her call ASAP.

Twenty minutes later she got a call.

'I've had the police here too,' Megan told her.
'They've just left. Remember – they can't start investigating the fraud case unless one of us makes a
complaint. As long as no one does that then there's a
chance to get the money back straight from Ellerman.
How are you getting on with drafting a statement for
him to sign?'

'I think I've taken everyone's case into consideration. I have stipulated that we all become equal
partners and decision-makers in his Spanish business.
Everything he does is run through us first and we get
total control of his funds for the business.'

'When will it be ready and when can you come
down?'

'I can come tomorrow.'

'They told me about poor Lisa.'

'Yes. It was a shock.'

'Are we suspects?' asked Emily.

'I think they're just trying to tie it all up in a time-
frame. If anyone's a suspect – it's JJ.'

Chapter 54

'Any news, Eb?' said Carter. Willis was looking at a message on her phone. They were in a lay-by on the moors, where Carter had pulled over to talk plans.

'It's a phone call about my mum again.'

'You want to ring the hospital?'

'No. I would rather just talk about the Ellerman case and I'll ring them later when we stop for a coffee on the way.'

'Okay – you're in charge.'

'Is your mum okay?' asked Tucker. 'She's in hospital?'

'Yes. It's all okay, thanks.' A heavy silence in the car meant that everyone got the message that Willis was dealing with things in her own way.

'I'll send the voice recordings up to Robbo,' she said as she opened her laptop.

'So what observations do you have of our interviews?' said Carter when she seemed to have finished.

'Okay.' She took out her notebook. 'My main observations on talking to Emily Porter yesterday and Megan Penarth today was that they were not telling us what was actually said at the meeting between the four women. They are closing ranks on us and I would guess that Megan Penarth is the ring leader.'

'But she didn't give him any money.'

'No, but she gave him something more important to her – she gave him her trust,' replied Willis.

Tucker was sitting in the back seat. He was thinking and staring out of the window at the moors. 'And ... correct me if I'm wrong, but she's a woman's woman and a little bit more. She took a shine to Ebony here,' he said.

'She was motherly ... I think.' Willis turned to look at him.

'No, Tucker is right,' said Carter. 'She was intrigued by you. She couldn't take her eyes off you.'

'In my opinion –' Tucker leant forward to talk to them between the front seats – 'she will want revenge. She's more angry than hurt. But she's become a representative for all of the women and all of their grievances with Ellerman.'

'What about Ellerman?' said Carter. 'What do we do about him now?'

'We have the women shutting us out and we have Ellerman with enough alibis to sink a ship. They want to deal with this themselves.'

'Even though we've told them he could be a murderer.'

'Yes. They don't seem to get it. They don't think he's capable.'

'Because he's not, maybe?' Willis looked across at Carter. 'Because one of them or more than one of them knows more than we think about the murders?'

'They didn't know about one another till the letter came?' said Tucker.

'Perhaps. We only have their words for that,' answered Carter.

'We need someone on the inside,' said Tucker.

'Harding.' Willis looked across at Carter. 'Could we ask Harding?'

'Ring her now and tell her we need her help.'

'Harding? She's one of the names on the list?' Tucker got out the list to look her up. 'Dr Jo Harding?'

'Yes. She's the pathologist attached to Archway. She's already agreed to help.'

'Were they close?'

'No. Harding's never close to anyone,' answered Carter. 'But they were having a sexual relationship at one time, briefly. Harding also knew Olivia Grantham in the same way. All three had sex.'

Willis phoned her. 'Dr Harding, we need you to talk to some of the women on the list. We're not getting anywhere with them.'

'Okay. Which one first?'

'Megan Penarth.'

'What's the line you want me to take?'

'Tell her you didn't invest any money but that you're angry and upset. We need her to trust you. But you'd better ring once and hang up. We don't want her thinking we put you up to it – we've only just left her place. Then, when you do get through, ask her for help to deal with it.'

'Okay, I'll do it. I'll let you know when it's done,' Harding said and hung up.

'Now, Eb, tell me to mind my own business, but I would feel better if you phone and find out about your mother. It might affect what we do today.' Carter waited to start the engine.

Willis picked up her phone, opened the door and got out of the car.

Carter watched her talking. She had become as thin as a reed. She lost weight so quickly. Her olive-coloured skin normally gave her a healthy-looking glow but not at the moment. She turned her face from the breeze that had sprung up. She was clutching the phone tight to her head, sheltering the mouthpiece with her hand.

'Is she okay?' asked Tucker.

Carter sighed. 'It's always difficult to tell with Willis. In all the time we've been partners, she's never really opened up to me about all parts of her life.'

'Her mother, you mean?'

'Yes, her mother, Bella. I know the facts but I don't know the feelings. I think she feels that if anyone really found those out she would enter a world full of chaos and unpredictability and she can't bear to be out of control.'

'She's a good detective.'

'She's brilliant at some things. But she also has large gaps in her knowledge. She cannot get behind it when it involves crimes of passion, matters of love. She doesn't really see it. It's still black and white to her. She's had no parental love.'

'What about boyfriends? Men in her life?'

'You'll have to ask her all that. She would hate me telling you anything about personal stuff. Talking about her mother is okay – she is in the public domain. But Ebony's sanctity would be a terrible thing to break into. I'm not sure how she'd recover. It's taken me over a year to gain her trust and friendship.'

They watched her put her phone away and walk back to the car. She had a look of sadness on her face. She was staring at the ground as she got in and put on her seat belt.

'Okay, Eb?'

Willis didn't look at Carter. She stared straight ahead. He started the engine.

'Yes, I don't have to go to the hospital. There's nothing I can do. She's earned herself an indefinite stay in Rampton.' Willis closed her eyes and laid her head back onto the headrest. 'She attacked a pregnant woman, cut out her baby.' Tucker reached forward and put his hand on her shoulder.

Carter put the car into gear and pulled out of the lay-by. 'We'll head to Exeter and drop off Tucker and then we'll hit the motorway home.'

A text came through from Harding. Willis read it:

We're in. I have an invite to meet her and a couple of the others.

After they'd dropped Tucker back in Exeter, Carter and Willis started the drive back to London.

'We'd better make sure Harding follows a brief,' Carter said, as they took the motorway north to Bristol. There were frozen fields either side of them as after the floods of autumn had come the cold of mid-winter. The day was already dark with layers of deepening grey.

'Is she dead, the woman your mother attacked?'

'Yes. So is her baby.'

'Christ – she's a monster.'

'Yes. I warned them when I was there. I could see it building in her. The business about finding my father – I should have handled that differently. That tipped her over the edge. She knew I wouldn't want him to see her. I couldn't risk his life being ruined. She knew I'd think that in the end.'

'I know that you handled it better than most people. You did it with a calculated approach. I know if someone could read your mother's mind they'd be in a very dark place, so don't think you should have seen any more than you did already. You need to keep sane, Ebony. You know all those years of your mother's neglect has left you much more stable than you deserve to be. Good job you were such a bright child that you could outsmart her.'

'I never looked on it like that. I always saw it as just managing. She's frighteningly clever.'

He reached over and gave her a jab on her arm.

'Guess who asked me if you had a boyfriend? Well, not directly.' She looked across at him, waiting for the answer. 'Scott, of course!'

'I hope you didn't tell him anything.'

'What like? She's only into men with train sets?'

'Stop being mean about Darren. You know it's more about the preservation of the old engines.'

'Huh! That's what he told all the women.'

'Anyway, we're not dating any more and we haven't been for six months, which is longer than it lasted altogether, so you can stop taking the piss now.'

Willis took a call from Zoe Blackman and put her phone in the speaker dock.

'Toffee is showing signs of coming round. His brain scan is looking positive. His eyes are fluttering in response to simple questions, but he's not talking yet.'

'Have someone stay with him at all the time,' Carter said. 'The only real lead we have to solving any of the murders is Toffee. If he gives us a name then we can hope all the cases will fall into place.'

'I will make sure he's not left alone.'

'What's happening with Simon Smith? Has he any more information for us?'

'I'm going to look for him now. He's here, because I saw his jacket. He may have slipped off for a coffee.'

'He could still have a lot more to tell us. If he and Toffee are friends then he might have let something slip. Ask him if Toffee ever used his laptop, ask him if we can have it for a couple of days.'

'I'll ask.' Willis ended Blackman's call but kept the phone in her hand.

'Shall I ring Robbo and see what's happening up there? Feels like ages since we were there.'

'Yeah – you and I are the same, Eb: too much green makes us feel uncomfortable. All this countryside makes me think I've dropped off the end of the earth.'

'Did Mahmet turn up?'

'Not yet.'

'Keep officers patrolling the estate. This should

bring him out. He's got to go to his own granddad's funeral. What happened to the dog?'

'He even tried to bite the gun that shot him.'

'Was he tagged in some way?'

'You mean an identity chip?'

'Yes.'

'No chance.'

'We must have Balik's prints on file?'

'Yes, we do, but they don't match any prints from the crime scene. Someone was wearing gloves; guess that was probably Balik.'

'I'll ask Sandford if we can still get a print from that. Glove prints have been admissible before.'

'Okay. How are you getting on with the PCs from the hostel of Faith and Light?'

'Wading through them.'

'Might be quicker to take Harding's laptop and do it that way.'

'I'll ask again.'

'Tell her she owes it to Lolly. It's the only way we're going to catch anyone for her murder.'

'What's the report from surveillance on Ellerman? Where is he right now?' asked Carter.

'He's been at home. He's decorating, we think. It's noisy inside. He's been sighted briefly in the garden, that's about as interesting as it gets. His wife comes and goes. Yesterday, one of the team followed her when she left the house.'

'What did they report?'

'She was out all day. She sat in a café with WiFi and, as far as the officer could see, she was working on a website design.'

'Did he see what it was?'

'He said it was in Spanish.'

'For Ellerman's Hacienda Renovations company?'

'I don't know. He didn't get a good look.'

'What has he got her doing? Designing him a website to stop us prying into that? If so, why is she doing it outside the house?'

'Ellerman must think the place is bugged.'

'It is.'

'Yeah, but we can't see what she's surfing in real time unless we put a Trojan on her laptop and that means getting our hands on it.'

'We can think about that.'

'Ellerman is playing clever with keeping the noise levels high in the house. We can't hear their conversations.'

'What else did she do?'

'She met the gardener and they went for a coffee.'

'Getting cosy with the hired help?'

'Possibly. It looked like they just bumped into one another but it could have been arranged. They spent forty minutes talking over coffee then they went their separate ways.'

'Is she the type to have an affair, do you think?'

'I think no one would blame her. She may be trying to get even, in a small way.'

'She'll have a long way to go to achieve that.'

Dee Ellerman picked up her phone and dialled.

'Hello, is that True Colours? Can I make an appointment with Paula, cut and colour? Yes, please, today if possible, the last appointment of the day.

Two hours will be great. See you then. My name is Trisha.'

Paula looked at her watch: it was gone five. She was having a friend over for dinner tonight whilst her girls were staying with friends and having a sleepover there. She'd dropped them off this morning on her way to work. Paula was secretly annoyed that she had a client so late in the day – it was already five and all the other stylists, even the junior, had gone home. She went round and made the salon ready to lock up in case the client was a 'no-show'.

The door opened and a petite woman with long dark hair in a plait walked in.

'Trisha?'

'Yes. Sorry I'm late.'

The two women looked at one another and it occurred to Paula that she knew Trisha.

'Have you been here to True Colours before?' she asked.

Trisha shook her head. Paula took her coat into the back room and returned with a gown. She slipped her arms into it, then she sat her down in front of the mirror. Paula took out Trisha's plait and ruffled her hair, to free it and get a better look at it.

'What would you like done?'

'Cut it short and colour it blonde.'

'Are you serious? You have beautiful hair. It's wrong to cut it, let alone colour it. Have you thought it through?'

'Yes. I've thought everything through.'

Two hours later and Paula had talked non-stop to

Trisha about her girls, about her man troubles, about her love of Spain and her hopes to have a salon out there. She held up a mirror so Trisha could see her hair from the back.

'Well, it's a transformation. You said that's what you wanted.'

Paula went into the back room to get Trisha's coat and, as she reached the coat down from the peg, she heard the key turn in the lock and remembered that she'd put the key ready to lock up before Trisha had arrived. She walked over and tried the handle of the door.

'Hello? Trisha, I seemed to be locked in. Hello? Trisha? Can you let me out, please?' She listened and heard the faintest movement on the other side of the door.

'Trisha?'

She heard the key turning in the lock again. When she opened it, Trisha was standing clutching a pair of scissors.

'Trisha, are you okay?' Paula took a step back.

'I thought I was going to have to use them to open the door to get you out.'

Paula frowned. She held Trisha's coat between them.

'Not those scissors, they're my hairdressing scissors; they cost a fortune.' She smiled warily.

'I used to be a hairdresser.'

'Did you, Trisha?'

'A long time ago, when I was young like you.'

'You're still young – now with that haircut, you look like a teenager.'

Trisha turned and looked at herself in the mirror.

'Yes, you're right. I don't recognize myself,' she said. 'I could be anybody.' She smiled.

'Precisely.' Paula took the scissors from her and put them down as she held up Trisha's coat to help her put it on.

'Now you can be anyone you choose.'

Chapter 55

Ellerman wiped the dust and dirt from his eyes as he scraped away at the wallpaper in Craig's room. He'd been working on it all day, non-stop. He had moved everything he could out onto the landing and covered the rest with sheets. He could see the hurt in Dee's eyes when he started, but it had to be done. He felt she knew it too. They couldn't stay in the house any more and live in a tomb. She had set up her space in the corner of his office. She had homework to do from her classes. She went out more than he ever realized before. But then, the last time he spent three consecutive nights at home, Craig had been alive.

Ellerman stopped working – he had felt his phone buzz in the pocket of his overalls. He looked at the caller ID. It was Megan. He paused, thought about it and then answered it.

'Hello, gorgeous, how are things in sunny Devon?'

'They are fine. I'm working too hard. I've just finished a big commission piece; I could do with a little distraction. Are you coming down my way soon?'

'Ahh. I'd love to. What did you have in mind?'

'What about tomorrow?'

'Thursday?'

'Yes, I thought we could spend a couple of days together, head to the coast, walk on the beach. It's cold but the forecast is for sunshine.'

'You don't know how marvellous that sounds. Can I ring you back later when I've juggled a few things?'

'Of course, but say yes – I feel like spoiling you. Great wine, great food.'

'Sold! What time do you want me down?'

'Late afternoon would be great – sixish; that will give me time to finish up the last of my work.'

'I'll be there, gorgeous.'

Megan came off the phone to Ellerman and opened up her list of numbers to call. She called Harding first.

'You have my address. Would you like to make an evening of it and come and stay?'

'Yes, I could – I don't have a lot on on Friday. That sounds delightful. What is the plan?'

'I'm inviting a few of the women from the list down. I think we should stick by one another – after all, we have a lot in common. You never know, good things might come out of all this. We might hit it off really well.'

'Sounds like fun.'

Megan phoned Paula and Emily next.

'I'll have to check I can leave the girls with my mum,' said Paula.

'You can sleep here, no problem. Have you heard from JJ?'

'Nothing.'

'Emily?'

'Yes?'

'Can you come down here tomorrow? Are you ready with the contract for us to look at?'

'Yes, the first draft of it anyway. 'Is it going to be too icy to drive home?'

'Possibly.'

'I've had car trouble recently. The steering went on me whilst I was driving on the lanes the other day. I could hire a car especially to come down or I could borrow one from the school.'

'Do it; but don't drive home anyway. I think you are going to want to stay.'

'What do you mean?'

'I'm hoping JJ might make an appearance.'

'Oh. Okay. I'll find that very strange, to see him with everyone else.'

'We will all find it strange, Emily, but it's the only way to sort it out. We need to confront him. I'm not telling everyone that he's coming. I sense that you won't be put off, but I think others will and I want us to end this on our terms, not his. We stand together and make him tell us what's going on. We get the truth. I want to see him squirm.'

Megan phoned Dee. Dee was walking back from the station.

'Dee Ellerman?'

'Yes. Who's this?'

'Megan Penarth.'

'We talked before ... You said you were Paula.'

'Yes. I'm sorry.'

'What do you want?' Megan was thinking what a difference a few days made. This sounded like a different woman. She was also trying to work out how Dee could possibly have known she was lying about being Paula.

'I have a proposition to put to you.'

'Go on.'

'I'm inviting you to Devon to meet some of the women who have been having a relationship with your husband.'

'I don't get it. Why would I want to do that? It sounds like a sick joke. Don't call me again. Leave me alone.'

'No – Dee, please don't hang up; just hear me out … we are all in this together. Even you. We can help one another. Come and meet us.'

'Everyone will hate me. I'm the reason why you all can't have JJ. Everyone will wonder why I don't just leave him. They will hate me.'

'No one has the right to judge you. We all just blame JJ. We know he's a past master at lying. I've invited him down here, Dee. He has no idea that there will be other women here. He thinks I never got the letter. I think you should come – we will all support you. We are all in this together after all.'

'How many of you will be there?'

'About four of us.'

'I can't possibly come. I can't do that. I won't tell him that I know where he's going and I wish you luck in confronting him but I can't do it, sorry.'

'All right, I understand it must be worse for you than anybody. If you change your mind you know where we are.'

Dee walked back into the house and heard

Ellerman still hard at it. She went upstairs and stood in Craig's doorway. Her husband stopped work and looked at her in amazement. He shook his head in disbelief but he didn't look pleased. That night he tried to make love to her. She went to sleep in the spare room.

Carter and Willis drove straight to the hospital to check on Toffee. Zoe was working on her laptop outside his room. She closed it and stood as they approached.

'Any change?' asked Carter.

'Very slight improvement, sir.'

Carter looked through the window at Toffee. He was sleeping, but he was no longer encased in a tangle of wires and tubes. He was breathing on his own. 'Have you managed to get near him?'

'Yes. I went in there with Simon Smith. He seemed to respond to his voice well.'

'What did Smith ask him?'

'He just asked him if he remembered what happened. Toffee just shook his head. We have to presume he doesn't know where he is right now.'

'Did he say anything at all?'

'He said something about loving Mimi. I asked Smith who that was and he said it was his sister.'

'Who's taking over for you tonight?'

'Gardner, sir. I'm going to pick up my mum from the hostel.'

'Any sign of Mahmet Balik?'

'We got an address for him; he's on one of the blocks towards the other end of the estate.'

'We'll get a search warrant issued tonight and get in there.'

'Okay, sir. I'll wait for your instructions and I'd like to come in with you.'

'We'll phone you when we have it.'

Zoe Blackman waited for Gardner to come and relieve her, then she drove to the hostel and parked up on the road outside. She was early but she wanted to go inside tonight and see how things were. Diane had said that particular clients were missing the PCs. Zoe wanted to see who she meant. As she walked across towards the hostel, she heard the sound of a chain dropping on tarmac. She stopped to listen and, instead of going inside the building, she followed the path around the church to the back, where the commercial buildings were. She saw Simon stepping into one of the buildings. He didn't see her as he flicked on the light switch and was about to close the door behind him when she managed to sprint the last few steps and catch it before it closed.

'Hello. Is everything all right?'

'Yes.' He tried to step back out quickly.

'What are all these?'

'My family's business, not mine. Nothing to do with me.'

Zoe took a few paces inside.

'Do you mind if I take a look?' Inside the building were ten cars under insulated covers.

'Well, yes – I was just checking that their battery leads were still okay.' Zoe lifted the corner of the cover nearest to them. A red Ferrari was beneath.

'What is this place?'

'It's just a storage facility for luxury cars. It means people who haven't the space or right conditions to take care of their cars leave them here under heated covers and I make sure they are kept ticking over.'

'You get to drive them?'

'I start them up. Shall we go?'

Zoe walked further into the facility. 'Do you mind if I take a look at some of the other cars? I find it really fascinating.'

'Maybe another time. I'm going to shut up here for the night.'

Zoe ignored him and lifted the cover of another car – an Aston Martin. She moved round the front to see the number plate: MER 100.

'I think I know this number plate – it belongs to a man named Ellerman, Mermaid Yachts. Do you know him?'

'I've heard of him. I've never met him.'

'Where do they come from, these cars?'

'Different owners. I have very little to do with it. It's a family concern. I just make sure they're all in working order.'

'Ready to use?'

'Yes, that's it. We finished?'

They walked outside. 'Have you had any more trouble from the gangs?'

'Not for a couple of days.'

'You haven't seen Mahmet Balik?'

'No.'

'Simon, the other day, when they were in the car park, I saw you give something to him; what was it?'

'I don't recall giving him anything. Excuse me, I'd better go and check that your mum is okay.'

'Why wouldn't she be?'

'Well, we have to watch the clients sometimes. Gangs get in and cause problems, injuries, people get hurt.'

Zoe phoned Carter from the car after she dropped her mother home.

'Ellerman's car is in the building at the back of the church. It's being looked after there. Smith gets cagier by the minute.'

'Okay, we'll bring him in after we search Balik's place. Get some rest and then join us at five in the morning. We'll catch him asleep hopefully.'

Chapter 56

At 4.30 in the morning the police van parked at the
entrance to Hannover Estate and Carter briefed the
officers inside.

'This is Mahmet's address,' said Carter. 'It's the
one he is said to use most. Now that his grandfather
is dead, we may have a chance of finding him at
home. If not him, then one or two of his deputies.
We are looking for weapons. We are looking for a
connection to the crime scenes. A tool provided by
Fiat, a jack with a bolt opener on the end, was used
to assault and kill Olivia Grantham and used at the
time that Lolly was killed in the lorry park. If you
find it then handle it as little as possible; we want
prints. Gloves also used during the attack. We are
looking for drugs, at least we can take the occupants
in for questioning – find me something to arrest Balik
for.'

'It's the middle of the night for Christ's sake!'
The sound of the door being bashed in woke the
neighbours, most of whom cared more about the early
hour than helping the police to make an arrest.

Carter went inside with Blackman. Willis watched from outside to make sure no one got out.

Blackman had Balik dragged out of bed, face down on the floor and handcuffed before he even had a chance to object. He wasn't alone in bed. The young woman with him tried to brave it out but she looked terrified.

'What's your name, miss?' Blackman asked.

'Rochelle.'

'How old are you, Rochelle?'

'Eighteen.'

'You sure?'

'Yes.'

'We will check, you know.'

'She better be eighteen. She told me she was.' Balik's face was pressed against the carpet.

'Quiet.'

'I'm fifteen. I don't want to be here. They forced me to stay.'

Blackman looked at Balik. 'You're under arrest.' She read him his rights.

Carter was called into the lounge area. Two more men were handcuffed and complaining.

'Sir?' A call went up from the bedroom. Carter walked into see the officer holding a small jack for a car. Outside, Willis was busy arresting a gang member who'd climbed over the balcony and was trying to make his way to the ground from there. He'd dropped ten feet and had a suspected broken ankle.

Carter came outside to join her – he looked at his watch.

'That's a good morning's work. I'm going back to

bed, Eb. If I hurry back, Cabrina may never realize I wasn't there. Then I'm going to my mum's for lunch but I'll be in contact all the time. After what Blackman saw at the hostel we need to consider bringing Smith in for a chat.'

'I think we should, guv, after we talk to Balik.'

'Okay, we'll interview him at three this afternoon and then decide about Smith.'

Carter drove home; it was just gone seven. The house was silent as he took his shoes off and crept up the stairs. He was so tired but his mind was still racing. As he passed Archie's bedroom door, he could hear him playing in his cot. Carter crept into the bedroom; it had the lovely smell of sleep. He undressed and got in beside Cabrina. He snuggled up to her and for a moment she was irritated because he was so cold and then she sighed and turned to wrap her arms around him.

Willis arrived at work. Robbo was pleased to see her. He had laid out his Haribo in colour groups. Willis knew why. He would allow himself one from each group, every ten minutes or so.

'Has Harding phoned you, Robbo?'

'Yes. She wants to chat to you.'

'Okay, I'll phone her now.'

'Be sure she understands she's not to take over the running of the group. She's only a spectator.'

'I'll tell her. Dr Harding?'

'Ebony? I'm packed up, just waiting for your call then I'm hitting the road. How long does it take to get there?'

'You have to allow four hours. Four and a half if you stop for coffee. You have a satnav?'

'Of course. I should be there by five then. Perfect.'

'Okay. If you run into any trouble, I'm going to be here in the office. Megan Penarth lives at the end of the village up a lane on the left. Ask in the pub if you can't find it.'

'Okay – will do. Now what is my objective?'

'To observe the other women. We want the truth about their investments. We want to know what Ellerman promised them. We want to know why they're not keen to tell us anything. But this is the first time, Doctor; the main thing is that they accept you, that they like you.'

'Why wouldn't they?'

'No reason at all. In fact, you must all be quite similar types in some ways; but that's not always a recipe for friendship, is it?'

'I get what you're saying.'

'Please take care when you're driving – the roads are icy.'

'I had them put winter tyres on my hire car – it's a four-wheel drive; I'll be fine.'

'Great. Any problems, I'm here.'

Willis came off the phone to Harding and looked across at Robbo. He was waiting to tell her something.

'Just got word from Intel. They found evidence that someone had been signing into the Naughties site from one of the hostel's computers.'

'How recently?'

'In the last week.'

'It can't be Toffee then.'

'Is Smith our man?'

'Looking possible. Smith and Ellerman together? A strange team. Is the only thing they have in common the fact that Ellerman keeps his car there?'

'Could Smith have taken the car and driven it down to Gillian Forth's?'

'I don't see why not. We need Balik to talk. We can put him in 22 Parade Street when Olivia was murdered; he had the weapon in his house. Harding saw someone matching his description attacking her car the night Lolly got killed and it's the same instrument.'

'Where is he now?'

'He's in Archway, waiting to be interviewed. Carter is coming back here at three.'

At three in the afternoon, Ellerman packed his bag in the boot of his Range Rover. He was whistling some tune that Dee didn't recognize. Dee had said nothing as she'd watched him go through the usual ritual. Suddenly he was not interested in redecorating Craig's room. From breakfast time on he had been coming up with reasons why he might have to leave today: this client, that client. The yachts had hit a problem in production. The client in Devon wanted clarification of this, modification of that.

'Bye,' Dee Ellerman said to herself as she watched him go from her place at the window in Craig's room, standing in the middle of the mess. She watched him go then she turned on the wallpaper steamer and began stripping off the last of the paper.

*

Mahmet Balik sat opposite Carter and Willis. His lawyer, Chapman, was sitting beside him. Carter asked the questions. But it didn't matter how many questions Carter asked, he got the same reply:

'Did someone pay you to go into 22 Parade Street?'

'No comment.'

'Does the name JJ Ellerman mean anything to you?'

'No comment.'

'You are facing charges relating to drug dealing and rape of a female under the age of sixteen. Do you want to add murder to the list of charges? Now is the time to speak out. The murder weapon was found in your possession.'

'No comment.'

'What is your relationship with Simon Smith?'

'No comment.'

'Your own grandfather was mauled to death by a dog that you set on a woman named Olivia Grantham. We have the proof. We have a match with the bite cast from your grandfather's body and that of Olivia's. Your dog. Your cowardly way of killing your own grandfather.'

'I object to your line of questioning,' Chapman said. 'I'll reword it...'

Balik's eyes burnt with hatred as he looked across at Carter.

'Don't bother ... No comment.'

They terminated the interview at four and headed back across to the Dark Side.

'He's not going to say anything unless we get him really angry,' said Willis.

'He's going to wait and see if the case crumbles around him first.'

'How can it crumble? The girl will testify.'

'Maybe. She will have to be moved, otherwise her family will be intimidated as part of the gang culture. Plus, the Fiat car jack needs his prints on them to make it happen. The drugs belong to his crew. In other words – we need him to want to talk.'

Robbo was just calling them as they walked back into his office.

'The surveillance team have lost Ellerman.'

'Where was he seen last?'

'Headed towards the M3, south-west. He's definitely going on one of his overnight trips. They said he had his bag.'

'Okay.' Carter took a deep breath. 'We'll hit the road again, just in case he turns up uninvited on Dartmoor. We can't afford to put Harding at risk.' He turned to Willis. 'Ring Scott and tell him we need him on stand-by.'

The roads were empty of traffic. The gritters were out. It was cold and bleak as they hit the road to drive south-west at 5 p.m.

Chapter 57

Harding pulled up outside the house and, before she had a chance to get out of the car, a woman appeared at the driver's window. Harding wound it down.

'Megan Penarth?'

'That's right. You must be Jo Harding?'

'Yes.'

'Did you have a good journey?'

'Not bad – it's blowing a gale down here, isn't it?'

'Yes. It's due to be bad tonight but it'll be still by the morning. Would you mind pulling in around the back of the house? There's plenty of parking there.'

'Of course not.' Harding drove round the side to the back of the house and parked up next to two other cars. Then she walked back round to the front of the house. She had a present for Megan, two bottles of Châteauneuf-du-Pape.

'I took the liberty.' She handed them to Megan. 'It seems rude to come empty-handed when you're being so generous as to host this.'

'How kind. Thank you.'

Harding stepped inside and saw two other women sitting at the kitchen table. She saw Megan set the wine next to two other gift-wrapped bottles and she smiled.

'Great minds, hey?'

Megan chuckled. 'Yes, as awkward as this is, meeting JJ's other women, you have to find it slightly funny that we must have a lot in common that we don't even realize.

'Okay – we're all here now. This is Jo Harding. Jo – here we have Emily there at the end of the table and Paula nearest.'

Harding smiled. 'Hello.'

'I have been waiting to announce another guest until you got here, Jo. We also have JJ coming.'

Emily looked down at her mug of tea. Paula looked up, panic-stricken. Jo Harding laughed.

'I'd better go,' said Paula, standing up. 'We can't all be here when he comes.'

'Yes, we can. This is the perfect solution to it all, Paula,' said Emily. 'Megan told me he was coming and I almost didn't come but then I thought – all together. A showdown.'

'Does he know we're here?'

'No.' Megan smiled. 'Do you really think he'd come if he knew?'

Paula sat back down. She chewed her lip nervously. 'I need a drink,' she said.

'Red or white?' Megan asked.

'Both.'

Megan opened a bottle of wine whilst Harding made herself comfortable. Megan put the open bottle on the table together with glasses for people to help themselves.

There was the sound of a message coming through to someone's phone. It was Megan's; she picked it up and read it. She looked up at the group.

'He'll be here in one hour. He's just stopped for fuel.'

'Oh, God ...' Paula poured out wine and took a large swig.

Emily poured out the rest of the wine into glasses and handed one to Harding. 'We need to use this time to decide things.' Emily took out the agreement from her bag.

'I've made a copy for each of us. Please read it and see what you agree with and what you don't. This is just a general agreement between us. I know it looks like it puts me in charge but it's just a template for the real thing.'

They read it through. Harding was a little uneasy at signing anything, but she knew it would mean she'd fulfilled her brief all the way. She had to infiltrate the group of women and that was exactly what was happening.

'Will he run when he sees that we are all here?' Harding asked when Megan drew near.

'I don't think so. He always parks here at the front. He'll see my car and that's all. Once he's inside, I'm going to lock the door.'

'I'm really frightened.' Paula shivered.

'Don't be,' Megan said as she went over and put her arm around her. 'We are going to come out of this a stronger group of people and we're going to make sure we all get what we want.'

'Which is what?' asked Harding. 'I mean, I see that

those of us who have invested money in the Spanish Hacienda company want to have some kind of input, some managerial control, considering their money has been used, but what else do the rest of us want from Ellerman?'

'Personally speaking . . .' said Megan, 'I want to hit him where it hurts – his pocket and his ego. I want him to look me in the eyes and admit he's a twat. Say that he's a pathetic loser who doesn't deserve anything good in life.'

'You want him to change?' asked Harding. 'You want to know him after tonight? Are you still hoping for a future with him?'

'Personally? No, I don't ever want to see him again after tonight.'

'But we're signing this to have control over the company. We will have to see him,' said Paula as she read the agreement.

'You will have to deal with the company, not him.'

'He must never be allowed to forget what he's done,' said Emily.

'I hope his wife leaves him,' said Paula.

'So do I,' said Megan. 'I hope she takes every last penny from him and he's forced to live in a bedsit somewhere.'

Ellerman saw the lights of the village appear in the pitch-black as he approached. As he parked up in front of Megan's house he saw the glow of candlelight coming from within. He knew the wood burner would be going, the Aga would be throwing out heat. There was no need to feel cut off. He parked up behind Megan's estate car and his car door nearly blew off its hinges as he opened it. He sheltered as he lifted the boot and took out his bag. He picked up the bottle of vintage wine that he'd been given by a client a few years ago. He'd forgotten about it until he was sorting through the papers in his office.

He knocked at the door and waited, being buffeted by the gales.

'Hello, gorgeous. Romantic ... candlelight, just for us.'

'Yes, perfect, isn't it?'

He put his bottle up next to the other wine as he came in and put his bag down. 'Ah ... you had guests, I see.'

Megan closed the door behind him and locked it.

'Not *had* – have.'

'Huh?'

'We have guests.'

Harding, Paula and Emily appeared in the archway that separated the kitchen from the sitting area and lounge.

'Oh ... I see,' said Ellerman. 'I get it now – what's this, a lynch mob?'

'More of a support group,' said Megan.

'I'm surprised to see you here, Jo,' he said to Harding.

'I couldn't resist it.' She smiled.

'Well, forgive me if I don't intend to play ball but I have better things to do with my time. Paula, I thought you and I had an understanding. Everything's in place. You let yourself be dragged into this. It's just mindless.'

'You lied to us, JJ,' Paula answered. 'You lied about so many things. I can't believe anything you say.'

He shook his head in disbelief. 'Emily? You can't be seriously expecting me to explain myself to you? Out of all the women here, I thought we knew one another. I've been a good friend to you – supportive – picked you up after your disastrous marriage ended. Now you turn on me?'

Emily didn't answer.

'You may as well sit down and have a glass of wine,' said Megan. 'We just want to talk. Every woman here deserves the right to speak her mind to you.'

'Who says?'

'We do.'

'You're speaking for everyone here now, are you?'

'Yes, I believe so.'

'What gives you the fucking right to do that?

'Emily?' Megan said. Ellerman was staring at her. She didn't look at him.

'Emily, could you show JJ the agreement, please?' said Megan. Emily placed it on the table. Ellerman picked it up and speed-read it.

'Huh . . .' He threw it down in contempt. 'I won't sign this – even if I did, it would mean nothing.'

'Not strictly true,' said Harding. 'We are all witnesses to it.'

'Oh, shut the fuck up, you nasty bitch.' He glared at her. 'This has nothing to do with you. I don't even know why you're here. Pathetic – all of you. I won't answer to a bunch of lonely, frustrated gold diggers who deserve everything they get. None of you mean anything to me. You can all go to hell.' He went to open the door and couldn't. 'Open it ...' he hissed into Megan's face. Harding stepped forward to support her and speak to Ellerman.

'Sit down. You're losing control. Sit down, for Christ's sake. There is no harm in talking to us.'

'Fuck off.'

He pushed Harding. She fell backwards and flinched as she hit the side of the kitchen table.

'Who the fuck do you think you are? All of you?' He turned and wrenched on the handle of the door. He caught hold of Megan by her arm. 'Open the fucking door. Get me the key to this door or I swear someone will get hurt here.'

'All right. Let her go,' Harding said coldly and precisely as she walked to the shelf and got the key to the back door and gave it to him. Ellerman pushed Megan back out of the way. He put the key in the door and unlocked it before turning to them.

'Never, I repeat, NEVER let me see your faces again. I am warning each one of you. I will come for you. You think you know me. You know nothing about me or what I'm capable of.'

He opened the door and left. Seconds later, they saw the lights of his car as he was reversing.

'Fuck that,' Harding said as she reached for her bag. 'No one speaks to me like that. No one threatens me and gets away with it.'

'Please – let him go.' Megan was still looking dazed and frightened.

Harding didn't wait to see who would join her as she went out of the door.

'We can't let her go on her own,' said Megan. 'We

said we were all in this together. We have to make sure she's all right. All of us.' She opened a kitchen drawer and took out three torches. Paula and Emily looked at one another. 'Okay ...' said Megan. 'You two stay here. We'll be back as soon as we can.'

She caught up with Harding at the back of the house and got into her car. Harding got to the top of the village and took a right. They saw Ellerman's car at the side of the old granite tramline that led up to the quarry. It looked as if it had spun off the road.

The rain sprayed like gravel on their faces as they got out of the car.

'Why isn't he in his car?' she said to Megan as they looked around in the dark for him.

'I don't know.'

'Where does he think he's going? Is he trying to get away from us on foot? Maybe his car has broken down?'

'He's going the wrong way. He's going up onto the moor. He must think this is a lane. We have to follow him.'

Harding followed Megan as they made their way by the light of the moon. The clouds were chasing fast and the moon came in bursts of light, reflecting off the granite road.

They reached the quarry but there was no sign of Ellerman.

Megan led Harding round to the back entrance of the quarry and they started their descent inside. High above them on the opposite side of the quarry, at the cliff edge, they saw a light and they heard something fly past them in the air and hit the brush.

She turned to see Megan holding the back of her hand against her face. 'What is it? Have you been hit?'

'Yes.'

'We need to get out of here,' Harding said as she saw the wound open up on Megan's cheek.

'This way.' Megan turned and they squatted low and moved under cover of the brush.

'Christ!' A missile glanced across Harding's back and another banged into the stone beside her. 'I can see someone up there. There's something moving. How can he see us? It's pitch-dark.'

They kept the granite off-cuts for cover as they made their way back up round the quarry.

'What the hell is he doing?'

'He's trying to kill us,' Harding said as they emerged from the cover of the banks and the wind battered them again.

A light flickered on the other side of the quarry.

'We're too exposed here. We have to run,' Megan said, turning her face from the wind so that she could talk. 'I can't see the light any more. We need to get back to the house and phone the police.' They looked down the way they had come.

'Do you have your mobile?' asked Harding.

'It won't work up here.'

'I must have left mine in my bag in my car.'

They kept close to the ground as they hurried down towards the village. Harding crouched by her car. Ellerman's car was still there.

'Why hasn't he left?' she hissed as she opened the back door. The light from inside the car flooded out. Harding reached inside and pulled her bag off the back seat. She found her phone and dialled Willis. She shouted into the phone as she crouched beside the car for cover.

'We're in trouble. I'm on the moor near Megan Penarth's. Ellerman's gone mad. He's trying to kill us.'

'We're half an hour away from you,' answered Willis.

'Hurry.'

Willis dialled Tucker's number.

'We need you to get out to Megan Penarth's. We just had a panic call from Jo Harding. Ellerman has turned up and he's trying to kill them. Can you get a rescue helicopter up there?'

'No way. We've got storms causing havoc here,' he answered. 'Where are you now? How far away?'

'We have just turned off the dual carriageway towards Bovey Tracey and are heading up to the moors.'

'You'll never make it that way. The river has burst its banks and there's widescale flooding and trees blown down. Turn round before you get caught in it.'

Carter swerved to avoid a tree that had fallen across the road. The sheets of rain pounded the wind-screen and debris snagged on the wiper as it bounced off the bonnet. Willis looked across at Carter for an answer.

'We don't have any choice – we have to try,' he called out as he slowed the car down and put it into first. The narrow lane had become a river.

'Turn round and I'll pick you up on the dual car-riageway in a four-wheel drive,' said Tucker.

'How long?'

'Half an hour.'

'Too long.'

'You'll never make it, Carter, listen to me; I know those roads.'

'Okay. Okay. We'll wait by the turn-off.'

Willis looked across at Carter, who didn't seem to be turning.

'Guv?'

'I know, Eb. I'm doing it. It's not that easy turning in floodwater. This road has changed into a river in the last few minutes.'

'Can we reverse?'

'No, we'll stall. The water will go up the exhaust. We have to go on and see if there's somewhere safe to turn round.'

'How can it just all happen so quickly?'

'The ground's saturated. We're caught in a flash flood.' Carter kept the car going in first gear as the floodwater rose up onto the bonnet. The car began to slide backwards.

'Christ – we're getting washed away.' They slid sideways down the lane. The back of the car was pushed into the hedge. The fallen tree stopped them moving any further as the water surged up as far as Willis's passenger window.

Carter revved the engine as he inched forward in first and then turned the wheel hard as he got past the tree trunk. Then he accelerated hard and the car sped back down the lane, carried with the fast-moving water. When they reached the pooling floodwater at the bottom they saw the lights of a four-wheel drive opposite them.

Carter wound down his window and shouted across.

'Is it too deep, do you think?'

Tucker put his head out of the driver's window.

'Give it a go. If it doesn't work you can wade through and I'll get ready to help.'

Carter looked at the swirling water ahead and then across at Willis.

'Open your window and get ready to jump out if you have to.'

'Guv, there's a steep drop my side.'

Carter leant across to have a look out of Willis's window.

'The trees will stop us going far. We can give it a go or get out and wade.'

'Okay. Let's try it, guv.'

'Willis – remind me never to come back to the countryside.'

'I definitely will.'

Carter kept the revs high and the car moving as he tried to find the lowest point of the flood, but the water was over the headlights. They shone in the muddy-brown river water.

'Christ, I'm relieved to see your ugly mug.' Carter got out of the car, onto dry land, and shook hands with Tucker. 'I thought you were going to have to send a boat not a Land Rover.'

'Yeah, I didn't want to panic you but there wouldn't have been much I could do if you went over the edge. You all right?' Tucker asked Willis, who was quiet.

'Just want to get going.'

'Okay. You get in, Willis, and, Carter, if you drive back to the main road and pull in at the lay-by, we'll collect your car as soon as we can. We'll take the other road up to the moor and hope we can get through the other way.'

After Carter had parked up he got into the cab of the Land Rover and sat next to Willis. He looked at the dashboard.

'Christ – this thing's got everything.'

'Let's hope so,' Tucker said as hail started pelting the windscreen. He drove down the dual carriageway and took the next turning off towards the moor.

Chapter 58

At the hospital, Detective Constable Zoe Blackman looked at the time – it was 9 p.m. She went to the vending machine in the hallway for some chocolate.

She was halfway back along the corridor when she noticed that the louvre blinds to Toffee's window were closed. She couldn't see him. She dropped the chocolate and ran the last few paces. As she opened the door she saw Simon's back to her as he leant over Toffee. He was holding something over Toffee's face.

'Simon?' He didn't look at her. He stayed leaning over Toffee. Everything about the way his shoulders were hunched and the tension in his neck told her that something was wrong.

'Simon, step away from the bed, please.'

Zoe took a few steps to come level with him and she reached out to hold his arm. She looked at Simon's face. He'd been crying. Toffee's eyes were open and staring at him.

'Sorry – I was just helping him get a drink.'

Zoe could tell they'd been talking.

'Toffee?' She looked at his face. He blinked.

'Yes . . .' His voice was croaky and it came out as a whisper.

'Is everything all right in here? Is Simon bothering you?'

Toffee didn't answer.

'I only wanted to say something to him, that's all.' Simon took a step back from the bed.

'What? What did you want to say to him?'

He didn't answer. Toffee's machines began squealing and within ten minutes he was pronounced dead.

Chapter 59

Harding left her car where it was as they raced back to the house.

'Whose car is that?'

There was a green Mini Cooper parked outside Megan's house.

Megan opened the door to see a short-haired blonde woman sitting at her kitchen table.

'Where's my husband?' Dee Ellerman looked behind them, as if she expected him to walk in as well.

'We don't know.' Harding came forward. 'We think he went up onto the moors.'

Megan got some kitchen towel and held it against her cheek to stop the bleeding. 'Where are Paula and Emily?' she asked, looking around.

'No one was here when I got here. The door was open,' Dee replied.

Megan looked at Harding. 'Perhaps they followed us? Maybe they decided to go and look for us?' Megan stared at Dee. 'Jo and I will go and take a look towards the moor if you stay here in case they come back. The police are on their way.'

Dee shook her head. 'Don't involve the police. You shouldn't have done that.'

'Why did you decide to come, Dee?' asked Megan.

'To see for myself, to face it all. But I don't want the police involved.'

'Stay here, Dee. We'll get back as quickly as we can.'

Outside, the wind buffeted them as they ran up behind the back of the house to the pony's field. Harding went one way, Megan the other as they looked for Paula and Emily. After fifteen minutes they met up again outside the house. The door was open slightly.

'They must be back.' Megan looked at Harding, relieved.

She pushed the door open and looked around the kitchen. She glanced back at Harding. There was no noise coming from inside the house. Megan nodded in the direction of the sitting room. Harding followed. It was empty. Beyond the lounge, the hallway and stairs up to the landing walkway and the bedrooms were completely dark. Megan turned.

'There's no one here. If we go back outside we stay together, okay?'

'Yes, one hundred per cent.'

It was pitch-dark. The wind had dropped, the road was speckled with hail. The moon emerged again – ringed with silver. The granite tramline once again stood out white against the dried moorland.

'Where would they have gone?' Megan asked as she held on to Harding's arm.

They walked upwards towards the Tor and dropped

down over the back, past the quarry, and stopped as something moved in their path. It was Ellerman. He was crawling towards them in the moonlight.

'Stay where you are,' said Harding.

'I need help. I'm hurt.'

'Stay where you are,' she repeated, as she motioned for Megan to wait, in case it was a trap.

He leant back against a rock and clutched his leg in pain. Something was sticking out of it.

'Please help me.'

Harding walked forward and knelt beside him. 'What's the matter?'

'I've been hurt.'

Harding looked at his leg. He flinched as she prodded the wound.

'Stay still, help is on its way.'

'I saw my wife's car. I tried to find her. Is she okay? She tried to run me off the road.'

'She was okay last time we saw her,' Harding said.

They heard a voice calling from above them.

'JJ?'

'*Run*,' said Ellerman. '*Hide*.'

'From who?' Harding looked around. 'From what?'

'Just do it – for Christ's sake.'

Megan looked around and started running towards the quarry. Harding followed. They got down to the base and hid amongst the rocks. Harding picked up a rock in her hand.

They looked up at the sound of the gate to the quarry opening. The sound was magnified in the stillness that had followed the storm. Illuminated by the moon they saw Paula being pushed forward by Emily.

'I know you're in here!' shouted Emily. The quarry rang with her voice. Megan and Harding kept quiet.

'You saved me the job of coming for you,' Emily shouted down at them.

Harding saw Emily standing, squaring up her aim on the clifftop, waiting for the clouds to part again, and then she took aim.

'Put the weapon down.'

It was Carter, standing at the gate to the quarry. Harding closed her eyes and sighed gratefully.

'You need to stop now.'

'Where's my wife? Did you find my wife?' Ellerman crawled forward towards Carter. 'I saw her car go past.'

'I'm here.' Dee stood ten feet away.

'Please, Dee, help me now. Everything I did was for you.'

Emily focused on Dee and then back at Ellerman.

Paula stepped forward. 'Dee?' She realized who it was.

Dee didn't move closer to Ellerman; she stayed where she was.

'I don't love you, JJ. I haven't loved you for a long time.'

Emily was agitated. 'You see? You need to start your life again, with me, JJ.'

Ellerman stifled his pain in his sleeve as he tried to move forward.

'Dee, please.'

'It's over, JJ. You destroyed the only good thing we ever had between us. I've found someone else now.'

In the moonlight his face was drained of blood. The

act of moving had shifted the arrowhead and punctured his femoral artery. He stood and staggered towards Emily.

'Help me. I need you.' He sank to his knees and his chin dropped to his chest.

Emily kept her bow pointed at Carter as she backed a few steps towards Ellerman. 'Help me up. We can still get away. We just have to get to my car.'

'Yes. I'm going to look after you. We only need one another. You'll see.'

Emily reached an arm down to help him up. He got wearily to his feet.

'Okay. We can make it. You ready, JJ?'

'I'm ready.'

He gripped her tightly and drove her forward over the edge of the cliff and the quarry filled with screams. There was a cracking sound in the middle of the deepest of the three lakes at the base of the quarry. The moon shone down on Ellerman lying on the top of the frozen surface as it slowly cracked around him. His eyes were open. His skull was smashed – blood leaked warm onto the frozen surface. Emily moved once, a spasm, then she sank with him into the black water.

Smith was in the cells by the time Carter and Willis got back from Devon. Carter and Willis stood outside the interview room.

'What's going to happen, guv?'

'We have all we need to convict Balik of Olivia Grantham's murder.'

'What about Smith's sister, Emily?' Willis looked at him incredulously. 'She murdered the women.'

'We don't know if it was her or Ellerman setting others up to do it and transporting them in his car. We have yet to find that out. Maybe we never will.'

'Pretty sure it was Emily: she taught Toffee to use the Internet, she had access to the PCs used to message Harding and the others.'

'Yeah, but I understand how things went wrong for her. I can see that she was a good person, just deceived one too many times. She needed help along the way when she didn't get it. She found it in someone like Ellerman,' said Carter. 'Ellerman was the root of all this.'

'Guv?'

We convict Balik, job done. Ellerman got what he deserved.'

'Case isn't closed.'

'No, case isn't closed, but I'm satisfied with the outcome.'

'What are we going to do with Smith?'

'He hasn't done anything wrong as far as I can see. He may be a twat but he hasn't done anything we can convict him of. He's lost his sister, that's enough.'

Chapter 60

In the morning, Alison parked her car as she always did on a weekday and got out and opened the rear door. She took out her coat, put it on and picked up her backpack and then she saw the dog limping out from behind the arch. She put her hand to her mouth to stifle a cry. The dog's eye was gone. It had massive wounds over its body. The skin was so ripped that she could see the bone of its shoulder. She stood there, watching as it limped towards her.

'Oh, my God.' She swallowed as the emotion stuck in her throat. The dog was coming towards her with a purpose. It could hardly walk but it was focussng on her and it kept coming. Alison looked around the car park but there was no one there to help. There was a homeless girl watching from the far side, her shawl wrapped around her head. She was staring but not moving.

Alison stood absolutely still as she watched the dog drag itself towards her and then she took a step towards it.

*

Sandy couldn't stand upright. Her balance was gone but she knew she had to reach the woman who gave her the food. She knew if there was one more task she had to do before she gave up, it was to try to save her master. She kept her eyes on the woman and limped towards her.

The dog continued to come forward. Alison took two more steps towards it and stopped. The dog turned and waited for her to follow. It limped back towards the far side of the arch and she followed. As she came level, she saw a man; he was shaking with fever and his face was mottled and swollen around deep cuts.

The dog collapsed by her master. Alison took out her phone and dialled for an ambulance.

Willis stared at the photos onscreen as she dialled a number.

'Hello?'

'Hello.' There was a slight time delay on the line. 'Is this Eddie?'

'Yes, speaking. I know who this is . . . this is Ebony, right? I got your email. I've been sat by this phone ever since. How are you doing?'

'I'm okay . . .'

'Thank you for the photos in the email. I could not believe it when I received them.'

'Sorry – it must have been a big shock. Not the kind of thing you think will happen.'

'No, not a shock, but it was a great surprise. It's not every day you find out you have a twenty-four-year-old daughter that you never knew about.'

'She never told you, did she?'

'No, I was young. I probably wouldn't have been much use but I would have done my best by you. I would have loved to have had a daughter. Well – it's never too late, huh? You will meet my sons and see how much you look like them; you're tall, right?'

'Yes. Five ten.'

'Just like me. My boys are both way over six foot.' Willis had a sudden urge to cry with happiness.

'But, Ebony – your mother. I read about the problems. She will stay in hospital, right?'

'Yes.'

'Good. She's a very sick woman. I am sorry for the life you must have had with her.'

'Yes.'

'You live in London now?'

'Yes, north London.'

'Have you ever been to Jamaica?'

'No, I haven't.'

'Ah … you will love it.'

Chapter 61

In April, the air had a sweetness to it. The quarry was a leafy green place.

'I thought I'd find you here,' Harding called down to Megan as she made her way down the side of the quarry in the spring sunshine.

'I left you sleeping.'

'What are you doing?'

'I'm just tending my husband's grave.'

Harding reached her and hugged her.

'Did he jump off here?'

'No. He couldn't bring himself to end it. After the cremation, I scattered his ashes in here. I feel close to him here.'

'I'm sorry to disturb you.'

'Not at all. I was talking to him about you.'

'What did you say?'

'I said I feel happy for the first time since I lost him.'

Fifi and Esme had matching white cotton dresses on. Paula had dressed them for the big day. They had bought the dresses in the market in Marbella. The girls had wanted flamenco outfits but Paula had said no – she explained that if they were to make Spain their home, they needed to give respect to the people that lived there. After all, Paula wouldn't only be cutting expats' hair. She would be opening the salon to everyone. It was the beginning of her dream. Over the door, the salon's name shone in bright red letters: *Truer Colours.*

Paula smiled as she wiped away a tear and pulled her girls close to her side and lifted her glass of sangria as a toast.

'To the future,' said a voice from her side. Dee Ellerman gave Paula a hug as she came close. 'Mike?' Dee turned to usher forward the man standing at the edge of the pavement admiring his handiwork. He was proud of the shop front. It had been a challenge.

'From gardener to builder, Mike.' Dee said proudly. 'You can be whoever you want to be.'

Acknowledgements

Thank you to so many people who gave their time and expertise generously and listened to my ideas for stories: Aengus Little, Carolyn Stephens, Neil Rickard, Dave Willis, Becky Long. All of whom are so important to the process of story writing for me.

Thanks to the usual suspects of friends and family who have to listen to my ideas time and time again and are invaluable in the development stage and the despondent stage and the gone completely mad stage.

To Della and the team at True Colours.

The teams: my agent, Darley Anderson, and his hard working women who take it personally if you don't buy my books, and the dedicated staff at Simon & Schuster. Massive thanks to them all.

Lee Weeks

DEAD OF WINTER

Victim, suspect, policeman.
When the lines blur, who do you trust?

When two bodies surface in the garden of a
rented house in North London, Forensics discover
fingerprints which link back to an unsolved crime that
no one in the Metropolitan Police wants to remember.

More than a decade ago, in an isolated holiday cottage
in Sussex, a family was found brutally slaughtered.
The prime suspect was Callum Carmichael, the father
of the family and a police officer from the Met's own
ranks. But without enough evidence to arrest him, the
case was hushed up and the trail left to go cold.

Now, with fresh proof that the killer is still out there,
rookie DC Ebony Willis is sent to find Callum Carmichael.
But Carmichael is an unknown entity and, with every
piece of information she tells him, she risks leading
a dangerous man closer to his prey.

Paperback ISBN 978-1-84983-857-3
Ebook ISBN 978-1-84983-858-0

Lee Weeks

Cold As Ice

There's a time to love, a time to hate,
a time to heal . . . and a time to kill.

On a freezing cold winter's day, the body of a
young woman is pulled from an icy canal in London.
To D.I. Dan Carter it looks like a tragic accident rather
than the work of a murderer. But D.C. Ebony Willis is
not so sure. Why has the woman's face been painted
with garish make-up and wrapped in a plastic bag?

Meanwhile cosmetics saleswoman Tracy Collins receives a
phone call. It's been twenty years since she gave up her
daughter for adoption, so when Danielle gets in touch, she
hesitantly begins to kindle a relationship with her and her
grandson Jackson. But when Danielle suddenly disappears,
Tracy is plunged into the middle of a living nightmare.

With the discovery of another body, it becomes clear that
Danielle is in grave danger. There is no time to lose and
Ebony Willis must take on the most challenging assignment
of her career – to play the role of the killer's next victim.

Paperback ISBN 978-1-84983-857-3
Ebook ISBN 978-1-84983-858-0

Lee Weeks
Cold Justice

The chilling new thriller featuring DC Ebony Willis

Coming November 2015

In Cornwall, Millie wakes up after a drug-laced party to
the realization that she has been raped. And it looks like it
involved her new boyfriend, Toby Forbes-Adams, who
has come down from London for the summer.

But the case is assigned to a corrupt local police sergeant,
who knows he can extort money from Toby's father,
a London MP, in return for his silence . . .

Fifteen years later, Toby's two-year-old son Samuel is
kidnapped on a London street and D.C. Ebony Willis and
D.I. Dan Carter are called in to find the missing boy.
They soon realize all roads lead to Cornwall and to find
the little boy they must finally get justice for Millie.

But someone is murdering the people they need
to speak to and time is running out . . .

Paperback ISBN 978-1-47113-363-3
Ebook ISBN 978-1-47113-362-6

LIKE YOUR FICTION A LITTLE ON THE DARK SIDE?

Like to curl up in a darkened room all alone, with the doors bolted and the windows locked and slip into something cold and terrifying...half hoping something goes bump in the night?

Me too.

That's why you'll find me at The Dark Pages - the home of crooks and villains, mobsters and terrorists, spies and private eyes; where the plots are twistier than a knotted noose and the pacing tighter than Marlon Brando's braces.

Beneath the city's glitz, down a litter-strewn alley, behind venetian blinds where neon slices the smoke-filled gloom, reading the dark pages.

Join me: **WWW.THEDARKPAGES.CO.UK**

AGENT X

@dark_pages